A TREACHEROUS PERFORMANCE

A Regency Cozy

LYNN MESSINA

potatoworks press • greenwich village

For the readers.

Chapter One

Having spent the better part of a decade trying to unload her orphaned niece on the first unsuspecting suitor willing to oblige, Vera Hyde-Clare was curiously reluctant to allow the young woman to marry the Duke of Kesgrave.

Naturally, her hesitance did not stem from any concern regarding his suitability, as a man of his standing was an impeccable choice for a husband. She was not entirely without reservations, of course, for the Hyde-Clares were a modest clan that had never sought to align itself with a duchy. Such a connection would bring all sorts of unwanted attention, and the *ton,* previously content to overlook the inferiority of the lace trimming on her daughter's ball gowns, would begin to inspect every aspect of their lives with careful precision. The small but necessary economies that made their life in London possible would have to be abandoned in favor of ostentatious quality, a development that would inevitably cause an uncomfortable increase in the family's monthly expenditure.

'Twas a distressing prospect, to be sure, but the strain her niece's matrimonial success would put on the household accounts was in fact the furthest thing from Vera's mind as she examined the young woman across from her in the breakfast room.

"Mere hours ago you suffered a deeply traumatic emotional event that few could have imagined," she said as the footman entered the room with a fresh pot of tea, "and nobody in the world, least of all the duke, would think less of you if you required a few days to calm your nerves."

Beatrice Hyde-Clare, whose usually wan cheeks were flush with excitement at the prospect of marrying the duke in only a few hours, regarded her aunt thoughtfully before responding. Although she felt no anxiety from her horrifying encounter with her parents' murderer the night before, she realized Vera might have a more difficult time digesting the new set of facts with which she had been abruptly and brutally presented. For twenty years, she had believed her brother-in-law had violently killed his adulterous wife and her unborn child in a fit of jealous rage, and now she had to accept another, wholly opposing truth—that the pair were victims of a deranged man's obsessive love. Incensed by Clara's refusal to return his affection, the Earl of Wem smothered the life out of her before subjecting her husband to the same treatment. Then, determined to hide his crime, he had dragged their lifeless bodies to the river and set them adrift on a fractured boat to make it appear as if they had drowned in a rainstorm.

The incident, already shocking in its wickedness, was made somehow worse by the fact that the earl had been an old friend of her father's from childhood. For years he had doted on the couple, affecting sincere concern for their welfare while silently nurturing a lethal fascination that would ultimately destroy them.

Vera knew the particulars of the earl's crimes because his lordship had described them in great detail while making his confession in the middle of Lord Stirling's ball. Indeed, the entire beau monde knew them as well, for neither Bea nor the madman who had killed her parents had realized a crowd had gathered to witness their exchange.

How unsettling it had been to turn away from the horror of Lord Wem and find herself the focus of several dozen curious gazes.

But Bea was not unsettled now.

Now all she felt was relief—relief at finally knowing what had happened to her parents, relief at finally *knowing* her parents.

For the vast majority of Bea's life, her aunt and uncle had withheld all information about Clara and Richard Hyde-Clare, fearing that she would display the same degeneracy as either one or both of them. They had been terrified she would turn out to be wanton like her mother or murderous like her father, and in their zeal to shield her from the excesses of her parents' moral failings, they themselves failed to provide her with love or affection. Hers had been a long and lonely childhood, with few opportunities to develop what were commonly described as the social graces, and she had sputtered and stammered her way through her first season before falling completely silent in her second.

And silent she would have remained if she had not looked up from the cooling corpse of an avaricious spice trader and met the shocked gaze of the high-handed Duke of Kesgrave in a deserted library in a country home in the Lake District six months ago. Inevitably, she'd concluded his grace had wielded the bloody candlestick to deadly effect and assumed he intended to dispose of her in the same manner. Somehow, in that moment of terror, when she thought her life was about to end, she discovered her voice and had used it ever since to tease and torment the duke. Fortunately, Kesgrave was just perverse enough to find that sort of behavior irre-

3

sistible and had accepted her proposal of marriage with grati-
fying swiftness—a proposal that had been made whilst Bea
was perched on the chest of the man who had only seconds
before tried to break her neck. That the duke had found
nothing untoward about her timing spoke of how well suited
they were and partially explained why she was disinclined to
delay their wedding because of the so-called deeply traumatic
emotional event of the night before.

Despite her determination to get married in—Bea glanced
at the clock—three hours and seventeen minutes, she did not
wish to insult her aunt, who had shown her more warmth in
the past two days than she had in the previous two decades,
and strove to come up with a reply that acknowledged the
validity of her concerns while dismissing them altogether.

Her younger cousin Flora, however, felt no such desire to
spare her mother's feelings and laughed at her lengthy speech
outlining her concerns about the imminent wedding.

"Well, clearly, not quite the *furthest* thing from your mind,
Mama," she said, her hazel eyes brimming with humor as she
reached for the sugar bowl.

Vera, unable to decipher either the source of her daughter's amusement or the basis for her remark, responded with
irritable impatience that she could not reply to the comment
without knowing the topic under discussion.

"The financial strain of Bea's matrimonial success," Flora
explained. "Were it truly the furthest thing from your mind,
you would not have mentioned it twice. It seems to me that it
is perhaps a *little bit* on your mind."

Although Vera could not deny the truth of this observation, for one part of her mind was always occupied with
financial matters, as her family well knew, she nevertheless
objected to being a source of amusement for her child and
chastised Flora for her rudeness. "My only wish is that Bea
begin her marriage to the duke with nothing but happiness

and goodwill in her heart," she explained with unexpected fervor, her eyes darting from her daughter to the cup of tea in front of her. "I would not want the ugliness of last night to mar what should be a wholly joyful event."

After twenty years in her aunt's indifferent care, Bea knew her limitations well and was hardly surprised the other woman could not bring herself to say these kind words directly to her. However unjustified they were, Vera's prejudices ran deep, and it would take more than one horrifyingly painful revelation to overcome them entirely.

Amiably, then, Bea thanked her for her concerns and promised her there was no reason to harbor them. "I feel curiously light, for it was the not knowing that weighed heavily on me. The truth, as they say, has set me free."

Certainly, Aunt Vera was reluctant to quarrel with the Bible, and she nodded briskly at the familiar aphorism. But even as she raised the teacup to her lips to have a sip, she couldn't resist amending it ever so slightly. "Ah, but the truth comes in degrees, my dear, and the shift in your perception of your parents has been so immense. Everything you thought you knew was wrong. Surely, you want to take a few days to grow accustomed to that new reality before everything changes once again."

It required no great understanding of the mechanism of the human mind to realize Aunt Vera was in fact talking about herself. For two decades, she'd embraced the fiction of Richard and Clara's perfidy, and just because she was now ready to let go did not mean the story was prepared to release her. She needed time to free herself from its grasp.

Bea was not without sympathy for Vera's situation, but she had no intention of allowing it to alter her plan to wed Kesgrave in—another peek at the clock—three hours and eleven minutes. She did not blame either her aunt or her uncle for believing the worst of her parents. They had been presented with evidence that had seemed inconvertible in its truth and, given the meagerness of their generosity, they did the only thing they could: subscribe to it wholeheartedly. Truly, she could contemplate their choices without any bitterness.

Well, she allowed wryly, without *much* bitterness.

Even so, their culpability was their problem, not hers—thanks mostly, she thought without irony, to their unwillingness to tell her anything about Richard and Clara. Perhaps if they had permitted her to know them just a little bit, she would have difficulty adjusting her perception of them now.

Bea saw no reason to point out this fact, as it would inevitably sound churlish, and merely smiled at her aunt. "I'm touched by your concern," she said with sincerity, "but I will be all right. Perhaps you should consider an unexpected benefit: Our hasty wedding might replace last night's theatrics as the on-dit of the moment."

Flora found this suggestion so amusing, the tea she'd been drinking dribbled down her chin as she laughed. "I think it is delightfulness itself that you are eager for the event to take place, my darling, but you mustn't allow it to delude you to reality. It will be weeks, if not months, before the beau monde talks about anything but Lord Wem's shocking confession of a double murder. Already this morning, Mama has received several notes requesting visits. The vultures are out in full force."

Aunt Vera blanched at her daughter's description of the *ton* as predatory birds and said only six notes had been delivered. "That is hardly 'several.' And three are from Mrs. Ralston," she said, as if the dogged interest of London's most persistent gossip made the attention somehow less acute. "But Flora's point is well taken. Delaying the wedding for a few days, perhaps a week or two, will give the scandal time to subside. Your marrying Kesgrave the morning after will only provide more fodder. Some people might be shocked by your lack of sensibility."

Flora, who was dabbing gently at her damp chin, insisted that wasn't her point at all. "I was simply explaining to Bea that her wedding isn't nearly as interesting as a double murder," she said before turning to her cousin and adding gently, "I do not say that to offend you. I trust you know that *I* find your marriage to Kesgrave to be the single most exciting thing that has ever happened to our family. I cannot wait to be cousin-in-law to a duke."

As Flora had already made several attempts to exploit her propinquity to Kesgrave, Bea did in fact know this and, tongue firmly in cheek, quickly assured the girl that no offense was taken.

Flora, finding genuine comfort in this communication, sent Bea a grateful look before appealing to her mother yet again for a wardrobe commensurate with her new station. "We shall go to Madame Bélanger, shall we not, for she is the finest modiste in London? I believe that is where the Countess of Abercrombie took Bea for her trousseau," she said, turning to her cousin for confirmation, although none was necessary. In the past few days, references to Bea's visit to Madame Bélanger had crept into Flora's conversation with alarming regularity. Regardless of the topic, every discussion eventually wended its way around to the skill and artistry of the French dressmaker. "And Miss Petworth shops there as well, so clearly it is the only place for a cousin-in-law to a duke to purchase her gowns."

At the mention of the exclusive Bond Street modiste, whose designs outpaced Mrs. Duval's modest creations by several pounds, Aunt Vera lost all the color in her cheeks. Tittering nervously, she chastised her daughter for her appalling lack of sensitivity. "Poor Bea has passed a very distressing evening and cannot bear to hear talk of such frivolous matters as dresses. We must be considerate of her feelings. Now, my dear, tell us how we may lighten your burden. Would it not help considerably if we all sat here in quiet contemplation?"

Naturally, Beatrice could not let such a self-serving remark pass without comment, and she was about to announce that nothing would calm her nerves more than listening to a conversation about silk ball gowns when her uncle entered the room. Ordinarily, he brought the newspaper to read during the morning meal, for he was as interested in the news as he was uninterested in his family. Today, however, in a radical break from custom, he carried a black leather-bound tome with him. Curious, Bea examined the book and noted it was a biography of Johannes Kepler.

Indeed, drawing closer, she realized it was the exact same biography of Kepler that she herself had been reading a little more than a week ago.

To be fair, *reading* was not quite the right word, for it had been during the two-week period when she had wallowed in despair of Kesgrave ever returning her regard and all she had done was stare at its pages for hours on end.

It was a curious choice for her uncle, who rarely showed an interest in literature, preferring instead to read newspapers and quarterly journals. Once, Bea had observed him flipping through a periodical devoted to the sporting pursuits of the country gentleman, such as fox hunting and riding, but after several disgusted grunts, he abandoned the endeavor and returned to his beloved *London Daily Gazette*.

As strange as her uncle's sudden interest in Kepler was, she refrained from comment, fearing any remark would be interpreted as a slight on his usual reading material.

Her aunt felt no such compunction and immediately took her husband to task for bringing a book to the breakfast table, where one was expected either to converse with one's family or seek edification about current events.

Russell, who had followed his father into the room, did not grasp the distinction his mother was making and observed that reading was reading regardless of the material.

Vexed by the cogency of her son's argument, Aunt Vera puckered her lips for several long moments before insisting the difference lay in the varying levels of involvement, for one was never truly engrossed by a newspaper. Russell, finding this logic specious, launched into a list of the various *Gazette* stories he had read during the past year that had consumed his interest. Flora rolled her eyes at the puffery and insisted that her brother had never read a single issue of the morning broadsheet, let alone found himself fully engaged in one of its articles. Naturally, he could not let that abuse stand and made his catalogue at double volume.

As the siblings bickered, Bea glanced at the clock and confirmed she had only three more hours and six minutes left as a resident of 19 Portman Square.

"What I find most interesting about Mr. Kepler is the way he saw the universe as a system of unified parts that are in harmony with each other," Uncle Horace said suddenly, eschewing his usual position at the table to take the seat next to hers.

The statement, uttered calmly, bore no resemblance to anything her relation had ever said to her before, and Bea stared at him, worried that the deeply traumatic emotional event of the night before had unduly affected him.

His eyes steady, he added softly, "I believe this is the foundation of all his discoveries. What do you think?"

It was an extraordinary question, and Bea grappled for an answer even as she struggled to understand her uncle's intent in posing it. Obviously, he was attempting to spark a conversation by seeking her opinion on a topic with which he believed she was familiar. That was remarkable in and of itself, for he was a man who liked his comfort and rarely made an effort to engage his own children, let alone the burdensome daughter of his deceased brother—a daughter, it must be noted, who would be removed from his care within a matter of hours. Finally, he would be released from an obligation he had never sought and long resented.

Hallelujah!

And yet his query signaled a desire to know something about her, perhaps even an eagerness to establish a relationship, and it confounded her that he would choose this moment, the morning of her wedding to Kesgrave, to make the effort. All those years of loneliness when she would have given her last breath for her uncle to take notice of her, and *now* he sought to engage her in a lively debate?

It was, she thought, an almost aggressively contrarian decision.

But of course it was not, for it followed immediately on the heels of many terrible revelations, the most painful of which was the grave disservice he'd done his niece by treating her as the daughter of a murderer. Finding her a constant reminder of his much-loved brother's horrifying end, he had shunted her to the side for decades, rarely sparing her a kind word or a moment of attention.

Knowing nothing of her parents' history, she'd always assumed his miserliness sprang from an honest and sincere place, an innate parsimony of the soul exacerbated by frugality and indifference. It had seemed so profoundly part of his character, she had never sought another explanation, and to discover the deep well of sorrow at its center, the vast hole filled with grief at what he believed to be his brother's nefarious deed, had been genuinely shocking. She had learned of it only a few days before, when Uncle Horace explained the devastation he'd felt upon realizing that Richard had ruthlessly drowned his wife and himself.

Lord Wem's grotesque confession, however, revealed the true depth of Horace's betrayal of his brother. Where he had been obligated by the bounds of blood and duty to provide comfort and kindness, he'd supplied only begrudging sustenance. Regardless of the unspeakable sin he had believed his brother guilty of, he still owed Richard's daughter love.

And now, it seemed to Bea, he was determined to offer it by asking her opinion on Kepler.

Horace Hyde-Clare had indeed been unduly affected by the deeply traumatic emotional event of the night before.

Bea, whose upbringing had not taught her how to handle small and sincere gestures of repentance, found herself speechless.

No, not small, she thought, noting the size of the biography, whose pages numbered well into the four hundred range. That he would embark on such a hefty tome as an act of contrition demonstrated both an earnestness of intention and a keen understanding of her character. She was a bluestocking through and through, and there was no better way to win her esteem than by holding an intelligent conversation on a subject she felt confident in.

Truly and deeply, she was touched.

As Flora continued to assert her brother's illiteracy, Bea grappled with how to respond to her uncle's query, for she could not think of a single intelligent reply. Of all the books he could have chosen as penitence, he'd settled on the one volume of which she had no functioning recollection.

To be sure, she'd carried it with her everywhere for almost two weeks, but had anyone actually seen her turning the pages?

No, they had not, because all she had done was stare vacantly at them.

And now she had to make a coherent observation on their contents.

It struck her as viciously unfair.

With her mind disconcertingly blank, she fished around for a title whose subject matter was adjacent. Salisbury's examination of Galileo's life had mentioned Kepler, had it not? It was the book that had originally whet her interest in the astronomer.

Worried that the silence had stretched a little too long, Bea agreed with his statement, echoing its premise and adding that geometry had a harmonic balance she found particularly pleasing. Then, briefly forgetting she had already arranged an activity for the afternoon, she resolved to go to Hatchards at once to purchase a new copy. She would stay up all night reading it and would present herself at the breakfast table in the morning ready to have a thoughtful and cogent conversation.

Uncle Horace professed a similar fondness for geometry and added that he had done quite well in the study of it at school.

"The orderliness of shapes appealed to me," he explained, before adding with only the slightest hesitation in his voice, "Your father also excelled in the subject, but that is not especially remarkable because your father excelled at everything. He was bookish like you."

'Twas a mundane admission by and large, and yet Bea's heart fluttered with pleasure at the notion that she and her father shared any similarities. Eagerly, she asked if he could recall any books in particular Richard had enjoyed, and her uncle paused for a thoughtful moment before making a tidy list that encompassed many interests and genres.

"And the autobiography of Benjamin Franklin, of course," he said with pointed emphasis. "He returned to that one over and over. He liked the way its author did not hesitate to acknowledge his mistakes and vow to do better."

A slight blush crept up his neck as he explained the appeal of the American polymath, but he kept his head straight and his eyes trained on hers.

Comprehending his intent, Bea smiled and leaned forward to share her memory of her father reading Franklin aloud to her in the study at Welldale house. Before she could say a word, however, Lady Abercrombie marched into the room with seemingly inexorable determination. Their butler, Dawson, trailed behind her, breathing slightly heavy from the exertion of chasing her up the steps.

"I told the countess you were not at home," he explained, his tone smoothly dignified despite the comical mix of exasperated irritation and abject apology on his face. "She would not abide by my authority."

Refusing to accept it now, her ladyship strode around the table and swept Bea up in a crushing embrace.

"Oh, you dear, dear girl, what a dreadful, dreadful time you have had of it," she said softly, her voice breaking as if she were desperately trying to fend off tears. "I have never witnessed such a ghastly display, and I watched Lord Abercrombie comfort his mother over the death of her pet guinea pig, so that is saying something. If I had known what grisly truths you would be subjected to, I would never have asked you to investigate your parents' murderer."

"*You* did this!" Aunt Vera said, gasping in shock. "By what act of perversity would you send an innocent young girl to investigate the wicked and sinister moral...failings...of..."

But Vera trailed off as she realized those words, which came so naturally to her, no longer applied to the situation and that it was only thanks to her niece's tenacity that they were in full possession of the truth after twenty years.

Bea, whose nose was still pressed against Lady Abercrombie's sweet-smelling shoulder, could easily picture the look of confusion on Aunt Vera's face as she sought to adjust to the new reality. Gently, she extricated herself from her ladyship's grasp to see Dawson tilting his head deeper into the room to more perfectly observe the scene. Noting his interest as well, her uncle thanked the butler for his efforts and suggested he return to his post.

"I cannot approve of your methods, Lady Abercrombie," Vera said stiffly, aware that some acknowledgment of the debt must be made, "and wonder at your judgment at giving such an improper assignment to any woman when there are law enforcement officers more equipped to assist in matters like these, but nevertheless, we are grateful for your interference. Without it, we would never have discovered Wem's treachery. I...thank you."

As gracious as the speech was, it was delivered with a rigid formality that anyone but the Countess of Abercrombie would find disconcerting. Her ladyship merely laughed with genuine amusement and insisted the other woman call her Tilly. "If we are to be family, we must not stand on ceremony."

The confusion this statement engendered in Vera's heart was acute, for there was nothing she aspired to more than intimacy with a noble and yet she could not bring herself to quite embrace *this* noble, who seemed to have little concern for the good name of the Hyde-Clares.

Then, as if discovering a loophole in a particularly dense contract, Aunt Vera said, "But we are not to be family."

The laws of genealogy, however, had no claim on the countess, who insisted Beatrice was like a daughter to her.

Vera, of course, could not let such a presumption stand and said with alacrity, "She *is* a daughter to me, and as such I do wish you had applied to me for the truth about Richard and Clara's death. I could have told you everything."

Even before the entire sentence was out of her mouth,

Vera realized the lunacy of such an allegation, for it could be read plainly in the expression on her face, but the habit of half a lifetime was too ingrained to be overcome in a single day.

Her daughter, showing little sympathy for the inflexibilities of a middle-aged mind, immediately pointed out the inaccuracy of her statement. "But you could not have, Mama, because what you believed was wrong. My uncle did not murder my aunt and then kill himself."

Now her ladyship gasped, for it was a shocking comment indeed, and she chastised Vera for withholding such vital information from her for *twenty years.* "Clara was my dearest friend. I'm sorry that did not please you, but you had no right —no right at all—not to tell me the truth about her death."

It wasn't the truth, of course, which Flora once again pointed out, but neither woman paid her any heed as they each warmed to their argument, Aunt Vera defending the decision to keep the family's great shame a secret and Lady Abercrombie scolding her for implying anything Clara did *was* shameful. Vera colored as she mentioned the affair with Braxfield, which caused the countess to scoff with contempt, for only a nodcock could believe Clara would fall for the sentimental drivel of that smug popinjay.

"Had you no respect for her at all?" Lady Abercrombie asked, seemingly distressed by Vera's low opinion of the friend she had loved, admired and missed for decades. "You were her sister!"

"'Twas the manuscript," Vera shrieked defensively. "If you had read it, you would not have doubted the affair either."

The widow could have no idea what manuscript she meant, but ignorance did not stop her from offering a scathing denouncement of this statement. Vera took a deep breath to respond, then suddenly let out a cry of alarm and dashed to the wall to press herself against the wallpaper.

Bea thought it was a singular act of madness until she noted the movement on the threshold and watched the Dowager Duchess of Kesgrave follow Dawson into the room. Mortified by her grace's presence, Aunt Vera was trying to hide an oil lamp stain from the exalted visitor's critical eye. Alas, she had only one body and the room was riddled with defects, such as the scratch in the tabletop and the frayed edge of Flora's chair. Panic swept across her face as she sought to recruit Bea in her campaign by tilting her head meaningfully and slightly waving her fingers with her right hand.

Although the direction was far from clear, Bea assumed her aunt was imploring her to cover the threadbare patch behind Flora, as placing her palm in the middle of the table would only draw attention to the mark.

She had no opportunity to comply, however, because her attention was immediately commanded by the dowager, who insisted on knowing the full details of last night's exchange with Wem.

"I cannot get a decent word out of my miscreant of a grandson, for he's too busy jumping from this thing to that thing, in preparation for your wedding today to provide me with a single useful detail about that atrocious scene we all witnessed," she said with contempt. "It goes without saying that I cannot remain wholly ignorant, and asking you for some explanation is not pestering you, regardless of how that scapegrace describes it."

Alas, she was thwarted in this simple goal by Mr. Hyde-Clare and Lady Abercrombie, who both found the information alarming.

"Today?" Uncle Horace asked, his expression an unnerving mix of surprise and sorrow. "I did not realize it would be so soon. I thought there was more time."

"Naturally, there must be more time," Lady Abercrombie

added with stern disapproval. "It's simply not possible for you to marry Kesgrave today. We haven't ordered your trousseau from Madame Bélanger yet, and I am planning to host a party in your honor. Nothing tremendously large, of course, just a small soiree with all the best people to introduce you to society, a little come-out, if you will, since you never had one."

Aunt Vera, who had listened to the beginning of this speech with sincere appreciation for the countess's unexpected support in delaying the nuptials, abruptly stopped nodding to protest this grossly inaccurate statement. "Bea *did* have a come-out. Her uncle still bemoans the expense of her court gown."

"I say, Vera," her husband objected, coloring so swiftly that the occupants of the room could not doubt the accuracy of the assertion.

"Of course she did," her ladyship said with placating kindness. "I misspoke, my dear, and for that I apologize. I should have said a *proper* come-out."

As full of respect as she was for her betters, Vera could not let the slight stand and she took three steps toward the countess before she recalled the stain, suddenly bare for all to see, and scurried back to the wall. Oblivious to any offense she might have given, Lady Abercrombie sought the dowager's support and discovered to her relief that her grace was also opposed to a hasty nuptial, for there was already a large enough scandal afoot and there was no point in adding broth to the flames.

Bea laughed, amused not only by the erroneous adage but the absurd scene as well. Her aunt, the dowager, Lady Abercrombie, every single person in London could talk, talk, talk their heads off, and it would make not the slightest difference in her plans. She would marry Damien in—another glance at the clock—two hours and thirty-six minutes.

But her determination dipped ever so slightly when she

observed the bereft expression on her uncle's face as he awkwardly clutched the Kepler biography to his chest.

Russell, who had fallen silent when the Countess of Abercrombie marched into the room, observed to no one in particular that surely adding something liquidish like broth to a fire would have the desired effect of extinguishing it.

The dowager, pinning the young man with her intimidating glare, asked him if he meant to support his cousin in her injudicious plan for a hurried wedding.

As Russell had never supported anything other than his own plight to possess a magnificent pair of horses and obtain a membership to Gentleman Jackson's, he shrunk from the accusation and promptly said no.

His father nodded with approval and gently advised Bea to consider putting off her vows for a little while. "Only a week or two," he added cautiously. "I don't think you fully appreciate how shocking the events of last night were to the *ton,* for never before has such an appalling scene been enacted in a ballroom. These are the people who you will live among, and there is nothing to be gained by pretending their opinions do not matter. You are scarcely aware of it, which is to your credit, but the fact that you managed to attach the duke has put quite a few noses out of joint. You were not considered a contender, you see, and that makes your triumph an affront to many members of the beau monde, which, in turn, makes you more vulnerable to malicious gossip. All we hope to do by delaying your marriage by a couple of days is give the *ton* an opportunity to grow accustomed to the idea. I firmly believe that will smooth the transition for both you and Kesgrave."

Inured to the arguments Aunt Vera had been making since she'd arrived at the breakfast room, Bea could not quite discount her uncle's reasoning. Nobody knew better than she how unlikely her relationship with the Duke of Kesgrave was, and as secure as she was in his affection, she was too sensible not to worry what marriage to her might mean for him. Obviously, nobody would give him the cut direct or eject him from White's, for he was far too wealthy and titled to offend directly. But people might whisper behind his back and make snide comments just beyond the periphery of his hearing.

She detested the thought of Kesgrave being mocked by anyone other than herself.

And his grandmother, of course. Naturally, the dowager, who had known him since birth, had a prior claim.

Although Lady Abercrombie found much to like in Horace's highly sensible speech, she could not help but take issue with his schedule. A week or two was a woefully inadequate amount of time to pull together the small soiree she had in mind. She would need a month at the least.

"But two would be better, of course," she added, "which would place your nuptials firmly in the summer, which is, I believe, a much more auspicious time to get married. But you will note how flexible I am being, my dear. I am willing to compromise my vision to ensure your happiness."

Before Bea could thank the countess for her tractability, Lord Stirling entered the room with Dawson at his heels. Greeting the company with one surprisingly curt nod, he directed his attention to Bea.

"You must forgive the intrusion, Miss Hyde-Clare," he said forcefully, "but I could not calm my mind until I called on you to see for myself that you were not adversely affected by last night's unpleasantness. You are well?"

Bea could see at once that he was genuinely agitated on her behalf and thought it was possible that he was more upset by the events of the previous evening than she. As unlikely as that was, it also made a strange sort of sense: For her, the exchange with Wem was the climax of a long, terrible story with a swift denouement that left her free to worry about how Kesgrave's butler would receive her. For Stirling and everyone else, it was only the opening chapter.

His lordship's arrival put Aunt Vera in a dreadful fix, for she could not stand pressed against the wall while there was a new guest to be welcomed and she could not step away and expose her lax housekeeping. She gestured wildly to Flora to come talk to her and as soon as her daughter complied, she positioned her in front of the stain and ordered her to remain still. Freed from her station, Vera slid her breakfast plate to the middle of the table to cover the scratch as she assured Lord Stirling of the lovely time they'd all had at his ball.

The gushing comment hung in the air for a moment before she realized how perfectly ridiculous it sounded, and she rushed to clarify that she meant *before* the little episode. That description, however, failed to do justice to the enormity of the incident, so she tried again, stumbling awkwardly as she said, "Th...that is, or, rather, I mean, th...that is to say, before the deeply traumatic emotional event that everyone found deeply emotional and traumatic. Before then, it was a lovely affair. The flowers...um...were, *in particular,* quite stunning."

Lord Stirling, who felt Vera's lack of composure displayed an appropriate sensibility, thanked her for her remarks and offered the name of his florist.

Bea found the exchange to be vastly amusing and, not wanting to offend either party by breaking into peals of laughter, bit her lip and looked away. She tilted her head toward the door and watched in fascination as Dawson, who had lingered on the threshold, one shoulder lounging nonchalantly on the doorframe, jumped to such sudden attention he banged his head against the wall. A moment later, Lord Braxfield strode into the room followed by a sheepish-looking Viscount Nuneaton, who, catching Bea's eye as soon as he crossed the threshold, shook his head helplessly.

"Ah, there, you see, they *are* accepting company," Braxfield said with satisfaction. "My nephew sought to convince me that you would not be entertaining callers after last night's imbroglio, but given the part I had unwillingly played in the drama, I knew it was my duty to ensure myself of Miss Hyde-Clare's welfare. And now I see you are a hosting a small party. And Nuneaton would have had me send around a note!"

The hint of disgust in his voice was pronounced, and Nuneaton dipped his head in acknowledgment. "It did seem preferable, Uncle, to entering the house uninvited and following the sound of Lord Stirling's voice. But obviously you know best."

Viscount Braxfield, either unaware of the sarcasm or indifferent to it, agreed with this observation and devoted himself to ascertaining how Bea had figured out that Lord Wem was responsible for her parents' death. He felt entitled to the information because she had visited him only the morning before to ask about his relationship with her mother. Wem had been convinced the pair were engaged in a torrid affair, and it was that belief that had sparked his murderous rage.

But the imagined liaison was merely the pretext, Bea realized, a fresh wave of sadness overcoming her as she contemplated their tragic end. Wem's mental faculties had already been in decline by the time he had struck out, and if his wrongheaded conclusion about Braxfield hadn't spurred him to act, then the next misconception would have.

Clara and Richard Hyde-Clare had been living on borrowed time for years, and although they were but faint wisps on the edge of their daughter's memory, Bea was grateful she had got five years with them rather than four or three.

As Braxfield persisted in his efforts to extract details from Beatrice, Stirling owned himself curious as to the viscount's connection to the matter and Lady Abercrombie thanked them for conveniently and beautifully proving her point.

"Four weeks," she said with a satisfied nod, "at the very least."

Uncle Horace asserted that two was sufficient, but the dowager agreed with the countess and insisted the room was filled with scandal broth, precisely as she had said.

Russell, perceiving again her confusion, explained that she meant fuel, which earned him the appellation of impertinent puppy from her grace. His mother, who had thought she had covered all the imperfections in the room, blushed hotly at the comment and regretted that she couldn't toss a tablecloth over her son. Flora suggested a compromise of three weeks while Lord Braxfield insisted on knowing the topic under discussion so that he may offer an opinion and Nuneaton leaned forward to apologize to Bea for failing to deter his uncle from visiting.

"But I promise you I made a valiant effort. Indeed, I haven't exerted myself so strenuously on another's behalf since I held my groom's riding crop while he changed the horse's shoe," he said over the cacophonous chatter that seemed to take over the room.

She laughed at the image of the elegant viscount, whose affect of finely honed disinterest seemed to slip a little more each time she met him, trying to dissuade his forceful uncle, and thanked him for making the attempt. "But there was no need," she added as she observed Dawson again in the doorway. Were they to be delighted with yet another visitor? Mrs. Ralston, perhaps, tired of waiting for Vera to respond to her missives? No, surely even the most persistent gossip in London was not so brazen as to show up at her target's doorstep demanding answers. Furthermore, Mrs. Ralston did not have pristine blond curls or, Bea noted with surprise, bear a striking resemblance to Miss Brougham, the mean-spirited miss who had ruined her first season. "The asylum had long been overrun by…overrun by—"

But it was useless to continue, for she couldn't possibly focus on what she intended to say when there was a facsimile of the dreadful Miss Brougham standing in the doorway.

No, Bea realized with a startled jolt, not a facsimile.

Miss Brougham herself.

Chapter Two

S o *many thoughts raced* through Bea's mind as she strode to the door to confront the spiteful creature who had undermined her social career, it was impossible for her to isolate any particular one. Her emotions were also in a tumult, and they seemed to swirl inside her, spinning and spiraling so that each feeling dominated briefly before being supplanted by the next: agitation, triumph, fear, curiosity, indignation, confusion, relief, anxiety, surprise, annoyance.

She had imagined this moment many times. Oh, indeed, she had, silently composing grand speeches that would reduce the malicious heiress to a quivering mass of shame at the offhand cruelty of her remarks. During her first season, when the sting of Miss Brougham's comments was still fresh and seemed to follow her everywhere, she had envisioned many such encounters, all of them ending with an abject apology and a pledge of friendship.

But that was years ago now, and her fury over Miss Brougham's ill treatment had cooled to mild umbrage. Without question, the girl's derision had turned Bea into an object of ridicule among the beau monde, which, with her self-effacing childhood, she was little equipped to handle. Ultimately, however, all the other girl's scorn had done was accelerate a process already in motion. The unimpressive Miss Hyde-Clare was never going to make a brilliant match, and even if she *had* managed to have a satisfying few weeks among the *ton,* acquiring a modicum of town bronze and a familiarity with several handsome gentlemen, including Mr. Byrne, who shared her interest in travelogues and science, her spot on the shelf had long been assured. Truly, Miss Brougham's mockery had merely made plain the foolishness of Bea's aspirations. Swept up in the excitement of her first season, she had allowed herself to forget her limitations and believe she could somehow attach a beau without the benefits of beauty, poise or wealth.

Obviously, that was not the case.

Mortification at her misplaced hubris made her awkward, and awkwardness made her silent.

That she had spent six seasons stammering incoherently in response to routine queries was not Miss Brougham's fault. It was a personal defect for which Bea took full responsibility. Furthermore, she could no more blame a marksman for having perfect aim than she could a songbird for singing.

And yet, as Beatrice drew closer to her archnemesis, as she observed the expression of polite interest on her pretty face, the familiar anger rekindled and she discovered it was still possible to feel infuriated by something more than a half decade old. It was merely the injustice of it all, for it had been so hideously unfair of Miss Brougham to single *her* out for disdain. Undoubtedly, there had been better targets among the *ton,* other hopeful young ladies with money, status and ambition who posed an actual threat to Miss Brougham's success. All Bea had was a spray of freckles across her nose and the meager belief that such a smattering lent a hint of appealing whimsy to her appearance. That single conceit was the extent of her vanity, the whole of it, part and parcel.

What swift work Miss Brougham had made of it by calling Bea a drab and dreary little mouse.

Squeak, squeak.

Compared with the wickedness revealed by Bea's recent investigations, such abuse seemed minor and unimportant. 'Twas only a little name calling, after all, and words could not cause physical harm. At the same time, she knew it was naïve to believe villainy always wielded a knife. Often, the greatest destruction was wrought by whispers and smears, by stories with just enough truth in them to resemble fact. Members of society vied constantly for dominance, and sometimes just the vaguest suggestion in the right person's ear was all it took to undermine a rival.

That was the crux of her uncle's argument for why she and Kesgrave should wait a week or two before marrying: After her extraordinary confrontation with Wem, society already had plenty of ammunition against her; it was fool-hardy to provide it with more.

Of the dozen thoughts that raced through her mind during the brief walk to the door, it was this one—about possibly postponing the wedding—that stayed with her as she raised her chin to meet Miss Brougham's frank gaze. 'Twas a disconcerting experience, for those light-brown eyes, glowing with interest, displayed not a trace of shame.

Surely, she felt *some* embarrassment—if not for turning Bea into a figure of fun six years ago, then for calling on her now, after the extraordinary events of the previous evening as if to gawk like an incessantly curious ghoul.

Forthrightly, Miss Brougham said, "I apologize for the intrusion, Miss Hyde-Clare, but my business could not wait. May we go somewhere to speak privately?"

Bea wanted to deny her. Of course she did. Here, finally,

was her archnemesis, the author of her misery, requiring a favor, and all she had to do to exact revenge was quietly shut the door.

Ah, but such an action would leave her *inside* the room, with its cacophonous swell of voices advocating for the delay of her marriage. Even now, above the din, she could hear Lord Stirling lament the shabbiness of ceremonies performed by special license.

Obviously, that opinion had not been offered without provocation.

Her aunt and uncle, as well as the countess and Kesgrave's grandmother, were building a case against her immediate nuptials, and Bea, fearing the weight of their argument, decided she couldn't bear to be in their presence a single minute longer.

She nodded abruptly and agreed to Miss Brougham's request. "Let us adjourn to my uncle's study."

Calmly, Bea led her down the hallway, too distracted by her weakening resolve to speculate as to the nature of the business the other woman could have with her. Instead, she was calculating the drawbacks of postponement, which included, of course, having to live with her relatives for another few days, but mainly consisted of being apart from Kesgrave for an unacceptable amount of time.

He had taken a long, slow, delightful leave of her only ten hours before in her aunt's front parlor, and already it felt as though it had been years since she'd beheld him. It did not help matters, certainly, that two of those hours had been filled first with a trickle of coercion from her aunt and then a veritable onslaught from the others, but she couldn't say if it was the desire to escape the absurdity or an impatience to share it that made the sensation more acute.

Bea opened the door to her uncle's study, which was a small room with an oak writing table buried under an unruly pile of ledgers and folders, and knew her aunt would be appalled at her for welcoming a guest into the cluttered sanctum.

Perhaps Aunt Vera would be so horrified by her niece's thoughtlessness, she would insist the girl vacate the premises at once. There, Bea thought, problem solved.

Regretting the unlikeliness of such a tidy end to her quandary, she gestured to a pair of armchairs near to the fireplace as she herself took a seat. "Please tell me how I may be of assistance."

Now that they were settled, Bea began to speculate about her visitor's purpose and could only conclude that she had come to mend fences. Against any reasonable person's expectations, the drab and dreary dormouse had nabbed a duke, and surely a society matron with Miss Brougham's finely honed instincts knew enough to ingratiate herself with a future duchess.

No, not Miss Brougham, Bea recalled suddenly. It had been years since the heiress had answered to that name, for she'd married a Mr. Norton of Salisbury at the end of her first season. Dutifully, she'd produced an heir and a spare, as well as an additional baby boy to inherit the estate in the case of utter disaster, and now hosted frequent dinner parties in her elegant town house in South Audley Street. Lady Jersey was an intimate and Countess Lieven a favorite, and Mrs. Norton often joined Mrs. Desmond in her box at the opera.

Plainly, a woman of her elevated standing could not be on unfriendly terms with the Duchess of Kesgrave. Amends had to be made.

It was an astonishing development for Bea, who, during all those hours of imagining the various ways Miss Brougham could apologize for her mistreatment, never once envisioned toadying sycophancy.

Naturally, Bea resolved to be gracious, not merely because

her unexpected high perch required kindness but also because the anger had passed as quickly as it had arisen. In truth, Miss Brougham's insults had ceased to plague her years ago, and as deeply satisfying as it would be to watch her onetime foe squirm in discomfort, Bea could not revive the outrage simply as a salve to her ego.

That said, she was not so high-minded that she could not take a *little* enjoyment in the fact that her very first opportunity to display the graciousness of her new station had been supplied by an old adversary.

Bea was almost inclined to thank the other woman for providing her with the satisfying experience before she even uttered a single word.

Mrs. Norton, her back rigidly straight against the worn leather of the chair, began by apologizing again for the intrusion. "I did not expect to find your house so full of guests... although perhaps I should have. I am sorry. My calling on you like this is highly irregular, and it would be less awkward if we had a connection or shared history. Perhaps if we had come out the same year...but by the time you were out, I was already married to Mr. Norton and had begun my confinement. Nevertheless, I am here now and determined to speak, as I believe you are the only person who can help me.

"I need help," she added firmly, quickly, as if afraid she might abandon her purpose if she didn't get the words out all at once. "I was at Lord Stirling's ball last night, and I witnessed your...ah, conversation...with Lord Wem. It was shocking, of course. Very, very shocking. I...uh...am terribly sorry about your parents. I did not know your history. It is... so sad...so...sad. Even so, your exchange demonstrated a talent for gaining information from a person who is disinclined to provide it, and I have need for just that sort of skill. Again, I am keenly aware of the unusual nature of this request and I would never have the audacity to come here and speak of it if I believed what happened last night was an isolated event. But, you see, there has been much...er...talk of late about the incident with Taunton at Lady Hortense's come-out, and while I, like everyone else, believed the matter had simply been an unfortunate mishap with one of the torches on the terrace, as Lord Larkwell had insisted, last night's proceedings have led me to reevaluate the matter. And Mrs. Ralston recently pointed out that you had been visiting Lakeview House when the unpleasantness with the spice trader occurred and she wondered if perhaps you had something to do with...well, with what happened to Lady Skeffington. Which is all to say that you appear to have considerable skill as an investigator, and I...I am in need of an investigator with considerable skill."

Bea laughed.

It was an awful way to respond, decidedly terrible, for Mrs. Norton's distress at raising the subject was readily apparent in the stiffness of her shoulders and the haste with which she spoke, the words pouring from her in a clumsy rush. Clearly, she wished to be anywhere but near the fireplace in Mr. Hyde-Clare's study asking his niece for help.

And yet Bea could do nothing to contain her mirth, for it struck her as a very great joke that the woman who had ruined her entire social career had absolutely no recollection of her. All those years nursing a grudge against Miss Brougham, and the malicious villain could not do her even the minor courtesy of remembering she existed. Had she insulted so many schoolroom misses she'd lost count or had Bea simply been that insignificant?

Very much the latter, Bea thought, struggling to regain control of herself.

How patently absurd to suppose Miss Brougham's interest in her all those years ago had been spurred by anything other than sheer expedience. For whatever reason, the heiress had happened to be in need of a convenient victim, and when she had looked around her, she had spotted Bea standing nearby.

It was that simple and impersonal.

Oh, yes, indeed, it was quite patently absurd to assume not only that her person was remembered but also that her forgiveness was sought.

Now I should truly thank her, Bea thought, for pricking my vanity at the precise moment it had started to swell.

And she had been engaged to the duke for barely a week! Imagine how large her self-regard would be after a full month. 'Twould likely rival the height and girth of an air-balloon.

Mrs. Norton's lips grew white as she pressed them together and waited for her hostess's amusement to pass, and Bea, perceiving the cruelty of extending what was obviously a deeply uncomfortable experience for the other woman, abruptly ceased her laughter.

"I am sorry," Bea said, leaning forward as if to take Mrs. Norton's hand in her own to emphasize the sincerity of her words. But obviously such intimate contact was inappropriate to their acquaintance and she wrapped her fingers around the arms of her chair. Then, unwilling to reveal the depths of her foolishness, she attributed her odd response to the events of the previous night. "As you yourself have pointed out, last night was quite shocking and I'm perhaps more unsettled than I realized."

Mrs. Norton nodded with understanding as a light shade of fuchsia suffused her cheeks. "I was right, of course. My timing is atrocious. I...I will just excuse myself."

"No, no, please," Bea said, reaching over now to still her visitor's movements. If Mrs. Norton left without explaining her purpose, her curiosity would never be assuaged and that was unacceptable. "Please, you must stay, for you are clearly in distress and I would like to be of service. Despite how it might look, I don't think it is entirely accurate to say I'm a skilled investigator, but perhaps I can assist you in finding a solution to your problem."

'Twas a blatant lie, for Bea knew herself to be a very skilled investigator and she did not doubt that once she was apprised of the facts she could easily apply herself to the situation. Obviously, the mystery itself was minor in nature, for Mrs. Norton would not sit so calmly before her if someone had died within the past few hours. And even with the theatrics of last night standing in testament to her talents, no society matron would be so ill bred as to present an unmarried lady with a corpse.

It was simply not good *ton.*

Quite clearly, then, Mrs. Norton's problem was a much simpler puzzle to solve, and if it weren't Beatrice's wedding day, then she would have been happy to accept the commission.

Ah, but no sooner did she have the thought than she wondered at its accuracy, for it seemed particularly foolish to believe that the Duchess of Kesgrave could blithely accept commissions from fellow members of the *ton.* Her aunt would have an apoplectic fit, and her uncle would turn an impossible shade of purple at the prospect of her interviewing the beau monde to uncover its members' secrets. Mrs. Ralston would delight in it, of course, for she adored a good scandal, and there could be nothing more scandalous than Kesgrave's wife setting herself up as a sort of amateur Runner.

Even Kesgrave, whose understanding of her investigative habit had been as astonishing as it was unfathomable, would draw the line at his duchess routinely scrutinizing homicide victims. He would never expect her to be a pattern card of respectability, of course, but there was only so much unconventionality a peer of his rank could withstand before five hundred years of breeding clamored to restore decorum.

To be fair, it was not the future she imagined for herself

either—being constantly in pursuit of murderers. As the Duchess of Kesgrave she planned to...she planned to...

But here her imagination failed her, for she had no idea what she planned to do as a duchess. She had been betrothed for little more than a week and had spent the vast majority of that time either investigating Richard and Clara's deaths or mourning the tragedy of their lives. The only opportunity she'd had to sit still and contemplate what her new status meant was when her aunt had provided her with a list of the servants it would soon be her responsibility to oversee. The catalogue had been so horrifyingly long and extensive, Bea had literally run away from the information, scurrying from the house and seeking refuge in the Countess of Abercrombie's promise of a mystery—a mystery that turned out to be her own parents' murders.

Now that Bea had learned the truth and brought the villain to justice, there was nothing for her to do but settle comfortably into her duchesshood, something she would do posthaste, as soon as she figured out what that meant.

Unaware of her hostess's sudden crisis of identity, Mrs. Norton thanked Beatrice for her generous offer. "You are so kind to indulge me. I am sure my little problems are nothing but a bother for you, and it is beyond anything for me to ask, for I have no claim on your time. Even now, I am of half a mind to apologize for the interruption and leave without imposing further. But I don't know where else to turn, and you have shown yourself to be so clever. I do wish I were more clever. Then I could resolve this matter on my own."

Bea refused to believe a woman who had established herself so effortlessly in society was without intelligence, but she saw no reason to cavil at the observation, which struck her as intentionally deprecating. To compensate for the awkwardness of the errand, Mrs. Norton was purposefully undervaluing her own intellect, and as Bea considered her response, she decided it was precisely the pose she herself would adopt in a similar situation.

"It is no bother, I promise you," Bea said calmly, even as one part of her brain remained focused on the thorny matter of her future. Kesgrave had assured her that his estates ran smoothly under their current stewardship and would continue to do so without any assistance from her. As his wife, she had only to please herself, and if that meant spending whole days in the library working her way through his very excellent collection, then that was what she should do.

Given that she'd yearned for little during her long years with her relatives other than an engrossing book and a quiet place in which to consume it, Bea was shocked to find herself unsettled by the prospect. What had once seemed like a refuge to her now felt like a retreat. By bracketing herself in the library rather than taking the reins of the household, she was ceding the ground before she even examined the territory.

Surely, she had more spine than that.

Immediately, she recalled the image of Kesgrave's butler in Berkeley Square, a man whose physical stature was as imposing as his manner. How superciliously he had stared down at her as she begged entrance to Kesgrave House. She had been dressed as a man at the time, to be sure, and the hour at which she'd called had hardly been decorous, but she had little hope of a warmer reception when presented as herself. Marlow's dignity was owed more than a mousy spinster with no wealth or status to recommend her.

In all honesty, she did not know if she was courageous enough to face his disappointment day after day.

But it was that uncertainty, of course, that made the daily confrontation an imperative. After so many years of shrinking from society, she could not cower in her own home. She would have to—

Realizing her focus had wandered from the matter at hand, Bea shook her head and pushed aside all domestic concerns. Mrs. Norton deserved better than her divided attention, she thought, smiling at the strange development, for prior to this very moment she could not conceive of Miss Brougham deserving anything of her save her anger and scorn.

Fortunately, Bea had missed nothing of import, for the woman was still expressing her gratitude for the gracious reception she had received at 19 Portman Square. "Honestly, I would have thought you too busy to concern yourself with someone like me."

Bea waved aside this further display of humility, which she assumed was also a pose, and assured her she had a few moments to spare—which was, she thought, only the truth, for the cacophonous meeting in the breakfast room was unlikely to disperse soon and she had no intention of returning to it.

"I fear it is going to sound horrendously far-fetched," Mrs. Norton announced, her color rising slightly at the prospect of relating an implausible tale. "To be honest, I'm not quite sure *I* believe it, and yet I cannot rest until all options are explored. You see, I thought it was just a bedtime story my grandfather liked to tell. It never occurred to me until I read his dying letter that it might be true."

She paused here, as if unsure she would continue, and Bea rushed to assure her that in her experience, many seemingly impossible things had turned out to be real. She did not take the opportunity to list them, of course, for it would never do to tell one's archnemesis the details of one's courtship.

"I appreciate that," Mrs. Norton said. "I'm just being silly. Really, there's no reason why I should not simply tell you everything and allow you decide on the probability for yourself. It begins with a man named Jean-Baptiste Tavernier. He was a jeweler."

Beatrice nodded firmly. "The seventeenth-century French gem merchant."

Her familiarity with the subject surprised her guest. "You know of him?"

"I do," she said. "He wrote about his extensive travels throughout Asia in a highly informative and engrossing book called *The Six Voyages of Jean-Baptiste Tavernier.* He was a keen observer as well as a gifted anthropologist."

"Ah, this is good," Mrs. Norton murmured softly. "This is very good. Perhaps now you will not find my story quite so difficult to believe. You see, my grandfather's father—that is, my great-grandfather Perseus Brougham—was also a merchant. He came from the north of England, where his people were farmers. Poor farmers. So he decided to leave home and join the Royal Mesopotamia Company. Eventually, he made his way to Persia and entered the tobacco trade. It was far from easy, for, as you can imagine, he had to contend with laborers who were coarse and ignorant, little better than savages, but he nevertheless managed to acquire allies. He found the local ruler, a man named Shaw, to be particularly helpful in his pursuit. But then the ruler lost his position in a tussle with some native. That was in the 1740s, in the middle of the decade."

Bea smothered a smile to hear the brutal murder of Nader Shah, in which fifteen of his own men conspired to chop off his head, described as a "tussle." An account of the attack had been given by the shah's personal physician Père Louis Bazin, who had barely escaped the chaotic aftermath of the assassination.

"Before his death, however, my great-grandfather had performed an important service for Mr. Shaw by warning him about a few grumbling discontents among his men, and in reward Mr. Shaw gave him a gem of tremendous value," Mrs. Norton said, then interrupted her story to sigh heavily. "You think I'm silly or, worse, gullible to believe such an outlandish tale. You must not deny it, Miss Hyde-Clare, for I can read it plainly on your face."

At once Bea objected to this characterization, for if anything was plain on her face it was utter amazement at the idea that the former Miss Brougham's ancestor was instrumental in the overthrow of one of Persia's most powerful rulers. Nader Shah's downfall had been predicated on his belief, wholly unfounded and assumed by many to be a product of his ill health, that his own royal guard was planning to kill him.

Perhaps that conviction was not without provocation after all.

Bea wondered if there was some scholar with whom she should share the information. She had no idea if the author of the historical tome she had read was still alive.

Across from her, Mrs. Norton took exception to her distraction, which she mistook for disbelief, and pulled her lips together in a moue of displeasure. "You think I'm the veriest fool for believing anything my grandfather told me. Very well. I accept your judgment now as I accepted it before and submit to you this letter he wrote to me before he died four months ago. I defy you to read it and maintain your position that it is naught but an extravagant story with which to entertain children," she said, withdrawing a letter from her reticule. "Please pay no mind to the ink smears. I fear I was rather overcome reading it."

As Bea could not quite say what the story was, other than a fascinating footnote to a well-known historical event, she did not respond to this accusation and silently accepted the proffered missive. As noted, the page was stained with blotches of ink, presumably marking where the tears of an overwrought Mrs. Norton had fallen. The handwriting was neat and even, and the words easy to decipher despite the many splatters that dotted the sheet.

My darling Maddie,

As the end grows nearer and I am forced to confront the truth of my own mortality, I find myself incapable of reconciling myself to the most difficult truth of all: I am to be deprived of the pleasure of looking upon your beautiful face one final time. My condition grows worse with every passing hour, and I know you will not arrive before I expire. Oh, my dear, dear Maddie, what a joy you have been to me during these lovely twilight years. I love all my grandchildren but you, who reminds me so strongly of my own dear, sweet Julia, with the purity of your soul, hold a special place in my heart.

Although we spent untold happy hours together, there are things I failed to tell you, important things that are necessary to your future and comfort. My mistake was in believing there was plenty of time. I'm sure all old men believe more hours remain than actually do. I had hoped you'd arrive at my bedside before it was too late, but this damnable storm has made the roads impassable, and there's naught I can do but say goodbye in this dreadfully inadequate manner. Although I leave you now, I know you will take consolation in the bounty of stories I told you during your childhood. You remember Mr. Akbar, don't you? He's in the garden now. Find him and you will want for nothing.

. . .

38

I must go, my love, for the candle flickers and the doctor says I must rest my weary head. Mourn for me but a little, for I have had a full life and more happiness than I deserve.

Adieu, you darling, darling girl.

In loving fondness,

Your Grandfather
   Augustus Brougham

Bea had several ideas at once—wildly outlandish ones that aligned nicely with Mrs. Norton's insistence on implausibility. Before stating them, however, she read the letter through again, skipping over the understandable lachrymosity of a dying man, and focusing thoughtfully on the mention of Mr. Akbar. It seemed far too pointed a reference to be a coincidence, especially in light of the other information she had already been given.

The former Miss Brougham required her help in locating a missing rose-cut, 280-carat diamond.

'Twas an extraordinary development.

Calmly, Bea said, "Your grandfather hid the Great Mughal diamond in an unknown location and you wish my assistance in finding it."

The expression on Mrs. Norton's face at this astute conclusion was an almost comical mix of amazement and annoyance, with which Bea was entirely sympathetic. How irritating indeed to believe you are about to astonish your listener with a profoundly shocking fact only to have your moment scuttled by the other person's intolerable cleverness. Kesgrave had done it to her more than once.

Mrs. Norton gaped at her for several long moments, her countenance losing none of its peevish surprise, before asking, "How in the world did you figure that out?"

Having no wish to insult her guest, Bea refrained from remarking on how simple it was to deduce and instead explained. "Akbar the Great, you see, oversaw the expansion of the Mughal Empire, so the inclusion of the name was a significant hint, which is, I believe, why your grandfather used it in the first place. Additionally, you started your tale with the mention of Jean-Baptiste Tavernier, who described the stone in his travelogue. He had beheld it while visiting India, but Nader *Shah*"—said with extra emphasis to indicate the name was not in fact Shaw—"took it several decades later when he invaded the Mughal Empire, as he considered it among the spoils of war. The story is recounted in a contemporaneous history written by an official envoy to the Persian court. The diamond was believed to have disappeared in the chaos that followed Shah's assassination, but apparently that assumption is inaccurate. Rather, the shah gave it to your great-grandfather, who brought it home to England and passed it along to his son, your grandfather Augustus Brougham, who did such a good job hiding it, you fear you will never find it."

Mrs. Norton's gaze narrowed as she slowly nodded her head. "Masterful, Miss Hyde-Clare, simply masterful. I must say, I severely underestimated you. Last night's performance was impressive, to be sure, but your ability to draw a conclusion from vastly disparate facts is genuinely a sight to behold."

Hearing the deeply upsetting events of the evening before described as a performance caused Bea to flinch and she stiffened her shoulders, aware that some insistent response was called for but unable to think of anything coherent.

Was that how other members of the *ton* perceived her exchange with Wem?

"Oh, dear, no," Mrs. Norton cried, noting the expression on her hostess's face. "I cannot believe those words just passed my lips. What a wretched creature I am! How thoughtless and cruel! You must believe, Miss Hyde-Clare, that I don't for a single moment equate that dreadful scene last night with theater. Truly, I do not. You must forgive me, or I will be despondent. Please, do say you forgive me. Do say it please. I cannot let you believe I'm so callous."

Years ago, Bea had imagined the other woman pleading for absolution in the same beseeching tone, and finding herself confronted with it now, in real life, not just in reverie, she could not resist the humor of the moment. The world was indeed a strange place.

"Yes, you are forgiven," Bea said, smiling as the insult slipped from her shoulders. And yet even as she relaxed, she found she could not entirely dismiss the ugliness of the thought and wondered if anyone really believed she had created that horrific scene with Wem in a bid for attention.

"Ah, you are an angel, Miss Hyde-Clare," Mrs. Norton said heartfully, her relief evident. "And now do say you will help me. I warn you, I will not be fobbed off with assertions that you are not suited to the task. You are clearly the skilled investigator Mrs. Ralston said you were, and I will listen to no more claims to the opposite. Modesty is, of course, a necessary trait in a gently bred woman, but displaying too much is just as discourteous as displaying too little. I am sure all it will take is one brief conversation with the fastidious Mr. Rose and you will discover everything."

Beatrice's anxiety returned at the mention of the famous

gossip, for it reminded her of her family's concerns about her hasty wedding to the duke.

No, not hasty, she decided with a defiant snap. Kesgrave had secured the special license almost a week ago. If anything, their pace was slow and cautious and, she thought, recalling the way he had kissed her goodbye in the early hours of the morning, fairly torturous.

She was eager to be a wife.

And yet she could not wholly dismiss the Mrs. Ralstons of the world, for doing so risked exposing the duke to ridicule. Doing a favor for one of London's most accomplished hostesses would further insulate him from scorn.

Bea could not dismiss the idea entirely out of hand.

"Mr. Rose?" she asked, unsure if she had missed a step in the conversation while she had been woolgathering.

"Yes, the solicitor my grandfather hired to oversee his affairs," Mrs. Norton explained. "That is whom my grandfather is referring to when he says Mr. Akbar is in the garden. I have spoken with him personally, but he refused to acknowledge the existence of the diamond, let alone reveal its true location. As I am not my grandfather's heir—that pleasure belongs to my Uncle Gareth, who neither knows of the jewel's existence nor requires it to spend his entire life in lavish luxury—he will not discuss any matter of succession or inheritance with me. He is a villain, Miss Hyde-Clare, a heartless villain to deny a dying man his final wish. I do not know how he can sleep at night, consumed by his horrible deeds. I have shown him the letter, which he acknowledges is legitimate, for he is well familiar with my grandfather's handwriting, and yet he remains impervious to sentiment or decency. But I am certain that he will not be impervious to you."

Mrs. Norton spoke with such confidence, Bea felt compelled to contradict her. "I really don't think—"

"No," her visitor said, interrupting with an emphatic

shake of her head and raising her right hand as if to call for silence. "I am loath to appear insensitive again, but I must remind you that last night you induced a murderer to confess his crimes in the middle of a crowded ballroom. A crowded ballroom, Miss Hyde-Clare, filled with the most illustrious members of society. Naturally, you are welcome to refuse the request. I hold no dominion over you and would never coerce any woman to do something she has no desire to do. But do let's dispense once and for all with the question of whether you are *able* to do it. From what I have observed during the past four and twenty hours, there is very little you *cannot* do."

Bea knew the stunning endorsement was undeserved—Wem had been seething for decades over what he perceived to be Clara's infidelities and had required only the slightest incitement to release his fury—but she could not deny the pleasure she felt in hearing it. In truth, she was dazzled by the praise, for it came from the woman who had heaped derision and scorn on her. If only she could travel back in time to her first season and whisper in her younger self's ear that one day the spiteful heiress would pay her the highest compliment and beg for her help.

That drab Miss Hyde-Clare would never have believed it.

And because it was true and because *this* drab Miss Hyde-Clare could scarcely believe it now, Beatrice said yes.

Chapter Three

The last thing *Bea wanted* to do was return to the breakfast room, with its strongly opinioned inhabitants unyielding in their calls for caution and restraint, but she could not bring herself to avoid it. If only she could have figured out some way to reconcile the cowardly act with her conscience! Then she could have sought the quiet solitude of her bedchamber and made sense of her warring emotions.

Alas, she felt compelled to be brave.

'Twas a sorry state of affairs, she thought resentfully, when a quiet spinster was obliged to make a good showing. *I am supposed to be shy and retiring.*

That was true, of course, for she had spent six seasons stuttering out one-word responses to benign questions, but she was also the woman who had just stared down the dreaded Miss Brougham. Surely if she could impress her arch-nemesis with her wit and daring, she could reason with a few squabbling family members.

Very well, she thought, determined to handle the situation calmly and firmly as she reached for the doorknob.

Inhaling deeply, she threw her shoulders back as if to screw her courage to the—

The room was empty save for the duke.

All at once, the air whooshed from her lungs as her heart knocked heavily against the wall of her chest, and she stood there, clutching the doorknob, her senses overcome by the sight of him. How handsome he was, with his bright blond curls, a little longer than fashionable, falling over his forehead and his blue eyes twinkling with amusement as he observed her surprise. He knew exactly how she felt, coming upon him like this—awash and overwhelmed—and she considered him silently as she struggled to catch her breath.

As he'd been clearly waiting for her, she expected him to offer a greeting, but he just watched her as she watched him, a fatuous smile on his face. She could only imagine the foolishness of her own wide grin.

It was absurd, she decided, the almost irresistible urge she felt to launch herself into his arms, as if they had been separated by long weeks, not mere hours, and she tightened her grasp on the doorknob as if to anchor herself.

Precisely because she felt so utterly besieged with pleasure at his presence, she sought to appear composed by artfully commending him on his exemplary timing. "Had you emerged from the comfort and safety of your home only a few minutes earlier, you would have found yourself beset by well-meaning relatives determined to bend you to their will."

Kesgrave's lips twitched as he regarded her thoughtfully. "It is somewhat difficult to tell because you have a habit of not quite saying what you mean, but I'm reasonably sure you just accused me of cowardice."

Although that had indeed been her intent, she blinked at her betrothed in innocent wonder and assured him she had meant nothing of the kind. "I was simply observing how convenient it was for you that you arrived *after* the fracas had ended," she explained as she loosened her grip on the door-knob, more confident now that she could control her move-ment. "Obviously, you could never have imagined that your grandmother would come directly here after you specifically ordered her not to, for she has a long history of meekly submitting to your commands."

"I cannot understand how I can love you so thoroughly when all you do is offer me insults," the duke said, contem-plating her gravely. "I will have you know, brat, that I did not arrive *after* the fracas. The fracas was still very much in full force when Dawson led me into the room, and the only reason it is empty now is that I vigorously ejected every last one of its occupants as they continued to quarrel with me about our injudicious plan to marry at once, including my grandmother, who had the temerity to complain that her hip joint ached too much for her to stand at present, even though yesterday she took an invigorating walk in Hyde Park with cousin Josephine over my objections."

Whatever clever reply she'd begun to formulate in response to the conundrum of his affection was entirely forgotten as Bea crossed the room in three brisk steps and flung herself into his arms. She could resist his blond curls, certainly, and withstand the tug of his twinkling blue eyes easily, but she was utterly powerless against the ruthless treat-ment of a beloved relative.

Kesgrave caught her with ease, only taking a single step back to adjust his stance, and crushed her against his chest. His lips captured hers, first tenderly, then fervently, and Bea snaked her arms around his neck to pull him closer. Her heart thudded insistently as she abandoned all thought to revel in sensation.

For several long, satisfying moments, the room was silent save for the ticking of the tall clock in the corner. Then Kesgrave raised his head, and Bea, fearing the clear-headedness that was the inevitable consequence of not kissing the duke, moaned in protest.

"No, please," she said, laying beseeching kisses along his jaw.

Alas, Kesgrave remained firm, and after succumbing to her pleas for another lovely minute, insisted they talk.

Grumbling about the tyranny of endless discussion, Bea took the seat next to him at the table and glowered darkly. "You are going to urge caution and restraint," she announced accusingly. In truth, she had no idea what his feelings were on the matter of their immediate nuptials, but the fact that he had been able to coolly end their embrace indicated an unwelcome lucidity. "You are going to parrot the clamoring mob and propose we wait a week or two."

Unable to deny it, Kesgrave nodded but promptly clarified that he would wait only one week. "Two is more caution and restraint than I am capable of showing. Naturally, I will leave the decision to you, as it is my fondest wish to satisfy your every desire. But for my own part, I will grudgingly admit that the clamoring mass raised some concerns that had not occurred to me," he explained, linking their fingers as he slid his chair closer to hers. "I do not believe I am revealing a deep and dark secret when I say you have a tendency to cloud my judgment. Recall, if you will, the mustache I wore to our interview with Taunton. I sent my valet back to the theater to fetch another one because the first specimen he selected was not luxuriant enough. I assure you, that is not the behavior of a man who can be relied upon to form a judicious opinion."

It was an affecting speech, to be sure, for Bea still found it remarkable that she had any influence at all on the Duke of Kesgrave's conduct, let alone such a profoundly debilitating one. But it was true, she knew, as nothing other than a diminished capacity to think clearly could explain the compulsion he'd felt from almost the very beginning to be in her presence.

Even so, he was far too arrogant to humbly submit to a browbeating by family and friends.

"You are the Duke of Kesgrave," she said resolutely.

He nodded his assent.

"You set the style," she said with rousing vehemence, repeating the very words he himself had uttered at various times to convince her of his vast importance. "The very moment you marry your betrothed by special license following a horrifying confession of murder, *that* becomes the fashion. By the end of the week, marquesses and viscounts would be eliciting horrifying confessions before marrying in haste."

Here, again, the duke nodded. "Agreed. We shall stay the course and marry this afternoon as planned. I am most grateful for your clear-headed appraisal of the situation, Miss Hyde-Clare."

Kesgrave was being sincere—yes, yes, Bea believed, entirely sincere and not all sardonic by calling her assessment *clear-headed*.

But, oh, did it feel like mockery, and she knew riding roughshod over everyone's concerns, including her own rather significant ones, was a ridiculous way to make a decision. She was deserving of his scorn.

Devil it!

On a deep sigh, she said, "Johannes Kepler."

Although this sudden conversation shift could have no particular meaning to Kesgrave, he said, "A most enlightened man."

"My uncle is reading a biography of Johannes Kepler."

Still uncomprehending, he gamely added, "A worthy endeavor."

A ghost of a smile appeared on Bea's lips as she stared

down at their clasped hands. "He's reading the book in an attempt to establish a connection with me. He wants to get to know me better and has settled on the biography of Johannes Kepler as the conduit."

"A surprisingly astute choice," Kesgrave observed.

Bea's heart contracted at the words, for they so closely echoed her own thoughts. "It is, yes, and I find that I am not unmoved by the gesture. I find that a part of me feels as though I am abandoning him and my aunt by leaving before they have had an opportunity to properly comprehend the truth about my parents. All those years they believed one thing and now, in the space of a few hours, they've discovered that they were victims—of Wem, yes, but also of themselves. They feel guilty and want to make amends. But it's not necessary. I cannot resent them for behaving terribly in a terrible situation. Really, I cannot," she said with increasing urgency as if determined to convince him. "I do not owe them anything, not even my forgiveness, and yet my uncle is reading Johannes Kepler and for some reason that makes me want to cry."

But she did not cry. Instead, she smiled sadly and looked up at Kesgrave, who moved his chair even closer so that his knees were touching hers. Then he held her hand more tightly and said, "You are an unnatural woman in many ways —your inability, for example, to grasp how truly impressive I am makes you deeply abnormal—but you are not inhuman. It makes you sad because it *is* sad. There's nothing wrong with deciding to give them another chance. Because you are making a choice, not submitting to an obligation. I think a week is a sufficient amount of time to discuss Kepler. After that, if your uncle wants to continue the conversation, he may come to Kesgrave House. He and your aunt will always be welcome."

The thought of Aunt Vera, with her insistence on mediocrity, running tame in the stunning Berkeley Square mansion caused Beatrice to giggle with unexpected exuberance, and she felt her anxiety subside. Only now that it had passed did she recognize the vague disquiet as grief.

Kesgrave gazed at her approvingly. "So we are agreed, then: Miss Hyde-Clare will wed the Duke of Kesgrave one week from today and nothing—no shocking revelations, no concerned family members, not even the Countess of Abercrombie's elaborate scheme to launch you into society with all the fanfare of a royal coronation. Oh, yes," he said at Bea's look of surprise, "I was subjected to the full plan in minute detail and was ordered to provide my list of guests by the end of the day. You did not believe me, did you, when I said I arrived mid-fracas. Indeed, I entered a fray so feverish in pitch that nobody, save Nuneaton, had noticed yet that you had left the room. Dawson was obliged to explain that you had gone into the study with Mrs. Norton. I trust, by the by, that the lady is well? Anyway, as I was saying, we wed one week from today and nobody shall stop us. Agreed?"

Recalling the chaos she had escaped, Bea laughed again, delighted to discover it had continued unabated without her, for it confirmed what she had suspected: Her person was incidental to the discussion. "Yes, it is agreed. Shall we shake on it like gentlemen?"

The duke, however, suggested a more pleasant way to seal the compact, and by the time the deal had been firmly set, Bea was sitting on Kesgrave's lap and they were both breathing heavily.

As before, Kesgrave was the one who called a halt to the delightful proceedings and he returned a protesting Bea to her chair before sliding his own seat several inches away from the table. "We cannot do that all day, brat," he said, then added with rueful amusement, "although that is precisely how I *had* planned to spend the day. Ah, yes, well you blush.

Come, now, let us think of some harmless occupation to distract us both. Tell me your thoughts on Kepler. What do you think of his argument for heliocentrism?"

Bea grinned and shook her head. "Oh, no, not Kepler. He will never do, for, in truth, although I carried the book with me almost constantly for two weeks, I never actually read a single word because I was despairing of you. This was during that period when you were too timid to scale my wall to declare yourself—I trust you recall that time—and all I could do was stare at the page and daydream of your handsome face. See? Now you are longing to kiss me again. Here, I shall slide my chair a few more inches away from you. Perhaps as a distraction, you can ask me about Miss Brougham."

Kesgrave's brow furrowed in confusion as this seeming non sequitur. "Miss Brougham?"

"Very good," Bea said approvingly. "Miss Brougham is my archnemesis."

Far from perplexing him further, this statement only amused him. "Your archnemesis?"

"Yes, Miss Brougham ruined my social career by calling me drab at the beginning of my first season," she explained plainly. "Whatever modest success I might have attained as an orphan with a very slight portion was scotched the moment she pointed at me with scorn and declared that I was a drab little mouse. And dreary. And sometimes both at once: the drab *and* dreary Miss Hyde-Clare. The *ton* thought this sally was outstandingly clever and adopted it with so much enthusiasm it followed me everywhere I went. I perceive the irony of that now—being so unremarkable that it was necessary to remark on it constantly—but at the time I found the derision humiliating and the humiliation crippling. Soon I was unable to answer even the most benign question without stuttering incomprehensibly, and I decided it was better to simply fall silent than to embarrass myself further."

As Bea spoke, she realized she had never said these words out loud before. Although the misery of her first season had felt to her like a grand, sweeping tragedy, in reality it had been a quiet little affair. A gentle shifting of trajectories, she realized now, so gentle nobody in her family had even noticed.

And why would they have, Bea wondered cynically. Miss Brougham's derision had merely aligned Bea's narrative arc with her relatives' expectations. They had known all along that her failure was predetermined.

Bea shook her head in silent rebuke at the direction her thoughts had taken, for there was nothing to be gained by reviving old hurts. 'Twas pointless indeed and served only to undermine any attempt at reconciliation with her aunt and uncle.

Ah, but letting go of the past was not as easy as simply resolving to let go. Not a half hour before, she'd sat next to the former Miss Brougham and decided she bore the other woman no ill will over injuries that had long since healed. And yet, as she heard herself recount for Kesgrave the events of her first season, she felt a fresh stab of pain as she recognized the depth of her isolation. She'd never said those words out loud before because she had never had anyone to say them aloud to.

It was mortifying, Bea thought, to realize that she could still discover new ways to feel bad about herself.

Kesgrave, who was either unaware of the morose turn her mood had taken or determined to overlook it, said, "Then I owe Miss Brougham a debt I can never repay, for you would not have been free to disparage me mercilessly had you made a match in your first season. The die was cast years ago, and yet I find my heartbeat slightly elevated as I contemplate how easily it could have gone the other way. Just a little less spite from Miss

Brougham, and I would have lived my whole life without you."

It was a lovely sentiment indeed, fateful and adoring, and it would require a lady with far more determination than Beatrice Hyde-Clare to remain sullen in the face of it. Her own heart beating at a slightly elevated pace, she dragged her chair close to his until their knees were once again touching.

How foolish we must look, she thought in amusement, our chairs so many feet removed from the table. Then she said, delight lilting in her voice, "It will no doubt relieve your mind greatly to know that in fact you can."

"I can what?" he asked.

"Repay your debt to the former Miss Brougham," she said, "for she has given us a case."

This answer provided no elucidation. "A case?"

"Yes, a case," she repeated, enjoying his confusion. She had known the word *case* would communicate nothing to him; that was precisely why she'd used it. "A case that requires our immediate investigation. You will note that I said *our,* for we are partners and I would never consider initiating an investigation without your assistance. The fact that I can say that sincerely is the clearest indication yet of my affection for you, as your ability to assume a convincing disguise is well below my standards. I submit as proof the mustache you donned to play Mr. Wright's law clerk, which you yourself recently pointed to as a troubling decision."

Although his eyes were alight with amusement, his voice remained serious as he thanked Bea for her willingness to overlook his shortcomings.

Naturally, she kept her own demeanor formal as she acknowledged his gratitude with a gracious dip of the head. "I am confident you will improve with my guidance."

"I wonder why I find that prospect terrifying," he said, affecting exaggerated fear with a shiver.

"Self-improvement is always daunting," she explained. "I trust you will agree to pursue the investigation. You can have no cause to object."

Now his sobriety gave way to laughter. "I can have no cause to object to my wife taking up so-called cases?"

Given that her skill at investigating—her ability to piece together an event from overlooked evidence and forgotten details—was the first and only thing she had taken pride in as a full-grown woman, she did not see the duke's rightful objection in quite the same amusing light. Obviously, she had no intention of continuing in that role after they married. During the investigation into her parents' deaths, she had felt quivers of unease and a new sense of alarm of the damage that would be done to both of them if she were caught imitating a solicitor or a steward. As her family had pointed out with unprecedented vigor just that morning, her behavior at Lord Stirling's ball already put her beyond the pale. Only her pending elevation to duchess had saved her from banishment to the farthest fringes of society.

So, yes, of course she would cease meddling in the affairs of dead men—even if it was a cause of some minor regret. No doubt she would discover she excelled at other things as well, appropriately duchess-y things such as...such as...

Here, again, her imagination fell short as she tried to contemplate what her life would be like as Kesgrave's wife.

To her relief, however, concerns about a murder-solving duchess did not pertain to the topic at hand, for, as she explained to the duke, a dead body did not figure into this particular case.

"That was the source of your alarm, was it not, when you made that unreasonable demand of me during the Fazeley affair? You traded your assistance for my promise that I would stop investigating the dead bodies that seem to fall constantly in my path. And, desiring your approval, I have done exactly that. There is no dead body this time," she said. Then, in the interest of the pedantry that was so dear to her beloved's heart, she quickly amended the statement. "Well, there *is* a dead body, Mrs. Norton's grandfather, but he has been dead for four months, and furthermore, has been buried so he cannot have fallen into my path. Or, for that matter, placed in my path. I know how strongly you object to that, as well. Paths in general seem to distress you. But happily there is no path at all."

As there was much to interest Kesgrave in this short speech, including the intriguing mystery as to what their case could be about if not the cause of Mrs. Norton's grandfather's presumably timely death, Bea was surprised when he asked with wry humor, "You desire my approval?"

Considering all she had done to thwart and insult him, she thought his cynicism was reasonable and did not cavil at his tone. Regardless of his perspective on the matter, the truth was rather stark, for she did in fact desire his approval dreadfully. Of course she did. For years there had been no one whose good opinion she'd sought. Her aunt and uncle had long made their apathy known, her cousins were indiscriminate in their judgments, and she had no friends. As unsettling as she found it to crave something so strongly, she was grateful that there was finally someone whose esteem she valued.

Nevertheless, she balked at revealing the true depth of her desperation and instead said, "Well, yes, your grace. Without it, I will have to disappoint Mrs. Norton, which would in turn be a grave disappointment to me, for I have my heart set on nobly and magnanimously providing my help. What is the point of being a duchess if not to condescend to one's archnemesis?"

Although Bea posed the question teasingly, she was in fact poking fun at herself and was quite taken aback when the duke, unable to let such provocation stand, insisted on demonstrating another satisfaction to be had as his duchess. He was so thorough in the display, he was obliged to return his betrothed to her own chair for the second time that morning.

Smiling ruefully at her from the other side of the table, where he had retreated, Kesgrave requested information about the case. "What need does the former Miss Brougham have of our investigative skills?"

Bea, who was much gratified by the distance he felt compelled to put between them, for it made her feel irresistible in a way she had not thought possible, explained that they were to find the location of the Great Mughal diamond. "Mrs. Norton's great-grandfather was given it by the Shah of Persia in exchange for confidential information. Her grandfather concealed it somewhere secret to keep it safe and unfortunately died before disclosing his hiding place. All this is speculation, of course, based on some fairy stories her grandfather told her as a child and a letter from him penned on his deathbed. The letter is intentionally vague, but she is convinced her grandfather's solicitor knows the diamond's location. She has applied to him directly for information, which he claims he doesn't have. Having witnessed my exchange with Wem last night, she's convinced I can manipulate Mr. Rose into telling me the truth without his even realizing it. I'm not sure it will be quite so easy to attain the information, but I appreciated the show of confidence from the woman who undermined my entire social career."

Before Kesgrave could reply, the door opened and Aunt Vera entered the room, a stern expression on her face that immediately softened to relief when she noted the width of the table between them. Smiling brightly, she apologized for the interruption. "But obviously it was necessary. The pair of you have been bracketed in here together for much more than a half hour, and we do not want to spur talk of our lenient guardianship. Nothing would be farther from the truth, as the Hyde-Clares are as stridently moralistic as anyone in society. Indeed, more so than many, for I refuse to allow your cousin to indulge in the brutal pugilism that is so popular among...ah...young...men."

Too late, Vera recalled that the Duke of Kesgrave was one of Gentleman Jackson's most accomplished sparring partners, and, blushing slightly, she affected a coughing fit that lasted just as long as she needed to come up with another example of immorality. On an awkward gasp, she settled on her friend Mrs. Lambert, whose slow payment of the fishmonger's bill was hailed as the greatest breach in decency since French beggars began chopping off the heads of their betters.

It was an absurd speech, a fact well known to its author, whose cheeks grew increasingly red the longer she rambled, her subject migrating from principles and scruples to kippers and mackerel. Determinedly, Bea avoided Kesgrave's gaze because she knew the moment her eyes met his, she would dissolve into a fit of giggles.

"But of course, an accomplished chef can make a meal out of anything that is available at the market and does not require the best cuts to create the best dishes," she explained, seeming to contradict an earlier point that argued that skill could not compensate for poor quality. "I am merely saying that as a society it behooves us to settle our accounts with the tradesmen in a timely fashion or risk having Parliament overthrown by dreaded Jacobins."

Although it was not entirely clear to her listeners that she had concluded her dissertation on morality, Kesgrave took advantage of the pause and eagerly agreed with her assessment. "Exactly so. Your understanding of politics as a function of one's appetite is as discerning a position as I have ever heard."

Aunt Vera preened happily at this praise, and after assuring the duke that she had arrived at her insights after extensive contemplation, asked if the outstanding issues of their nuptials had been settled satisfactorily. "I trust you have convinced Bea of the wisdom of waiting."

Kesgrave dipped his head and announced that he had.

"Wonderful," she said approvingly. "I shall inform your grandmother and Lady Abercrombie that you have decided to be sensible. I assure you both, you are doing the right thing. A wedding in June is much better than a rushed, patched-up affair."

"I have agreed to wait a week," Bea said before her aunt could launch into either a lengthy diatribe against hasty weddings or an extended tribute to the merits of a long betrothal. "After much consideration, I have decided that you and my uncle are right in your insistence that we give the *ton* an opportunity to adjust to the shocking events of last night. I believe a week is a sufficient amount of time for the *ton* to start to make that adjustment, and there's no reason why the *ton* cannot continue with the adjustment after my marriage."

If Aunt Vera understood that Bea was in fact talking about her husband and herself, she gave no indication of it in her response, which sought to stretch the delay by a month, then a fortnight, then a week. Bea considered the expediency of succumbing to one extra day in order to provide her relative with a feeling of successfully overcoming her intractability, but a brief glance at Kesgrave's handsome face—blue eyes alight with mirth, soft lips tilted up in amusement—dissuaded the effort. Seven days were already too many.

When it became clear that Bea could not be budged from her original counteroffer of a single week, Aunt Vera sighed and adopted a different tact, agreeing to let the matter rest for the moment. "We have so many other things to discuss and we can return to this tomorrow morning, after you have had a decent night's sleep. No doubt you are exhausted after the deeply traumatic emotional event of last evening. Come, let us adjourn to the drawing room, where we may discuss the needs of your engagement in comfort," she said, before directing a congenial smile at Kesgrave. "Naturally, you are invited to join us, your grace, but I cannot believe the substance of our conversation would interest you. You must have many important things to see to yourself. Please do not let us detain you."

As it was clear their tête-à-tête was at an end, Kesgrave readily agreed to this statement and Bea realized that she would have no further opportunity to discuss Mrs. Norton's missing diamond. Their investigation would come to a standstill before it had even begun.

Determined not to let that happen, Bea opened her mouth wide and yawned loudly, as if suddenly exhausted.

"Oh, my, I am sorry," she said, raising a hand to cover her mouth as she feigned another yawn. "I fear you are right, Aunt, and that I am indeed quite tired. My sleep was much compromised by the deeply traumatic emotional event of last evening and I am well in need of rest. You won't mind terribly, will you, if I forgo conversation in the living room in favor of a nap? I suddenly feel as if I could sleep straight through to dinner."

Aunt Vera, who had slept very poorly herself the night before, applauded the plan and insisted she would follow suit. "Just a brief lie-down, you understand, for I have far too much to do to while away the entire day in repose. But you, my dear, should feel no compunction in doing so. Perhaps when you wake, we can resume our discussion about the date of your nuptials. I am confident you will see that next week is simply not feasible."

Knowing there was nothing to be gained by refuting this comment, Bea nodded vaguely, then bid the duke goodbye.

"And do not forget you have a meeting with Mr. Wright in"—
she quickly calculated how long it would take her to don her
male disguise, sneak out of the house, hail a hack and arrive
in Berkeley Square—"two hours."

Her aunt tittered disapprovingly. "Really, Beatrice, how
foolish you are. As if his grace would be so remiss as to forget
an appointment with his own..." But here she trailed off, for
she did not know what function the man served.

"Solicitor," Bea supplied.

Alas, Kesgrave spoke at the same moment. "Steward."

Aunt Vera's furrowed brow had less to do with the
discrepancy between the answers than with her niece's
presumption in speaking for the duke. "I am sure Mr. Wright
is an excellent steward," she said with unnecessary placation.

Kesgrave agreed that he was and promised to pass along
her good opinion when he met with the man in two hours at
—and here he paused briefly to look at Bea—his residence.

Bea confirmed the location with a nod.

"I'm looking forward to it," Kesgrave added with a
fleeting smile.

Aunt Vera applauded this attitude and wished Mr. Hyde-
Clare were as enthusiastic to meet with his own steward, who
was, as a matter of extraordinary coincidence, also called
Wright.

Unsure that the entirety of her message had conveyed
itself to the duke, Bea added that she hoped Mr. Wright's
assistant had recovered from his setback enough to be in
attendance too.

"Goodness gracious," Aunt Vera said, "what happened to
Mr. Wright's assistant? Nothing too egregious, I trust."

"Indeed not," Bea said mildly. "Merely a mustache injury.
It was dire for a while, but in the end only his vanity was
hurt."

Although such a grievance was not commonplace, her

aunt nodded as if she were quite familiar with it while the duke assured them both that the junior steward was fully healed and would in fact be attending the meeting.

Satisfied, Bea feigned another effusive yawn, announced she could barely keep her eyes open, and dashed out of the room before her aunt could say another word. It was time to begin her investigation into the location of the Great Mughal diamond.

Chapter Four

Although she had assumed the identity of a solicitor several times in the course of her murder investigations, Bea had never actually visited the offices of one before and was slightly taken aback by the comfort and comparative luxury of Mr. Rose's rooms at 22 Savoy Street. The building's plain facade hid an interior swathed in a giddy mix of fabrics, colors and patterns that managed to create a soothing setting in which to conduct business. Somehow, the settee, with its pink daisies against a charcoal-gray jacquard, blended effortlessly with a rouge wallpaper print of peacocks and rabbits. The pervasive calm of the atmosphere was further aided by the strong hint of lavender that filled the room—cloying, to be sure, but not smothering.

By contrast, the man himself met every expectation she had of what a solicitor should look like: medium height, slight build, owlish eyes behind thick spectacles, ink-stained cuffs. He was a little younger than she had anticipated, nearer to Kesgrave's age than her uncle's, but seated behind a sleek cherrywood writing table, its slender legs tapering to elegant claw feet, he struck her as the consummate professional. It was hardly surprising that this demur lawyer had resisted Mrs. Norton's efforts to discover the location of the missing diamond. As an upstanding member of the Chancery, he would not violate the laws governing inheritance to give information to someone who was not the true heir.

Bea regarded him thoughtfully as she settled into the proffered chair, a thick brocade in a rich purple shade, and apologized again for intruding on him without warning. He had been abroad when they arrived, seeing to a matter in Westminster, but had returned promptly, as his clerk had promised. "We would never do so if the issue were not so pressing," she explained in the deep tenor she had refined during the course of her previous investigations. It always surprised her how easily she could affect a convincing masculine persona, and she knew a large part of it was the fact that people saw only what they expected to see. Having been introduced to a man, they failed to perceive slight slips into a higher register or features that were perhaps a bit softer than they should be. It no doubt helped that she had a somewhat mannish form, particularly in the shoulders, which her aunt had long ago deemed ideally suited to fencing.

"No matter, no matter," Mr. Rose said, waving his left hand as if swatting a fly to the side. "I understand the capricious nature of business and how problems often occur at the most inopportune moments, which is not to say this is one of those times. Having accomplished my morning errand, I am entirely at your disposal for"—he consulted his pocket watch —"a full forty-five minutes. Now do tell me how I may be of help."

Bea appreciated everything about this statement, from its use of the collaborative term *we* to the assumption of his usefulness. It made her far more hopeful that they would leave with the information they sought, as her optimism had plummeted when she'd perceived his rigid dedication to the law.

"As I said, my name is Mr. Wright, and this is my associate, Mr. Stephens," Bea said, tilting her head to the side to indicate Kesgrave sitting beside her. For the ploy, he had donned a simple brown suit similar to the one he'd worn when pretending to be a lowly law clerk. On that occasion, she had pointed out with mild disapproval the inappropriate excellence of his clothes, for nowhere was a cuff worn or a hem frayed. How exactly he had attended to the oversight, she did not know—perhaps by asking his valet to abrade the fabric, perhaps by purchasing an outfit directly from a law clerk—but he now looked a little more careworn and a lot less regal. She lauded the effort, but even with the missing buttons and threadbare elbows, it was impossible for Kesgrave to overcome the air of privilege he effortlessly carried. It was in his bearing, in the straight ridge of his shoulders and the direct line of his gaze. Here, clearly, was a man who had never averted his eyes to earn the approval of anyone.

"I am the head of the modern artificial curiosities department at the British Museum, and Mr. Stephens works as my assistant," Bea said, tilting her head as she appraised the solicitor. "You strike me as a man of culture. I trust you have been to Montagu House?"

As if pained by the confidence in her tone, Mr. Rose rounded his shoulders as he admitted with quiet embarrassment that he had never had the pleasure. "But it is an oversight I have every intention of rectifying as soon as possible."

Bea nodded in full sympathy of his plight, but in actuality she had been depending on his lack of familiarity to make their ruse more believable. "That is a pity, truly a pity, for we have many objects and treasures that are well worth your time," she said before launching into a description of the processes by which animals from foreign lands were preserved for display at the museum. Her tone, didactic and dry, was an almost exact facsimile of Mr. Goddard, the supercilious librarian who had refused her access to the British Museum's archive on account of her sex.

Fortunately, Kesgrave had materialized seemingly out of nowhere to settle the matter in her favor—though not to her satisfaction, for she could not accept the insult to her kind without seething at the small-mindedness.

Recalling the injustice roused her annoyance, and she momentarily forgot she was only pretending to be as boring as the tedious Mr. Goddard and related in great detail the process by which the wire bodies were constructed. Next, she planned to explain the method for treating animal hide but Kesgrave interrupted. "I wonder if giving too precise a description of the procedure will deprive the exhibition of its grandeur and awe."

It was a stunning observation, indeed it was, and Bea struggled to contain her mirth. Grinning at her assistant, Mr. Stephens, would almost certainly undermine the impression of sober-minded professionalism she was trying to present. Oh, but how wildly it amused her to have the meticulous Duke of Kesgrave take *her* to task for being excessively detailed in her account. He, with his pedantic soul, compelled by maritime tradition always to recite the order of navy ships according to their appearance in battle. For him to object to a surfeit of particulars indicated with unequivocal certainty that she had veered far off course.

"Goodness gracious, have I let my enthusiasm for our collection run away with me again?" she asked with a self-conscious laugh that was only partially calculated. "I fear it is a hazard of what we do, for our work of preserving treasures for subsequent generations is so important. Actually, that is the reason we are here today."

It was, Bea decided, a rather smooth transition and boded well for their scheme. Pretending to be administrators of the British Museum had been Kesgrave's idea, and naturally she had been hesitant. Posing as solicitors hired by Mrs. Norton had struck her as far simpler and wasn't it always better to adopt the simpler plan? The category of lawyer required little in the way of specific knowledge because it was a broad enough grouping to encompass all sorts of behaviors. But an administrator would have to know something about over-seeing a department and the museum itself.

Feigning that knowledge would be more difficult.

Kesgrave readily conceded this point but countered that the advantage to be gained from the element of surprise more than compensated. "Mrs. Norton has already applied to Mr. Rose for the information, has she not? Mr. Rose will be expecting her to make another attempt and for that effort to be a variation on the original. If we introduce ourselves as her solicitors, we will be doing the very thing he is prepared for. But if we utilize the Stewart stratagem he will not be prepared. Indeed, he will not even know the second attempt is happening."

"The Stewart stratagem," she repeated flatly as she eyed her betrothed with deep mistrust.

"Yes," he said with a firm nod, "the Stewart stratagem. It was a trick employed by the head of the second infantry division, Lieutenant-General William Stewart, during the Peninsula War."

As comprehensive a reader as Beatrice was, there were gaps in her education, most notable among them battlefield strategies. History and travel and science were much more interesting subjects than dreary accounts of troop movements. For this reason, she couldn't entirely deny the validity of the Stewart stratagem. At the same time, she thought assigning a title to an extemporaneous idea would be an ingenious way to give it consequence, and she could not decide if Kesgrave would sink to such subterfuge. She knew *she* would if the notion had occurred to her and helped her win an argument.

Testing him, she asked for details of the stratagem and knew by the delighted look that overtook his face that it was indeed a legitimate military maneuver. Nothing pleased him more than lecturing on a topic with which he was intimately familiar, a trait she had discovered on their second night at Lakeview House, when he had rebuked his host's deplorable knowledge of ships under Nelson's command during the Battle of the Nile by listing them all for the edification and boredom of the company.

Unaware of Bea's fond recollection of their early courtship, the duke explained, "The stratagem centered around the Maya Pass, which Stewart hoped to capture for the British, as taking it would cut the French forces off from the larger army farther north and leave them nowhere to retreat. Stewart knew the French would expect an ambush at the pass, for it was the most obvious way to cut off their retreat, so he pulled his men from the area and moved them to an old fortress nearby. Amaiur overlooked another pass, one much more difficult to cross because the terrain was steeper, but the route was actually shorter."

Bea could only imagine the expression on her face as she listened to this account—a mixture, to be sure, of amused condescension and fondness at his inability to resist the urge to pontificate—and was not surprised when he paused his explanation to defend the necessary specificity of his narrative. "If you don't know the particulars of the situation, you won't understand why the scheme prevailed. It all depended on the implausibility of this second pass. If Stewart's decision appeared irrational, then the French would not have been persuaded. Fortunately, the French marshal, Jean-Baptiste

Drouet, Comte d'Erlon, perceived the tactical advantage and relocated his forces accordingly. He moved his men under the cover of night, hoping to surprise Stewart. But Stewart moved *his* forces, thus evading the French and capturing the pass. That is using the element of surprise and the advantage we need to establish with Mr. Rose."

Beatrice allowed that there might be some usefulness in applying the Stewart stratagem to their situation and asked what he proposed. His answer was why she had introduced them as members of the modern artificial curiosities department.

Now, as she prepared to explain to Mr. Rose the true purpose of their visit, she acknowledged the benefits of Kesgrave's scheme. Approaching a target from the side was far more devious than meeting it head-on, a conclusion bolstered by the fact that Mr. Rose displayed no concern or suspicion at the mention of treasure. He merely lifted his chin to a curious angle and said, "Indeed"?

"Yes, it is at the heart of all we do—preserving treasures found both at home and abroad. It is so easy for these precious things to be destroyed through neglect or careless-ness. Fortunately, our organization is large and well funded, so we are able to have teams in many countries on several conti-nents. This is how we know things," Bea explained before leaning forward and lowering her voice slightly, as if revealing a secret, "and one of the things we know is that you should be concerned."

As this network of informants was a fiction Kesgrave improvised on the carriage ride to the office, Bea would not have been the least bit amazed if Mr. Rose scoffed with scornful dismissal at the prospect of a vast web of mysteri-ously knowledgeable museum administrators.

But her host did not sneer. Instead, he rubbed his chin thoughtfully and regarded her with interest.

Much encouraged by this display of curiosity, Bea continued, "Through our sources, it has come to our attention that an item of very great value is in danger of being stolen."

This was, Bea thought, a statement with a clear implication, but it sparked no light of understanding in the solicitor's eye. So she added with pointed emphasis, "An object of very, *very* great value."

Alas, understanding still eluded him.

Smothering a sigh, she all but spelled it out. "A jewel, in fact."

Comprehension was immediate, and Mr. Rose stiffened his shoulders sharply against the back of his chair. He made no move to speak, content, it seemed, to wait for Mr. Wright to explain himself further. Bea, however, thought the moment needed to be more dramatic, so she raised her hand as if to forestall his comment and ordered him to remain silent. "I am not here to talk about the object in question. My goal is only to ensure that you have taken the necessary precautions to keep it safe. Everything else falls outside my purview as the head of the modern artificial curiosities department. Do you understand?"

Naturally, the sensible response to such a query was no, for much of what Bea had said defied comprehension. But Mr. Rose, after several moments of silent contemplation, nodded slowly and said, "I do, yes. But I must ask: Are you very sure the object is at risk? What information has your organization uncovered to give rise to this alarm?"

It was a reasonable line of inquiry, and although neither Bea nor the duke had anticipated the question, she knew enough about the gem trade from Jean-Baptiste Tavernier's travelogue to provide an answer.

"A jewelry dealer in London was contacted regarding the possibility of cutting up a very large stone," she said. "As large stones are distinct and easily identifiable, the best way to disguise a stolen one is to cut it into a dozen smaller gems. Aware that something nefarious was most likely afoot, the jeweler alerted us to the query. It is possible that the stone in question is not a diamond, and be assured we are talking to other possible targets as well. We at the British Museum never take risks with valuable artifacts."

Fortunately for their scheme, Mr. Rose found this explanation plausible. "Yes, I can see why you find that concerning, and I appreciate your taking the time to warn me. I must admit I find it difficult to believe that the...ah, object...in my possession is in danger. I was visited recently by a young lady who insisted she had a claim to the stone but was unable to present documentation that clearly attested to that fact. I explained I could be of no help to her, as she was not the rightful heir, and she took her leave without argument. You are not suggesting, are you, that this woman would conspire to steal the stone?"

Bea, who had not expected Mr. Rose to introduce Mrs. Norton into the conversation at all, was momentarily taken aback by how much easier it would be to gather the necessary information than she had expected. She'd assumed the solicitor would evade the topic or claim ignorance of the stone.

As he was forthcoming, she decided to change tactics and become reticent. Affecting great surprise, she turned to her colleague, Mr. Stephens, and said, "Could this mean...?"

Deliberately vague, she left the thought unfinished.

Confusion darted across Kesgrave's face as he wondered what she intended to imply, but quickly enough he grasped her ploy. "It does seem to indicate..."

He, too, trailed off enticingly.

Perfect, Bea thought, delighted with how smoothly he'd returned her volley. "We should probably...?" She tilted her head quite purposely toward the door in a clear intimation that perhaps it was time to take their leave.

Mr. Rose found this exchange of half-finished sentences quite agitating and, correctly interpreting Bea's look, insisted they could not leave until they shared what they knew. "Is it Mrs. Norton? Is she behind the threat? That cannot be. She's highly decorous and well respected among society. She would never sink to the level of theft. The Great Mughal diamond's original owner was her great-grandfather, and it is an heirloom of great value and historical importance. To steal it from her uncle would be to steal from her own family, and I cannot believe she would be so without conscience," he stated firmly, before rounding his shoulders and looking at Bea with uncertainty. "Is that what you believe?"

As retreat had already brought such satisfying results, Bea continued with the gambit. "It is not for me to say what I believe or don't believe. Our purpose in visiting you was only to give warning, which we have done. Now we will do the same with others whom we think might be at risk. We thank you for your time."

Bea nodded to Kesgrave to signal he should stand up, but before either of them could rise, Mr. Rose said, "Yes, yes, of course. I understand and appreciate it. But, please, the news you have given me is very distressing and I require a few moments to gather my thoughts. I hope you will bear with me."

Graciously, Bea leaned back in her seat and told Mr. Rose to take all the time he needed to assimilate the information. She made it sound as if she were doing him a favor, but of course she had no intention of leaving before she'd discovered where the stone was hidden. "I am sure you have no cause for apprehension, Mr. Rose," she added reassuringly, "for you strike me as an intelligent man. You would not take foolish chances with something of such great value."

If anything, this compliment increased his anxiety and he nodded absent-mindedly as he clasped his hands together. "That is true, yes, quite true. But, you see, I did not make the arrangements myself and in fact had nothing to do with the object. My client entrusted the secreting of it to his groom, a man named Richard Flowerdew, in whom he had absolute faith. That is why I am unsure how to proceed. Your belief as well as Mrs. Norton's that it is I who knows the location of the jewel seems to indicate that it is perfectly safe in Mr. Flowerdew's hiding spot. The thieves cannot extract the information from him because they don't know he exists. Ah, but am I being foolhardy in my assumptions? Perhaps a little too confident? So I should warn him of your concerns. Or would doing that alert the thieves to his existence, therefore making him a target? And if he is at risk, am I not as well, for everyone supposes that I know where the stone is. Does that make me vulnerable to coercion? Will I be held at knifepoint and compelled to tell them where the diamond is?" he asked, his hands shaking now as he contemplated the grim possibility. "Oh, what a very messy muddle, to be sure."

Bea, who felt decidedly confident in her conviction that he was not at any risk, urged him to remain calm and called upon the network of museum agents who had led her to his door to further soothe his mind. "Our informants thought it was highly unlikely that you had the diamond or knew of its whereabouts based on a variety of factors, including the fact that few men truly trust their lawyer, but we decided it would be prudent to visit you regardless. As I said, it is our policy to be thorough. All precautions must be taken even if some are less necessary than others."

Grateful, Mr. Rose nodded and spoke at length about the importance of being careful as it related to his work writing contracts. "For there are so many opportunities for matters to go awry. So much of the meaning in the law resides in the details and even the smallest mistake can have sweeping ramifications."

As eager as she was to leave now that they had the right name, she sat patiently through his pontifications because she imagined he was rambling more out of relief rather than a genuine desire to explicate a difficult aspect of his occupation. Having been the cause of his disquiet, it only seemed fair to be part of its reprieve.

Nevertheless, sitting there quietly when there was the matter of the former groom to discuss with Kesgrave created an almost physical ache in her body.

Mr. Flowerdew!

Yes, of course *that* was the garden to which Mr. Brougham had referred in his final letter to his granddaughter. It was redolent of life and vigor, a vibrant patch populated with plants of all species and varieties, not just roses. Bea wasn't at all surprised that the former groom had not presented himself as an option to Mrs. Norton, for members of the household staff were frequently underestimated or overlooked. If Mr. Rose had not been maneuvered into revealing the truth, Bea wondered if she would have discovered it on her own. It was doubtful it would have occurred to her to look beyond the obvious answer.

Fortunately, the duke's ruse had worked beautifully, and now she would have the pleasure of astonishing the former Miss Brougham with her resourcefulness and ingenuity. Obviously, the other woman would not have requested her help if she had not believed she could achieve the goal, but she could not have imagined her achieving it so quickly. No doubt she'd assumed the task would be difficult.

And perhaps it would be—for someone else.

Even knowing the spiteful heiress had no recollection of their shared history, of the malice she had aimed indiscriminately at a young schoolroom miss with neither looks nor status, did little to dampen Bea's pleasure at proving so neatly and effectively that she was neither drab nor dreary where it mattered—in the intellect.

How, then, to convey the news, she wondered as Mr. Rose turned his attention to the havoc wreaked by a poorly placed comma. Should she content herself with sending a note or enjoy the gratification of an in-person account? The latter offered the ability to witness Mrs. Norton's amazement firsthand, which certainly had its appeal, but presented challenges that would cause delays, such as changing out of her male disguise and coordinating their schedules. Bea had no way of knowing if the society matron was at home for calls that afternoon.

A letter would allow her immediate if indirect gratification.

Bea accepted the compromise and began composing the note as Mr. Rose discussed the necessity of hiring an assistant to proof one's contracts. Although he spoke quite highly of several people who had passed through his employ in recent months, he interrupted his speech to ask if the modern artificial curiosities department or perhaps the large institution of the British Museum had a reliable reader it could recommend.

"I am sure it will come as no surprise to you when I say it's very difficult to find reliably competent associates," he lamented and paused briefly to allow his listeners to lend their support to this statement. Then, taking their silence as tacit agreement, he nodded understandingly and launched into a plaint against printers, who overcharged for their services.

Ardently, he detailed the arbitrary pricing of ink, and Kesgrave, who was accustomed to inflicting boredom, not suffering from it, could stand it no longer. He rose abruptly to his feet with the imperiousness of five centuries of breeding and bid the solicitor good day.

Mr. Rose broke off his grievance to stare in awe.

Amused, Bea stood as well and apologized for her associate's curt goodbye. "Mr. Stephens is very diligent in his responsibilities, and although I am sure he is as reluctant as I am to end this pleasant interlude, he is also eager to return to his duty. Thank you, Mr. Rose, for your time and patience. You have been a great help."

The solicitor took no offense at the haste of their departure and stood up to escort them to the door. "I understand feeling passionate about one's work, as I can be quite zealous myself upon occasion," he said, then added with a sheepish grin, "Indeed, I have a slight tendency to run on when I talk about my profession, which you probably noticed. If I have kept you from your business with my rambling, I most sincerely apologize."

Bea, whose conscience twinged slightly at the anxiety they had caused their host, rushed to assure him that he had not. But Kesgrave, speaking at precisely the same moment and feeling no conciliating compunction, suggested that the solicitor's fondness for tedious pontificating might explain his difficulty in retaining qualified staff.

At once, Mr. Rose turned a bright shade of fuchsia, but he kept his gaze level and thanked the duke for the critique of his performance. "I will certainly keep it in mind," he said with tactful civility.

Kesgrave's brusque nod, which Bea had seen many times during their stay at Lakeview House and had been directed at her on several occasions, was a masterstroke of indifference and impatience. Clearly, he was done affecting the servility required to play a convincing museum clerk and had reverted to form. A twenty-minute sermon on the challenges of the law profession was more than he could withstand. Bea, who had been subjected to far worse tedium during her twenty years under her aunt and uncle's roof, found this lack of discipline as amazing as it was amusing.

As if to provide a demonstration of her own self-control, Bea waited until they were both comfortably settled in Kesgrave's carriage before dissolving into a fit of giggles. What an incongruent picture he had made—the high-handed duke exerting his rightful authority from the careworn suit and modest mustache of the lowly Mr. Stephens. Of course the solicitor had stared in wonder at the astonishing display, for humble clerks of any persuasion typically did not brandish unrestrained entitlement.

As the carriage lurched into the road, Kesgrave observed mildly, "Say what you will about my own tendency to pontificate—and knowing you, you will say much and all of it heartless—but I do not allow my thoughts to meander from topic to topic as new ideas occur to me. My scope is limited, and I am disciplined."

Conceding the validity of the duke's point, for he did in fact ruthlessly constrain his lectures to the matter at hand, devoting, for example, a full half hour to the Royal Navy's warships at the Battle of the Nile and never once diverting his attention to Napoleon's fleet, Bea tried to contain her amusement. But her efforts at respectful sobriety were undermined entirely by this well-timed reference to discipline and her waning laughter redoubled.

The duke bore the insult nobly, examining his own threadbare cuff with apparent indifference while waiting for the torrent to pass. He did not point out how beautifully his idea of using a variation of the Stewart stratagem had worked, a forbearance she genuinely appreciated and one that forced her to concede that he might have some discipline after all.

Because he did not ask for the compliment, Bea felt compelled to offer it, thanking him for helping her attain the information with as little fuss as possible. "As you may recall, sometimes an operation calls for a dramatic intervention in order to gain access to the information. Fortunately, that was not necessary because of your suggestion."

Kesgrave raised his eyes to hers and said, "By 'dramatic intervention,' you mean your pretending to swoon so that I may search the files in his cabinet?"

"No, I mean *your* pretending to swoon so that *I* may search his files," she clarified.

"Yes, of course," Kesgrave said, his lips twitching. "You are, after all, my superior."

'Twas only a sally, a teasing comment in reference to their assumed identities as employees of the modern artificial curiosities department, not, she knew, an actual statement of his position, for the Duke of Kesgrave considered himself subordinate to no one. And yet there was just enough sincerity in his tone to give her pause, and her heartbeat suddenly ticked up at the implication of genuine respect. Looking at him in the darkened light of the carriage—the rueful grin so similar to the one he had worn after the interview with Taunton—she felt an inexorable rush of affection, and finding him as irresistible now as she had then, she slid closer. Staring deeply into his eyes, moved, impossibly, by the light that she knew glowed only for her, she lowered her lips to his.

Ah, but no, she thought, as the gentle brush of his mustache tickled her face, I am far too clever to make that mistake again.

Gently, she pulled at the edge of the mustache to remove it. Given how easily it had come off during a previous kiss in a carriage, she had naturally assumed it would yield now to the slightest of pressure. When it did not, she pulled harder. Still, it resisted so she tugged at the fiendish theater prop with more and more force until she had finally wrenched it free. Catapulting freely, her hand struck the side of the carriage with a decided thwack, which caused her to cry out in pain at the same moment the duke yelped, "Ouch!"

Mortified, she stared as Kesgrave raised a hand to examine his upper lip for damage. Unaccountably, she felt laughter well up inside her. That...that *damnable* mustache had humiliated her again.

It was more than she could bear, and she succumbed to another bout of giggles, horror and humor uniting with so much vigor she could barely breathe. She was certainly incapable of choking out an apology. But she did feel sorry, so dreadfully sorry, for unintentionally scraping off his skin.

Kesgrave, clutching her by the shoulders in hopes of calming her, asking with genuine bewilderment, "How can I love someone so absurd?"

Bea, who had asked herself that question many times, managed to contain her mirth enough to say, "I assure you, your grace, I am as befuddled by the development as you and can only wonder when you will come to your senses."

It was just an offhand comment, for she didn't truly believe his feelings for her defied all explanation—at least she did not believe that anymore. With a better understanding of him and a sharper sense of her own appeal, she knew now that that his affection was the only rational response he could have to the situation, for his perverse pleasure at being held to account by an upstart spinster was well documented.

But Kesgrave could not know she was merely teasing and instantly looked contrite. "I am the sanest I have ever been," he assured her.

Naturally, such romantic drivel could not go unrewarded, and Bea, picking up from where she had left off prior to the debacle with the mustache, pressed her lips against his. Within moments, the kiss turned heated, and worried that she would lose her own precarious grip on control—so much for her recently vaunted discipline—she pulled away.

Regretfully, she sighed heavily and asked, "Did I really agree to one week?"

Kesgrave chuckled softly. "Alas, my love, you did."

"I trust next time you will talk me out of such foolishness."

"I promise you there will not be a next time," he said confidently. "But come, let us not think about what was lost but rather what was gained—that is, an opportunity to prove your vast superiority to your archnemesis. How do you plan to inform her of your success? A letter via a messenger or in person? If you would seek my opinion, I would advise the former, as it is much easier to be exquisitely condescending in a note. Without question, it can be done in person, as I have demonstrated on several occasions, but a letter allows you to control every aspect and therefore can be particularly cutting."

Although Bea had already settled on sending a missive because it was the faster method, she found his reason to be equally appealing and immediately asked for tips. If there was anything the duke excelled at, it was puncturing the pretensions of toad-eaters.

Happy to have his expertise sought, Kesgrave launched into an enthusiastic lecture that exhaustively detailed his reliable method for deflating impertinent mushrooms. To Beatrice's delight, it lasted not only the rest of the journey to Portman Square but also several dozen minutes after they arrived.

Chapter Five

B*ea had not been present* in the breakfast room when the détente between Aunt Vera and Lady Abercrombie had been struck, but she was nevertheless obliged to abide by its terms.

"I am sorry if it seems unfair to you, my dear, but decisions are made by those who stay in the room long enough to make them," her aunt explained as Bea protested the need for quite so many new gowns.

Certainly, as a young miss fresh from the schoolroom she had pined for the pretty frocks the other girls wore, with their lovely pearl rosettes and elegant lace trim, and, yes, of course, when she had pictured herself dancing in the arms of a handsome beau, she always twirled in the finest silk. But even in her most outlandish reveries, she rotated among a few beautiful dresses, not a full dozen, for she was as moderate in her tastes in fantasy as she was in real life.

Alas, the Countess of Abercrombie knew nothing of moderation, and it was she who had been given control of Beatrice's trousseau. It was the only concession her ladyship had been willing to accept in exchange for her abandoning her scheme to introduce Bea to society.

Or, as Aunt Vera would say in a shrill voice, *re*-introduce.

"Do you think I am happy with the arrangement?" her aunt asked in a low voice, an overly bright smile on her face as she nodded at Madame Bélanger, who was consulting with the countess over fabrics for the three riding habits her ladyship insisted were necessary for a duchess. Every so often, Lady Abercrombie would call to one of the shop assistants to bring something richer, more opulent, and poor Aunt Vera would flinch as if pricked by a pin or something equally as sharp. "Let me assure you I am not. You know as well as I do that Flora will never be satisfied with Mrs. Duval's thoroughly adequate work once she has seen the mastery of London's finest modiste up-close and will pester me relentlessly until she, too, is brought to this establishment for several new items. And how do you think Russell will receive the news of his sister's Bond Street wardrobe? With calm delight? With gracious acceptance? No. He will insist at once that he be allowed to visit Weston, and now I am spending an entire year's worth of candles on clothes for them on top of standing this huge expense for you. To be sure, I find the whole thing wretched beyond bearing, and yet I am here, advising you on which colors look best with your wan complexion without uttering a word against it. The least you can do, my dear, is the same."

Striving to look slightly chastened, Bea said, "Yes, ma'am."

Aunt Vera, mollified by the subdued response, nodded with approval. "As unpleasant as this experience is, it is little compared with the discomfort of letting Lady Abercrombie present you to society as if you were a green miss having her first season. If the circumstances were different, it would not signify, for the countess is welcome to take whomever she wants under her wing. But in the wake of Wem's confession, it simply will not do. We are already the subject of so much gossip. People are wondering what we knew and what we withheld from you." Here, her color rose sharply, for she and her husband had known quite a bit and withheld it all from their niece. It turned out that everything they thought they'd known was wrong, but the inaccuracy of their beliefs did not nullify their decision to hide them from her. "Mrs. Ralston has intimated that some people might think we conspired with Wem to gain control of the estate, which is patently absurd, for although Welldale House is a lovely home, it has a shocking number of rooms that all require upkeep. Not to mention the grounds, with their ornamental garden and sweeping park. It is a hideous thing to say, exceptionally hideous, and not at all true. We had no idea what Wem had done and believed him when he told us of Clara's infidelities. You understand that, don't you? We had no cause to question his word. He was your father's oldest friend. He had known him since childhood."

Hoping to calm her aunt, who seemed genuinely worried that she might be swayed by Mrs. Ralston's mendacious gossip, Bea wrapped one arm around her shoulder and promised she would never believe such vile speculation.

Indeed, she would not, for hiding among Clara and Richard's things in a trio of chests stored in the attic were her father's investments, untouched by either his brother or sister-in-law. As miserly as her relatives were, they had never drawn on the inheritance of the orphan girl left in their care to alleviate the financial burden she presented. It was a laudable impulse, to be sure, and yet how much happier Bea's life would have been if her aunt and uncle had cashed in a few stocks to pay for basic provisions such as a decent mount or a dress with lovely pearl rosettes and elegant lace trim. Their refusal to touch her parents' money coupled with their own innate parsimony meant she had often had to do without, and that deprivation had made her feel as if she herself were without value.

And now poor Aunt Vera was being forced to rectify two decades' worth of stinginess in a single visit to the modiste!

Bea would have laughed at her aunt's predicament if she herself weren't so unsettled by the Countess of Abercrombie's conception of an appropriate trousseau. There was something about the tenth morning dress that was akin to the eighth footman her aunt had included in her list of household staff she would have to oversee as Kesgrave's wife. Like Aunt Vera's seemingly endless list of servants, her ladyship's boundless wardrobe of clothes hinted at the immensity of her future as the Duchess of Kesgrave.

Although Vera Hyde-Clare submitted to Bea's embrace without protest, she was far too accustomed to keeping her niece at arm's length to endure the proximity for long. Twisting her shoulders awkwardly, she slipped free, took a step to the side and said with unfamiliar cynicism, "I am sure we all know who Mrs. Ralston means when she says 'some people.' It is mostly she and her daughters."

Bea rather doubted the group included the daughters, but she nodded in general agreement and tried not to cringe as Lady Abercrombie, satisfied with her selections for walking dresses, turned her attention to promenade dresses. Having reached the ripe old age of six and twenty without owning a gown specifically tailored to be seen and admired whilst strolling through Hyde Park, Bea did not think such an item was necessary now. Surely, one of the dozen walking dresses her ladyship had already ordered was elegant enough to suffice.

Next to her, Aunt Vera shuddered in horror as the countess sought Madame Bélanger's opinion on the correct number of promenade dresses to order—three or four. Naturally, the modiste suggested the higher number, then paused slightly before wondering if perhaps five was not better.

"Ze park can be filthy, with mud and dirt everywhere, *n'est-ce pas?*" she pointed out. "It takes very little for ze hem to be ruined."

Persuaded by the rigor of the argument, Lady Abercrombie agreed with five.

Aunt Vera moaned as though in pain and then muttered softly, as if to remind herself of the necessity of her suffering, "A second come-out hosted by her ladyship would provide fodder for the gossips. They would point to her generosity as proof of our frugality and our failure to present you properly the first time, which would draw harsh attention to our guardianship and cause people to question our choices. This is better. I am at peace with our compromise."

But clearly she was not and continued to quietly catalogue the advantages of the arrangement. Bea contemplated offering to cover some of the rapidly mounting costs with the money left by her parents and wondered how such a proposal would be received. She knew her relatives would be grateful to spend less on her behalf, for the habits of a lifetime were hard to break, and yet she could not entirely dismiss her aunt's newfound self-consciousness about their shabby treatment of her. With Mrs. Ralston's maliciousness echoing in her ears, she might take offense at the implication of clutch-fistedness. Her uncle, as well, had been unreliably generous of late, insisting that no expense be spared in regards to her trousseau, a statement that had as deleterious effect on his wife's nerves as Madame Bélanger's insistence on the need for five promenade gowns.

Her aunt repeated, "I am at peace," as Lady Abercrombie asked to see heavier fabrics appropriate for traveling dresses, and Bea, succumbing to an antic sort of anxiety, began to laugh.

"Miss Hyde-Clare?" a voice called uncertainly, then with more conviction, "Miss Hyde-Clare! I am so pleased to see you."

Beatrice turned to find the light-brown gaze of Mrs. Norton peering at her. Aunt Vera, who, prior to her association with the domineering and spendthrifty whirlwind that was the Countess of Abercrombie, would have been delighted to find her niece on agreeable terms with a society matron with deep ties to the hostesses of Almack's, recoiled in alarm at the familiarity.

Darting an apprehensive glance at Bea, Vera greeted the newcomer, who was accompanied by her mother. Her salutation was eagerly returned, and Mrs. Brougham remarked on the amiability of the weather, a topic particularly dear to Aunt Vera's heart.

"Oh, yes," she said gratefully, "it is everything that is delightful. Mr. Hyde-Clare went for a ride this morning, and we are going to go for a drive this afternoon in the park, for one can never rely on such pleasantness to last. Indeed, clouds have already begun to gather. They are seemingly harmless now, white and fluffy, but heaven knows how quickly they can turn thunderous."

Mrs. Brougham, sharing her pessimistic bent, immediately agreed to this assessment and observed the slight chill she had felt upon exiting her carriage only minutes before.

As the older women aired their concerns about the weather, Mrs. Norton slipped her arm through Bea's elbow and drew her head close. "I am glad for this chance meeting, for I very much wanted to thank you for your assistance. I am still agog at how quickly you sorted out the confusion regarding my grandfather's cryptic comment about gardens. I thought for sure it was Mr. Rose. To discover it is Flowerdew, the groom I have known for my entire life, is still astounding. I would ask how you did it, but having observed your interrogation of Lord Wem, I suspect I already know. You truly are a wonder, Miss Hyde-Clare, and I am desolate we did not have cause to get to know each other sooner. I am certain we would have been fast friends."

Although Bea was as susceptible to flattery as any young woman who had been exiled to the fringe of society for six long seasons, she knew Mrs. Norton's compliments were motivated as much by sycophancy and gratitude as they were by sincere admiration. She was the future duchess who had helped her locate a diamond of staggering value. Of course the other woman thought they would be friends.

Despite these cynical thoughts, Bea regarded her with a genial smile and assured her it had been her pleasure to lend her assistance three days ago—which was true. As Kesgrave himself had noted, proving oneself vastly superior to one's archnemesis was an especially delectable sensation. "Have you had a chance to talk with Mr. Flowerdew since the discovery? Is he more forthcoming than Mr. Rose?"

Mrs. Norton's expression darkened and her lips turned down in a pout. "No, he is not! And I am very cross about it, for he has known me since I was a small child and is quite aware of my grandfather's affection for me. I swear, it is the veriest quandary."

Bea did not find it surprising that a groom would be reluctant to reveal the location of one of the most valuable gems in creation. At the same time, there was little he could do with the diamond, for what she had told Mr. Rose about the disposal of a large gem was accurate: It was almost impossible to dispense of one discreetly without breaking it down into many smaller, less conspicuous gems. Would Mr. Flowerdew have access to that sort of skill?

Considering the problem, she asked Mrs. Norton if she had shown him her grandfather's letter, which made his intentions known.

Although Bea considered this approach to be a fairly self-evident tactic, the surprised look on Mrs. Norton's visage made it clear it had not occurred to her. "Of course I must show him the letter! How could I not have thought of that myself? Really, I am so appallingly obtuse! My only excuse is that Flowerdew's refusal to listen to reason frustrated me to such a degree, I could barely recall my own name," she explained with a deprecating sigh. "Thank you, Miss Hyde-Clare, for helping me *again*. You are quite a marvel."

Although Bea knew suggesting the most obvious solution was far from impressive, she was too polite to say so. "You are welcome."

Mrs. Norton, who continued to regard her with amazement, said, "I don't suppose—" But she did not finish the thought, abruptly cutting herself off with a violent shake of her head. "No, you have already been so helpful, and you are here to select your trousseau, are you not?"

As the munificence broadly on display made her deeply uncomfortable, she agreed and hesitantly added, "Lady Abercrombie is helping, as she was my mother's dearest friend and has strong opinions about what is needed."

"How very wonderful," Mrs. Norton enthused. "I am sure she knows exactly what a duchess requires. At your advanced age, your instinct is most likely to be utterly pragmatic and get only a few dresses and one riding habit. Oh, but this isn't the time for calm-minded practicality, for you are going to be a duchess. A duchess, Miss-Hyde-Clare! And you will have many beautiful gowns and be so very important. Really, my dear, did you ever dream you would rise to such grandeur? Think back to your first season—can you even remember it? —and imagine telling yourself that one day you would be a duchess. A duchess! I'm sure the earlier you would swoon from shock. I swear, sometimes I feel like I will. I am so surprised by the happiness I've found in my own union. Mr.

Norton is everything I dreamed of as a young girl and sometimes I can scarcely believe we will have been married six years this summer."

Bea, whose equanimity had already been weakened by the breadth of her trousseau, dearly wished the other woman would stop saying *duchess* in that worshipful tone. The exaltation made marriage to Kesgrave seem like something foreign and far, another country or a distant shore, not the binding together of two people who loved each other, which was, ultimately, a simple thing.

And Mrs. Norton's exhortation to consider the astonishment of her earlier self! No other remark could be more carefully calculated to increase Bea's unease, for the earlier version of herself would have indeed fainted to hear of the news. That Bea, whose perception of being a duchess mirrored Mrs. Norton's, would have been in awe of this Bea.

Now, *that* was a most unsettling idea to contemplate.

Unaware of the other woman's growing discomfort, Mrs. Norton continued. "To think I was on the verge of asking you to help me again! Here you are, engaged in one of the most exhilarating activities a newly betrothed woman can do— selecting your trousseau—and I wanted to drag you away to cajole my grandfather's former groom into revealing the location of the Great Mughal diamond. What an absurd creature I am! Please," she said imploringly as she tugged Bea's arm, "you must not let my idiocy dissuade you from being my friend. I promise you I usually display much better judgment."

Bea felt her agitation increase with every word Mrs. Norton spoke and could easily imagine the other woman's response if she announced that she would much rather interrogate Mr. Flowerdew than remain where she was. Amazement! Horror! True befuddlement!

Choosing her trousseau was not exhilarating for Bea—it

was terrifying—and now, because Mrs. Norton had put it in her head, she could almost hear her younger self tut-tutting in disappointment at the poor-spirited spinster she had become.

It was, Bea thought defensively, a most unfair charge, for she had always been a poor-spirited miss, even in her first season. At least now she had the ingenuity and temerity to identify murderers.

As Bea struggled to stop quarreling with a fictional version of herself, an enterprise as ridiculous as it was futile, Lady Abercrombie gasped in delight. "This cashmere is perfection," she said, running her fingers caressingly over the fabric. "Bea, you simply must feel it. The texture is divine. We will take three shawls in your most vibrant colors. Let us discuss cloaks. She must have a long, heavy, hooded one for the winter months and one that is lighter for the autumn and early spring."

Bea did not rush to do her bidding, but the lure of perfect cashmere was more than Mrs. Norton could withstand and she brushed her hand lovingly over the silken cloth.

"Oh, indeed, yes, quite divine," the heiress said, echoing the countess's approval. "Are you sure, Lady Abercrombie, that three are enough? Considering how frequently I lose my own shawls, I think four would be better."

Her ladyship needed no further inducement and promptly agreed, causing Aunt Vera to whimper quietly as she calculated the cost of the extra cashmere. Instantly solicitous, Mrs. Brougham enquired after her health, and noting the paleness of her cheeks, suggested she sit down. Aunt Vera weakly objected while accepting a seat from one of the shop assistants, and Mrs. Brougham, endorsing her daughter's observation that shawls were easily misplaced, wondered if perhaps a fifth would not be best.

"As a precaution," she added.

The wisdom of this was generally lauded, with Madame

Bélanger noting the difficulty of keeping track of many items in one's wardrobe. "Gloves in particular," she said. "A duchess can never have too many pairs of gloves."

Her ladyship immediately concurred with this observation and added that the modiste's skilled embroiderers elevated the plain white glove to a work of art.

Aunt Vera visibly recoiled at the prospect of spending additional funds to decorate items that were sure to be lost, while Bea feared that Madame Bélanger's observation would prove to be literal. At once, she pictured herself in a room filled increasingly with white gloves, gasping for air as lovely silk pairs rose higher and higher, above her mouth and nose, smothering the life out of her.

It was only in her head, the sensation of suffocation, and yet it truly felt to her as if the walls were drawing nearer.

She needed to leave.

Sliding her own arm through her archnemesis's elbow, she said, "I will do it."

Mrs. Norton, scarcely able to pull her eyes from an illustration of an exquisite scarlet cloak, looked fleetingly at Bea. "Do what?"

"Help you with that important matter," she explained, aware that she was the absurd creature now. She did not care, for she needed to breathe, and that was impossible in the cloying confines of Madame Bélanger's shop. It was all of a mad piece anyway, the lavish trousseau her poor aunt was being forced to buy. All those outfits, the dozens of dresses and shawls, so that she may bury herself in her finery in the library at Kesgrave House.

She would be the most splendidly attired coward in history.

"Oh, but we cannot go yet," Lady Abercrombie protested. "We still have so much to do: spencers and pelisses and scarves and chemisettes. So many decisions yet to be made."

"Naturally, I would love to stay, but Mrs. Norton's matter is pressing and I did promise to assist her with it," Bea said, clutching meaningfully on the other woman's arm.

Mrs. Norton understood at once and announced that the matter was very pressing. "Almost dire, I would say."

Her mother stared at her with a thoroughly baffled look, no doubt trying to comprehend how something so urgent could arise seemingly out of nowhere.

Bea turned to Lady Abercrombie and deferred all wardrobe decisions to her. "I trust you implicitly and I think we can all agree that your taste is impeccable. I remain in awe of the perfection that is your drawing room."

"All?" Aunt Vera echoed, her cheeks paler than ever.

"But what could be so dire, dear," Mrs. Brougham said, "that you would leave Madame Bélanger's establishment without selecting a new morning gown?"

Mrs. Norton opened her mouth to respond and then, her mind clearly empty of ideas, turned to stare at Bea. Equally without a ready lie, Bea stared back for one long humming moment before saying, "Embroidery."

"Embroidery?" Mrs. Brougham repeated.

"Yes," Bea replied, stretching out the word as she darted a glance at her fellow conspirator, who appeared as disconcerted as her mother. Clearly, she would get no help from that quarter. "An embroidery project. A very special one for...her husband. Yes! For Mr. Norton. They are celebrating their sixth wedding anniversary in the summer, and she is making a special gift for him."

It was just enough information for Mrs. Norton, and now she picked up the thread. "You know how much John loves to hunt, Mama. I am embroidering a set of his handkerchiefs with images of Pugnacious, his beloved foxhound. I am finding it quite challenging to get his head exactly right, and

Miss Hyde-Clare offered to assist me, as she is a skilled embroideress."

Aunt Vera, who would allow her niece few talents, could not cavil at this description. "If there is anything Bea can do well, it is sit quietly in a room and sew," she observed, her expression still skeptical, however, at the oddity of the commitment.

Likewise, Mrs. Brougham remained perplexed. "But you were so insistent only an hour ago that you needed a new morning gown today."

Mrs. Norton smiled. "And I still do. Why don't you remain here and select it for me? You know exactly what I like, for we have similar tastes. Perhaps Lady Abercrombie would be kind enough to drive you home?"

The countess, whose eagerness to resume sampling fabrics plainly conveyed her conviction that she could more easily compile a future duchess's trousseau without the future duchess herself, asserted immediately that there was plenty of room in her carriage.

Bea, whose compulsion to leave would not have been denied no matter how many reasonable objections were levied against it, tugged Mrs. Norton gently on the arm and bid her aunt goodbye. Running out of the shop would be inexcusably coarse, so Bea had to content herself with taking long strides as she crossed the floor. Her companion could barely keep up, and it was only when they were in the other woman's carriage, after the groom had firmly shut the door, that she allowed herself to exhale sharply in relief.

Mrs. Norton began to laugh. "The look on my mother's face! The poor darling was confused and no wonder. I have always been an indifferent embroideress. It was one of the things she despaired of my ever doing correctly, and now I have sworn to make John handkerchiefs to celebrate our marriage. She must think I bear him a terrible grudge."

The other woman's amusement was irresistible, especially in combination with the overwhelming relief Bea felt at being temporarily free of the tyranny of her trousseau, and as she started to giggle herself, she experienced the oddly disconcerting sensation of laughing with one's archnemesis.

"I am a horrible daughter," Mrs. Norton said as her gales began to subside. "I am a horrible, wicked daughter for taking such pleasure in my mother's perplexity. I welcome your judgment, Miss Hyde-Clare. Express it freely."

As Beatrice had spent the vast majority of the past decade silently mocking her relatives, she did not think it was appropriate that she cast any stones now. Instead, she confessed her own limitation with an embroidery needle. "My aunt believes I am somewhat proficient simply because I am less inept at sewing than I am at the other activities at which a gently bred lady should excel. Alas, it was the first and only thing I could think of, and I apologize if I've got you in a muddle from which you will find it difficult to extricate yourself."

Mrs. Norton waved her hand dismissively. "It is no bother. If my maid finds sewing Pugnacious into the handkerchief beyond her ability, I will hire a skilled seamstress. I own, John will be surprised, for I have been flagrantly obvious in my distaste for Pugnacious—I trust the name reveals why—and have been disinclined before now to memorialize him. And if anything, it is I who owes you the apology. You have abandoned very important business to help me with a trifling matter. Your generosity is overwhelming, and I cannot thank you enough."

Although Bea felt the impulse to assure her there was nothing generous in her craven desire to escape, she merely nodded and looked out the window. Observing the unfamiliar surroundings, she asked where they were going.

"Milford Lane," Mrs. Norton said. "After my grandfather died, Flowerdew accepted a position at a public stable there.

93

It is small, so it's manageable at his age. My father begged him to stay on, for he had served us well for many years, but he had long wanted to move closer to his son's family and had remained out of obligation to my grandfather. As he is the only one who knows where the Great Mughal diamond is hidden, it will come as no surprise when I say my grandfather trusted him implicitly. All we need to do is convince him that telling me where the stone is now is an expression of Grandfather's trust, not a betrayal of it."

As simple as the other woman made it sound, Bea knew it was quite a difficult task. "Should we not return to your home first in order to retrieve the letter? It is the strongest part of your argument and evidence of your grandfather's intentions."

"Good gracious, the letter!" Mrs. Norton cried as she began to laugh again. This time, however, the sound was tinged with scorn, not humor. "It slipped my mind *entirely*. I warned you, did I not, that I was the most absurd creature? Of course we should have gone back to my house to fetch it. Only now we are so close..." Her thought trailed off as she looked out the window and considered their location. "What do you think of our sallying forth regardless? Making an honest effort without it so that we may have something to fall back on if we fail? I know this will embarrass you dreadfully, but I have complete faith in your ability to elicit the information. Flowerdew will be powerless against you."

Contrary to Mrs. Norton's expectations, this statement did not embarrass Bea. If only the emotion it engendered in her chest were so benign as embarrassment! What a relief that would be. Alas, her seemingly implacable confidence created dismay and distress and not a small amount of panic. It dismayed and distressed and panicked her so much she wanted to order the driver to stop and allow her to disembark from the carriage. What Mrs. Norton believed her capable of exceeded all reasonable expectation of what a person could do. Wem's unlikely confession in the middle of Lord Stirling's ballroom was the result of a strange confluence of forces that could not be reliably reproduced —and even if they could, it would require hours of thoughtful planning, not a few minutes in a speeding carriage.

It was madness.

Oh, but Beatrice could not tell her that, not the former Miss Brougham, who was regarding her now with the light of respect glowing in her eyes.

And still the panic!

She was merely a mortal woman commanding no magical powers to compel men to say the words she wished to hear. That this society matron who had dismissed her as drab and dreary seemed to believe otherwise was astounding.

If only our earlier selves could see us now, Bea thought sardonically, her sense of humor rescuing her once again from despair. Mrs. Norton's surfeit of faith, irrational and groundless, was perhaps exactly what she deserved for desiring an apology for so many years.

Feeling slightly less apprehensive, she considered the problem dispassionately and decided that failure was in no way assured. Wem's confession *was* an extreme example of what was possible, but she had managed to elicit vital information on several occasions. Most often her success came from allowing people to speak uninterrupted, tracking their comments closely and figuring out how seemingly minor facts fit into a larger picture.

There was no reason to assume she could not apply those strengths to the situation with Flowerdew.

But there was another element, she realized, and that was the assessment she did of each situation to decide the best way to approach a subject. In every case, she had entered the conversation with a specifically tailored point of view and persona. Rarely had she conducted an interrogation as Beatrice Hyde-Clare.

She needed a stratagem now.

As if determined to deprive Bea of every last scrap of her composure, Mrs. Norton looked out the window and observed they would arrive at their destination in a few minutes.

"And then this episode will be concluded in a very satisfying manner," she added. "Miss Hyde-Clare, I am very grateful you consented to accompany me today."

Bea nodded absently and called up what she knew about the situation in order to formulate a hasty plan. In one way or another, the whole situation seemed to hinge on trust: Mr. Brougham had entrusted the diamond to his longtime groom, who in turn refused to trust the granddaughter. Bea's purpose in making this visit was to convince Mr. Flowerdew that Mrs. Norton was worthy of his trust. If the groom retained his full faculties—and there was no reason to believe he didn't—then he would expect her to argue in favor of Mrs. Norton's trustworthiness. What he wouldn't anticipate was her making the opposite case.

Ah, but why would Mr. Flowerdew trust *her*?

That was the rub, Bea thought.

Clearly, she needed to devise an identity that positioned her as an ally of his, not Mrs. Norton's. 'Twas a daunting proposition, to be sure, one made more challenging still by the fact that she was dressed as herself and had had no opportunity to research her target.

What did she know of grooms other than their skill with and fondness for horses? Rogers, who oversaw the stables at Welldale House, frequently—

Abruptly, the carriage stopped.

"Finally," Mrs. Norton said as if the journey had been arduous and long, "we are arrived. And there is Clement with the door. Do watch yourself as you climb down, Miss Hyde-Clare."

As Bea alighted smoothly from the carriage, some of the trepidation that had overwhelmed her during the drive began to fall away. All her concerns remained, for she still had no idea how she would introduce herself to the groom or earn his trust, but she felt oddly invigorated by the challenge ahead of her. She'd had no time to prepare, that was true, but she retained her wits and they had been equal to the task before. She was confident that they wouldn't fail her now.

The two-story building in Milford Lane that housed the stable was tidy and compact, with stalls facing the street much like a mews.

"There is a small courtyard through here," Mrs. Norton explained as she led the way, opening a green door and passing through. "The grooms live above the stalls, but Flowerdew has apartments on the first floor."

Indeed, the courtyard was compact, with three sets of stalls forming a U along the perimeter, and Bea imagined about a dozen horses in total stabled there at any given time. It was a modest but successful enterprise.

As Bea observed her surroundings, Mrs. Norton strode across the courtyard and arrived at a second green door. "His rooms are right through here," she announced as she grasped the doorknob and entered the building without pausing to knock or announce her presence in any way.

Noting the other woman's audacity, Bea wondered if perhaps that was not part of the problem. Had Mrs. Norton marched into Flowerdew's residence with a sense of entitlement, as if it were merely an ancillary structure to her grandfather's estate? Had she declared her ownership of the diamond with the same proprietary boldness she seemed to feel toward his front parlor?

If Mrs. Norton was part of the problem, then she could not be part of the solution.

At once, an idea began to form in her head. It was vague yet (a variation on the museum ploy...a network of informers had warned her...Mrs. Norton known to be conspiring... perhaps Bea worked for a jeweler), but it would never develop into an effective plan if Mrs. Norton barged in on the groom and demanded he listen to her friend.

Indeed, Flowerdew must not know Mrs. Norton was there at all.

Hurriedly, Bea caught up with her in the narrow hallway and grabbed her arm.

Taken aback by the rough handling, the other woman pulled her brows together in a ferocious scowl before her features lightened. Then, misinterpreting Bea's intervention as reluctance, she said with rousing conviction, "Come, Miss Hyde-Clare, you will not turn timid now, for you are no longer that drab thing. Show a little duchess backbone."

Then she smiled encouragingly, and Bea's entire body jerked in recognition, for it was wrong, all wrong. Everything.

What exactly? How?

She couldn't say. She had no idea.

But she knew one thing with overwhelming certainty: Miss Brougham remembered her. She had feigned complete ignorance.

No, it was more than that—she had made a great show of having no recollection of their shared first season.

If the effort had been deliberate, then it could have only one cause and that was to ensure the situation unfolded in a particular way.

Her archnemesis was manipulating her.

To what end?

Ah, yes, that was the question, Bea thought, her mind

buzzing with possibilities. Obviously, her intent was nefarious. Nobody planned an elaborate scheme with good intentions and this was an especially intricate plot—coming up with the story about the diamond, finding someone to masquerade as Mr. Rose, making sure to meet by happenstance at the modiste.

So many steps and each one required effort and consideration.

What step were they up to now?

Mrs. Norton, unaware that she had made a misstep, placed her hand on Bea's shoulder and gave it a reassuring squeeze. "You'll be brilliant, I know it. Now let's beard this lion in his den, shall we?" she asked as her fingers reached for the door to the left. "Then we will celebrate your success with tea and rout cakes."

Whatever evil plan was under way, its culmination lay on the other side of that door, Bea realized. Refusing to be its victim, she turned her shoulder sharply to extricate herself from Mrs. Norton's grasp and walked briskly in the other direction. She wanted to race through the narrow hallway to the door but also realized the importance of appearing composed in the event someone encountered her in the courtyard. Running as if chased by the devil would raise eyebrows and alarms.

While Bea told herself to remain calm, Mrs. Norton, who assumed her sudden reversal was merely a cowardly bout of faintheartedness, demanded she stiffen her spine and return at once. Bea ignored her appeals and marched ever closer to the door. She was only a foot from the exit when Mrs. Norton screamed.

Bea's stride hitched because the cry was shrill and piercing, riven with a sort of bottomless intensity, as if it came from somewhere deep and dark, and she was not a monster. The scream terrified her.

It's only a ruse, she assured herself, resuming her march to the door.

But then Mrs. Norton shrieked again and again and again, and the sound took on a wild, uncontrollable note as the woman's frenzy seemed to grow exponentially, doubling and tripling and quadrupling until it filled the narrow hallway.

Calling herself a fool, knowing it was a mistake but having no capacity to stop herself, Bea spun on her heels and darted back down the corridor to Mrs. Norton. Closer now, she could see other signs of distress—shaking limbs, falling tears, fingers clutching the frame of the door so tightly her knuckles had turned white—and realized it was real. Her fear and panic were genuine.

No longer worried about the trap that had been laid, Bea raced past the hysterical woman and shot into the room. It was a small space, dark and cramped, with an imposing wardrobe along one wall and a bed against another. Light entered the chamber in a wide sliver through the slim window over the bed and fell on the lifeless eyes of Mr. Rose.

Bea gasped, as shocked to find him there at the stables on Milford Lane as she was to find him in that condition. He was to have been the instrument of her destruction but how, in this dingy room, with its fractured light and shabby furniture? He could not have come there expecting—Bea stepped closer to get a better look at the wounds—to be run through several times with a....knife?

Sword?

Perhaps a sharp cane?

Definitely something with a point.

Truthfully, she found it impossible to think clearly with Mrs. Norton's cries growing increasingly loud and intense, as if her horror was made worse by Bea's dispassionate appraisal of the scene.

But I am not dispassionate, Bea thought, wondering what

the better term would be. She was not shaken by the grue-some scene itself, for she had seen far worse in her investiga-tions, but she was agitated and frightened by its cause. Somehow Mr. Rose's murdered corpse fit into someone's plan to destroy her.

Bea could not begin to figure out how with Mrs. Norton's terrible screams filling the room, and hoping to calm her, she pressed a comforting hand on her shoulder. The other woman recoiled at the contact, then submitted meekly as her shrieks turned to whimpers. As docile as a baby, she allowed herself to be led from the room, and Bea, grateful for the small mercy, closed the door behind them.

There, she thought, on a sigh, relieved that she could now start to make sense of the debacle and decide the best way to extricate herself from further harm.

And then, as if in a nightmare, the front door to the building opened and London's most determined gossip stepped inside.

Chapter Six

Bea felt an unfathomable desire to laugh.
   She knew intellectually that the events that were
unfolding as if in a terrifying dream were truly happening. She
was actually in Milford Lane, Mr. Rose was actually dead, and
Mrs. Ralston had actually just arrived. It was all real and
actual and dreadful in ways she couldn't begin to calculate but
knew viscerally would ruin her future. Everything was falling
apart here and now, and all she could do was stare.

And yet as certain as she was in the reality of the
moment, she could not quite free herself from the sensation
that she had fallen into the middle of a play.

It was a farce, was it not?

A Drury Lane farce complete with players and property?

Mr. Rose told them that very thing, solemnly thanking
the duke for the critique of his performance.

That was precisely the word he had used: *performance.*

Indeed he had, yes. He'd described it in just that way
because that was exactly what the exchange had been for him
—a play in which he had been hired to perform a part—and
for days now the show had been staged around her, a satirical

comedy that got its bite from the guileless ingenue having no idea she was the star of the production. All that was missing was the audience.

Oh but no, it wasn't missing, for Mrs. Ralston was there to witness the denouement and she was the same as a packed house at Covent Garden.

It was here—with the revelation of Mrs. Ralston's purpose—that Bea's desire to laugh became truly debilitating, for if she succumbed now to the irrational impulse, she would never recover. By the time she regained control, her life, like her reputation, would be in tatters.

All these thoughts flittered through Bea's head in the few seconds it took for Mrs. Ralston to recognize her and register her shock. Seeing the look of astonishment overcome the other woman's face, Bea affixed a smile to her own and resolved to get through the encounter with unflagging warmth and preternatural calm.

Beside her, Mrs. Norton whimpered with increasing intensity and Bea feared she might collapse entirely, a turn that would deal a fatal blow to her plan to brazen it out.

Grinning with impossible brightness and keeping her eyes well trained on Mrs. Ralston, Bea pinched the forearm of her archnemesis and said with gentle menace, "You will compose yourself, or I will ensure that your reputation is destroyed just as thoroughly as mine. Do you understand?"

Mrs. Norton let out a low plaintive whine, which Bea had no choice but to accept as agreement, for Mrs. Ralston had overcome her shock and was now walking toward them.

Affecting pure delight, Bea met her in the middle of the narrow hallway and shook her head as if unable to comprehend her good fortune. "What a most felicitous coincidence, Mrs. Ralston. I cannot imagine how it was contrived."

As the accomplished gossip was clearly wondering the same thing, the question did not raise her suspicions and she replied honestly. "I stable my horses here, with Mr. Josiah, and received a note informing me there was a problem with my husband's mount. Georgie is dear to Mr. Ralston's heart so naturally I came right away to see what the matter was. And what is your business with Mr. Josiah?"

Bea gave her the only answer she could think of in the moment, although it was inadequate. "I'm looking for a stable for my horse."

As she feared, Mrs. Ralston could not accept this without questioning the necessity of her hiring a public stable. "Kesgrave House has a very stately and commodious stable. I cannot believe there isn't room for one more mount."

"Oh, indeed, yes, there's plenty of room in the stables at Kesgrave House, for everything about the home is stately and commodious," Bea agreed, purposely speaking at length to give herself time to think. "But we are not married yet, so it would never do for me to stable...uh, Apple Blossom there and we do not have room in the mews in Portman Square. You see, the problem arose when my uncle bought me the horse as a present to celebrate my betrothal. In his excitement, he might have been a little precipitous."

The change that came over Mrs. Ralston at the word *precipitous* was stunning, for in a flash she went from mildly curious to deathly interested and it was as though a literal fire of interest sparked in her eyes.

But her tone was almost absentminded as she said, "Oh?"

When Bea had employed the word *precipitous* to describe her uncle's fictional decision to buy her a mount, she had merely meant to say he had acted prematurely. But now, observing Mrs. Ralston's keen attention, she realized it could also mean he had acted rashly, maybe too rashly for a situation that could prove volatile.

Perhaps if she let slip a sensational on-dit, the telltale

would leave the premises without asking too many questions and discovering the cooling corpse of Mr. Rose.

"Well, yes, but it's my fault, for I mistakenly gave him the impression that the duke was eager to wed at once," Bea said with what she hoped was endearingly oblivious candor. "But of course we must heed the advice of his grandmother, who feels that short engagements are ill-bred and for foreigners. She has advised the duke to consider a Christmas wedding, which makes sense despite my aunt's concerns. I am sure the dowager is not withholding her approval."

As intended, Mrs. Ralston found this tidbit irresistible and repeated it with almost voracious curiosity. "The dowager is withholding her approval?"

Bea blinked several times in an attempt to appear at once surprised and a little stupid. "Goodness no, why would you think that?"

Now it was Mrs. Ralston's turn to affect innocence, and she pressed her lips together as if swayed by the protest. Then she said, "No reason."

"Because of the uncertainty of my betrothal—the length of it, that is," Bea said, hastening to clarify, lest there be any misunderstanding, "I am in need of a stable for Apple Blossom. If it was to be for only a few weeks, we could make do with the mews in Portman Square. But several months is too long. So we are here to discuss the matter with Mr. Josiah, but he appears to be away from home at the moment."

Mrs. Ralston accepted this explanation with a nod and looked beyond Beatrice to the other woman in the hallway, whom she considered silently for an interval.

A long interval.

Indeed, a very long one—so long that Bea, whose back was to Mrs. Norton, felt a frisson of anxiety about the composure of her archnemesis. Had the wretched creature failed to collect herself despite the threat of social ruination?

Bea itched to turn around and look, but showing undo concern might raise more questions than it settled. She forced herself to remain still.

Finally, Mrs. Ralston said, "Mrs. Norton, is that you?"

Slowly, Bea exhaled the breath she had been holding and said, "When she learned of my dilemma, Mrs. Norton kindly suggested Mr. Josiah's stables as a solution. I was quite grateful because Uncle Horace had suggested sending him to Welldale House."

Mrs. Ralston returned her shrewd gaze to Beatrice and said with thoughtful consideration that she had not known the two women were of particular acquaintance. "I would not have said you were friends at all."

Behind Bea, Mrs. Norton laughed, a faintly hysterical giggle that teetered fleetingly into maniacal before steadying.

But the brief, unrestrained chortle, which was really more of a guffaw, drew the interest of the famous London gossip, who examined Mrs. Norton with a quizzical look.

"My goodness, yes, we've known each other for ages," Bea announced, perhaps a little too loudly in her eagerness to bring the attention back to herself. Aware of the slip, she determined to modulate her voice and added more smoothly, "We had our come-outs the same year."

"Did you?" Mrs. Ralston said as if searching her own memory for confirmation. "I do not recall."

Before Bea could collaborate her own story, Mrs. Norton responded, "Yes, we had our come-outs in the same year."

Her archnemesis spoke firmly, evenly, her voice revealing none of the frenzy of only a few minutes ago, and Bea allowed herself to turn around to inspect her. There were traces of her recent ordeal, such as red rims around her eyes and a faint shaking of her left hand, but for the most part she seemed to be her usual self. Bea thought it was unlikely Mrs. Ralston would notice anything amiss unless she was particularly looking for it.

The thought provided little comfort because the scandal-monger was always looking for it.

"Oh, yes, of course," Mrs. Ralston said thoughtfully. "I think I did know that."

"Of course you did," Mrs. Norton said comfortingly as she walked toward them in the hallway. "It is widely known. What is less known is that Beatrice introduced me to my husband. I owe her a great debt I can never repay. Naturally, I would have offered to board Apple Blossom in South Audley Street, but our stalls are far too tight to squeeze in another horse. But my father has relied upon Mr. Josiah's services from time to time and found them to be superior, so I knew it would be just the solution. Unfortunately, the proprietor is absent, so we will have to return another time. It is so fascinating about Georgie."

"Fascinating?" Mrs. Ralston asked, taken aback by the description.

"Well, yes," Mrs. Norton said as she slipped her arms through the gossip's and started to lead her to the front door. "The message, I mean. It's a mystery and a fascinating one at that. Whoever could have sent it? No matter. I am sure Georgie is fine, and we will go check on him right now to confirm it."

Mrs. Ralston started in surprise, making it apparent to both women that she had forgotten all about her husband's beloved steed. It was hardly shocking that such a mundane matter had slipped her mind with all the scintillating information to be gathered. No doubt she could hardly wait to race back to Mayfair to start telling the beau monde to expect the Duke of Kesgrave's inexplicable betrothal to the spinsterish Miss Hyde-Clare to end at any moment.

Bea felt a twinge of remorse for casting the lovely

dowager duchess as the villain again, for she had done so during the investigation into her parents' death as well, but there was nothing for it. As a famous high stickler, she was tailor-made for the abuse.

Mrs. Ralston led them to Georgie's stall, and it was apparent to all of them at a glance that no harm had befallen the horse, whose black coat was so shiny one could almost see one's reflection. Nevertheless, his owner was reluctant to leave without having a word with a stable boy, and Mrs. Norton, displaying a deviousness that should not have surprised Bea given how easily the other woman had moved her around the chess board, hurried the gossip along by insisting she remain.

"You must feed the dear love some carrots," she said, holding out a satchel containing several dozen that were clearly meant for the whole yard. "And perhaps sing to him. My own horse is particularly fond of 'The Soldier's Adieu.' Do you know it?"

When Mrs. Ralston confessed she did not, Mrs. Norton began to sing it. It was a high-pitched tune, and her skill fell well short of capturing its appeal. Whether that was intentional, Bea had no idea and was merely grateful a few minutes later, when the notorious scandalmonger got into her carriage.

Bea and Mrs. Norton made a show of climbing into their own coach as if they too were about to depart. Then they waited for her to leave. They sat silently, on opposing benches, and while Bea was annoyed at Mrs. Norton's refusal to look her in the eye rather than stare trenchantly down at her own hands, she was grateful for the respite. In the interval since discovering a great machination was afoot, she had not had a single moment to think about what had occurred. The corpse of Mr. Rose had scarcely registered with her brain before Mrs. Ralston was striding into the hallway.

What a perfectly horrid fifteen minutes.

Had it really only been fifteen minutes? she wondered. She had taken carriage rides through the Hyde Park that felt shorter.

Fully aware of how very close she had come to disaster, Bea dreaded the thought of reentering the house with every fiber of her being. The forces that were at work to destroy her reputation were most likely still in play and would inevitably strike again.

The safest place for her now was away from Milford Lane.

How ardently she wanted to run.

But there was the dead body, Mr. Rose or Mr. Flowerdew or Mr. Whoever lying in his own blood in the weedy spring light of the narrow window. She could not flee to save herself and leave him there alone. It was not merely the immorality of abandoning a victim that prevented her escape. No, it was another compulsion, a sensibility of what she owed to herself and her avocation as a woman who had decided that identifying murderers was to be her occupation.

She had inserted herself into matters that only marginally related to her because she could not bear to watch them unfold incorrectly. She was too clever to stand idly by while mistakes were made, and in that process, in that deliberate intrusion, she had acquired skills. She could not simply forsake them now because the situation was inconvenient and dangerous.

If there was information to be gathered from the site of the murder, then she was obligated to look for it. Regardless of the personal risk to herself, she had to go back.

A cold hole seemed to open in the pit of her stomach, and she closed her eyes, wishing silently for Kesgrave to suddenly appear.

What foolishness, she thought.

But there was comfort in it as well, for knowing how thoroughly he would disapprove of her returning to examine the corpse lent a hint of defiance to the act. From the very beginning of their association, he had made his opinion of her habit of investigating dead bodies very clear, and as soon as he saw the opportunity, he had coerced her into promising to cease it.

She had overcome the pledge by arguing the circumstances proscribed had yet to repeat—Fazeley might have fallen into her path as the duke said, but Mr. Wilson had been nudged here.

And this one had been purposefully placed.

Knowing that someone's life had been taken merely to cause her pain made her ineffably sad.

You do not *know* that, she told herself. You only *think* it.

'Twas a fair enough point, and there was only one way to find out the truth.

Sighing deeply, she opened her eyes, stiffened her back, reached for the carriage door and said pragmatically to her archnemesis, "Come on, then."

Mrs. Norton glanced up from her clasped fingers and stared at Bea as if confused by the command. "Come on where?" the blank look seemed to say. And then enlightenment struck and she lost all color in her face.

"What?" she shrieked.

Bea had no patience for the dramatics and thought the astonishment was entirely out of line with the situation. Why else had she thought they were waiting for the other carriage to leave if not for the opportunity to inspect the dead man and his environs? Nevertheless, she explained calmly, "We cannot leave without examining the scene."

As Bea had expected further demonstrations of shock and disbelief, she was taken aback when Mrs. Norton began to laugh. Briefly, she thought it was an expression of genuine humor, but almost immediately the sound took on the unsettling cast of unrestrained chortling. Mrs. Norton was on the verge of losing her equanimity altogether.

Bea, hoping a measured response would help calm the other woman, kept her gaze steady. It worked, in a fashion, for eventually the gales waned enough for Mrs. Norton to glare at her with fervent dislike and ask with disgust dripping from every syllable, "What kind of...of...*ghoul* are you?"

It was the wrong thing to say.

Oh, yes, it was absolutely the worst thing she could say to the woman she'd been manipulating for days.

Although her heart felt as though it would explode from the ferocity of her fury, Bea spoke softly, gently, even serenely. "Let me ask you, Mrs. Norton, what kind of ghoul are you that you would create an elaborate lie to gain a woman's assistance on an entirely fictional matter? What kind of ghoul are you that you would use a woman's generosity and willingness to help against her? What kind of ghoul are you that you would lure a woman to her ruination? What kind of ghoul are you that you would scheme and plot with a murderer? What kind of ghoul are you that you would take the life of one person in order to destroy another's?"

Somehow, despite the enraging litany, Bea remained calm. It was as if the coldness of Mrs. Norton's calculation had washed over her and engulfed her very soul. It helped, she thought, that her archnemesis's composure had crumbled entirely and now the vile schemer sat pressed against the corner of the carriage, trying with little success to disappear into the wood as tears streamed down her face.

It gave Bea no satisfaction to see her terror or grief, but it did make for an interesting study in contrast.

"Given that we are both ghouls," Bea continued, her tone more matter-of-fact now than aggressively smooth, "albeit of different stripes, only one thing can happen now. I, in my ghoulishness, must examine the victim, whom I will call Mr. Rose, as that was the name by which he was known to me, for information that may help reveal the identity of his attacker. You, in your ghoulishness, must accompany me because I cannot allow you to report back to your coconspirators without first thoroughly questioning you, which I cannot do until after I have examined Mr. Rose. I will own that being near the man whose life you helped brutally end is probably an extremely unpleasant experience for you, but I would argue that perhaps you should have considered that possibility before you helped brutally end a man's life. So do please come, Mrs. Norton, for I have found this outing far more wearying than expected and my energy has begun to wane."

Bea climbed out of the coach and, seeing that Mrs. Norton remained unnaturally still, held out a hand in encouragement. "There you go," she said soothingly as if talking to a small child. "Do come along. The sooner we go in, the sooner we come out."

Conceding the futility of trying to make herself disappear into the structure of the carriage, Mrs. Norton slid hesitantly forward in her seat and allowed Beatrice to help her down. As they entered the courtyard, she asked, her voice still shaky but stronger than before, "How did you figure it out?"

"You called me a drab thing," Bea said.

"No," she corrected, "I said you were a drab thing no longer."

Bea nodded, granting the minor distinction. "Nonetheless, it was a tactical mistake when you had earlier professed to having no recollection of me at all. Obviously, you did and it was easy enough to piece together the purpose of the lie when Mrs. Ralston appeared. There is one reason and one reason only to embroil her in your efforts, and that is to ensure a story is spread as far and as wide as possible. It's hardly surprising you slipped up when you did. You were so close to your goal—I was mere steps from the bedchamber—and yet still so far away. How very frustrating it must have been for you to have your quarry stop short like that."

"How very self-righteous you are!" Mrs. Norton cried.

It was, Bea thought, a particularly reckless charge from a woman who had forfeited any high ground she might have had.

"Yes, yes, I am, quite self-righteous," she said with extravagant affability. "It comes, you see, from being the victim of a plot to maneuver me into a compromising situation to destroy my reputation and end my engagement to Kesgrave. Next time, make yourself the victim and you may be self-righteous as well."

But Mrs. Norton did not wait for next time. "I *am* a victim...a victim of a...a...heinous crime. Mr. Rose was not supposed to be killed like that. He...he was supposed to compromise you, as you said, and...and Mrs. Ralston was supposed to arrive just in time to...to corroborate my story. I have been manipulated too! Someone used me, just as they used you. If Mrs. Ralston had seen the body, then my reputation would have been ruined just as assuredly as yours—worse, perhaps, for I am an intimate of Almack's patronesses and have entrée to all the best houses while you...while you..."

Belatedly, Mrs. Norton realized that hurling insults at her...er, fellow victim...was not the way to earn the other woman's sympathy.

"While I am just a drab thing," Beatrice supplied crushingly.

Mrs. Norton, however, did not cower but said scornfully, "You are going to be a duchess. You may relinquish your victimhood now."

The temerity of the charge was so huge and sweeping, Bea actually found herself breathless in response. How dare the

Machiavellian schemer who had been controlling her movements for days position herself as a victim while deriding Bea for feeling ill used!

Through the compact courtyard now, Bea opened the green front door for Mrs. Norton and followed her into the house. They had been gone for only twenty minutes, and yet the light was already different. The sun had sunk partially behind the building next door, lengthening their shadows in the hallway.

"This is preposterous," Mrs. Norton muttered as she halted at the threshold of the bedchamber. She refused to go further. "You may be ghoulish in there, and I will be ghoulish out here."

Bea accepted the arrangement without quibbling because the room was small and a second person—well, technically, a third, keeping in mind its original occupant—would make it crowded. Additionally, treading around the mess on the floor required care, and she felt confident her archnemesis would cheerfully stomp on the murder weapon just to annoy her.

Ah, yes, the murder weapon, Bea thought, deciding that was the best place to start. How, precisely, had the victim been killed?

As she had noted before, the dead man lay prone on the bed, its wildly disheveled linens indicating that a great struggle had occurred. Mr. Rose had not succumbed to his fate without a fight, she thought, noting that a slim bookcase and a sizable mirror had been destroyed in the tussle. Shards of both, as well as the books themselves, were scattered liberally throughout the room. None, however, had blood on them, which suggested Mr. Rose had suffered the hole in his stomach at the end of the altercation.

Evidently, a knife in the gut was the stroke that finished it.

No, not a knife, she realized, seeing now, up close, that

there wasn't a single hole in his belly but four deep pokes evenly spaced. The killer had used a tool of some sort, one he most likely had not brought with him, for if the murder had been planned with care and concision, neither the bookcase nor the mirror would have been shattered. Although the element of surprise did not ensure a tidy crime scene, it certainly helped contain things.

The question then became: Had he taken the instrument with him?

She began to search under the piles of clothes that had been emptied from the clothespress and from the wardrobe until she discovered what she was looking for: brass fireplace tongs. She had no doubt it was the correct item, for both arms were covered with blood, but she carried the tool to the body and aligned the prongs with the wounds to make sure they matched.

They did.

Good, she thought, turning her attention next to its placement under the clothes, which clarified the sequence of events. The killer had stabbed Mr. Rose in the stomach twice with the tongs, threw them on floor and then emptied the wardrobe. And the clothespress, she noted.

That was the correct order, was it not?

She could conceive of no other explanation, for it seemed far too implausible to infer the wardrobe had been knocked open during the struggle and its entire contents dislodged. Perhaps some of the clothes inside but not every single garment.

Someone was looking for something, and having failed to find it in the clothespress, they had searched the wardrobe. Or vise versa.

Whatever the missing item was, Bea was certain Mr. Rose had died for it.

She could only assume it was something of great value.

Satisfied with her understanding of the proceedings, she returned to the bed, stumbling over a worn copy of a book on the care of Thoroughbreds that had rolled on a sleigh bell. Given the mess, it was only to be expected and yet slightly embarrassing due to her assumption about Mrs. Norton carelessly trampling evidence.

Her balance restored, she peered closely at Mr. Rose, whose state of dishabille—a muslin shirt gaping open at the neck, unstockinged feet—was to have been her undoing. Although the scene had not gone as Mrs. Norton had intended, and would not have because she had figured out her game, Bea still felt a shudder of alarm at what might have been.

"Good God, Miss Hyde-Clare, you are taking longer than my maid to arrange my hair in the coiffure Caliste," Mrs. Norton said plaintively, "and Molly is only just competent at making plaits. Please finish up so that we may go. I cannot believe Mr. Josiah will remain out for long. As soon as he returns, he will call the constable, I am sure of it, and he will do a proper inspection. No doubt *he* will be quite cross at *you* for disturbing the scene with your gruesome interest."

Ah, yes, Mr. Josiah, the actual owner of the Milford Lane stable, Bea thought, quite curious as to where the man was and how his absence had been contrived. His staff of stable boys was also curiously missing. Certainly, such an arrangement would have cost someone a great deal of money.

As soon as they returned in the carriage, she was determined to find out from Mrs. Norton who her malefactor was.

But first she had to assure herself that she had not missed anything of significance and inspected the body for additional wounds. There was a trio of scratches on his neck, and a bruise had started to form on his cheek, further evidence of a bout. There were no deep cuts, however, which might mean that he had been unconscious when his attacker stabbed him with the fireplace tongs. The fact that there were no soot marks on the bed linens, only a swathe of blood where it had settled after leaving his body, collaborated her supposition that it had been the deployment of the tongs—one thrust, then two—that had ended the struggle.

"It would be remiss of me not to mention that Lady Marsham is joining me for tea at four," Mrs. Norton said, her tone taking on a slightly cross note as she explained that it was almost three now. "If my butler tells her I am not 'at home,' she will think I forgot about our engagement and be quite cross with me. If we could avoid that outcome, I would be most grateful."

Regardless of how long Bea lingered over the corpse of Mr. Rose, Mrs. Norton would not keep her appointment with her ladyship. With all that had transpired, Bea thought that was rather obvious, and if her archnemesis did not realize it, then her understanding of her own predicament was somewhat deficient.

Nevertheless, she straightened her shoulders and stepped carefully around the mess, for she was done with the inspection portion of her investigation and ready for the interrogation.

Sweeping past Mrs. Norton, who had propped one shoulder against the wall in a most informal fashion, Bea advised her to space her events more liberally the next time she decided to ruin a young lady's reputation.

"Far be it for me to say it, for I am only the victim—and a drab one at that—but your ability to plan correctly seems to be somewhat lacking," she added as they stepped out into the afternoon light of the courtyard.

Chapter Seven

I f *Bea could identify* any positive aspect to narrowly escaping total ruination only to be confronted with the violently murdered corpse of her intended seducer, it was that it left her far too unsettled, angry and distracted to be in awe of the imposing butler of the stately mansion that would soon be her home.

Standing on the doorstep of the duke's Berkeley Square residence, her left arm looped through Mrs. Norton's right to tether her firmly to her side, she smiled at the barrel-chested behemoth who oversaw Kesgrave House and said with brisk informality, "Ah, yes, my good man. We have not yet been introduced, but I am Beatrice Hyde-Clare, the duke's betrothed, and this is my guest, Mrs. Norton. We have most urgent business with his grace so do please alert him to our presence immediately."

As Bea had already had one encounter with Marlow—though the butler did not realize it because she had been dressed as a man—she knew how his heavy black brows could appear to pulse in disdain and she watched them bounce now as he tried to settle on an appropriate response. He was clearly repulsed by her audacity and wanted to deny her access, but he could not quite bring himself to behave so shabbily to a future duchess.

His future duchess.

Marlow's hesitation was all the invitation Bea needed, and she brushed by him to enter the house, hardly pausing to be intimidated by the stunning entranceway, with its pristine white arches. "We will be waiting in the drawing room."

Although Marlow had stepped to the side to allow them entrance, for he couldn't physically impede the movements of the woman who would soon be mistress there, he said with menacing civility, "His grace is away from home this afternoon, and if you leave your card, he will be sure to see it with the others."

Mrs. Norton thought this was a wonderful plan and tried to gain enough freedom of movement to withdraw a calling card from her reticule. Bea tightened her grip and told the butler they would wait as he sent for the duke.

Plainly ruffled by her refusal to be appropriately rebuffed, he stared at her with a mix of indecision and offense on his face, and Bea, hoping to speed the proceedings along, suggested he fetch the duke's steward. "Mr. Stephens is a sensible fellow. He will agree that the duke must be sent for, or is Jenkins here? Jenkins will vouch for me, I'm sure of it."

Her familiarity with the household staff further disconcerted the butler and after another moment, he relented. "You may wait in the drawing room. I will have tea brought in."

Having been in the house once before, she knew precisely the location of the drawing room, but rather than stride purposefully there, she decided to ingratiate herself a little—and it was, she knew, only a very little—by allowing Marlow to lead them at a sedate pace. He gestured to an elegant settee nestled in an arched recess adorned with colorful tiles and said tea would be delivered presently.

As soon as he left, Mrs. Norton tugged herself loose from Bea's grasp and whispered with harsh disapproval, "How positively *mortifying*. We are clearly not welcome here. We should have left our cards and returned at a more felicitous time."

Her color was high, signaling the sincerity of her humiliation, and Bea stared at her aghast that *this* was the thing that embarrassed her. The woman had lied and manipulated Bea on multiple occasions in a vicious attempt to destroy her reputation and end her engagement, but overcoming a butler's objections was the dire breach of etiquette?

Truly, it was too great a hypocrisy to comprehend.

Hoping the housekeeper would provide rout cakes or scones with the tea, Bea sat down on the settee and stared at the clock that had ticked so mercilessly the last time she had waited in the room. On that occasion, she had intended to invite Kesgrave to break into Viscount Braxfield's townhouse to search for her mother's missing bracelet, an anxiety-producing prospect that had turned out very well in the end.

Mrs. Norton declined the comfort of the settee and paced awkwardly around the room. "If you would just let me—"

Bea raised a hand to forestall her. "No."

"But as I said in the carriage—"

Again, Bea refused to allow her to explain her part in the ploy and the malevolent forces behind it. As impatient as she was to discover the truth, she had realized almost immediately that she didn't want to hear another word without Kesgrave.

"As the intention of the plan was to end my betrothal to Kesgrave, the harm you sought to do was to the both of us," Bea said firmly, offering a variation on the explanation she had given several times during their journey through the streets of London. "We will await his grace."

The tinge of pink that connoted her embarrassment drained from Mrs. Norton's cheeks as she contemplated the force of the duke's wrath, and she sat down on a mahogany chair with scroll arms.

Only a moment later, a footman arrived with a tea tray, its delivery overseen by a thin woman of modest height, with a flat nose and inquisitive brown eyes. The curiosity in her expression and the presence of tea cakes on the salver seemed to imply to Bea an awareness of her identity.

Naturally, word had spread among the staff.

"You are indeed the treasure his grace said you are, Mrs. Wallace," Bea announced in genuine delight, for she was both famished and determined to show herself to be anything but the indecorous clump-peeper she was sure Marlow had described her as. "I fear this is a most unusual introduction, and I hope you will forgive me for intruding like this. I would never have thrust myself upon the household if the matter were not of the utmost urgency."

"Yes, miss, it is most unusual but a pleasure nonetheless," the housekeeper said politely.

Although Bea would have liked for the other woman to inject a note of warmth in her tone, it was not an inauspicious beginning. "Thank you."

After Mrs. Wallace left, trailed by the footman, Bea poured and offered a cup to her archnemesis, who grumbled that she was supposed to be having tea at that very hour with Lady Marsham.

"How very cross she will be!" Mrs. Norton said with simmering outrage. "She is quite fastidious with her commitments and might not accept another invitation. It is very vexing, Miss Hyde-Clare, very vexing indeed, and I won't soon forget it."

Bea thought her ability to worry about only herself despite engaging in a callous and destructive scheme indi-

cated that she would be at best lightly scathed by her ladyship's displeasure.

"Then we may be grateful you have something to fret
about other than the duke's response to your machinations,"
Bea said with an overly bright smile.

Mrs. Norton's teacup clattered against its saucer as her
hand trembled.

Satisfied, Bea settled in to wait for the duke, noting the
excellent quality of the tea cakes and supposing it would not
be the worst thing in the world to oversee such accomplished
kitchens.

Twenty minutes later, the Duke of Kesgrave swept into
the drawing room in buckskin breeches, top boots and a
light-colored tailcoat. His hair was slightly disheveled, and
Bea wondered if he had been out for a ride in Hyde Park or
perhaps sparring at Jackson's.

"This is a delightful surprise, to be sure," he said smoothly,
sketching a bow before taking a seat next to Beatrice on the
settee. "I'd hoped I would have the opportunity to thank you
for your treatment of my betrothed, Mrs. Norton, but I could
not believe it would come so soon."

At the utterance of the word *treatment,* the society matron
started guiltily and shrunk back in the chair. She could not
know that his gratitude was sincere and naturally assumed he
was toying with her.

Bea hastened to clarify the situation, for she had waited
long enough to learn the name of the person who sought her
destruction. Her explanation, however, was almost immediately interrupted by Mrs. Norton, who could not contain her
astonishment at the fact that the duke already knew about
the Great Mughal diamond.

"You *told* him?" she asked, professing horror at the
apparent betrayal. "But that was to be *our* secret."

As the comment was patently ridiculous, Bea ignored it

and continued, "The story about the diamond was entirely fictional. Since word of my investigative skill has spread, a mystery was created to manipulate my actions. Mr. Rose was an actor hired to play a part, first as the solicitor, then as my lover. The plan was to culminate today with my being discovered in a compromising situation by the indefatigable Mrs. Ralston in a shabby room on Milford Lane. Something, however, went—"

Before she could get to the genuinely concerning part of the story, however, Bea was cut off by the duke, who ordered her to repeat herself. His voice was as cold as ice, indicating a simmering anger, but his face was a mask of calm.

"Excuse me?" Bea asked, not at all sure she understood the request.

"You will say those words again so that I may be quite sure I heard them correctly, for they seem inconceivable to me," he explained, his tone somehow several degrees chillier than before.

In the mahogany chair, Mrs. Norton clutched the scroll arms with white knuckles.

Bea complied with Kesgrave's request, speaking quickly so that she may arrive at the murdered corpse of Mr. Rose. "Something, however, went egregiously—"

But Mrs. Norton, unable to bear the anxiety any longer, jumped to her feet and said with beseeching fervor to the duke, "I was trying to *save* you!"

"Save me?" Kesgrave asked mildly.

Taking his determined calm as encouragement, she said, "Yes, *save* you. Everyone knows you were hoodwinked into proposing at the Larkwells' ball. She set herself on fire with the express purpose of trapping you. The dowager herself has arranged a long engagement to allow you time to extricate yourself. And I was only trying to provide you with a solution you would be too noble to attempt yourself. I thought you would be grateful."

Although much of what Mrs. Norton said about the beau monde's understanding of her engagement had recently constituted a humiliating nightmare for Bea, that afternoon she had discovered the true meaning of the phrase when Mrs. Ralston strode into the narrow hallway at the stable yard. As a consequence, she was able to listen to the speech and feel only amusement at the faint but perceptible whine in Mrs. Norton's voice at not being appreciated for her heroism.

Kesgrave must have noticed it too, for the moment his eyes met Bea's, he began to laugh. She immediately joined in, to the displeasure of their guest, who insisted quite petulantly that none of this was funny.

Agreeing with her assessment, the duke ceased his laughter and said, "No, it's not funny. It's stupid. It's stupid and dangerous and maddening, and I have half a mind to tell Norton every salacious detail and order him to exile you to the country for a decade. But I won't because I know what you are, Mrs. Norton, what you have always been. You are a dull and stupid woman who *knows* she is a dull and stupid woman. And Bea is bright and clever and that is a personal affront to you because the dull and stupid are always affronted by the temerity of wit."

Outraged, Mrs. Norton opened her mouth to protest the insults but, as if to prove his point, immediately closed it because she could not think of anything to say.

Kesgrave laughed once more, this time with derision, and warned Mrs. Norton to never interfere again in his and Beatrice's life. "Or you will suffer grave consequences," he said sharply. "Do you understand me?"

Mrs. Norton rushed to assure him that she very much did. He nodded. "Good. Then leave. Now."

The society matron, aware of how lightly she had got off

considering the actual events of the day, wasted no time in complying with his wishes. "Yes, of course, your grace. Thank you, your grace," she said, her eyes staunchly tipped down as she stared at the floor. "You are most generous and kind."

Bea decided the woman must truly be stupid if she believed she would actually pass through the doorway before Kesgrave knew the whole of the story.

"Do sit down, Mrs. Norton," Bea said with weary impatience, then turned to Kesgrave to explain. "She cannot leave because I haven't told you the worst part yet."

Having dealt with the intended ruination of his betrothed with admirable calm, he was unable to handle the prospect of more with equal equanimity. With his eyes flashing hotly, he looked at Mrs. Norton with vehement dislike and yelled, "There is a *worst* part?"

Bea, noting the rim of white along his tightly compressed mouth, realized she had never seen him truly angry before. During all of their arguments, he had maintained that insufferable air of ducal superiority and arrogant detachment. But now he seemed like a street brawler, insensible to reason and inured to logic.

And he knew nothing of Mr. Rose's corpse yet.

Worried not so much for Mrs. Norton's safety as for the duke's dignity, Bea said, "Let us consult."

She made the statement firmly, resolutely, as if they had an established custom of consultation and the duke would know precisely what she meant. Observing her options, which were limited by the shape of the room and the amount of furniture in it, she settled on an alcove between the fireplace and a marble statue of Athene. Crossing the floor, she gestured to Kesgrave to follow, and he did, after glaring menacingly at Mrs. Norton. He did not order her to stay where she was, but his meaning was clear.

In the privacy of their makeshift office, Bea explained the

events of the afternoon in greater details than before: Mrs. Norton's appearance at Madame Bélanger, the deserted stable, the realization that Mrs. Norton did indeed remember her, the discovery that her archnemesis was playing a very deep and dangerous game.

On the verge of describing the other woman's hysterical reaction to Mr. Rose's unfortunate end, she broke off suddenly and reconsidered her approach. Given the ease with which dead bodies seemed to appear in her life, one could be forgiven for thinking she was in some way responsible for the reoccurrence. It was patently false, of course, for during her tedious convalescence from the assault she had suffered while investigating Fazeley's death, she had devoted quite a lot of time and effort to thinking up ways to find murder victims in need of vindication and had failed to come up with a single viable idea. Short of advertising in the dailies or getting hired by the Runners, it was simply impossible to locate a mystery in need of solving in London.

But the duke was not entirely swayed by happenstance, and it struck her as prudent to take a moment to ensure he knew she had respect for their pact—nominal respect, to be sure, but respect nonetheless.

"Before I continue, I want to be certain you understand that I did not seek out this event," she said plainly. "It is something that has befallen me, your grace. *Befallen,* not fallen. It is an important distinction, and I should like to hear that you comprehend it."

Although she had been brief in her narration, she had not been succinct enough for the duke, who said impatiently, "Yes, yes, I do. Now tell me the rest, Bea. Now."

She nodded as if agreeing to his request but added, "And you do know, Damien, that I consider you an equal?"

As thoroughly exasperated as he was by her and this

seeming non sequitur, his lips nonetheless quivered in amusement. "I do, brat, and I'm flattered."

"It is important to me that you know that because I would never launch an investigation into a murder without consulting you first. We are partners," she said with sober intensity. "That being the case, your grace, I must tell you that this afternoon I launched an investigation into a murder without consulting you first. It was an unavoidable necessity, and I hope you can forgive me."

Despite his temper being so threadbare, he did not yell or vent his spleen or even stare daggers at the back of Mrs. Norton's head. He merely sighed resignedly and said, "Oh, hell, Bea, another dead body?"

"Another dead body," she said with considerably more eagerness than her betrothed, "of which I made a full inspection before leaving."

Kesgrave displayed no surprise at her thoroughness and simply inquired about the cause of death. Bea answered in as few words as possible, briefly describing the four puncture wounds in his chest caused by the fireplace tongs, which, being covered in blood, seemed like the only viable source of the holes. Although she could feel his anger rise again when she described the terrifyingly close shave she'd had with Mrs. Ralston, he did not interrupt and spoke only when her tale was complete.

"Tell me who did this, Bea," he said, his voice low and smoldering with fury. "Obviously, Mrs. Norton is but a pawn, for she is too cabbage-headed to arrange a theater outing, let alone an elaborate ruse."

Ah, yes, Bea thought, delighted that her own curiosity was to be satisfied at last. "That is indeed the question. But before we discover the identity of the Machiavellian conspirator behind the plot, would you care to hazard a name? I have only one guess and that is Lord Taunton, for I cannot think of anyone else who would wish me ill. But he is on the Continent and sufficiently cowed by your threats of penury for his family."

Startled by her restraint, Kesgrave stared. "You haven't asked her yet?"

"We are partners, and as such I would not pursue the investigation without you," she said. "Did I not just explain all this? I made a particular point to be pedantic about it so you would be sure to understand."

Her comment earned her a smile, but she could not say if it was the dip into pedantry or the sentiment itself that pleased him. She felt fairly certain, however, that had Mrs. Norton not been in the room, she would have been subjected to a lavish kiss from her betrothed.

"Come, then," he said, "as I have no names to wager. Let's find out."

Bearing in mind the woman's eagerness to reveal her accomplice during the carriage ride to Berkeley Square and their brief wait for the duke, Bea assumed acquiring the information would be easy. Alas, now that the moment had arrived, she turned strangely reluctant to talk.

"To be perfectly frank, I am reticent to speak in the presence of his grace, for I do not wish to cause him pain," Mrs. Norton said kindly.

It was, Bea thought, a rather audacious thing to say for the person who had made an effort to terminate his engagement by destroying the reputation of the woman he loved. Nevertheless, she calmly explained that the society matron's concern was not necessary. Unless the perpetrator was in fact the Dowager Duchess of Kesgrave, the only emotion the duke would feel was anger.

But Mrs. Norton, witnessing this display of misplaced confidence, shook her head sadly and said learning her associate's name would remind him of all the beauty, grace and elegance that had slipped through his fingers when he fell prey to Miss Hyde-Clare's machinations.

Bea, her reserves of patience woefully depleted by the various challenges of the day, could not form a coherent reply and simply groaned in disgust as she dropped her head to the back of the sofa.

Kesgrave's frustration was equally keen, but he regarded Mrs. Norton steadily and asked with quiet forcefulness for the name.

"Tavistock."

'Twas a stunning disclosure, and Bea, whipping her head up, immediately straightened in her seat. "Lord Tavistock?"

Mrs. Norton, darting a glance at Kesgrave, nodded almost with shame and said, "Lord Tavistock."

Her answer made the villain's identity crystal clear, and yet Bea required further clarification. "Lord Tavistock as in Lady Victoria's father?"

Obviously, it was an absurd question, for there were hardly two gentlemen bearing that appellation currently enjoying the London season.

Mrs. Norton, interpreting her response as the sort of frenzied insecurity any plain young woman who had reached above her touch would feel at the mention of the Incomparable her beau had previously courted, could not resist a small, gleeful smile. "Yes, Lord Tavistock, the beautiful, graceful and elegant Lady Victoria's father."

Her satisfaction was further increased by the expression on Kesgrave's face, which, as she had expressly warned, was a mix of surprise and regret.

Naturally, Mrs. Norton was determined to be gracious in her victory, for the scheme, which had appeared to have failed wildly in its purpose, had eventually wended its way around to its ultimate goal: hurting Beatrice Hyde-Clare.

Drawing her eyebrows close and pursing her lips together,

Mrs. Norton regarded her victim with an air of piteous understanding and determinedly sought her gaze, as if attempting to assure herself the poor dear was all right. Bea fully expected her to sit down on the settee and press Bea's head against her shoulder whilst softly murmuring, "There, there."

It was a hollow performance, as Mrs. Norton had neither the intelligence nor the humanity to successfully affect sympathy. It was also entirely unnecessary, for Kesgrave was not lamenting the terrible fate he had succumbed to on the terrace during Lord Larkwell's ball. Rather, he was contemplating how grossly he had miscalculated the situation with Lady Victoria, whom he had determined to bring into fashion as a favor to her family. Although he had danced attendance on her during the early weeks of her first season, he never had any intention of courting her, something he had felt certain she and her father had understood. It had merely been an act of kindness for a neighbor with whom he rubbed along well.

But now he was examining the agreement from another perspective and realizing Tavistock had been far loftier in his objective. He'd asked the duke to show interest in Lady Victoria, yes, but he had expected that interest to lead to something more. He thought Kesgrave would either develop feelings for her or recognize the value of taking a beautiful heiress as wife. The request to bring her into fashion had been only a ruse.

It was a staggering revelation for the imperious Duke of Kesgrave to discover he had been a naïve fool.

At least that was what Beatrice assumed he was thinking as he digested the information Mrs. Norton had supplied. It would account for both the surprise and regret she saw on his face.

Unable to sustain even feigned compassion, Mrs. Norton dropped her gaze from Bea's and lent her consideration to the salver, thoughtfully selecting a tea cake. As she watched the other woman nibble politely, Bea decided it was not surprising that her appetite appeared to have returned. Previously, she had been anxious about the duke's reception of the news, but now it was out and his response was all she could have hoped for.

Mrs. Norton lifted the silver pot and, refilling her own cup, asked Beatrice if she would like more tea. "You look horribly parched."

Atrocious woman, Bea thought.

Kesgrave, ignoring these antics, asked Mrs. Norton why Lord Tavistock had approached her with his plan.

"He knew I was sympathetic to your plight," she explained, "as I had expressed concern after the Larkwell affair. I was perhaps a bit zealous in my alarm because I recalled Miss Hyde-Clare from my first season and knew her to be manipulative in her ways. I do not blame her, of course, for a woman with as few positive attributes as she has to compensate for her shortcomings in some way."

Bea, who had known herself to be not only a drab mouse for much of her adult life but also a compliant one, could not comprehend the madness of this charge. "*I* was manipulative?"

Her archnemesis nodded firmly. "You feign surprise as if you don't know it is true."

Despite Mrs. Norton's conviction, Bea knew the idea was laughable. If she had had any ability to bend people and situations to her will, she would have extricated herself from her aunt's grasp years ago. "I defy you to cite a single instance of my being manipulative."

But Mrs. Norton had her example at the ready and immediately discharged it. "You told Mr. Norton that anyone who enjoyed reading *The Old English Baron* was a veritable peagoose."

Bea stared in amazement, at once unable to deny the accusation and unsure why she should want to. It was a most benign comment and patently true, for the novel was a poor imitation of *The Castle of Otranto,* which the author herself acknowledged in her preface.

"See, you are doing it right now," Mrs. Norton cried triumphantly.

"What?"

"Manipulating the situation to make it appear as if you have done nothing wrong," Mrs. Norton said. "But it is all a hum. Everyone knew Mr. Norton was devoted to me, and you made every effort to scotch his proposal because you wanted him for yourself. You flirted shamelessly with him and called me names behind my back. As my fondness for gothic novels was well known among the *ton,* there could be only one person whom you mocked with your comment. Mr. Norton might have been fooled, but I was not."

Bea wanted to laugh at the wanton vanity that presumed intimate knowledge of her likes and dislikes by every member of the beau monde, but her own obliviousness to these undercurrents pointed to enough personal self-absorption to quell her amusement.

Briefly, Bea considered explaining that her perceived offenses were only a misunderstanding, for her comment regarding *The Old English Baron* had not been meant as a condemnation of all gothic novels, of which she herself was a devotee. Indeed, it had not even been a condemnation of all works by Clara Reeve because she had thoroughly enjoyed *The Progress of Romance,* her engrossing history of prose fiction. It had genuinely and truly been a critique of that one book, and Bea stood by her opinion, for *The Old English Baron* was entirely derivative and only a peagoose could enjoy it over the original.

But Mrs. Norton's response to her peccadillos—name

calling, beau flirting—were so out of proportion to the crimes, Bea knew she was not open to a rational conversation about old hurts.

Therefore, Bea nodded as if accepting her guilt and asked when Tavistock approached her.

"At Lord Stirling's ball, after your appalling abuse of Lord Wem," she said, shaking her head in disgust. "I cannot say if his lordship is guilty of the crimes to which he confessed—perhaps he harmed your parents, perhaps he did not—but the shameful way you took advantage of what is obviously an infirm man aged well beyond his years who is not entirely in control of his faculties was disgraceful. I was quite candid in my disapproval, as was Lord Tavistock. It quickly became clear that we had to act at once to save his grace." She turned then to look at Kesgrave and professed deep remorse at the dead body. "I had nothing to do with that and know nothing about it."

The duke ignored the comment. "You visited Bea the morning immediately following the Stirling ball. If you had joined the plan only the night before, how was Tavistock able to implement it so fast?"

"Immediately following Miss Hyde-Clare's disgraceful pursuit of you at the Larkwells', Mrs. Ralston shared with his lordship her suspicions about her investigative tendencies. As he had his own concerns about Miss Hyde-Clare's decency, he quickly devised a plan, hiring Mr. Rose and arranging rooms at 22 Savoy," she explained. "He had even employed an actress to appear at Miss Hyde-Clare's door with a letter from her grandfather, but after the Wem fiasco he sought me out and asked if I would be willing to assist him in his endeavor. His plan would have a far better chance of succeeding if the call was made by someone of the same world whom Miss Hyde-Clare already knew. She would trust me implicitly, whereas she might first investigate an actress who was not convincing enough, especially given her proclivities."

As the logic was irrefutable, Kesgrave nodded. "And Mr. Rose's brutal slaying? How was that arranged?"

Mrs. Norton's face turned ashen at the reminder of the bloodied corpse. "Arranged, your grace?"

"By Tavistock."

"No, no, no," she said, shaking her head fervently, her composure starting to slip as she realized the duke believed she had engaged in a truly wicked scheme. "That wasn't part of the plan. That was never part of the plan. He was supposed to be alive, and as soon as Miss Hyde-Clare stepped into the room, he was to carry her to the bed and lie on top of her. And then, only a moment later, Mrs. Ralston was supposed to enter and I would scream as if shocked and she would come running and witness the same scandalous scene as I. Nobody was supposed to get hurt. I don't know how it happened, and if you could have seen him, your grace, lying there in the bed, with all that blood, and his eyes, his eyes staring blankly. I don't know how something so awful could have happened."

Tears started to slide down her cheeks, and she clenched her hands together. "It was all going so well, for I had found Miss Hyde-Clare at the modiste and convinced her to accompany me to Milford Lane with only a modicum of effort. And when we got there, everything was exactly as Tavistock said, so I had no concerns. There was only a moment, a slight moment in the hallway when she grabbed my arm, that I thought the plan might not prosper, but I realized she just needed a little encouragement. And then...and then...I opened the door and saw him lying there and..."

Unable to bear the memory, she broke down into heated sobs.

Although many of the details Mrs. Norton had revealed were new to Bea, none of them altered the narrative as she had lived it and she found nothing particularly upsetting. Kesgrave, however, had not been in the hallway with Mrs. Norton encouraging her to enter a room to be attacked by a partially dressed man.

His anger was incandescent.

Bea met his eyes over the weeping form and said gently, "No. No. As you observed, she is dull and stupid. To that I would add she is sad and petty. There is no punishment you can mete out that is worse than her having to go through life being dull and stupid *and* sad and petty."

Although inconsolable, Mrs. Norton was not insensible and she lifted her head to protest this litany of abuse. "How dare...you say...such horrible...things about me," she demanded, the severity of her outrage undercut by the shallow breathing and hiccups brought on by her bout of tears. "I am...too smart to...be taken...in by the...likes of...you. Can his grace...say the...same?"

Bea was grateful for the wildly imprudent comment, for it shattered the intensity of the moment. "You see my point?" she asked, unable to smother the amusement in her own eyes and relieved to see the answering glint in his.

"I do, yes," he said smoothly, "but I would advise you to think more creatively, something at which you usually excel. For example, being denied entry to Almack's, while not as poetic as your punishment, is unquestionably worse."

Mrs. Norton, whose cheeks were splotched with red from the exertion of her sobs, turned stark white. "No."

"Yes," Kesgrave said firmly.

She turned to Bea and pleaded with her to reason with him. "Please. If you care nothing for me, think of my children. Their social success depends on mine. If the patronesses decide to revoke my vouchers after being such intimate friends, it would set off a storm of gossip and lead to my utter ruination."

Alas, *ruination* was the very worst word she could have said in the duke's presence at that particular moment, and he rang the bell to call for a footman. The butler himself appeared.

"Ah, Marlow, very good. Our guest is ready to go. Please ensure she makes it safely to her carriage and departs the premises as quickly as possible," he said.

Either realizing the futility of arguing further or possessing too much dignity to do so in front of the servant, Mrs. Norton nodded. Then she sighed heavily, as if defeated by a force far greater than she, and called on generations of breeding to make a courteous exit. "I thank you, your grace, for your generous hospitality."

He accepted the comment with a dip of his head, watched her leave, and after a brief word with Marlow, shut the door on his unwanted guest with visible relief.

Chapter Eight

As soon as the drawing room door had closed, Bea complimented the duke on devising a punishment so well suited to Mrs. Norton's crime. "I would love to be hiding behind a curtain in the room when she tries to explain to her husband why their vouchers have been revoked. I do not think she is equal to the challenge of coming up with a reasonable-sounding excuse."

Nodding, Kesgrave agreed that the woman would inevitably bungle her story and posited that he would soon be subjected to an unpleasant conversation with her husband. "I mean no offense," he added, "but you have appalling taste in archnemeses."

Bea laughed and assured him that none was taken. "I will have to see about what I can do about finding a better quality of enemy. Or perhaps I should consider forgoing all enemies. I must own, Damien, I find it excessively exhausting."

She was about to throw herself languidly on the settee in exactly the manner Lady Abercrombie had prescribed for sufferers of lovesickness, but Kesgrave interceded, pulling her into a crushing hug. He pressed his lips to her ear, her cheek, the line of her chin, all the while murmuring, "I'm sorry."

Bea could think of nothing less worthy of forgiveness than the wonderful feeling of his lips against her skin, but she knew he was apologizing for something else. As she was no more eager to cease their activity or break their contact or confront the messiness of their near future than he, she tilted her head to allow him better access to her neck.

When the activity threatened to get out of hand, Kesgrave raised his head, pressed a soft kiss on her forehead and led her to the sofa. Before he sat beside her, he reopened the door to the drawing room.

"I do not think five minutes with it closed will invite endless chatter, but any more than that would be courting trouble," he explained. "Now, let us sit here like civilized members of the *ton* drinking lukewarm tea without complaining, so that I may apologize properly."

"*You* apologize?" she asked, lifting an eyebrow in surprise. "I know as the Duke of Kesgrave you like to think the sun sets at your command, but I brought her here. I'm the one who should apologize."

"Yes, you brought her into my home," he agreed easily, "but *I* brought this nightmare to your door. Everything you suffered today was because of me. Your reputation could have been ruined today because of me. You could have been brutally attacked today because of me. You could have been killed today because of me. I was blind to Tavistock's ambitions, which was a grave and unforgivable oversight. As you frequently enjoy pointing out, I hold myself in very high esteem and in doing so I should have realized Tavistock would not be content with just securing my attention for his daughter. It is obvious now that he'd hoped to join the two families. But I did not and you suffered for it. I am very sorry."

Bea listened to this speech, which contained several objectionable conclusions, not the least of which was the assumption that she had been in physical danger, and exclaimed with irritation, "Fie on you, sir!"

As he had expected a more charitable response to his list of mea culpas, most likely, Bea thought, because he so rarely issued one, Kesgrave blinked in bewilderment. "Excuse me?"

"You have no idea how dearly I wished while sitting across from you at the dinner table at Lakeview Hall and listening to you drone on about one deadly dull topic after another to see a look of debasement on your face," she said. "And now here it is—utter debasement!—and you have contrived it in precisely such a way that I can get no enjoyment from it at all. So, yes, fie on you!"

Cautiously, the duke said, "I would apologize again, although I am not entirely sure what for other than being knowledgeable about the French Revolutionary Wars, but your tone indicates it will only provoke you further."

"You are insightful, your grace. Indeed, you are insightful to an often disconcerting degree. But even you are not omniscient," she said with sharp emphasis. "You cannot hold yourself responsible for not knowing the unspoken thoughts of any person, let alone a man whom you considered to be a friend. It is hubristic, which I will accept because I knew you were arrogant when we became betrothed, but it is also stupid and *that* I did not consent to wed. If I want to tether myself to foolishness, I might as well say dash it all and become Aunt Vera's companion."

The expression on Kesgrave's face changed several times while she spoke, circling through confusion, outrage and annoyance before settling on amused. "Very well, brat, I rescind my apology on the grounds that my understanding and insight are not infinite, although I remain firm in the belief that I should have been more cynical of Tavistock's request. What you call omniscience, I would describe as a lifetime of learning the value of a dukedom," he explained. "However, it strikes me as egregiously unfair that you get to apologize for Mrs. Norton while I'm forbidden from doing so for Tavistock."

"At the risk of being pedantic—and truly, Damien, for the first time ever I say that with absolutely no intention of teasing you—the difference is, I brought her into your home," she said, then added, "And I mean that literally. I showed her into your drawing room and let her eat your housekeeper's wonderful tea cakes. I subjected you to her horribleness, I forced you to endure her awfulness, and *that* is what I'm apologizing for. But I take no responsibility for the very fact of her existence or my inability to foretell her destructive pettiness, as those things are beyond my control. Now, you are perfectly welcome to apologize for Tavistock after I meet him and he issues several cutting remarks on my unsuitability as a duchess."

"It was a worthy attempt, Bea," he said, shaking his head, "but it won't do. Slipping in a confrontation with Tavistock at the end of a needlessly long-winded explanation will not cause me to overlook it. You are not meeting with him. He means you ill, and I won't expose you further to his evil intent."

Obviously, the decision was not his to make, for it fell to her to decide what evil she was or was not exposed to further. Nevertheless, she protested his comment because every word of her explanation had been necessary. "What you were supposed to take issue with was my faulty logic, for if I introduce myself to Tavistock, then you remain blameless. That, your grace, was the semantical burrow you were meant to dig as a distraction. Alas, now we must have a quarrel." She sighed heavily and stared at the empty plate with its miserly scattering of crumbs. "Is it possible to request more tea

cakes? I fear I am quite famished, and without proper rein-
forcements, I will not be able to argue with my usual
alacrity."

Kesgrave stood at once and tugged the bell pull, noting,
however, that it was in his best interest to deny her sustenance. "Your being weakened by hunger is probably the only
way I will win one of our quarrels."

Bea airily dismissed this conceit as beneath his dignity, for
he had too much pride in his verbal acuity to win by deprivation. Kesgrave admitted that certainly once held true, but
after several months of her acquaintance, he was prepared to
take his victories where he could.

"Brought already so low and the parson's mousetrap has
yet to snap shut!" she said with pronounced sympathy. "It is
little wonder Lord Tavistock is trying to save you."

But the duke was not prepared to make light of the situation, and his frown was fierce as the footman carried in
another tray with a fresh pot and tea cakes piled high.
Undaunted, Bea launched into an argument detailing why she
had to be present at the confrontation with Tavistock and
made the case so persuasively to herself that she ended the
polemic by insisting Kesgrave himself should abstain from
attending.

"You will only make him standoffish and defensive," she
said, "which will accomplish nothing."

Kesgrave ardently disagreed with this line of reasoning
and asked her what in particular she thought he hoped to
accomplish other than seeing the man who sought to destroy
her pay for his transgression.

"Identifying the person who murdered Mr. Rose," Bea
said. "Tavistock hired him so he is the natural place to begin
our investigation. It's too early to rule anyone out, of course,
but I think it's very unlikely that he himself killed the man.
What would the advantage be? The only danger the actor

LYNN MESSINA

posed was the information regarding the scheme itself and that was shared by Mrs. Norton. Why hire someone to perform a service and then kill him before he did it? It simply defies logic. Furthermore, the killer had been looking for something, and it's highly implausible that Mr. Rose possessed something of enough value to tempt Tavistock to kill for it. No, it's much more probable that Mr. Rose was murdered for a matter completely unassociated with his work for his lordship. I wonder if Mr. Rose was even the intended victim. It was Mr. Josiah's bedchamber that was searched, so perhaps he was the target. After all, it is unusual for someone to be in the room of a man with whom he has no association. But if that is true, wouldn't the murderer have realized he had the wrong victim? Had he never seen him before? If so, why kill a complete stranger? Or did the two men look alarmingly alike? Could they have been twin brothers? And is that why Mr. Josiah allowed Tavistock to hire out his stables for the scheme? Because it was a family affair?"

Bea concluded the long list of items she hoped to accomplish in her interview with Tavistock and raised the teacup to her lips, pleased to discover the brew had cooled enough for her to drink it. "As we know almost nothing about the victim, there is a tremendous amount of information to be gained from Lord Tavistock, who will be less inclined to give it with your standing there glaring thunderously at him," she explained, before adding that his desire to glare thunderously was entirely understandable and something of which she had no intention of depriving him. "I am merely pointing out the prudence of your waiting until after we have our answers to confront him."

Kesgrave, patiently sipping tea as she exhausted her argument, looked at her over the rim of his teacup and said, "I am going with you, Beatrice. That is the end of the discussion."

She sighed heavily as if frustrated by a particularly

disheartening defeat and hid her smile in the teacup, hoping very much that it was indeed the end of the discussion, for it had finished in a very satisfying place.

"You may cease pretending to be disappointed," he added mildly, "when we both know you have got exactly what you want. And don't think you hoodwinked me by switching to an inane argument so that your original premise seemed reasonable in comparison. I simply realized as you made your comprehensive list of questions for Tavistock that you would not rest until you had the answers. If I do not allow you to come with me, you will go separately as Mr. Wright, which is far more dangerous."

If Bea had not actually made the decision to call on the peer in the guise of a solicitor, it was merely because the need had not arisen. She had been confident that she could sway her betrothed with reason. That she had unintentionally applied a sort of extortive pressure was a delightful revelation.

Even so, she could see Kesgrave's anxiety for her safety in his posture and hated that she'd had a part in making it worse. Hoping to alleviate his apprehension, she said, "You know Tavistock better than I, so I won't say you have no cause for concern if you feel it, but I do think the risk is relatively low. Consider how convoluted his scheme was: hiring an actor, renting a stable, recruiting Mrs. Norton. He was clearly unwilling to strike at me directly, which would have been much more efficient. And now that the great plot has unraveled and his part in it exposed, you would never fall in line with his plans even if a terrible tragedy befell me. So the only reason he could have now to hurt me, and that would be to exact revenge for not blithely going along with his scheme to compromise me. But even that doesn't really make sense, for the failure was not even my fault. If Tavistock wants to resent anyone, it should be Mr. Rose's killer, which makes helping us identify the murderer in his best interest."

As she spoke, Kesgrave's countenance lightened, and when she rambled to a finish, he asked if that was the tack she planned to take to gain Tavistock's assistance. "If so, I think it would be more persuasive coming from Mr. Wright than the woman who ultimately thwarted him."

"Again, I would contend Mr. Rose's killer ultimately thwarted him, but, no, that is not to be my tack. I intend to employ no strategy or ruse. I will speak to him forthrightly. I believe the term you recently used was a *frank conversation*," she added as she glanced at the clock and noted it was approaching five. "Let us be on our way. The hour grows late and my family will start to wonder where I am."

Kesgrave smiled. "It's about time you worried about your family. According to your own account, you have been gone for three hours. Noting your lack of consideration, I sent your aunt a note informing her that you were with me. For the sake of propriety, we are in the company of my cousin Josephine—although, given how you traipse through the city dressed as a solicitor and your own maid, you show as little respect as you do consideration for propriety."

Recalling the episodes to which he referred, Bea laughed and said, "It is a shame Tavistock expended so much effort in trying to ruin me when all he had to do was wait a few days until I ruined myself."

Naturally, her betrothed was not as amused as she by her exploits, which he called reckless and she described as ingenious, and a spirited debate ensued regarding the future duchess's behavior that was ended by the appearance of the duke's groom.

"Sorry to interrupt, ye grace, miss," Jenkins said with a shy smile at Bea, "but ye wanted to know when he got back. He returned fifteen minutes ago."

"Very good, Jenkins," Kesgrave said, nodding abruptly. "We will leave immediately."

Bea was gratified to discover the reason for the duke's lack of urgency and, taking one last tea cake for the journey to Bedford Square, followed him out of the drawing room. Standing next to the front door was Marlow, who, black brows raised in chilly displeasure, made her feel keenly aware that eating a pastry in the stately hallway of the elegant mansion was not very duchess-like behavior. At once, she felt a childish impulse to hide the confection behind her back and only managed to resist the urge by reminding herself she was a fully grown adult who did not require the approval of the butler.

If anything, the butler should require *her* approval.

Brave words, Bea thought as she climbed into the carriage. Then, pondering the matter, she said to the duke, "Jenkins likes me."

Although he appeared struck by the apparent introduction of a new topic, he could not deny its truth. "He does, yes. He is impressed with your spirit; says you've got bottom."

As the number of people in the world who thought Beatrice Hyde-Clare had courage was vanishingly small, she took sincere pleasure in the groom's approval. "Given that he regards me positively, I would be most grateful if you would ask him to say something complimentary about me to Marlow," she announced, pausing a moment to consider the sort of comment that would best counter the abrasive impression she had made that afternoon by issuing orders and demanding entrance to the home. "You can ask him to say something anodyne and encouraging such as: I believe you will find her to be a most biddable mistress."

Kesgrave, his lips quirking at the request, flatly rejected this proposal, adding that he would not embarrass his loyal servant for anyone, not even her.

Trying not to resent his refusal, which was issued without any serious consideration, Bea reminded herself of the complexities of a gentleman's relationship with his groom. Although she knew very little about it, she imagined it could be as fraught as his bond with his valet. With a nod of understanding, she said, "Very well. I suppose you can make the comment."

"I?" he asked in sweeping astonishment, as if she had proposed something truly shocking, such as strolling down Bond Street in his dressing gown.

Naturally, she did not appreciate his needlessly dramatic response, and bristling with offense, said, "Yes, *you* can tell Marlow that you believe I will make a most biddable mistress. Upon reconsideration, it is in fact the better arrangement. It will carry more weight coming from you, as you know me slightly better than Jenkins."

"Slightly?" he said, succumbing entirely to his mirth. "I know you only *slightly* better than my groom?"

She found his ability to be easily distracted by a trifle to be genuinely exasperating and sighed with hearty frustration. "Moderately better, then," she amended. "Regardless, a kind word from you would help improve Marlow's opinion of me. We did not meet under the most opportune circumstances this afternoon, and I worry that he thinks I am overbearing."

Kesgrave's opinion on the matter could not be immediately ascertained because he was still laughing too hard to form a coherent sentence. Finally, his gales subsided enough for him to decline the honor. "As much as I want to smooth your way—and I assure you, nothing would make me happier than your effortless adoption of your role as mistress of Kesgrave House—I will not endanger my relationship with the staff by telling them a bald-faced lie."

"Devil it, I *am* biddable!" she said angrily, for she had spent twenty unresisting years under the thumb of her aunt.

Surely, that was enough for an informal endorsement of her character.

Her furious insistence on her own docility further amused the duke, who said between chuckles that he felt sure she had no cause to worry. "You made an excellent impression on Marlow, who was confused by your refusal to cower at his scorn. Even my grandmother withers when he uses his most dampening tone and ferocious scowl."

"Really?" she asked, not convinced that he wasn't placating her with a fiction, for the butler, whose disdain had never faltered, had seemed far from perplexed.

"Indeed," he said firmly. "I have it from Jenkins, who got it from Mrs. Wallace, who heard it firsthand from Brennan, who witnessed the way you browbeat Marlow."

"Browbeat?" she asked tartly, displeased by the image that had formed in her head of her repeatedly thumping the imposing butler with a broom. "I'm sure that is not an accurate description of our interaction."

"No, do not back down now," Kesgrave said. "Marlow responds to strength. After your impressive showing, he most likely thinks I don't deserve you. Perhaps, my love, you can say a kind word about me?"

Although Bea expressed concern that such a statement might undermine her standing in the new household, she promised to consider it. "You will note, I trust, how I did not immediately say no to your request even though I will ultimately deny it? That is what we call proper conduct or decorum, your grace."

Before he could respond to her exquisite condescension, the carriage slowed to a stop, and Bea felt her anxiety, which had receded during the ride, increase sharply. It was, she thought, strange that she was so apprehensive about confronting Tavistock, for she had had several brutal skirmishes in recent months with men who wished her ill. She had been clunked on the head with a rotting plank and tossed in a decrepit shack, beaten on a public thoroughfare, and throttled on Lord Larkwell's terrace during a ball. This encounter could be no worse than those, for she would not be subjected to violence, and yet she felt chilled by the cold calculation of Tavistock's abuse. All the other attacks, propagated in a heated moment, had been committed when the opportunity presented itself.

Kesgrave, displaying no unease, exited the carriage with familiar grace and helped her climb down. Tavistock lived in a white edifice with arched windows on the first floor and three shallow steps leading to the door. It was an impressive townhouse, larger, certainly, and more ornate than what the Hyde-Clares enjoyed in Portman Square, and Bea found her disquiet rise, for how could the owner of such an august residence resent her? She was far beneath his notice.

And she knew the question was disingenuous, for it was her lack of standing that made her success so galling.

Almost as soon as Kesgrave had knocked on the door, the butler answered and welcomed them warmly, an indication, Bea thought, of the duke's familiarity with the family. In a matter of moments, they were shown into the drawing room, offered tea and informed that his lordship would be with them momentarily. He also invited them to sit down, but Bea was too restless to do something as sedate as sitting.

She did not have to pace for long because Lord Tavistock entered almost immediately. He was dark like his daughter and robust despite generous jowls that seemed to pull him down.

Having been apprised of the events by one of his associates—Mrs. Norton, presumably—he wasted little time in pleasantries and launched at once into an expression of his disappointment that his scheme had not worked out as he planned. To Bea's utter amazement, he displayed no sign of shame or embarrassment, only philosophical disappointment at the vagaries of fate.

"'Tis a salutary lesson for me to be reminded that you can make every attempt to account for every variable in a situation and yet something unimaginable can still make your plan go awry. Hobson being killed like that—" He broke off to shake his head, marveling. "It's the damnedest thing. Never in a dozen years could I have compensated for that eventuality. It is a disappointment, to be sure, but I am confident, Kesgrave, that you will consider this episode in the spirit in which it was conceived, for you must know that as a father I could not let you slip off the hook so easily. You do not have a daughter of your own yet, but God willing, you will one day, and then you will comprehend the insult done to my own when you threw her over for a plain, inconsequential spinster like Miss Hyde-Clare. It was insupportable, and given how little you could have truly wanted it, I knew there would be no harm in trying to right the ship. Alas, the vessel has capsized entirely, and that is a disappointment. I trust, your grace, that you bear me no ill will. As I said, I am a father and it is my sacred duty to address an injustice that has been done to my family."

Bea stared aghast at the lord, incapable of properly comprehending the staggering insolence of his speech. She could not comprehend his tone, which had a cast of geniality about it, as if his appalling efforts had been done in the spirit of friendly good-fellowship. She could not comprehend his words, with their slight chastisement of the duke for making him exert himself at all. She could not comprehend the languidness of his demeanor as he flicked open his snuffbox with a thumb and unhurriedly raised the powder to his nose.

It was all so incomprehensible.

Indeed, the only thing she did understand was Kesgrave's response, for as soon as Tavistock stopped talking, he said, "I do bear you considerable ill will," and struck the other man in the face. The blow landed on the left side of his jaw, above his considerable jowl, and wrenched his head to the side. His whole body twisted from the force, and he stumbled against a bergère before falling to the floor. He landed firmly on his behind and, holding his chin, stared up at Kesgrave in horrified wonder, unable to believe the violence of the duke's response. His eyes darted to Bea, then to Kesgrave, then back to Bea, then to the duke again, as if trying to discern something in the space between them.

Kesgrave's relaxed stance reflected none of the pugilism of the past few moments, and she admired the elegance of his presentation, for even while he was driving his fist into Tavistock's face, he seemed to hardly move at all. His arm had swung out, connected with skin and returned to his side as easily as raising a teacup to his lips.

It was an impressive display, and Bea thought she finally understood why Russell was so desperate to take instruction from Gentleman Jackson.

Bea rather thought she wouldn't mind a lesson or two herself.

Silently, Kesgrave regarded his neighbor, his fingers on his right hand twitching slightly, as if itching to re-form as a fist. Tavistock was still too stunned to speak, and Bea imagined him reviewing his recent speech and being unable to locate what exactly he had said to create such a furor.

Could a peer not ruin the reputation of one inconsequential spinster without arousing a duke's anger? Was that no longer permissible? When had the rules of civility changed? When had it become unacceptable for a father to behave with whatever immorality he deemed necessary to avenge his daughter's honor? What pale imitation of itself had the kingdom become that the dictates of basic decorum no longer applied?

Imagining these thoughts, Bea felt a wave of amusement and was grateful for it, as she had been much troubled by his words. He had said little that Mrs. Norton herself hadn't said —or, for that matter, her own family—but, unlike them, he'd given her no consideration at all, not even wincing at the discomfort of being required by circumstance to embarrass her. It was as if her humanity didn't even rise to the level of callousness.

To say she'd been deeply demoralized by his attitude would be to vastly understate the case. Having already felt herself to be a dreg at the bottom of a barrel, she was mortified to discover she was in fact under the casket itself.

But now her sense of humor reasserted itself, and she could almost smile at the absurdity of poor, befuddled Lord Tavistock struggling to understand why he could not insult another man's betrothed with impunity.

O, unfair world!

'Twas about to get more unfair yet, Bea thought, as she crossed the room to where he sat on the floor nursing his jaw. Looking down at him, she said coolly, "Do allow me to introduce myself, Lord Tavistock, as I don't believe we've met. I am Miss Hyde-Clare. No, you do not have to get up. I understand you are incapacitated at the moment."

In fact, the peer had made no move to stand for the introduction, but her implication that he could not was all the incentive he needed to make the effort. It was no easy task, and he wobbled several times before finally steadying himself. The chair he had fallen against remained within easy reach, but he refrained from using it as a crutch.

He opened his mouth to speak and winced from the pain. Then, as if determined to ignore the throbbing, he said with careless spite, "Knowing you are far too well bred to hit a man in the presence of a lady, Kesgrave, I can only conclude you agree with my assessment of her."

Kesgrave regarded Tavistock calmly, but his fingers twitched at the insult, and Bea, recalling the ease with which he had knocked Taunton unconscious on the Larkwell terrace, stepped forward. She had no desire to stand idly by for however many minutes while he recovered his senses.

"My lord, as you have chosen to speak frankly, I will return the favor," she said with pragmatic assurance. "Although I have seen no sign of intelligence in you this afternoon, the fact that you arranged such an elaborate scheme indicates you have some cognitive ability. I would ask you to apply that aptitude to this situation, for, as far as I can tell, your plan is to provoke Kesgrave into pummeling you senseless. While I'm sure that strategy has much to recommend it, I would strongly urge you to reconsider the advantages because we are not leaving your drawing room until our curiosity has been appeased so all you will accomplish is giving yourself a terrible headache." Then she turned to the duke and asked mildly, "Is that correct, your grace? Or will there be other adverse effects from the abuse? Might his lordship suffer lapses of memory over a long period of time or find himself less able to think clearly? Despite reading a biography of Jack Broughton, I fear I know very little about bare-knuckle fighting."

"It depends on several factors," Kesgrave said, matching her straightforward, conversational tone, "such as the force of the blow, the softness of the skull and the amount of time the subject is insensible. It is certainly not unheard of for a boxer's brainbox to undergo permanent damage after a particularly punishing bout. But it's impossible to say for sure. If Tavistock wants to find out for certain, I am happy to oblige him."

"See?" Bea said approvingly. "Kesgrave is determined to be reasonable, as am I. Neither one of us would dream of standing in the way of a gentleman's right to get himself repeatedly knocked unconscious. That being the case, it would be remiss of me not to point out once again that your being insensible will not speed our departure. The best and easiest way to persuade us to leave is to answer our questions."

But Tavistock did not appreciate getting advice from an insignificant miss in the comfort of his own drawing room, and he glowered at the duke, as if it were his fault he was forced to endure the indignity.

Kesgrave returned his scowl with a blank stare.

Although neither man seemed inclined to break the impasse, Tavistock was far too insulted to remain silent for long and after a minute or two, he growled peevishly.

"You think you are very clever, don't you, Miss Hyde-Clare. A veritable wit!" he said snidely. "And perhaps you are, for you did nab the elusive Duke of Kesgrave. I had thought I had come up with the perfect ruse by asking him to squire my darling Victoria around London during her first season, but you, madam, you have shown me what true deviousness is. You are to be commended." Now he dipped his head in sneering tribute. "My poor Victoria never stood a chance."

The duke stiffened at the attack, which took aim directly at Bea, and his expression hardened. But his betrothed, who was grateful to have risen to the level of acknowledgment, took no new offense.

"Lord Tavistock, we are no more happy to avail ourselves of your hospitality than you are to offer it," she said calmly, for there was no value in letting her impatience show. "Now, we can continue down this path, with your issuing insults and Kesgrave's answering them with violence, but you strike me as too practical to waste your own time on such futility. The afternoon wears on, and I am confident you have something else you'd rather do than argue with us. All we need are a few answers and then we will go."

As much as his lordship detested the prospect of giving Beatrice anything she desired, he allowed that, yes, he had an appointment in an hour, for which he required time to change. Aware that there was nothing to be done but to get through it, he invited his visitors to have a seat and, his mood turning philosophical again, observed with earnest regret how disappointed Kesgrave's father would be with his son's descent into mawkishness.

"Now that was a man who appreciated a coldly calculated scheme," he said fondly. "There was not a sentimental bone in his entire body. The way he treated his own tenants, as if they were cloths to be wrung dry—it was inspiring. I could never match his hard-heartedness, as exemplified by my scheme. If the fifth duke were alive, Miss Hyde-Clare, you would never have been lured to a stable to be ruined but simply made to disappear."

As troubling as his account of Kesgrave's father was, Bea knew now was not the appropriate time to linger over it. Nevertheless, she could not suppress a distracting twinge of remorse over her inconsideration. She had been so consumed by her own orphanhood, she had never thought to ask Kesgrave about his.

Tavistock shook his head, as if to clear the old duke from his mind and sat down in the bergère. "Very well. Ask me what you wish to know so that we may bring this disheartening episode to a close," he said as if resolved to be sensible, but almost immediately his tone took on a regretful cast as he lamented the poor timing of the actor's death. "If only Hobson had been slain after his work for me had been done!" He sighed deeply and looked to Kesgrave. "In that circumstance, I assure you, we would be having a very different conversation."

"No," Kesgrave said firmly, "we would not."

But Tavistock refused to believe the duke would have

continued in the betrothal after London's most notorious gossip had gleefully carried back the tale of Bea's shocking liaison with an actor. "Mrs. Ralston would have described Hobson's state of undress in almost loving detail and placed Miss Hyde-Clare tightly in his embrace no matter how many feet apart they might have actually been. No man could withstand that, especially not a Matlock. The family name is everything, and that harpy would have dragged it through the mud."

Although Kesgrave's expression remained bland, his eyes were chips of blue ice when he spoke with aggressive mildness. "Let me be clear, Tavistock, so that there can be no misunderstanding in the future or possibility of another attempt. There is nothing you can do that will sunder my bond with Miss Hyde-Clare. The only thing you will accomplish is inciting my fury, and then you will discover that my appreciation for a coldly calculated scheme rivals my father's. Do you understand?"

At this question, Tavistock's color rose in his cheeks, making his comprehension known, and he began to grumble under this breath about the duke's churlishness, for the situation was not so sordid that it required threats. "I am a parent, am I not? I had to do something. She is my daughter, after all."

Bea's appreciation of the ridiculous, never far from the surface, reemerged as she noted the air of aggrieved father he wore. How dreadfully unfair to be held to account for what was ultimately just another mundane obligation of parenting! Coordinating the ruin of an innocent woman was no different from ensuring Lady Victoria had enough pairs of gloves to see her though the season.

Kesgrave, however, was not amused, and before his expression could turn thunderous, Bea took the reins of the conversation.

"Tell us about the actor—Mr. Hobson, as you just called him," she said. "Where did you find him? How did you arrange for his hire?"

Given that Tavistock's only thought for the actor had been the many ways his violent murder had upended his plan, Bea was hardly surprised to observe the impatient boredom that overcame his features. Slowly, however, that changed to suspicion. "Why?" he asked, clutching the arms of the chair. "Why does it matter to you where I found him? What interest could that be of yours?"

"A man was viciously killed today while performing a service for you," Bea said plainly, well aware that his lordship had already discovered her investigative bent. It had been central to his plot. "Are you not curious to know why?"

"Curious to know why?" he echoed, as if genuinely baffled by the concept. "What interest could I have in a miserable actor's wretched fate? It has nothing to do with me, and Josiah has already taken care of the matter by making it appear as if the man tripped in the courtyard and landed on a rake. A unfortunate tragedy, to be sure, but no business of mine."

As Bea already believed Tavistock to be among the most terrible people she'd ever had the displeasure to meet, she was shocked to discover her opinion of him could sink lower. And yet there she was, disgusted anew by the cool way he lauded the stable owner's callous treatment of the murdered actor. It was fiendish to consider a man's death only by the inconvenience it caused.

Smothering her anger, Bea asked him how he knew.

Tavistock tilted his head, still bewildered. "How do I know what?"

"That this has nothing to do with you," she replied. "It is possible that some element in your scheme exposed him to danger."

This idea had never occurred to him, and he was quick to dismiss it by pointing out that Hobson was most likely killed by one of the dozen unsavory characters he interacted with on a daily basis. "The man was an actor at one of the lower-quality theaters in the city, a showhouse on the Strand called the Particular, which falls well short of Drury Lane or the Haymarket, and he did not keep the best company. I am to understand he was an exceedingly rough fellow, and he certainly drove a hard bargain. Rodwell was forced to triple my offer to gain his compliance."

"You did not meet with him yourself?" she asked, aghast that he would ask an underling to perform such an ignoble task. Surely, he would seek to hide the depths of his depravity from his servants.

Indeed not, for he stared back at her in horror at the suggestion. "Meet with him myself! I do not know how you imagine one employs an actor to do one's bidding, Miss Hyde-Clare, but I assure you, it is not like hiring a valet. What cause would I have to pollute my house with his presence or do you propose I visit him in his lodgings? Or," he asked with a snide laugh, "do you imagine I would frequent the filthy underbelly of a theater? Perhaps call on Hobson in his dressing room? No, I did not meet with him myself. I sent my steward, who, after being ruthlessly browbeaten on the price by the dreadful brute, arranged the matter."

"If the quality of the theater did not meet your standards," she asked, confused further by the lax manner by which her downfall was arranged, "why not seek someone from Drury Lane or the Haymarket? What led you to Mr. Hobson in the first place?"

As benign as the question was, his lordship responded fiercely, his eyes flashing in disgust as the color in his cheeks rose again. "You impertinent hussy! How dare you ask me that?"

Incapable of understanding the violence of his response, she looked to the duke for edification, which he promptly provided.

"His mistress referred him to the Particular," Kesgrave explained, demonstrating none of their host's modesty or reluctance. "He has been keeping an actress in a house near the Thames—Savoy Street, I recall now—for these past six months. She belongs to a theater near to the Particular that is set up in much the same style, the Athenaeum."

If Lord Tavistock had retained any modicum of respect for the Duke of Kesgrave after his appalling revelation of sentimentality, it was eradicated entirely by this blatant want of discretion. "I will not confirm your supposition and can only feel relief now that my daughter was not saddled with a man who has so little respect for the proprieties. You are an embarrassment to decency."

Naturally, he spoke without irony and felt no contradiction lay at the heart of his own gallantry, for it fell well within his code of moral conduct to compromise an innocent female to further his own ends.

Bea would have liked to have been surprised by the display of male hypocrisy because that would have meant it was somewhat of a novel experience. Alas, she had come across many maddening examples in the course of her investigations.

"Summon your steward, then," she said imperiously.

Tavistock straightened his shoulders and said with indignant refusal, "I will not."

Kesgrave, however, assured him quite emphatically that he would.

Glancing pointedly at the brass inlaid wall clock, Tavistock reminded his visitors that Bea said she had a few questions for him. "She did not mention interrogating my entire staff."

"Did your entire staff meet with Hobson?" Bea asked.

"Don't be absurd!" his lordship growled.

"Then I do not need to interrogate your entire staff. Just Mr. Rodwell," she replied calmly. "Now summon him at once so that we may have the pleasure of removing ourselves from your company as soon as possible."

Although Tavistock desired to be done with them as well, he pulled his lips into a tight line, as if offended by the sentiment, and rang for a footman to convey his message to Rodwell. While they waited for him to appear, Bea inquired about his arrangement with the stable owner.

Peevishly, he insisted that the pact he made with Josiah had no bearing on the actor's death.

Bea wanted to be amused by his air of mistreatment, for it was outrageous that the man who had tried to ruin her only hours before felt a few questions in the tragic death of his own hireling were a terrible imposition, but it was simply too galling.

Nevertheless, she revealed none of her annoyance as she reiterated her earlier point, insisting that it was impossible to say at that juncture what was or what was not a factor in Hobson's death. "Anything could be related, anything at all, and only a fool would dismiss even the most minor-seeming detail out of hand. Now again, please tell me the nature of your arrangement with Mr. Josiah. How did you contrive his absence? Was he aware of what would transpire in his bedchamber whilst he was gone?"

But Tavistock, who allowed no man to call him a fool, let alone a spinster without consequence, leaned back in his chair and stared at her malevolently. "You are right, Miss Hyde-Clare, that I should not discount any possibility, and thinking about it carefully now—considering, as you say, even the most minor details—I cannot help but wonder at your involvement in Hobson's demise. You claim to be asking

these questions out of concern for the victim, but how do I
know you are not just trying to find out if you yourself are
vulnerable to discovery. You are, in fact, the only one in this
story who has a reason to wish Hobson ill, Miss Hyde-Clare...
or should I call you Mr. Wright?"

As soon as he said the name of her alter ego, Bea realized
that her ability to think clearly had been impaired from the
moment she had seen Mr. Hobson's bloodied corpse on the
bed. If the actor had been hired to play Mr. Rose, then her
guise as an administrator for the British Museum had been
for naught. He had known all along who she was, and of
course he had reported that information back to the man
who'd hired him.

Obviously, that should have occurred to her sooner, but as
she contemplated it now, she wondered if it was problematic
that Tavistock knew about Mr. Wright. It was unconven-
tional, certainly, for a woman to don men's clothing, but
Caroline Lamb had made a practice of dressing as a page boy
and society had tittered only slightly—possibly because her
ladyship had quickly progressed to more scandalous behavior.
Even so, Bea's reputation was hardly pristine, for prevailing
on a lord to confess to a double murder in the middle of a
London ball was quite outré. The new on-dit, should Tavistock decide to circulate it, would cause at worst a minor stir.

Ah, but that wasn't the rumor Tavistock was threatening
to circulate now. Rather, he was intimating that Beatrice was
responsible for Hobson's murder.

Thoughtfully, she acknowledged it was not an altogether
illogical tack for him to take, as sending her to the gallows
would be an especially reliable way of ending her betrothal to
Kesgrave.

Nevertheless, Bea suffered no tinge of concern at Tavistock's ludicrous implication—nor, it appeared, did the duke,
if his response was to be judged by his silence—because she

had examined enough crime scenes to know the importance of evidence. Pointing one's finger at a patently innocent woman without substantiating proof would rebound dreadfully on the accuser.

Slightly disconcerted by the underwhelming response to his revelation, Tavistock said, "Yes, that's right. You did not know it, but Hobson saw easily through your disguise, which he described as quite a feeble attempt. Your eyebrows are too dainty, he said. In possession of your secret, Hobson threatened to tell the duke everything if you did not pay him several hundred pounds. Not having the money and worried that the blackmailer would never be satisfied even if you did, you stabbed him repeatedly in the stomach until he was dead. You are a blackguard and a deceiver, Miss Hyde-Clare, and now Kesgrave knows the truth."

So saying, Tavistock looked at the duke in expectation of wide-eyed shock and found nothing, not even mild interest. His lordship scowled at him with petulant displeasure and insisted that Mrs. Ralston would not find the story at all implausible. "After all, you did attack Taunton with a torch on the Larkwell terrace, so your history of violence is well established. Oh, indeed, yes," he said, warming to his subject. "Mrs. Ralston is convinced something quite nefarious happened at the Larkwells', especially since Taunton abruptly quit London immediately following the incident. It would require very little exertion on one's part to make her wonder at the fate of an actor and even less to embroil you in the drama. Just a few words in her ear posed as a question: What *was* Miss Hyde-Clare doing at Josiah's stable? Did she truly *not* know the actor who was killed? It's all *very* curious, isn't it?"

Although Bea readily dismissed this ploy as a half-hearted attempt to unsettle her—more of a requisite effort than a sincere one—Kesgrave shot to his feet, grabbed Tavistock by the cravat and lifted him a full inch off the floor.

Speaking very slowly, as if trying to convince a small, recalcitrant child to go to bed, the duke said, "As we just had this talk only a few minutes ago, I find it extremely disheartening that I am required to repeat myself, Tavistock. You will do nothing to undermine Miss Hyde-Clare's reputation, do you understand me? Nothing. If her name is attached in any way to Mr. Hobson's untimely death, I will make it my purpose in life to see you ruined—your estates bankrupt, your family impoverished and you reduced to begging on the streets of the Devil's Acre to earn enough farthings to buy your beloved daughter a crumb of stale bread."

Tavistock's face turned purple as his feet kicked in the air, and as if flicking away a fly, Kesgrave tossed him carelessly back into the chair.

His lordship gasped for an easy breath as he said, "But... but Mrs. Norton! I cannot be responsible for what she says."

"On the contrary," Kesgrave said smoothly, "you can indeed. As you had the misjudgment to embroil her in this affair, it is your obligation to ensure her silence. Now do tell Miss Hyde-Clare the details of your arrangement with Josiah, for I can no longer stand the stench of this room."

Bristling at the insult, Tavistock tightened his jaw and immediately flinched at the pain. "This afternoon, Josiah and his staff visited Tattersalls to look at horseflesh on my behalf. There are several options I am considering for Victoria and required consultation. He was well compensated for the exertion, and although he did not know the details of what would transpire in his absence, he would never be so presumptuous as to wonder. Indeed, upon finding Hobson, he efficiently arranged the matter with the rake and sent me a note informing me of the development and providing an enumerated list of the further expenses incurred on my behalf. Naturally, I will reimburse him the cost of new sheets and blankets, for he should not have to stand the cost of Mr. Hobson's misadventure any more than I should have to suffer the inconvenience."

Bea longed to be shocked by Mr. Josiah's monstrous indifference to human life, but she could not find it surprising that a man of Tavistock's ilk associated with similarly immoral people. "And that was the first you had heard of Mr. Hobson's demise? Mrs. Norton did not alert you to the trouble?"

"Of course she did not," he said stiffly. "She is far too well bred to broach the subject with me, for she rightly understood that it was none of my concern. Her note merely said that our plan had not prospered and she suggested I explore another avenue that does not involve her, as her role in the affair had been exposed. I was quite cross at her inability to pull off the thing, which I had so meticulously planned, but then I learned of Hobson's fatal attack and realized fate had failed me, not Mrs. Norton."

His tone turned mournful, and he sighed pitifully, almost as if he were trying to invite commiseration. Bea, always delighted to make an absurd situation more ridiculous, murmured soothingly and assured him that she was confident his next attempt to compromise an innocent young lady would go much better. "You will no doubt destroy her utterly."

"Bea!" Kesgrave said, not at all amused. "I trust it goes without saying, Tavistock, that you will not ruin any innocent young ladies."

Before his lordship could agree, the door opened and his steward entered the room. Rodwell, who was above sixty, walked with a slight stoop but was otherwise robust, with a high forehead and rounded cheeks that turned bright purple when he spotted Bea. Then, tilting his head slightly, his gray eyes encountered the duke and his face lost all color. In an instant he was white and, thoroughly shocked, he darted an angry, almost hateful look at his lordship for subjecting him to an interview with his victims.

Blithely unaware of his employee's disapproval, Tavistock ordered his steward to recount his dealings with Hobson. "And do be as concise as possible. I am already late for my club."

Mr. Rodwell tried to comply, but rather than limit his response to as few as words as possible, he spoke at length with unsettling swiftness, beginning with his first interaction by note. "It was a brief note, very brief, and simply said that I had an assignment that Miss Yates thought he would be well suited for and would he be interested in meeting with me to discuss it. He responded at once and said he was always happy to entertain proposals and could I come by the theater before that evening's performance. I reported that auspicious response to my lord and went to the Particular. The timing of our conversation was not ideal, as it was an hour before the show began and people were buzzing about in preparation. Hobson, who was used to the commotion and appeared not to notice it, directed me to his dressing room, where he said we may talk freely. During our discussion we were, in fact, interrupted several times by various actors and staff members, which I found disconcerting, but Hobson was focused and attentive throughout it. When I finished explaining the plan, he called it ingenious and said he relished challenging roles. I took both his enthusiasm and his professional conduct as further auspicious indications that my lord's scheme would succeed."

Here, he faltered because *success* in this case meant Miss Hyde-Clare's ruination and it was foolhardy to praise that course of action as desirable in the presence of the duke himself. He swallowed loudly, as if gulping a cupful of air, before continuing.

"Hobson began to plan his character, a necessity, he said, to any great performance. Mr. Rose would be a simple man with austere tastes who had lost his wife to consumption six years ago and was raising four children on his own. He thought a barren room would be appropriate for Mr. Rose's office, but I explained that we were using your mis...um, that is, Miss Yates's rooms on Savoy Street and they were far from barren. He sighed with what I thought was inappropriate disappointment and said he would adjust his character accordingly. I showed him the letter that his lordship composed regarding the missing diamond, and although it was a very fine missive, he said it lacked dramatic tension, so he rewrote it himself. I was greatly offended on my lord's behalf, for he is an excellent correspondent, at once ingratiating and informative, but Hobson would not listen to my protests. He rewrote the letter and threw the original in the bin. I tried to object further, but he wanted to discuss money —how much was this little gem worth? I was confused at first, assuming he meant the diamond, which did not exist, as he very well knew, for he had just rewritten the letter himself, but he meant the part. I stated the amount my lord was willing to pay. He said it was inadequate to the role and bid me good day and he took the discarded letter out of the rubbish bin and explained it was suited to the shabby production we were mounting."

Mr. Rodwell's tone rung with insult and he apologized profusely to his lordship as if he himself had made the charge. Tavistock nodded his head irritably and urged him to finish his narrative swiftly.

"Nothing my lord does is inferior, and I tripled the offer at once," Mr. Rodwell explained.

Despite his impatience, Tavistock could not let this travesty pass without comment. "You *volunteered* the excessive amount? Hobson did not bend you to his will through an intimidating mix of coercion and threats of physical violence?"

Even as he flinched at the displeasure, Mr. Rodwell remained firm in his conviction that he had behaved correctly. "As your employee, it is my responsibility to hold you in higher esteem than you hold yourself, my lord, and defend you against all detractors. You *were* mounting a superior production. Hobson agreed to the new price and said that playing a mild-mannered solicitor who was really a practiced seducer was a comprehensive and complex challenge. Indeed, he described the role as a substantial meal—an indication, I thought, that he would provide a convincing performance. I turned our attention to the payment schedule and held firmly to the arrangement his lordship had outlined, despite Hobson's attempts to change it to his advantage. Therefore, we agreed that he would get a quarter of the sum immediately, another quarter after the meeting at the solicitor's office and the last half after the encounter at the stable yard. Then I gave him the settled-upon amount, plus additional shillings for his wardrobe allowance because all superior productions require proper costuming, and left."

Tavistock's brows darkened at the discovery that his steward had allowed himself to be gulled out of even more money, but he held his censure and merely dismissed him from the room. Bea, however, forestalled his exit by asking the day of his visit and next inquiring about the interruptions. Could he recall how many times people entered the room and who they were?

His lordship sighed churlishly and looked at Kesgrave in amazement, as if completely incapable of understanding why any man would desire a wife who asked so many questions. Was not the point of marriage to beget legitimate heirs while attaining silent connubial accord?

Mr. Rodwell, who had to lean forward to hear Bea's questions, as he was a little hard of hearing, vacillated on the number of interruptions. Three, he said firmly, before immediately correcting it to four. But, no, that wasn't right because he relayed the plan in a single, uninterrupted speech, so perhaps there were only two? Two felt like too few. Three had to be the right number. Unless it was four.

"Truly, it's too difficult to say," Mr. Rodwell concluded.

Although Bea appreciated his sincere attempt to give an accurate accounting, she thoroughly enjoyed how his indecisive rambling caused Tavistock to vibrate with impatience. Long after her curiosity had been satisfied, she posed question after question simply to discomfit him further.

"And how did Hobson's draft of the letter differ from the original?" she asked.

"It was vastly inferior," Mr. Rodwell said unhelpfully, "for as an actor he could not match the clarity of my lord, who is a skilled correspondent as well as accomplished orator."

Bea resisted the urge to roll her eyes. "I don't doubt that Lord Tavistock has argued convincingly for the abuse of orphans in the House of Lords, but I meant in the particulars. How did the two letters differ? Make a point-by-point comparison."

Tavistock growled at the request, and Kesgrave shot him a warning look as the steward confessed he was unable to recall specific differences. "In general, Hobson's letter was more vague and mysterious and perhaps a little confusing, whereas my lord's missive was the epitome of concision. As I said, he knows how to communicate with simplicity and lucidity."

Nodding, Bea looked at the clock and noted it was fast approaching six. As much as she wanted to remain for another full hour to inconvenience his lordship, she knew she had to return to Portman Square before her family began to wonder where she was. Nevertheless, she lingered several minutes to lecture Mr. Rodwell on the immorality of

LYNN MESSINA

arranging the ruination of an innocent female, insisting that his mother, God rest her soul, would not only be appalled by his behavior but saddened as well. "I'm confident she raised you to treat ladies with respect."

Kesgrave, interpreting the change in topic as an indication she had gathered all the information she could, asked if she was finished with her questioning. "You have completed your interrogation of Tavistock and ascertained all that you require?"

Bea agreed that she had.

"Very good," Kesgrave said before he raised his fist again and plowed it into the other man's face, definitively knocking him unconscious and possibly breaking his nose. As Mr. Rodwell screeched in horror, the duke offered Bea his arm and escorted her to the carriage.

Chapter Nine

Bea *tended to think* of her cousin Flora as a pretty ninnyhammer, but the girl was actually quite astute and her suspicions of the former Miss Brougham were well founded.

"She is not your usual style," Flora said the next morning as the two women sat in the front parlor engaged in separate occupations.

In between her cousin's interruptions, Bea was trying to read the biography of Kepler she had got from the lending library so that she could hold an intelligent conversation with her uncle. Flora, who deeply resented being excluded from yesterday's shopping expedition to Madame Bélanger's by her mother, was flipping though the most recent issue of *La Belle Assemblée*. She was determined to gain her mother's approval for a new gown and wanted to be prepared with the latest style.

Ordinarily, Bea would never bet against her aunt's frugality, but lately Flora had figured out an approach that seemed to be truly infallible: drawing attention to a minor imperfection in her dress—a pulled thread or a tiny stain—and wondering aloud what the Dowager Duchess of Kesgrave would think. Then she would dismiss her own concern. "I'm being silly, of course. She will never notice. Her eye for detail is not that highly developed."

Flora had enacted this very scene at least twice a day since the fracas in the breakfast room following Lord Stirling's ball.

Having observed the performance on multiple occasions, Bea was genuinely impressed by her ingenuity.

Now she tilted her head at her cousin, considered her remark regarding Mrs. Norton and said, "I don't have a style, usual or otherwise."

"Well, yes, darling, that is true," Flora conceded. "But if you did have a style, it would not be Mrs. Norton. She is snide and sycophantic."

Bea, who would have added selfish to the list of character traits, said, "All right."

"And she is no admirer of yours," added Flora, who was too young to know anything about her cousin's sordid history with the society matron. Her proclamations were based on more recent transgressions. "On the night of your engagement, at the Larkwell ball, I overheard her telling Lady Marsham that you were too drab to be a duchess. Then she called you the duchess of drab and laughed wildly as if it were the cleverest sally."

It required very little imagination for Bea to picture the exchange, and she agreed with her cousin's assessment of Mrs. Norton's wit. "I am sure she was just disappointed because she hoped he would make a match of it with Lady Victoria."

Flora scoffed at this explanation, for it would necessitate the woman to care about someone who was not herself. "And given how very beautiful Lady Victoria is, I find it quite hard to believe that Mrs. Norton was worried about her welfare."

"Perhaps she was worried about the duke's welfare," Bea

pointed out. "Many seem to feel I have done him a rotten turn by consenting to be his wife."

Affronted on her cousin's behalf, Flora tossed the magazine to the side—a dramatic but sincere indication of her affection—slid across the settee and wrapped her arms around Bea. "I have seen the way he looks at you when he thinks nobody is watching and can assure you that you have done him a lovely turn. The rotten thing would have been to refuse him."

"Thank you," Bea said, submitting to her cousin's embrace while wondering how to gently extricate herself so that she may return to her book. She was scheduled to meet with her uncle in an hour and was only little more than halfway through the volume, which focused a lot of attention on Kepler's early years in Weil der Stadt. She had just got to his defense of the Copernican system, placing the sun at the center of the universe.

Flora, however, was not ready to relinquish her hold and said, "Despite this general disgust for you, Mrs. Norton came here four days ago to have a private conversation, and then yesterday, she appeared suddenly at the modiste and you went off with her for hours and hours."

Bea, who knew how carefully orchestrated her archnemesis's every step had been, found this description of her arrival as if by fiat humorous. Nevertheless, when she spoke it was merely to correct her version of events so that they aligned with the fiction she and the duke had established. "Not hours and hours. 'Twas merely for one hour. Then I spent the rest of the afternoon with Kesgrave's delightful cousin Josephine."

But Flora continued as if Bea had not spoken. "Now, I am not so naïve as to the way of the world that I don't understand why a snide and sycophantic toady like Mrs. Norton would suddenly try to endear herself to you. Even a drab duchess is still a duchess. And yet I cannot help but feel she has another motive for her friendship, a secret one. Could there be a wager about you in the betting book at Brooks's?"

Of all the possible explanations her cousin could have come up with to explain Mrs. Norton's strange interest in her, the betting book at Brooks's was by far the most outlandish and Bea laughed in delight at her imagination. "Naturally, for only the lure of possible great wealth could induce the woman to befriend me," she said with a light giggle.

The teasing comment horrified Flora, who pulled back with a stricken look on her face and insisted she had not meant to imply anything so cruel. "Merely that you should be wary of her friendship. I am not convinced she has your best interest at heart."

As Bea knew how very ill Mrs. Norton wished her, she felt guilty for shaming her cousin and, laying her book to the side, grasped the other woman's hands in her own. "You are kind to be concerned, and while I think a wager about me in the betting book is highly unlikely, I will tread cautiously around Mrs. Norton. Does that put your mind at ease?"

Flora said that it did. "And please do not take my criticism of her to be a criticism of all toadies, for I think the prospect of the leaders of the *ton* currying your favor just because you are to be a duchess is above all things delightful. Now let us discuss something happier such as your trousseau. Mama returned from Madame Bélanger's so agitated by the experience she could not decide if she needed to lie down or take several turns around the square. In the end, she oversaw the reorganization of the linen closet, and now bathing towels are on the bottom shelf and blankets are on the top."

With a languishing glance at the Kepler biography, Bea launched into an account of the shopping excursion, detailing the seemingly endless list of items deemed necessary for duchesshood by Lady Abercrombie. Flora's eyes flew open with wonder as she described ordering four cashmere shawls, and Bea decided there could be no harm if she happened to "forget" one on her cousin's bed. Having survived for six and twenty years with only one shawl, she felt confident she could scrape by with three.

As slight and insubstantial as Bea considered the topic, her cousin was wholly enthralled and easily filled the hour with dozens of queries about color, fabric and design. She was lauding Bea's decision to add embroidery to the hem of one of her new walking gowns—although, to be clear, Bea had no recollection of making any decisions—when Uncle Horace entered the room with his edition of the Kepler biography under his arm. Rather than interrupt and remind Bea of their scheduled appointment, he sat down in a chair adjacent to the settee and made every appearance of listening intently.

Bea found his interest puzzling and could only assume he was hoping to get a better sense of how much money he had been obliged to spend on her behalf, for her aunt's accounting could not have been very coherent if she had been driven by agitation to rearrange the linens. Given his financial invest- ment, she expected him to show either scorn or displeasure for the ornamental details his daughter gushed over, for they had steadily increased the price of each piece. Instead, he nodded sagely, as if appreciating the wisdom.

Indeed, he did.

"It is far too easy to dismiss fashion as inconsequential," Uncle Horace said, "but I have found that I always enter a room with more conviction if I know my cravat is tied in an impeccable Waterfall."

Flora praised this observation for its insight and under- standing before noting that she had long admired his Water- fall. "And your Barrel, which is always quite pristine."

Although he was usually impatient with his children, whom he considered to be frivolous in their interests, he thanked her and smiled.

It was, Bea thought, a rare moment of father and daughter comity.

But it was not only a moment, for her uncle remained for a full hour in gracious discussion, and Bea marveled again at how sincere he was in his efforts to make amends for twenty years of apathy. That he would expend any energy at all in trying to convince her that he had strongly held opinions about hem lengths was remarkable.

Unable to linger indefinitely, Uncle Horace rose, thanked the ladies for an invigorating discussion and gestured to the book on the settee cushion. "We will resume our conversation of Kepler next time."

"Yes," Bea said with a firm nod, resolving to finish the biography swiftly despite the distraction of Hobson's murder.

And yet she would not have an opportunity to make significant progress in the book now because she and Kesgrave were scheduled to resume their investigation in a half hour. Although her family had not been given the correct description of the outing, believing that she was to visit with another Matlock cousin, they knew she had to leave soon and Flora urged her to dash upstairs to change out of her morning dress.

Complying with her cousin's directive, Bea returned to her room and considered the challenge of selecting an outfit. As she would leave the building not only through the front door but in the company of the duke, she could not don a disguise for their excursion. Their plan was to search Hobson's room before proceeding to the theater to interview his associates. As the Duke of Kesgrave and his betrothed could not be seen interrogating members of the Particular without causing a mild scandal, they had decided to pose as the owners of a small playhouse in Bath who were looking to make an investment in a London theater. Such a part, she thought, would require an unexceptional gown.

Fortunately, her entire wardrobe was comprised of unexceptional gowns.

When she descended again, Kesgrave was waiting for her in the parlor and answering questions about his cousin Amelia, upon whom they were purportedly calling.

"She is the daughter of my grandfather's brother," he explained.

"Josephine's sister, then?" Aunt Vera asked.

"No, Josephine is the daughter of my grandfather's sister," he said.

Her aunt nodded solemnly. "But Amelia *does* have a sister?"

"A brother," Kesgrave amended patiently. "Two, actually. As does Josephine and another brother as well."

"And how many siblings did your paternal grandfather have?" Aunt Vera asked.

The matter was of such consuming interest to her relative that she did not notice anything amiss with the duke's attire. Had she been a little more observant she would have perceived the oddly out-of-date cut of his coat, with its straight cutaway and broad lapels. In place of donning modestly made clothes, of which, Bea assumed, he was not in possession, he had worn an older style.

He looked, she thought, convincingly like a successful man who had not recently invested funds to ensure the upkeep of his wardrobe.

It was the perfect note to strike.

Hoping to spare the duke the obligation of reviewing his entire family tree, Bea entered the room and insisted they depart right way. "It would be rude to keep your cousin Amelia waiting."

Kesgrave rose at once and affirmed that his cousin was not one to wait patiently for tardy visitors. "She gets churlish and leaves the house so that her staff can honestly announce that she is not at home."

Aunt Vera sighed and said how very gracious it was of his family to put aside their disappointment and be so welcoming to her niece. "I am grateful for it, as I am sure Bea is as well."

Smiling, Bea informed her aunt that she was grateful to anyone who did not secretly conspire to compromise her reputation in a bid to end her betrothal.

This strange and cryptic remark silenced her aunt, which allowed Flora the opportunity to assure Bea that she must not fret over the minor tear on the left side of her dress just below the waist. "I am certain it is too small for even the dowager duchess's eagle eye to notice."

Her mother visibly started at the mention of the famous high stickler, and Flora made an inadequate effort to hide her grin.

Once they were in the carriage and en route to the theater, Bea chastised the duke for forgoing the opportunity to awe Aunt Vera with the impressiveness of his ancestors. "If anyone is determined to be overwhelmed by the administrator of an obscure governmental office charged with ensuring the quality of sealing wax, it is my aunt."

"The clerk of the hanaper collected fees and other moneys for the sealing of charters, writs, and patents," he corrected.

"Yes," she said, nodding with approval, "like that."

Kesgrave smiled and said he'd assumed she was eager to search Hobson's things. "But next time I will make a precise catalogue of all six lords privy seal just to tweak you."

"And do be sure to describe your cousin Josephine's extensive collection of needlework boxes," she said, noting that she had been subjected to its wonders by his grandmother and it was riveting storytelling.

Laughing, the duke lamented the lost opportunity to bear

witness to that exchange, for he could only imagine Bea's suffering had been quite acute.

A few minutes later they arrived at a modest brick building with a wrought-iron gate on a small street in Covent Garden, where Hobson rented a room in a boarding house. It was too soon for Mrs. Rudge to have advertised for a new lodger, but the widow with four small children was far too busy managing her brood and providing for her tenants to ask questions. She merely ascertained if the applicants would be able to afford ten shillings a week—plus supplemental charges for blacking (four shillings), coals (twelve and sixpence), meat (half a crown per pound) and eggs (three pence each)—and led them to the room. As she opened the door, she explained that the previous lodger's things would be removed by the end of the week and if they saw anything that they would like to hold on to, they should propose an amount. Then she was gone, returned to the tumult of her kitchen before Bea could share the story she had invented to explain their circumstance.

It was just as well, she thought, as the duke was far too imperious to make a believable apprentice in any profession, let alone the law, and his clothes were too nicely tailored to justify the economy of renting a single room for the two of them.

Bea felt this doubly so when she entered the accommodation, for the space was almost too cramped for just one person, dominated as it was by a bed that pressed against a curtain. Behind the worn damask was not a window but an alcove stuffed with clothes arranged by various means: some items hung from a bar, others rested on a shelf, still more were draped over a stool that had been squeezed into the corner. It was chaotic and messy, and after a thoughtful glance, Bea suggested Kesgrave examine the contents, as he would be better suited to noting if anything was amiss, as he, like the victim, was a man.

As she had inspected several male wardrobes in the course of her previous investigations, this was obviously a pretext to avoid an unpleasant task and she was surprised when the duke contented himself with darting her a disgruntled look. Calmly, as if squeezing between the headboard and the wall did not impugn his dignity in any way, he turned sideways and slid through the narrow space. Bea turned her attention to the table, which had a half-filled mug of coffee on it, as well as an empty plate with pastry crumbs, a dirt-stained handkerchief and a half dozen pages of what appeared to be a play. She read the top sheet, which marked the start of act one, scene five, and detailed the exchange between a marquess and his guardian, who expressed his staunch disapproval of his ward's profligate spending on clothes by calling him a fop. The young lord offered a series of one-word protests that rhymed merrily— *stop, chop, drop, flop, plop*—and Bea giggled when she got to the last one, which was only an inarticulate grunt of frustration: *gwop*.

Finding no indication of the author, she wondered if the play could have been written by Hobson and searched the room until she found a notebook, which provided a sample of his handwriting. As she'd suspected, the styles matched.

Their victim was not only an actor but a writer as well—a development that was hardly surprising given his eagerness and determination to revise Tavistock's letter, which he felt lacked dramatic tension.

Bea returned the script to the table and studied the notebook, which she had opened indiscriminately. Now she read its contents, observing that it seemed to be a list of chores and reminders: Mend breeches, get more coal from Mrs. Rudge, meet Latham for dinner. The next page was a similar catalogue, although slightly more interesting because it recorded a debt of two guineas owed by Fairbrother.

So Hobson was a gambler.

That was, she thought, an avenue worthy of exploration, for a gamester who got himself deeply in debt risked bodily harm if unable to settle.

She flipped through the book, looking for evidence of money owed by him, but could not find anything substantial. The only person he seemed to wager against was this Fairbrother fellow, and in the six instances she found, he had emerged the victor. In total, he had won six pounds from the other man, which was not an insignificant sum. Whether that was an undue burden on Fairbrother depended on his circumstance, and she resolved to identify his person and assess his situation as quickly as possible.

Next Bea inspected the jars and canisters on a shelf near the fire, and finding only nibs and a few farthings, looked through a small stack of books on the narrow windowsill. One was on the elements of drama, which seemed appropriate given his playwriting proclivity, and the other two were novels from Minerva Press.

Discouraged, she sighed and asked Kesgrave if he had discovered anything of note.

"Other than an unsettling lack of respect for orderliness and linen?" he asked as he slipped out of the closet space. "No, I did not. You seem to have fared better if your laughter is anything to go by. Don't think I didn't notice your amusement while I was being squashed between the headboard and a greatcoat."

"I did have some luck, yes," she admitted, "but not with the source of the humor, which was a snippet of a play that Hobson was writing. He appears to have been something of a gambler."

"Ah," Kesgrave said, comprehending at once the possibilities such a development provided. "Then let us proceed to the Particular to see if we can discover who holds his vowels. I would suggest a brief conversation with Mrs. Rudge, but she doesn't strike me as the observant type. She didn't flinch when we asked to rent a room that has been vacant for less than four and twenty hours."

Bea agreed with this assessment, and although she knew the lack of curiosity and awareness was almost certainly due to the four small children hanging off her skirts and the seven impatient lodgers awaiting tea and laundered sheets, she wondered if the distracted air was a pretense to hide her immorality.

"Perhaps she and Hobson were entwined romantically and, fearful that he was being unfaithful to her, she followed him to the stables. The scene she discovered there affirmed her worst suspicions and she ran him through with the tongs in a fit of jealousy," she said as the carriage rambled to the corner of Leighton Road and Bow Street. "She would not be the first woman to lose control in such a way."

'Twas an outrageous suggestion, to be sure, but Kesgrave did not dismiss it out of hand. Rather, he considered it on its merits and posited the various ways a woman of her situation could slip the obligations of motherhood and hospitality long enough to visit a stable several miles away in the middle of the day. He proposed a helpful family member who watched the children and an efficient maid who washed the pots and plates from breakfast before stoking the fire for the evening meal. Perhaps the oldest child, a blond-haired girl of about six, was precocious and looked after her younger siblings. Or maybe one of the lodgers was happy to help out in times of need.

Thoughtfully, he considered the matter, and Bea, reminded again of the seriousness and esteem with which he regarded her, fell a little deeper in love.

Chapter Ten

As *Beatrice's estimation* of the Particular was based solely on Lord Tavistock's description of the theater as an inferior playhouse populated by unsavory characters, she was surprised to behold a pristine building with a stucco facade, overflowing window boxes and four fluted Doric columns that supported a portico engraved with the theater's name. It had been established over a decade ago by Michael Drake, a dye manufacturer, and his daughter Mary, who oversaw its daily management and penned many of its entertainments. Known for the quality of its farces and burlettas, the Particular, accommodating an audience about half the size of Covent Garden, was thought to earn its owners a tidy profit.

Jenkins watched Bea and the duke exit the carriage with a frown of concern because he recalled the last time he had delivered them to a building near the Strand: Miss Hyde-Clare had been brutally attacked on the street, her face suffering several blows that immediately darkened and swelled to bruises.

"You are lovely to worry," Bea said placatingly, "but there

LYNN MESSINA

is no need for concern. We are just here to ask a few questions."

"Ye were just asking a few questions last time," he mumbled under his breath as he complied with Kesgrave's order to move the carriage, which looked too fine to belong to a gentleman from the country.

The doors to the theater were unlocked, and entering, they stepped into a vestibule with a grand staircase to its left and a pair of doors to the right. They slipped through the doors into the box-lobby, which was decorated with pilasters painted a deep burgundy red and a statue of Shakespeare. They passed through the space to a narrow hallway that led to the office occupied by the manager and owner.

Kesgrave knocked on the door, and it was answered a few moments later by a woman two decades older than Bea wearing a dark gray dress and sporting a splotch of ink on her forehead.

She spoke quickly and precisely in a soft tone that belied the haste of her words. "Good afternoon. Vendor meetings are Thursday mornings and do not require an appointment. Interviews for staff positions are held on Tuesday morning and do require an appointment. Ticket sales are via the office on Adams Street to the left. Noise complaints are to be submitted on the first Monday of every month. We are pleased with our company and as such are currently not auditioning new actors. Thank you for your interest in the Particular. Good day."

Bea, taking her cue from the older woman, who was about to shut the door firmly in their faces, said with the same apparent haste, "You see, Mr. Harper, it is exactly as I said: a well-run theater with no time for dillydallying. Miss Drake is so busy carrying out her obligations, she had no time to entertain our offer. That is exactly the attitude one wants in a manager, and I fear now we are making a dreadful mistake.

We should not be here to ask her to let us invest in her theater but begging her to come run ours, for she is clearly a superior being. It is a delight to see such a competent woman. As you know, Mr. Harper, I am surrounded by incompetent men. Not you, of course, but our manager and stage director. It is a pity, certainly, that she has no time for us. But do let's leave our card and hope she calls on us before we depart London."

Although Bea's head was turned toward Kesgrave, her eyes were tilted to the side so she could observe Miss Drake's reaction to this rambling speech. As she'd hoped, she noted a glimmer of interest.

Smiling at the other woman, Bea added, "That is all right, isn't it? That we give you our card? Nowhere in your recitation did you include instructions for aspiring investors so we are not sure how to proceed."

Miss Drake narrowed her brown eyes warily, clever enough, Bea thought, to suspect a trick. "Investors?"

"Investors, yes," Bea said, smothering the first kick of guilt she felt at the deception, "from Bath, where my husband, Mr. Harper, and I run a theater about half the size of the Particular called the Adelphi. We are in London to find a theater to invest in, as we think it is time to expand our interests. After an exhaustive search, we have settled on your venture as the ideal enterprise to place our money. We understand, of course, if you are not interested in taking on investors, as it is a complicated matter, and we are fully prepared to graciously accept your refusal. To that end, we have identified a second opportunity. The Athenaeum is not as profitable as the Particular, but it is the size we are looking for and it has potential."

Scoffing with disdain, Miss Drake said, "The Athenaeum is a crumbling pit with an undisciplined troupe of players and a poorly trained staff. It is a wonder it hasn't burned down."

Bea's grin widened at this information, for she knew contempt could spur reckless behavior. "Ah, yes, that is correct. It is pandemonium at the Athenaeum almost daily, which is why Mr. Harper insists that we consider it. Our investment would have a greater impact in such a chaotic situation. Here, certainly, you could do wonderful things with the money, but ultimately, it would just make you more successful. But at the Athenaeum, the money could mean the difference between turning a tidy profit and burning the building down. Mr. Harper relishes a challenge. I, on the other hand, relish interacting with competent women."

Miss Drake nodded thoughtfully and professed herself willing to listen to an offer—but only listen, for her father, who was the actual owner of the theater, would make the ultimate decision. Delighted, Bea glanced meaningfully at the duke and stepped inside the office, which was larger and more comfortable than she had expected. A bookshelf pressed against one wall, with a writing table covered with papers, quills and ink stains adjacent. Bound ledgers were piled on an oval side table that was next to an embroidered chair, which was also stained with ink.

"Please sit down," Miss Drake said, brushing a wisp of hair to the side and leaving another daub of ink, this time near her ear.

Bea took the chair by the bookshelf, leaving the two at the work table for Kesgrave and the owner, and she examined the exhaustive collection of plays while the duke discussed the particulars of the investment. All the greats were represented—Shakespeare, Sheridan, Johnson, Heywood, Marlowe, Congreve, Farquhar, Aeschylus, Sophocles, Euripides, Aristophanes—as well as many lesser playwrights whose works she was not familiar with. She pulled a slim volume from the shelf called *Christus Redivivus* and noted it was in the original Latin. She read the dedication, then glanced briefly at several pages. It was a resurrection play.

Across from her, the duke reviewed the general terms of Mr. and Mrs. Harper's offer. As the proposal's sole purpose was to gain them access to the company, there was no need to be strident or miserly with the conditions. In fact, there was every reason to make the offer as generous as possible. But Kesgrave, the steward of a large estate, could not to be profligate even as a pretense, and his offer to invest in the Particular, though fair, ultimately tipped in his favor.

Proving to be a keen businesswoman, Miss Drake noted the advantages to the Harpers and warned Kesgrave that neither she nor her father would agree to several of the provisions. "Fifteen percent ownership of the theater, for one thing, is too much. At best, I can see my father consenting to half that."

Kesgrave allowed that some aspects of the agreement could be negotiated, including the percentage of ownership, but he could not go as low as seven and a half. "I would accept twelve."

"My father would counter with nine."

Bea returned the Nicholas Grimald play to the shelf and selected another bound copy: *La Serva Padrona,* an Italian burletta by Giovanni Battista Pergolesi, with a libretto by Gennaro Federico. She flipped to the opening scene, but she knew very little Italian and her familiarity with Latin helped her only minorly. She put that book back and turned her attention to the pages on the work table in front of her. Reluctant to appear unduly curious, she examined the sheets without touching them, noting that they seemed to be pages from a comedy about a maid who was mistaken for her mistress. The maid, striving to mimic her employer's melliferous voice, says yes to a marriage proposal from—

The exchange continued on the next page, and forgetting

her goal to appear respectful, she shifted papers around looking for the rest of the scene.

Angelique...Angelique, she thought, checking each sheet for the name of the maid. No, that page started with a speech by a character named Samuel......that one was a bill for candles...that one was a play that featured a jester trying to juggle with one hand...that one was a sketch of the front and back ends of a donkey costume worn by two actors...that one was a play about a marquess who spends too much money on waistcoats...that one was a reminder to mend—

Her hand pausing in midair, Beatrice dropped the note about the torn curtain and picked up the sheet with the marquess vehemently defending the necessity of diamond-studded buttons. Naturally, she recalled the manuscript she had read at Hobson's lodgings only an hour before. It also contained a spendthrift marquess with a taste for expensive clothes.

Patently, it could not be a coincidence.

Miss Drake, noticing her interest, observed that *The Fretful Peacock* was one of their most successful plays. "It ran for sixty-eight performances."

Making note of the title, Bea asked if it contained a delightful rhyming exchange based on the word *fop*.

The owner grinned widely as she said with genuine pleasure, "You have seen it?"

"Yes, of course," Bea said.

This affirmative reply pleased Miss Drake even more, and she lowered her voice as if revealing a secret. "At the risk of descending into vulgar braggadocio, I am compelled to admit that I believe it is one of my finest works."

Taken aback, Bea said, "*You* wrote it?"

Now Miss Drake was surprised, for if the Harpers had truly investigated the theater, then they would know she was the authoress of many of its production.

"Well, yes, I knew you wrote *many* productions," Bea said quickly, "but I didn't realize you wrote *so* many. I wonder how you find the time, as you are already so busy managing the theater. Frankly, I am in awe."

Miss Drake accepted the praise with a cursory nod and insisted that writing successful plays was an aspect of managing the theater. "Perhaps the most important aspect. The Particular would not still be operating twelve years later, let alone doing so well that investors from Bath would show an interest, if our material was mediocre."

Lauding the practical-minded approach, Bea asked if any of the cast members were of an equally literary bent. "I believe actors acquire a finely honed sense of the dramatic from performing in so many plays."

Laughing lightly, Miss Drake said that none of the actors in the company fancied themselves playwrights, which, she confessed, was a great relief. "It would cause much discord among the ranks if one player wrote a particularly sparkling part for himself. As it is, I am almost constantly deluged with requests to increase the size and scope of a role. Sometimes I get requests to make the villain more villainous or the hero more heroic, which is particularly galling because then the character becomes a lampoon of himself."

As Bea had seen pages from *The Fretful Peacock* in Hobson's room written in the actor's own hand, this assertion did not strike her as wholly true. It was possible, yes, that he had decided to copy the script in the pursuit of some worthy goal—in an effort to learn the mechanics of composing a play, for example—but given the quality of the paper, she could not reconcile the expense of such a habit with its benefit, which would be minor at best. If one were truly interested in learning the craft, reading the plays of accomplished playwrights would be a more practical solution.

Nevertheless, taking credit for the achievements of

people in your employ was not an entirely unknown practice, especially among artists. Rubens and Van Dyke, even Rembrandt, had assistants in their workshops who frequently executed their vision while they turned their attention to the next project.

Perhaps the owner had a similar arrangement with Hobson: She came up with the general plot and characters of a story and he wrote the actual lines. If that were the case, her claims of authorship would be accurate if not complete. The fact that she did not mention the actor's contribution, however, implied the agreement was not quite aboveboard.

No, Miss Drake was hiding the truth, which made Bea inclined to think she was more of a plagiarist than a collaborator.

Even so, that did not make her a murderess.

Thoughtfully, Bea agreed that players who had strong opinions about their characters could be challenging to work with and quickly invented a story to illustrate this point. "We are a small company and as such tiny disagreements inevitably cause huge problems. Our biggest challenge as owners is ensuring amiability among the cast. Sometimes among actors there can be issues with egos, but I am sure I don't have to tell *you* that."

Miss Drake demurred, insisting that her company, though also small, rubbed together well. "We have a nice balance of personalities, which is vital for fostering an esprit de corps."

Realizing that the owner would not readily admit to tensions among her troupe, Bea congratulated her again on her excellent management skills. "I am agog at your success. I fear at the Adelphi we have much drama and tears. I tell them to save the Cheltenham tragedies for the stage and yet they do insist on enacting them in the greenroom. You must tell me your secret for avoiding calamity. The Particular strikes me as a happy place."

At this statement, Miss Drake started visibly and looked down at her hands, which were clasped tightly on the table. "Oh, dear, I fear I have given you the wrong impression, for no life is free from calamity, especially ours today. You see, we found out only a few hours ago that one of our dear actors had suffered a tragic accident. He...Robert...Mr. Hobson...he was visiting a stable yard and tripped and...and impaled himself on a rake. He was, I am told, running away from a horse, a wild one that had broken lose, and wasn't looking where he was going. He lost his footing and fell...onto the rake. There was—" She broke off, unable to continue without taking a deep breath. "I am told there was a lot of blood. It's truly awful."

It required no great theatrical skill for Bea to gasp in horror, for she was genuinely shocked that Mr. Josiah's dashed-off explanation for Hobson's death had actually held together. She had thought for sure that a constable would examine the placement of the wounds in his stomach and note that the holes and spikes did not align.

Evidently, she held the parish constable in higher esteem than he deserved.

Bea expressed her sympathy and lamented the fleeting-ness of life. Kesgrave also offered his condolences, and Miss Drake, struggling to appear composed—or, Bea thought, appearing to struggle to appear composed—bit her bottom lip as if to hold back tears. It was impossible to judge the sincerity of her reaction, for the other woman was at once a former actor with the training to affect emotion and a theater manager who had recently lost a member of her company. Either explanation would justify her agitation, for having run Hobson through with the fireplace tongs in a fit of unre-strained fury, she could now regret the excessive violence of her response.

"You must excuse me," Miss Drake said, dabbing her eye

with a handkerchief, "for this unbridled display. We only learned about his death a few hours ago. The stable yard sent over a groom with the message. It is difficult to adjust. I find myself worrying about who will assume his roles in the performances this evening and then getting angry at the triviality of the concern when a man has lost his life."

Bea nodded sympathetically. "Yes, I am sure it's quite challenging to balance your personal feelings with the requirements of the theater. Was he at the stable yard at your behest? To fetch a prop for one of your plays?"

"Good gracious, no," Miss Drake said with noticeable relief. "I would feel quite cut up with guilt if he had been there on an errand for me. Actually, I have no idea why he was at the stable. Robert did not keep a horse and showed no interest in owning one. Perhaps he was visiting someone there."

A note of confusion entered her tone, and Bea assumed it was genuine, for it was entirely possible to follow someone to a destination without knowing why he was there. "Is that usual—for one of the actors to leave the theater in the middle of the day? Were there not rehearsals that required his attendance?"

Although Bea was only attempting to get a sense of Hobson's movements on the last day of his life, Miss Drake detected a hint of censure in the question and rushed to assure the potential investor that her players were quite diligent in their work. "Our schedule varies from day to day, depending on where we are in the process of preparing a production, but nobody wanders off during rehearsals. Yesterday, for example, we did our first full-costume rehearsal for *Jacopo the Courageous,* which premieres next week. Then we took a break to allow the company to rest, and the various crews—scenery, wardrobe, property, mechanical, etcetera— met among themselves to discuss the design requirements for a show that debuts at the end of April. After the break, the company did a reading of the play I am currently working on. Robert did not appear at that reading, which made me cross, and when he missed that evening's performance, I was prepared to dispense of his services. It is very distressing to realize all that time he had been dead."

Bea murmured consolingly, for it would indeed be upsetting to know you had been thinking ill thoughts about a deceased man. Nevertheless, she was there to gather information, and the only way to do that was to discover where Miss Drake had been during the interval between rehearsals. If her presence at the theater could be firmly established, then she could not possibly be the murderer.

"What were you doing during the break?" Bea asked.

Startled by the question, Miss Drake looked at her with her brows tightly drawn. "Excuse me?"

"When someone I know passes, I find it helpful to imagine them thinking of me in a familiar place. Familiarity is comfort, is it not?" Bea said soothingly. "Where you were at the time he suffered his accident."

Although she looked doubtful such a tactic would provide any solace, Miss Drake admitted she had been in her office working on the script for *Jacopo the Courageous.* "The director had requested revisions, so from one to three I was here, addressing his concerns. It is actually where I am most frequently, so if Hobson thought of me at all, it would inevitably be in this very chair with my head bent over this desk," she explained, a deprecating smile appearing suddenly on her face as she acknowledged that the thought actually *did* make her feel a little better.

It was impossible to say who was more surprised by this development: Bea or Miss Drake. The former, however, nodded wisely, as if her method for dealing with grief had never failed to work, and wondered if anyone at the theater could attest to the veracity of the latter's claim. The easiest way to find out would be to ask the woman forthrightly, but there was simply no way to word the question without appearing strange or in possession of an ulterior motive.

Bea decided it did not matter at present, for they had learned several useful things from the interview, including the interval for which they had to account for all the suspects. Miss Drake had said that the various technical staffs had been in meetings to settle details for an upcoming performance, which meant they could not have murdered Mr. Hobson.

If someone from the theater was the killer, then it was either Miss Drake or her actors.

Although she was eager to conduct further interrogations, Bea forced herself to sit calmly in Miss Drake's office and ask if the director was satisfied with the changes.

The theater owner sighed. "I believe so, but it is hard to know for certain, as we did not rehearse the play this morning. The message from the stable arrived before we could begin, and I allowed the company to retire to their dressing rooms to compose themselves. It seemed cruel to allow them no time to adjust. That said, they will of course perform tonight, as tickets are already sold and moping about won't bring Robert back. And with that in mind, I think we should take that tour now," she said matter-of-factly as she rose to her feet, "and you can meet the players. As I'm sure you know from your own experience, a theater is only as good as its actors and the Particular's actors are wonderful."

Kesgrave agreed with this comment as they left the office and made several shrewd observations about the importance of finding reliable retainers, insights gleamed, Bea could only assume, from a decade of stewardship.

Having read the memoirs of La Clairon, the celebrated French actress who had originated many famous roles during her long career, Bea had some idea of what to expect from a tour of the unseen parts of a theater, the compartments and contraptions that made a production seem effortless and sometimes even a little magical. Nevertheless, she was taken aback by the sheer amount of rooms that were required to tell a believable story. Dressing rooms alone numbered almost in the double digits; there were five full-sized ones, plus four small cubicles for rapid costume changes. Additionally, there were four work rooms, three scene rooms, one greenroom, and nine recess areas to the left and right of the stage for actors to wait between scenes. And then, of course, there were the store rooms—so many store rooms, Bea thought, as Miss Drake led them down a winding staircase to the cellars, where even more space was devoted to the stowage of costumes, scenery, and property.

When they reached the bottom of the staircase, Miss Drake lit several wall sconces and a narrow hallway with a gravel floor was revealed. She took a dozen steps into the corridor, opened a door and walked inside, indicating with a gesture that Bea and the duke should follow.

"The cellar is a warren of little rooms, of which this one is fairly representative," she said, raising the candle so that they could see their surroundings more clearly. The chamber was indeed small, with rough stone walls about ten feet across in each direction. It contained shelves, a wardrobe and several rough-hewn trunks stacked on top of each other. "I will not waste your time with a meticulous catalogue of each room, but I wanted to show you an example of how prudent we are with our resources. The vast majority of articles we use for any given production are things we have already used and have tailored to fit the new circumstance. Here, we are in one of the store rooms used for costumes. There are four rooms in total devoted to costumes in the cellar. Three others are filled with props, and two larger rooms hold our scenery."

Bea looked around, at the shelves haphazardly arrayed

with masks—dozens of masks, from the Venetian *medico della peste,* with its birdlike beak, to a demon head with distorted features. In the flickering light of the candle, arranged in no discernable order, the assortment took on a vaguely night-marish cast, and she felt as though she were standing in a grotesquerie. Vaguely terrified by the display, she shuddered.

Miss Drake, noting the direction of Bea's gaze but not her discomfort, nodded with approval as she walked over to the shelf to shed more light on the demon head. "Ah, yes, this is a perfect example of Mrs. Tapsell's ingenuity. You see a demon head now, but this costume was originally a donkey's head for *A Midsummer Night's Dream.* Our wardrobe designer turned it into a lion's head for *The Flower or the Forgery,* and then, when our Dr. Faust needed to look like a demon in last year's production of *The Devil Awakens,* Mrs. Tapsell altered it again. And it will remain here until we have a new need for it."

In the full glow of the candle, the demon looked even more threatening, for what little resemblance it bore to an ordinary human head was eliminated. Now she could see its sickly green complexion and oddly hollow burnt-orange eyes, and she tilted her gaze away, toward the comical Pulcinella mask, its crooked nose and brash colors softened by a thick layer of dust.

Kesgrave lauded Mrs. Tapsell's frugality and asked about the cellar's ventilation, noting that dampness and frost could easily undermine the integrity of the stored items. It was, Bea thought, a deeply prosaic comment and one she found highly reassuring in both its mundane consideration of the ghastly room as just another place to store items, varying little from a wine cellar or an icehouse, and its affirmation of his character, for who else but the pedantic love of her life could stand in an unsettling cabinet of horrors and think of drainage.

Miss Drake, preening more from the question than the

compliment, congratulated the duke on his astute observation before launching into a detailed description of how the moisture in the cellar was regulated. Inevitably, this explanation led to follow-up questions on Kesgrave's part, and the subject kept the pair well occupied for five minutes while Bea struggled to contain her unease.

It was mortifying and ridiculous, she knew, to be so dismayed by the masks all around her, for they were naught but a collection of materials: papier-mâché, silk, feathers, plaster. Reduced to their elements, they were as uninteresting as a bedsheet and yet she could not quite calm her nerves. It was the dark hollows that stared emptily where eyes should be, she decided, and when Miss Drake announced with regret that she could not linger because the hour grew late, Bea was the first one through the door.

"I have so many tasks to perform before we open," Miss Drake said as they wound their way back up the staircase, "and, as you can imagine, I am behind my usual schedule because of our great tragedy. As we are dedicating tonight's performance to Robert, I must also find a moment to sit down and write a proper tribute. I will introduce you to Mr. Smeeton, my stage manager, and he will make the presentations to the company."

Mr. Smeeton was in the property storeroom inspecting the items to be used onstage for that evening's afterpiece, a pantomime involving Mephistopheles and a cracked chamber pot. He was most displeased with the condition of the katana used in the second act. Although it was made of wood, it looked dauntingly fierce to Beatrice, but the stage manager insisted it was too shabby to convincingly appear as though it could pierce porcelain. Miss Drake concurred with his assessment and suggested they substitute a fencing foil, a practical recommendation that Mr. Smeeton agreed to with great reluctance, as the change in weapon would undercut the verisimilitude of the scene.

Miss Drake conceded the validity of his point while immediately noting that Mephistopheles's requirement of a chamber pot already strained credulity. "What is one more improbable event?"

Although the stage manager did not appreciate her cavalier attitude, he was denied the opportunity to argue further by the introduction of the Harpers. At the prospect of potential investors, his thin face lightened and he offered an enthusiastic welcome—no doubt, Bea thought with amusement, imagining all the fake katanas he would be able to keep on hand with an influx of capital.

"Aye, I'd be happy to make introductions," he said agreeably, his voice slightly roughened and bearing the mark of an upbringing in East London. "We go curtain up in a few hours so no time for tea and scones. But plenty enough time to meet everyone briefly."

Miss Drake thanked him for his help and assured him she would make sure the property mistress fetched a fencing foil from the storeroom in the cellar.

"A *proper* fencing foil," he said with pointed emphasis, and Bea wondered what an improper fencing foil was and how many times the property mistress had fetched one out of inattention or ignorance.

"Of course," Miss Drake said calmly.

Satisfied, Mr. Smeeton led Bea and Kesgrave from the room. "At this hour, the actors are usually finishing up the morning rehearsal, but as I'm sure Miss Drake told you, nothing today is usual. It was such terrible news to get, about Hobson's death, and I felt awful, just awful, because the moment before I had been urging Miss Drake to let him go because he had missed last evening's performances without any notice at all. He just simply failed to show up, which is unacceptable. And I was already in a state because we had lost *another* actor yesterday to an accident. Mr. Fairbrother's leg was crushed when the scenery fell on it—a rampart. He was barely able to limp out of here. So then I was short two men for the performance. I had to move Mr. Chatterley into Mr. Fairbrother's role and Mr. Gofton had to take Mr. Chatterley's role and Mr. Steagle had to fill in for Mr. Gofton, which left six minor characters without an actor to play them. I cut two of them from the story and dragooned Clark—one of my scene painters—to play the others. The crux of the problem was the afterpiece, which has a donkey in several scenes. A donkey needs two actors, one behind the other."

Mr. Smeeton rambled on, detailing the challenges of rapidly tailoring a donkey costume made for two actors into a costume for one actor with an inordinately long torso, and Bea marveled at the coincidence of two actors suffering grave injuries in a single day. It seemed to her highly unlikely that the incidents were unrelated, and she wondered if this Fairbrother—whose name she recalled from Hobson's notebook as being in debt to him for six pounds—had been hurt in the altercation that had killed Hobson.

"I would like to hear more about this accident," Bea said when the stage manager paused for breath. "How did the scenery fall on the actor? Was it known to be unstable? Were there witnesses to the collapse?"

The stage manager grimaced, as if realizing belatedly how slapdash such an incident would sound to a potential investor. He'd been too consumed by the organizational challenge it had presented to notice. "Absolutely not, no. The rampart was firmly secured and solidly built. It definitely did not fall due to careless construction."

"Then what did cause it?" Kesgrave asked.

Mr. Smeeton opened his mouth to answer, then immediately shut it and shook his head. "I don't know, but it wasn't the builders' fault. The men who build our sets are superior craftsmen. Truly, I can't explain how it happened since I wasn't there. Nobody was there save Mr. Fairbrother and Mr. Chatterley, who were rehearsing on the stage when disaster struck. I confess, I had no idea they were even on the stage, having assumed they had retired to their dressing rooms along with the other actors. And of course the leaders of the different departments were not present because they were conducting meetings in their workshops. We all came running at once. As soon as we heard Mr. Fairbrother's desperate cries, we all dashed over to discover what had happened. Except Miss Drake. She was too engrossed in her writing to hear him."

The information contained in this brief speech was more than Bea could have imagined learning from a single source, and she wondered how to ask follow-up questions without alerting Mr. Smeeton to her true purpose.

"Goodness gracious," she said, drawing her brows in concern, "what a calamity. I suppose it unsettled the rest of the day's schedule, especially if it happened at the beginning of the break interval."

"It happened at the end," Mr. Smeeton explain, "around a quarter to three. Luckily, the departmental meetings were already drawing to a close."

Two forty-five, Bea thought, recalling that she and Mrs. Norton found Hobson at two fifteen. As Milford Lane was a twenty-minute walk away, the fact of person's presence on the stage a half hour later did not exclude him or her from suspicion.

"Can you confirm that actors were in their dressing rooms?" Bea asked. "As you freely admit you had no idea Chatterley and Fairbrother were on the stage rehearsing, how do you know where any of your actors were?"

Blanching at the implied disapproval, the stage manager

nevertheless managed to keep a tight smile on his face and explain that his actors were all responsible, upstanding and reliable people who did not require his constant attention. Then he added that he could attest to the fact that Mr. Latham had indeed been in his room, for he had checked on him at two o'clock to see if he was ready for his tea. "That is to say, I *peered* into his darkened room and noted he was still asleep. I do that every day—not at two, of course. Rather, an hour into his nap. He takes one every day, for he finds the exertion of perfecting a character to be quite exhausting. So I checked on him and noted he was still asleep under the blanket. But as for the others, no, I cannot account for their whereabouts. My obligations are manifold, and I believe my time is better spent attending meetings and addressing concerns than closely watching the movements of the troupe. You are free to disagree," he said, his tone at once defiant and pleading. His eyes were tilted down, as if afraid to confront the disapproval of the potential investor.

As Smeeton had eliminated yet another suspect, Bea was far from disapproving and congratulated him on how well he balanced the obligations of his job.

Flustered by the compliment, he beamed and began to list all the responsibilities he oversaw as stage manager. Bea listened with half an ear as she reviewed the list of people about whom she needed to gather information: Miss Drake, to be certain, had a motive for wishing Hobson ill if the charge of plagiarism proved to be true, and Smeeton was unable to account for her movements during the time in question. Likewise Fairbrother and Chatterley, for the timing of the rampart accident was too suspicious to accept without questioning. That the debacle had no witnesses raised eyebrows, and she wondered if it had been staged in an attempt to hide the true source of the actor's injury. Milford Lane was close enough that Fairbrother could have gone to the stable, confronted Hobson, returned to the theater, and destroyed the backdrop to provide a reasonable explanation for his grievously wounded leg with plenty of time to spare.

Had Fairbrother acted alone or was Chatterley his conspirator?

Given his debt of six pounds, Fairbrother had a reason to want Hobson dead, for his obligation was now at an end. Based on the information in her possession, Bea could devise no motive for Chatterley. It seemed more likely, therefore, that Fairbrother had acted alone. Then, finding himself gravely harmed in the disastrous encounter, he'd obtained his friend's assistance upon his return to the theater.

How had he convinced his friend to wreck the scenery to disguise his guilt? Perhaps by promising him money?

Bea shook her head, for the man was already in debt and would have a hard time convincing Chatterley that he could reasonably take on more.

Maybe he had promised the other actor his part in the play?

Or could Chatterley have simply offered his help out of generous concern for his friend?

Regardless of the method by which Fairbrother may have secured help, it was only one aspect of an outlandish theory. Bea realized that and yet she could not dismiss it entirely, for it had the advantage of explaining the oddity of the ruined rampart. Mr. Smeeton swore that the solidly built set could not have fallen on its own, and she believed him. If the destruction did not occur naturally, then it had to been spurred by human action.

While Bea appraised the situation with Chatterley as an accomplice to the murder itself, Kesgrave asked if Fairbrother would require a long recuperation.

A frown returned to Mr. Smeeton's face as he confessed he had no idea how long Mr. Fairbrother would be unable to perform. "But he is of hearty stock, very hearty. I'm sure he'll be back soon." As confident as his words were, however, his tone was uncertain, and he shook his head, as if to dislodge a very unpleasant thought. Then, recalling his assignment to introduce the Harpers to the company, he apologized for keeping them standing in the middle of the hallway. "I'm not sure what I was thinking, other than I am a little addled by recent events. Come, let us go at once."

Chapter Eleven

L eading them through a stairwell that climbed to the upper boxes, Mr. Smeeton brought them to a narrow corridor and stopped when they reached the first dressing room. He knocked softly on the door, calling the actor's name gently.

"Typically, Mr. Latham takes his restorative in the late morning or early afternoon depending on our rehearsal schedule. Given the upsetting news about Mr. Hobson, I have no idea if he will be awake or asleep right now. Everything is a muddle," he said, clearly distressed by the uncertainty the unexpected death had caused. Then, as if realizing the potential investors might not be as familiar with the company as he supposed, he rushed to explain that Mr. Latham was one of two principal male players at the Particular. "Mr. Fairbrother is the other, and we have four supporting male actors. Well, three now, with Mr. Hobson's misfortune. Mr. Latham is quite vital to our success. If a rampart crushed his leg, we would have no show, for he is quite our best performer. He can make any part, even the most poorly conceived one, believable."

A commanding baritone bid them to enter, and the stage

manager, complying at once, opened the door. Bea walked into the room and noticed at a glance that it looked quite similar to her aunt's sitting room, with its worn settee and dressing table buried under various articles and papers. It was larger, certainly, and contained a welcoming trio of comfortable chairs arranged around a table with a neat stack of newspapers and journals. Brightly colored costumes hanging from hooks along the far wall attested to a wide-ranging repertoire and included everything from an elaborate royal robe in the deepest purple to a simple shepherd's outfit with a woven woolen tunic. By all indications, Mr. Latham, who appeared to be midway through his thirties, had recently played a king, a barrister, a coalminer, a jester, a lion and a milkmaid.

Below the jumble of garments were three bins overflowing with even more costumes as well as items of various sizes—stage pistols, gloves, paws, spectacles, hats—that rounded out a character's wardrobe.

In the center of the room, his mien determinedly noble as he awaited his visitors, a cup of tea raised halfway to his mouth, Mr. Latham sat calmly, and observing him, Bea had little doubt that he could successfully imbue any part with credibility. With his raven black hair swept dashingly across his forehead and his large brooding eyes, as dark as obsidian, he had the sort of gothic good looks that weakened one's ability to think clearly—a valuable trait for an actor.

Bea, who had spent years unable to formulate replies to even the most benign queries about the weather or her own health, considered herself immune to the stunning effects of beauty. The pervasiveness of her awkward stammers indicated that the defect was internal, not external, a fact that had deeply frustrated her aunt, who could not understand how anyone could be intimidated by an insipid ape leader like Miss Shaw. Surely, Bea was not so missish that she couldn't exchange a few coherent pleasantries with a plain-faced woman of eight and thirty who was an unbearable burden on her brother?

But as Bea stared into the dark pools of Mr. Latham's eyes, lavishly fringed with thick lashes, she discovered she was somewhat susceptible to a handsome appearance, for her first thought was he could never have murdered Hobson. A man with a gaze as melting as his did not require violence to get what he wanted. All he had to do was arrange his features into a sympathetic pout and say please.

Please spare me the effort of exerting myself unduly and kindly impale yourself on these brass fireplace tongs. There's a good fellow.

The duke stepped forward to greet Mr. Latham, and Bea realized that Mr. Smeeton had introduced the pair of them while she had been woolgathering. It was a most disconcerting revelation, for she considered herself well adept at conducting conversation whilst simultaneously ordering her thoughts. Looking away from the sculpted perfection of the actor's nose, she was further flustered to observe the amusement on Kesgrave's face.

Damn his eyes—he had observed the whole thing!

Resolutely fending off a blush, Bea extended her hand in what she considered to be a business-like manner. Unaware of her intention, Mr. Latham raised her hand to his lips and pressed a kiss on her gloved palm.

"Despite the utter devastation of this day—I trust Smeeton has explained that my dear confidante Robert has suffered a terrible fate—it is a pleasure to meet such a lovely investor," he said smoothly, lingering over her hand several seconds longer than what was generally considered polite. "Indeed, it seems as though you have appeared solely to lift my spirits and for that I must thank a kind and generous god."

"Mr. Latham and Mr. Hobson were great friends," Mr.

Smeeton explained as Beatrice sat down in the chair to which the actor gestured. "His death will hit him the hardest."

"Indeed, yes," he agreed, "and here I was, trying to imagine how I would get through this evening's performance without him to bolster my mood and then you and Mr. Harper appeared. My disposition feels lightened already. Do tell me, madame, what alerted you to our modest little show-house? My portrayal of Apollo in the *Dagerwood Inheritance,* perhaps? Writing in the *Farmers Chronicle,* Gabriel Yates described my rendering of a sympathetic surgeon as 'revelatory,' and John Mellon called it a 'wonder' in the *London Midmorning Ledger.* Or was it my depiction of King Anaconda in the *Tale of the Amazonian Prince*, which has been described both as a 'comic masterpiece' by William Wieland in the *St. James Sun* and a 'dramatic tour de force' by Oscar Hickman in the *Brighton Packet.* To have one performance described in seemingly contradictory terms is what we in the theater call range, and few have the ability to accomplish it. I am humbled to have my skill recognized."

As Bea had never seen Daniel Latham perform, she could make no judgment regarding his range, but she knew it could not be as extensive as he hoped, as he clearly lacked the capacity to affect humility.

This limitation had no bearing on the stage manager's appreciation for the other man's talent, and he seconded his perception of himself by insisting there was nothing Mr. Latham could not do. "He has originated all the great roles at the Particular. We are very lucky to have him."

Mr. Latham ardently affirmed the veracity of this statement with an insistent nod. "And now you, madame, may be just as fortunate if you decide to go forward with your plan to invest in our delightful theater. I trust this meeting makes you more committed than ever to doing so, but you mustn't make any hasty decisions. Wait until you see me tonight, when I breathe remarkable life into Matthew Carson in *The Rapacious Valet*. *The Cheapside Advertiser* described my depiction of rapaciousness as 'startling' and 'astounding,' and the *London Every-So-Often* marveled at my ability to expand the definition of *rapacious* to include generosity."

As Kesgrave's handsome form had grown only more and more appealing the better acquainted Bea had become with his intelligence and humor, she'd naturally assumed the opposite to be true as well—that one's dullness would deaden one's beauty. And yet Latham's dark eyes continued to sparkle from seemingly bottomless depths, forcing her to conclude that vanity must have its own ineffable glow.

Bea smothered a smile and, resisting the urge to look at the duke for fear of giggling uncontrollably, congratulated the actor on his wonderful notices.

Naturally, Latham took her admiration as an invitation to entertain her with additional reviews, of which he seemed to have an inexhaustible supply. Bea listened politely until he paused to take a sip of his rapidly cooling tea and then quickly offered her sympathy on the passing of his cherished friend.

"It is such a horrific accident," she said. "Do you have any idea why he was at the stable?"

Latham sighed heavily, turned his head away, toward the other side of the room, with its frayed settee and polished mirror, and then looked at her with firm resolution. "Given the circumstance, I can draw only the obvious conclusion for such a sordid setting and say he was there for a tryst."

"A tryst?" she repeated, as if surprised but of course she wasn't, for she was to have been Hobson's trysting partner.

"It pains me to say it because Robert was such a dear companion whom I held in the highest esteem, but the truth cannot be denied just because it is unpleasant to me. No, I must be brave and face it," Latham explained with a hefty sigh. "The fact that he would arrange this secret assignation while publicly courting Miss Andrews proves he was not quite the honorable man I believed him to be. My despair at his death is doubled by my inability to call him to account on his dastardly behavior toward a valued member of our troupe."

As jealousy was a long-enduring motive for murder, Bea sat up straighter and leaned forward in her chair. "Miss Andrews?"

Appreciating her interest, Latham smiled with pleasure and said with relish, "Helen Andrews. A delightful young woman. Quite the charming ingenue. She's been with the company for—" He broke off and looked at the stage manager. "How long has it been now? One year? Two?"

Visibly discomfited by the turn in the conversation, Mr. Smeeton coughed lightly and mumbled that he could not recall.

"No matter," Latham said dismissively. "She has been with us for at least a year, and Hobson, who was immediately smitten by her flaxen-haired beauty, courted her assiduously. I had *thought* he was on the verge of proposing, but if he was making stable yard appointments, then my understanding of the situation was clearly incomplete. What about you, Smeeton? Were you expecting an announcement at any moment as well?"

The stage manager coughed again, more forcefully this time, and insisted Miss Drake would not appreciate his gossiping with potential investors. "She asked me to show the Harpers around, not entertain them with idle speculation. Now let us proceed to the next dressing room. We have interrupted Mr. Latham's rest long enough."

Having found an attentive listener, Latham was no more willing to let her go than Bea was to leave and apologized for the stage manager's impatience. "He cannot help himself. As the keeper of the schedule, he is merely doing his job when he insists on moving us along. But try as he might, he cannot control everything. You are welcome to stay as long as you like, speculating about Hobson's intentions toward Miss Andrews and telling me about your wonderful little theater in Bath. The Adelphi, was it?"

Smeeton smiled tightly as he agreed with the actor's assessment of the situation. "Of course, they must stay as long as they like. My concern was only for you, Mr. Latham, for the rigors of portraying Matthew Carson in *The Rapacious Valet* are great and you have yet to take your afternoon nap. I was merely concerned about your performance tonight. But if you are not worried, then I am not worried."

It was comical, the competing impulses this statement engendered in Latham's breast, and Bea watched in amusement as he struggled to overcome his own vanity. In the end, he succumbed and agreed that he must allow them to leave so that he may rest. "I hope you will forgive me for cutting this lovely interlude short, but my art requires sacrifice."

"Yes, of course," Bea said, smothering the giggle that rose in her throat.

"As much as it pains me to admit it, Smeeton is always right," Latham said, escorting them to the dressing room door. "I don't know what I would do if he ever left me—quit the theater forever, I suppose, and remove to a cottage in the Cotswolds to raise roses with my mother."

Mindful of his obligation to Miss Drake, Smeeton quickly disavowed this comment, insisting that he had no intention of going anywhere, and furthermore, Mr. Latham had no plans to grow flowers. "His mother lives in Clare Market," he said, naming one of the roughest neighborhoods in London. Few things bloomed in Clare Market, least of all flowers.

Although Bea could not like the forceful way the stage manager had guided them into the corridor, she understood his concern, for if she had been genuine in her intention to evaluate the company for an investment, she would have been alarmed several times over by now. The accident with the scenery was concerning on its own because it implied inferior craftsmanship as well as a lack of supervision, but add to that a licentious behavior among cast members and a lead player threatening to quit performing altogether and it was a worrying level of chaos.

No wonder Mr. Smeeton was anxious to hurry them along.

Bea wanted to seek out Miss Andrews immediately but followed unprotestingly as he lead them to the dressing room next door. To her delight, she was introduced to Mr. Chatterley, another promising suspect.

In stark contrast to Mr. Latham's situation, the supporting player shared the space with two other men of his stature, and although the room had more occupants it contained fewer things. There were no bins for storing assorted items, a handful of hooks, and only two chairs, one of which was immediately vacated for Mrs. Harper's comfort.

Chatterley stood out among his fellow actors because of his height, which well exceeded six feet, and his brightly colored orange hair. The two men with whom he shared the dressing room, however, were not exactly short either—Caleb Gofton and Westmacott Steagle were as tall as the duke—and the room felt cramped.

Steagle, who had jumped to his feet at once to offer his chair, professed himself eager to hear about the Adelphi, for he too was from Somerset. "I grew up in Pensford, but it has been an age since I've visited. Tell me, do the Sydney Gardens still serve Sally Lunn Buns at midday? I remember them being quite divine."

Having never been to Bath, much less to its pleasure gardens, Beatrice had no idea what pastries were served at what time, but she felt it reasonably safe to answer the query in the affirmative. 'Twas not as though anyone in the room would contradict her.

Even so, she paused briefly after speaking as if in anticipation of a hearty objection, but all she heard was Steagle's yearnful sigh.

Gofton, who was at least two decades his junior, scoffed at such wistfulness and insisted the treat could not be better than the teacakes sold at the Lamb's Head in Dean Street.

"I bet you a shilling each that neither compares with my own mother's scones," asserted Chatterley, whose closely cropped hair was nevertheless disheveled.

Mr. Smeeton tutted with disapproval over the wager and insisted the Harpers had not visited the Particular to listen to the company quarrel over the best place to purchase pastries.

"My mother doesn't charge me," Chatterley said with a mischievous smile that revealed a dimple in his left cheek.

Bea commended Chatterley on the restoration of his spirits after so many recent setbacks, as resilience was vital to an actor's success.

Wincing, he pitched his head at a sad angle and confessed that it was difficult to appear cheerful with Hobson's unfortunate passing. "He was a good fellow, well liked by everyone. It is hard to believe he is gone, served a bad turn by a dastardly rake."

Steagle scoffed at this description, claiming it was a revised version of the actual facts, which plainly stated that Hobson had been well liked by Latham, to whom he toadied with assiduous determination, and mostly tolerated by the rest of them. "And Latham only indulged his endless fawning because he hoped he would write better roles for him."

"More substantial roles," Gofton added, "what he often describes as a satisfying meal."

Steagle nodded. "A vital necessity, for it gives Latham something to chew other than the scenery."

The three actors broke out into delighted guffaws at this sally while Mr. Smeeton turned deep red and insisted they could not linger. "It is almost four o'clock, and we must hurry if we are to meet the entire company before the curtain rises at six. Do let us continue, Mr. and Mrs. Harper."

Bea respected the stage manager's desire to move them along, and if she were in his position, she would have made the same attempt in hopes of distracting them from Steagle's remark. Alas, it was already too late, for she had gleaned enough information to comprehend the meaning and refused to leave before her curiosity had been satisfied.

"Write better roles for him?" Bea asked, wrinkling her brow in confusion. "Was Hobson a playwright as well? Miss Drake did not mention it."

Mr. Smeeton's face turned an impossibly bright shade of purple as Steagle cheerfully explained that Hobson was the actual author of the plays their esteemed owner claimed to pen. "We all know it to be true."

"No, no," Mr. Smeeton insisted in a hushed tone, as if lowering his voice in fear of being overheard. "You all *suspect* it to be true." He turned to Bea and added almost pleadingly, "It is only a rumor, Mrs. Harper, and you know what it is like to work in a theater. Rumors everywhere! It is a product, I believe, of working so closely together. There are no secrets, so we are compelled to invent them."

"That is true," Chatterley conceded. "We do know everything about each other. Smeeton, for example, suffers from a terrible rash every time he eats strawberries."

The stage manager, who had been nodding gratefully at the agreement, suddenly opened his eyes wide as he realized the acting troupe knew about his difficulty with the fruit. "So that is why everything I've eaten in the past week has caused me to break out into red spots!"

Chatterley made no response other than to giggle wildly.

Steagle tsk-tsked with disapproval and apologized for his associate, who was given to high-spirited pranks.

"More like mean-spirited," Smeeton muttered.

"Ah, but did not our Chatterley heroically rescue poor Fairbrother yesterday?" Gofton asked with only a hint of mockery. "Pulled him from the wreckage with no thought of his own safety."

Chatterley ceased his laughter to accept the praise with a surfeit of dignity and assured everyone present that he would do no less for them should they find themselves in the regrettable situation of being prone under a rampart.

Smeeton harrumphed at this display of pomposity, Steagle rolled his eyes, and Bea asked how that might be arranged.

Disconcerted, Chatterley looked at her. "Excuse me?"

"Prone under a rampart," she explained. "How does one find oneself in that position? The scenery was well secured, was it not, for it had stood for several dozen performances. What caused it to topple like a child's toy castle?"

Although the way she had worded the question clearly horrified Smeeton, he could not suppress his interest in the answer, as he also sought a greater understanding of the incident.

Chatterley was momentarily at a loss—an indication, Bea thought, that the story about Fairbrother's injury might indeed be a fabrication—before enthusiastically settling on an explanation. "Exuberance!"

"Exuberance?" Bea asked.

"Oh, yes, exuberance," Chatterley said eagerly, "for Fairbrother quite threw himself into the role, playing Mysore with such exuberance he drove himself right into the rampart, knocking over one of the supports and bringing down the entire set. He sustained a terrible injury and the scenery was all but ruined, but I must say his performance was stupendous. Never have I felt Mysore's fear and desperation so fully."

"Bravo," Steagle murmured.

Chatterley colored slightly but did not otherwise address the remark, which struck Bea as curious as it was cynical. Apparently, Steagle distrusted the story as much as she did, which made her wonder what cause he had to doubt it. It certainly seemed unlikely that a rampart that had withstood abuse for several weeks would topple at a bump, and yet she could not believe he suspected his associates of conspiring to murder Hobson.

At the same time, Steagle, as a member of the theatrical company, would know all about the grudges that festered among the actors. As Smeeton had said only a few minutes before, there were no secrets among the company.

If there were tensions between Fairbrother, Chatterley, and Hobson, then Steagle would know about it. He'd mentioned Hobson's sycophancy toward Latham, which resulted in the latter getting better, more substantial parts in the plays the former wrote. Perhaps Fairbrother and Chatterley, desiring better roles for themselves, resented the preferential treatment and confronted Hobson. The argument, beginning calmly and reasonably, could have deteriorated into a violent altercation that ended in the tragic and unintentional death of Hobson.

But if the intention was only to have a rational discussion, then why choose to conduct it at the stable yard? Given that the three men shared a dressing room, the far more obvious place would have been on their own settee.

No, Bea thought, the fact that Hobson was followed to Milford Lane indicated an intention that was considerably more nefarious.

Inevitably, that thought led her back to Fairbrother's debt.

Regardless of how she examined the situation, the fact of the matter was the injured actor had a greater motive for wanting Hobson permanently removed from the company. Perhaps she was being too harsh with her assumption as to why Fairbrother would have followed him to the stable. Maybe his purpose in confronting him there had been innocent enough—desiring to keep his debt private, he sought to have the conversation away from the theater. Hobson, however, was unwilling to be fair, and an argument erupted, growing increasingly vicious until Hobson lay dead on the bed, fireplace tongs protruding from his stomach.

Horrified by what he had done, terrified of the consequences and half mad with the pain from his injury, Fairbrother dragged himself back to the theater and somehow recruited Chatterley to his cause.

Hoping to discover more information upon which to base her theories, she asked if Mysore was a so-called substantial meal of a role and who would assume it in Fairbrother's absence.

"Chatterley," Gofton said with a trace of bitterness. "We flipped a coin—cross or pile—and he won, which is fair enough. I still contend, however, that I would make a better villain. Chatterley's sense of humor is too keen. He almost laughed during the death scene last night."

"'Tis true," the actor conceded. "I was supposed to fall onto the table after I am struck in the face, but I rotated too much and landed in the wheelbarrow. My legs flew into the air and I could barely get myself out again."

"Our owner was not pleased that you made *her* character likable," Steagle observed dryly. "I could see the ferocity of her scowl from the side of the stage."

Beatrice stared at the three men, her eyes opened wide in

shock. "And you are absolutely sure she did not write the play? Is it not possible that Hobson was trying to take credit for her work?"

Gofton scoffed at the naiveté of the suggestion and assured her there was no misunderstanding. They knew conclusively the play had been written by Hobson because no woman could write anything so adroit and insightful as *The Rapacious Valet.* "Or any of the other works she claims to have composed. We don't want to upset her, so we pretend to believe it. There's no reason to upset her, for she is the owner of the theater and you know how women can be—vindictive and spiteful when their feelings are injured. It is better to simply allow her to think she has hoodwinked us. But if you are going to invest your capital in our little showhouse, then you must know the truth. Hobson is the author of our most popular melodramas, farces and burlettas. Without him, we are none better than the Athenaeum."

Mr. Smeeton found this statement to be so upsetting he could manage barely a squeak of protest, but he objected, Bea knew, only to the perception of his employer as immoral, not to the horrendous assessment of the female character.

Chatterley laid an encouraging hand on the stage manager's shoulder and urged him not to fret so much. "I'm sure our sensible owner has stashed away several years' worth of works in anticipation of this event. We need only dip into her ready supply for our next opus."

While the stage manager insisted there was no supply, ready or otherwise, the actors speculated about the kind of play Miss Drake would write.

"It would feature a prince, a missing chest of gold and an ill-treated maiden," said Gofton.

"No, no," countered Chatterley. "A wizard, a lost diadem and an ill-fated maiden."

"A wizard *and* a unicorn," said Steagle.

Chatterley clapped his hands in approval and insisted he would much rather play the bottom of a unicorn than the ass of an ass.

His cheeks turning a bright purple, Smeeton stammered a profuse and passionate apology to Mrs. Harper, who, he felt, had never been subjected to such vulgarity in her life. "They are usually better behaved them this, and I cannot say what has come over them other than they are deeply troubled by Mr. Hobson's passing and perhaps Mr. Fairbrother's accident. It does seem as though in the past four and twenty hours the theater has fallen under a dark cloud," he said, then immediately reconsidered his language, for he did not mean to imply that the theater was cursed. "We have merely had some bad luck, but that is over now, for you and Mr. Harper are here."

"Excellent toadying, my good man," Chatterley said.

Smeeton's face darkened fiercely, and although he opened his mouth as if to hotly protest the comment, he calmly suggested they carry on with their tour. He claimed the hour was growing late, which was no doubt accurate, but it was clear from his discomfort that he was eager to quit the room before one of the actors said something truly regrettable.

After they made their goodbyes, Smeeton led them from the room and past a third dressing room on the men's side of the stage, which caused Bea to pause and ask if it would be occupied during Fairbrother's absence.

"Chatterley assumed he would have access to it," he said, "but I quickly disabused him of that notion. Exposing him to a temporary luxury would do nothing to improve his character and would only create division within the ranks."

Bea applauded his practical approach and wondered to herself if Chatterley could in some way be responsible for Fairbrother's condition, for he seemed to have gained the most from his friend's incapacitation. Possibly, the two violent events happening in the same afternoon was simply a stroke of bad luck as Smeeton had decried.

There was no way of knowing without interrogating Fairbrother, which she would do at the earliest opportunity. If she could be persuaded that the wound had actually been caused by a falling rampart, then she would eliminate both him and Chatterley from her list.

As Smeeton led them down the hallway, Bea asked if everyone in the company knew Hobson wrote the plays for which Miss Drake took credit.

"Suspects," he immediately corrected. "We...that is, *they*... only suspect. As I said, it is merely a pernicious rumor. It cannot be true. It is Latham who started it, swearing that Hobson had told him while in his cups and pledging him to secrecy. But that story must be false because Hobson knew Latham far too well to believe for a moment that he would keep his secret. As soon as he has any tiny sliver of privileged information, Latham cannot contain himself until he has found someone to whom he can hint wildly. If Hobson genuinely had a secret to protect, Latham is the last person he would tell. *That* is how I know it is not true. I trust you will pay it no heed and not allow it to factor into your decision regarding the Particular."

Guiding them through the scene rooms, he gestured to a staircase that led to the galleries and rather forcefully pointed out the notable architectural features, such as the Corinthian columns and coved ceiling. Then he explained that the ladies' dressing rooms were on the other side of the stage, well away from where the men were housed. "I can only assume the arrangement is the same in your theater, as it is important for everyone that the proprieties be observed."

"Of course," Bea said, well aware of the difficulties many women suffered as members of the theatrical profession. Aunt Vera would no doubt stare in horror at the prospect of her niece mingling with actresses, whom she regarded as fast and unscrupulous, but Bea knew it was wrong to lump all female performers together. To be sure, La Clairon had been little better than a courtesan, succumbing to the advances of Charles Alexander, Margrave of Brandenburg-Ansbach, who provided her with a comfortable living midway through her career. But she had read enough admiring biographical articles of actresses in *The Ladies' Monthly Museum* and *La Belle Assemblée* to know that many of them plied their trade honorably. Mrs. Edwin, of the Lyceum, for example, possessed a reputation so unsullied that the Duchess of York had condescended to be her patron.

"And here we are," Smeeton said as they arrived at yet another dressing room door. "But before I knock, I must warn you—"

Whatever caution he was about to issue, however, was forever forestalled by the door, which suddenly swung open.

Chapter Twelve

The room's inhabitant was a lovely woman, tall and willowy, with dark brown hair, well-proportioned features and an eager smile that warmed her green eyes.

"Goodness gracious, Mr. Smeeton, it's about time you got here. I have been waiting an age to meet our new investors," she said as she stepped aside to welcome them into her dressing room. "Mr. Latham insisted that you had requested to meet only him, but I knew that could not be correct. As experienced members of the theater world, which you clearly are, you had to know that the female principal is as vital to a production's success as the male lead. In fact, some would argue more vital, as it can be challenging to find an actress whose talent is equal to her morals. Now do come in and sit down so that we may grow acquainted." She gestured to a cozy grouping of embroidered armchairs arranged next to a low table set with tea service for three, a clear indication that she had indeed been expecting them. "You may go, Mr. Smeeton, as the Harpers are safely in my hands now."

The look of distress on the stage manager's face as he

contemplated the tea tray was almost comical. "But Miss Drake asked me to escort them around the theater."

"And so you shall, my good man, so you shall," she said firmly, "for I have no intention of wandering the halls of the theater so close to the start of the performance. You may return here in thirty minutes."

"Thirty minutes?" he asked, gaping in amazement. It was almost four-thirty now.

Responsive to his surprise, Miss Calcott asked how long the Harpers spent in conversation with Mr. Latham.

"Perhaps a half hour," he answered absently, his attention anxiously focused on the mahogany table clock on her vanity. "Most likely shorter."

"I appreciate your caution and agree that we cannot take any chances," she said agreeably to Smeeton's obvious confusion. "You may collect your charges in forty-five minutes. Now do run along. The curtain rises in less than two hours and you have much to see to. I noticed a new tear in the curtain. Perhaps you can fetch a sewing needle."

As much as the stage manager wanted to protest the treatment, he seemed incapable of finding the words and shuffled toward the corridor with one final, beseeching glance. Impervious, Miss Calcott closed the door in his face and smiled brightly at her guests.

She moved, Bea thought, with the sort of liquid grace one frequently observed in a dancer. It was difficult to judge her age in the glow of the flickering candles, but Bea suspected the vivid light of the sun would reveal fine wrinkles around the eyes. Perhaps she was in the second half of her fourth decade.

"Now let us talk before he returns," Miss Calcott said as she sat down and poured the tea into cream-colored teacups with a delicate rose pattern. "There is no way he will give us the full forty-five minutes, and we have much to say to each other. I will begin by telling you I know exactly what you are up to with this story of being investors."

Resisting the almost overwhelming urge to look at Kesgrave, Bea kept her gaze steady and her movements smooth. Unless the actress was part of Tavistock's scheme, she could not possibly know their true intent. Even if she recognized Kesgrave—a prospect that was not an impossibility, given his age and the proclivities of most gentlemen—it was highly unlikely she would conclude the duke was there to investigate the murder of a lowly actor.

Injecting humor into her tone, Bea said, "You do?"

"Oh, yes, of course. You do not want to invest in the Particular; you want to buy it," Miss Calcott revealed with a knowing grin. "Do not bother to deny it, for I won't believe a word. And because I know the theater could prosper under new ownership, I am prepared to have a conversation with you about its advantages and disadvantages. And I will do so honestly without quoting my notices ad nauseam. I trust Mr. Latham alerted you to the mediocre reviews he drew for the *Dagerwood Inheritance*. The reporter for the *Farmer Chronicle* did in fact describe his performance as 'revelatory' but only so far as he found it a revelation that a surgeon could perform an operation without the use of his second hand. Mr. Latham is not the sharpest needle in the sewing kit, but nevertheless he is a draw. Audiences adore him, especially women, who find his dark, gothic looks to be brooding and mysterious. I count him among the assets of the theater."

"How very charitable," Bea said, genuinely amused.

Miss Calcott denied the charge and insisted she was merely being practical. "I would love to pretend that acting is only a matter of talent, but one's appearance has as much to do with one's success as one's aptitude. I would also put Mr. Fairbrother in the asset column, as he has a good look for the theater—not handsome like our Mr. Latham but striking in an interesting way. His face is narrow, which makes him look a little wolfish and cruel. But I assure you, he isn't cruel. A little impetuous and easily led astray, but he's also young yet, still a few years shy of his thirtieth. He likes to gamble, which is problematic because he isn't very good at it. Even I have wagered against him and won, and I know nothing about how to improve my odds. But he is a very good actor, talented and hardworking."

"Impetuous?" Bea asked as she leaned forward. "Is that what you think happened yesterday when the rampart collapsed on him? He behaved impetuously?"

"Now that is a conundrum," Miss Calcott said wryly, "and I will not embarrass myself by presuming to speculate about what happened. Ordinarily, our stage scenery is indestructible, and I assure you the craftsmen who built it are highly skilled. Yesterday's accident was an anomaly. As the future owners of the Particular, you must have no worry on that score."

"As *possible* future owners of the Particular," Bea amended. "We have not made our decision yet."

"Of course you haven't," Miss Calcott graciously allowed, "for it is far too soon in our discussion for you to have arrived at a sensible conclusion. Let us resume our list of assets before moving on to the liabilities."

"Naturally, you fall into the assets column," Bea said amiably.

Miss Calcott, however, shook her head and said, "I am rapidly approaching my—"

She broke off suddenly and lifted a hand to forestall questions. Then she rose to her feet, lifted her chair and carried it to the door, where she placed it under the knob, effectively rendering it unusable.

Scarcely a second later, a knock sounded at the door and a woman with a high, sweet voice asked if she may enter.

"Of course, Helen," Miss Calcott called, then waited a few seconds before trying to turn the knob. "Oh, dear, the door seems to be jammed."

"Again?" the woman named Helen asked.

"Yes, again," she answered, somehow managing to sound genuinely helpless as she lodged the bergère even more firmly into place. "I cannot imagine why this keeps happening to me. No one else in the theater is forced to suffer thusly. Could you be a dear, Helen, and fetch Mr. Vokes? I would be ever so grateful."

"Yes, of course, darling," Helen said. "Do stay calm and don't panic."

Although the other woman appeared to have left, Miss Calcott remained another moment longer and pressed her ear against the door. Then she retrieved the chair from her vanity and rejoined Bea and the duke.

Raising a teacup to her lips, Miss Calcott explained that she could hear Miss Andrews approaching because the walls to the dressing rooms were as thin as paper. "I would add inferior construction to the list of liabilities. The building is sturdy enough—I don't mean to imply that it will suddenly crumble around our ears—but the acoustics were designed by an architect with a poor understanding of the discipline. Sound barely travels from the stage to the upper boxes, and yet in the dressing rooms you can hear a script drop to the table. You will see for yourself tonight when you watch the performance," she promised before taking a delicate sip of the brew. "Now where was I before Miss Andrews decided to intrude on our gathering? Ah, yes, I was adding myself to the liabilities list, for I am approaching forty at a terrifying clip and the bloom is much off the rose."

Bea, who had enjoyed her antics with the chair and mentally filed the ruse away for future use, felt compelled to disagree.

Miss Calcott dismissed her concern with an airy wave of her hand. "You must not fret. I said 'much off,' not 'removed entirely.' I still have a significant number of Lady McBeths left in me, but new theater owners might prefer a Cordelia who can stretch into a Tatiana and I fear I no longer have that—to borrow one of Mr. Latham's favorite terms—range."

As they had no intention of buying the Particular, Bea wanted to put the other woman's mind at ease, but even as she opened her mouth to speak, Miss Calcott briskly continued. "Now to consider the other liabilities."

"Miss Andrews, perhaps?" Bea said in light of her recent behavior.

The actress laughed self-consciously. "Oh, dear. I fear you have reached the limits of my cleverness because I'm not really sure into which column Helen should be sorted. She is a wonderful actress, very natural and talented, and she's quite beautiful—flowing blond tresses, delicate frame and adorable button nose. But she is also painfully silly and naïve, and I fear she will be led astray by the first man to show an interest in her. Indeed, she almost was, but he revealed his true colors before it was too late."

"You are referring to Mr. Hobson's courtship," Bea said, recalling what Latham had said.

"I am, yes. The poor dear is heartbroken," Miss Calcott said softly. "At first I thought she was overreacting, for it is not unusual for a man, especially an actor, to wander off for an hour and not tell his sweetheart where he's going. I told her she would have a long and miserable life if she wrung her hands in distress every time her husband left the house. But when he came back a few days ago reeking of lavender perfume, I realized her cynical understanding was accurate. He denied it, of course, insisted she had grossly misunderstood the situation, swore he was merely working to settle their future, and then grew terribly self-righteous at her lack of trust and faith in him. He became very distressed and insisted she would learn the truth soon enough. To be fair, it was a convincing performance, but he gave it while emanating that cloying lavender scent and Helen remained resolute, which is to her credit. I thought she would believe his story that he was working in secret to settle their future, but even she is not such a peagoose as to fall for a plumper like that."

Listening to Miss Calcott's tale, Bea felt an odd pang of sympathy for Hobson, for he had spoken nothing but the truth—had he succeeded in finishing the assignment for Lord Tavistock, then he would have indeed secured funds with which to establish a home for him and his future wife. And yet she knew how shockingly immoral the task was and that if he had managed to accomplish his goal, her own reputation would be in tatters. A man willing to build his domestic happiness on the ruins of someone else's was not worthy of her compassion.

"The poor dear indeed," Bea murmured kindly as she wondered again if the young actress could have been driven by jealousy to run her lover through with a pair of fireplace tongs. "Is she devastated by the news of his death?"

Miss Calcott sighed deeply and held the cup of tea to her lips for a long moment. "Indeed not, which is very strange. I thought for sure she would be ridden with guilt for not reconciling with him while she still had the chance—wails of 'Oh, why didn't I believe him?' and 'I am sorry, my love.' But she is curiously lighthearted about the whole thing, and I worry that she doesn't fully comprehend the finality of the situation."

It was possible, Bea thought, that Miss Andrews's delicateness extended to her mind but the opposite was also plausible: that she understood far too well the decisiveness of his death because she was the one who'd dealt it.

"I cannot pretend I am not worried about her," the

actress continued. "Inevitably, the surprise will recede and the truth will be impossible to deny, and she will be full of self-recriminations. I am grateful he met his end in that ramshackle stable yard, for it makes it just sordid enough to prove conclusively he was up to no good. I will be able to remind her of that once the wailing begins."

"You are a good friend to resent him so deeply on her behalf," Bea observed, wondering if this dislike could have spurred her to violence.

For a moment, Miss Calcott looked surprised, then she laughed lightly at the suggestion that she held any personal enmity toward him. "You are giving me too much credit. Ultimately, all I care about is my own comfort and dread a protracted period of mourning in which I am obligated to provide solace. The truth is, I liked Robert. He learned his lines quickly and efficiently, never wasted time arguing with the director and wrote reasonably entertaining burlettas and farces. His melodramas left something to be desired, as they always contained too many drawn-out fatalities. A word to writers everywhere: Protracted death scenes are not the only way to make an audience feel deep emotion. Needless to say, that the Particular's playwright had a ruinous confrontation with a rake is another liability."

Bea was not surprised that Miss Calcott knew Miss Drake's secret. It seemed to her as though there was very little the capable actress did not know. She had no doubt the other woman could wield the brass tongs with efficiency and skill. But competence was not enough to earn one a spot on the list of suspects. One required a reason to wish the victim harm and the opportunity to cause it.

"The catalogue of liabilities is growing distressingly long," Bea observed, "and I must confess I am a little disconcerted by the two-hour interval that interrupted yesterday's rehearsal. At the Adelphi, we do not allow such a lenient schedule, for we think it makes the actors a little indolent. Mr. Latham, for example. I understand he takes a nap every afternoon."

Miss Calcott narrowed her eyes and tilted her head. "I see what you are doing and it will not work."

Resisting the urge to issue a general denial, Bea blinked her eyelids several times in a display of innocent confusion and asked what she was doing.

"You are attempting to get me to say a word against Latham, so that you may count him among the liabilities, for his salary is the Particular's single largest expense," she explained, revealing an unexpected familiarity with the details of the theater's expenditures. "Try as you might, you will not succeed. He is a chucklehead, yes, and most definitely lazy. He is also greedy and would empty Miss Drake's pockets for her last farthing if he could just figure out how to turn her upside down to shake it loose. But the fact remains that he is hugely popular with the audience. People come to see him and in the process catch a glimpse of me. As I said, I care only about my own comfort and Latham provides it."

Although Bea did not doubt Miss Calcott could be piti-less in her calculations, she thought her claims to selfishness were more satirical than sincere. Nevertheless, Bea decided to take her at her word and considered the ways in which Hobson's death increased or ensured her comfort. On the face of it, however, it appeared to have done just the oppo-site, for now she was obligated to provide emotional succor to an overwrought colleague and the theater would have to locate another author of mildly amusing burlettas and farces.

Opportunity, Bea thought again. Speculation about motive was futile if the suspect did not have the opportunity to commit the murder.

Lifting a brow, she said with arch cynicism, "I suppose that means you spent the interval resting as well?"

Miss Calcott found the idea risible and laughed dismissively. "Spend an afternoon napping while the wardrobe designers and executors are deciding on our costumes for our next production? My dear Mrs. Harper, I don't know how many times I can repeat myself without being a tedious bore, but my dedication to my own comfort is resolute—and in this case I mean my actual comfort, not a state of mental tranquility. If I am not there to represent my own interests, they will deposit me into a corset so tight I can barely recite a sonnet. In *The Abandoned Inamorata,* when I played the mouse queen, they gave me a set of whiskers that caused me to sneeze incessantly. No, I would never sleep through a meeting of the wardrobe department."

"I trust the wardrobe mistress finds your input valuable?"

The other woman stared at her in astonishment and insisted that the Adelphi must be an extraordinary theater if the wardrobe staff welcomed interference from the actors. "Mrs. Tapsell turns red at the very sight of me. Truly, you must ask her how much she appreciates my opinions. Although, if you value your own comfort, I would advise you not to."

Naturally, Bea would do just that at the earliest opportunity.

Then, hoping to eliminate Miss Andrews from her list in the same neat stroke, she asked if the other actress attended the meetings as well. "Or does it fall to you to safeguard her—"

But Miss Calcott held up her hand again, in that same way of requesting silence, and Bea broke off midsentence. The actress dashed to the door, slid the chair from under the knob and placed it against the wall. Then she removed a fur-lined robe from a hook and tossed it onto the cushion to give it the appearance of having been there for a while and returned to her seat. She was lifting a teacup to her lips when the door opened easily and a confused Miss Andrews peered into the room in the company of a stocky man holding a screwdriver aloft.

Affecting surprise, Miss Calcott gasped in delight and said, "You fixed it! And just when I began to fear I would miss tonight's call. Thank you, Mr. Vokes, you are so decidedly clever."

Although he had nothing to do with the door's sudden ability to open without resistance, he basked in her praise and assured her it was his pleasure to be of help. Then he asked if there was anything else he could repair while he was there.

She looked around the room for a moment, as if thoughtfully contemplating the condition of all the items contained within it, and said, "I think everything is all right and tight at the moment. But you are ever so kind to ask."

Miss Andrews, whose lovely appearance included eyes the color of cool light azure, an appealing trait Miss Calcott had failed to mention in her description, thanked Mr. Vokes as well for his help, although somewhat falteringly because she was not quite sure what he had done. Then she took two steps into the room to join the prospective investors in a cup of tea, but her progress was immediately halted by Mr. Smeeton's cry of alarm.

"Do not take one step more!" he said, darting into the room. "We cannot risk another malfunction. No, Miss Andrews, you must return to your dressing room to prepare for tonight's show, and I will take charge of the Harpers. Miss Calcott, I advise you not to shut the door entirely. If you feel a particular need for privacy, as I'm sure you will when it comes time to change into your costume, you may join Miss Andrews in her room."

Miss Calcott smiled at the stage manager and insisted the door had been fixed by the capable Mr. Vokes. "You may lack confidence in him, but I do not."

The carpenter simpered at the compliment, while Smeeton stared doubtfully at the door and Miss Andrews stepped farther into the room to introduce herself to the Harpers.

"I have never been to Bath," she said, "but have longed for ages to take the waters. I hear it is an enchanting city, particularly from Mr. Steagle, who grew up in the area."

Before Bea could make a vague if benign comment, Smeeton dashed across the floor to insist that he must escort Bea and the duke to their box now to view the performance. "As it must be in your own theater, the interval directly preceding the opening of the house is a particularly chaotic time and we must give the actors an opportunity to prepare."

Although his tone was beseeching, Bea detected a note of fixed determination just beneath the surface and decided against openly thwarting him. Defying his authority in front of his staff would only create unnecessary resentment, which would make his assistance harder to gain in the future should they need it. Rather, she deployed the single greatest weapon she had against intractability: Kesgrave's pedantry.

"Indeed, yes, we must adjourn to our box," Bea said agreeably. "It is quite providential that you should mention theatrical boxes because Mr. Harper nurtures a particular passion for them and delights in telling their history."

Mr. Smeeton, not yet perceiving how this would be to his misfortune, nodded politely and murmured, "How very interesting."

Kesgrave, however, comprehended at once and sent her an amused look. "The boxes?"

"Yes," she said with a firm nod, "the boxes."

Shaking his head slightly, as if somehow surprised that he could still be surprised by the depths to which she could sink him, he launched into a detailed account of the evolution of theater design, beginning with the theater of Epidaurus, which was situated in a sanctuary dedicated to Asclepius. "He was the ancient Greek god of medicine, and the theater was located at the southeast end of the plot. The sanctuary itself was built to the west Cynortion Mountain, which is near the town of Lygourio, population one thousand two hundred and six. The theater of Epidaurus is notable for both its acoustics and aesthetics, therefore making it the best example of a classical theater we have in the modern world. It dates to the fourth century B.C."

As Smeeton looked for an opportunity to extract himself from the conversation without giving grievous offense to the prospective investor, Bea greeted Miss Andrews kindly and noted that the actress did not appear to be unduly distressed by Hobson's death. If she was mourning the love of her life, she was doing an excellent job of hiding it.

It was, Bea thought, a curious response, but rather than probe the actress's seeming indifference right away, she sought to discover where she had been during the interval. "Miss Calcott was just regaling me with the tale of the wardrobe meeting yesterday. Tell me, did you attend as well?"

"Good gracious, no!" she said, her voice pitched in horror. "I would sooner have breakfast with a roomful of hungry lions than meet with Mrs. Tapsell. She is a beastly woman. Very good with a needle and undoubtedly shrewd with fabric, but altogether beastly. I think it is lovely that Maria is willing to beard the lion in her den. She is so devastatingly brave, and I am in awe of her. I took the opportunity to go shopping for ribbons at Coddlington's, for I was desperately in need of a new pink satin ribbon. My last one has been worn dreadfully thin from use. I promised Maria I would get her one in coquelicot because that shade of red is so flattering to her complexion. She looks wonderful in strong colors, and Mrs. Tapsell knows it too, which is why she always puts her in primrose. Because she is beastly."

"It happened only the one time," Miss Calcott pointed out calmly, "and I was playing Princess Sunrise."

Miss Andrews was unconvinced. "Then she should have put you in a jonquil gown and allowed you to shine. No, she is beastly and you will not convince me otherwise."

"I trust your shopping expedition was a success?" Bea asked, thinking that it would eliminate her neatly from the list if she could produce her purchase as proof of her outing.

"Oh, yes, very," she said with a happy grin. "I found the most lovely satin ribbon in an exquisite shade of blossom. It quite picked up the blush in my cheeks. And the red that I found for Maria! It was beyond all things divine. I was so very pleased. Only the most vexatious thing occurred. When I went to pay for the items, I discovered I'd forgotten my reticule. I'd left it sitting on the table in my dressing room! You know how often that happens to me, Maria."

But Maria confessed she did not.

Miss Andrews trilled lightly, as if her friend had not spoken, and said, "I have the most atrocious memory and am always forgetting this thing or that. Robert always ob... observed"—here she faltered slightly as if belatedly realizing what she'd said—"I would forget my head if it wasn't attached to my body. But what did he know? He always thought he knew more than me, but I have excellent recall. I am able to memorize my part in every play *and* Maria's in case I am called upon to stand in for her."

Her tone was defiant, but she wore an expression of vague despair, and Bea feared that she might start to cry at any moment. As she stood there, struggling to control her emotions, Miss Andrews looked young and delicate, her narrow frame barely able to hold her up. It was impossible to imagine her skewering Hobson with the fireplace tongs not once but twice. Surely, she was far too frail to overcome a man of his superior height and build.

Ah, but if she had surprise on her side, she might have been able to gain the upper hand and subdue him with a modicum of effort.

Bea knew her theory did not correspond exactly with the crime scene itself, which indicated an aggressive fight and then a frantic search, but Miss Andrews had the most cause for wishing the victim ill of any of the suspects and had been unable to supply evidence of her shopping trip.

"Now we may jump ahead to the first century A.D., when the Romans built the Colosseum, which was an amphitheater," Kesgrave continued didactically. "As an amphitheater is different from an ancient Greek theater in several ways. For one thing, it had seating all around. Contrast that with Epidaurus, which had seating in tiers on only one side of the performance area."

Poor Mr. Smeeton, torn between two opposing urges—the desire to cut Harper off midsentence and the compulsion to earn his approval. Somehow, he even managed to appear slightly interested in the topic, as if he'd always wondered how the parterre had evolved from the arena.

Miss Andrews reiterated that she had excellent recall, very, very excellent recall, and with each assertion her grip on her emotions slipped a little more until she looked as though she were about to dissolve into a heap of tears in the middle of the floor. Clearly, she could not take the stage in a state of distraught misery, and Miss Calcott, hoping to forestall both a collapse and the obligation of propping her back up, called for Mr. Smeeton.

"I do apologize, Mr. Harper, but Miss Andrews urgently requires our stage manager's bracing presence," she explained matter-of-factly. "I would try to help her myself, but I would just coddle the poor dear and that's the last thing she needs right now. Here, Mr. Smeeton, do take her arm and escort her back to her dressing room. I would advise a splash of cold water on her face, but of course I would never tell you how to do your job."

Smeeton immediately stepped forward to comply with her request, but he also cast a longing glance at the duke, for he would rather be bored to flinders by changing proscenium widths than deal with a hysterical female.

"I am all right," Miss Andrews said, smiling bravely to show him he had nothing to worry about. But her lips quavered unconvincingly.

As Smeeton led her out, Miss Calcott offered to show the Harpers to their seats.

Bea longed to consent to this plan but knew they could not linger, for it was almost half past five and she had been away from Portman Square for the whole of the afternoon. If she did not return soon, her aunt would begin to worry and perhaps send a note to the dowager. If she did, Bea's lie about spending time with Kesgrave's cousin might be exposed. The revelation in and of itself would not be a particularly devastating one, as it could have no impact on Bea's welfare, but it would cause unnecessary fuss. Her relatives, with whom she was attempting to build a sort of trust, would be hurt and offended. Inevitably, they would worry that her mental faculties were failing, for even though her aunt and uncle understood intellectually that her parents were not a sinking morass of moral turpitude, they could not simply stop believing something they had known to be true for twenty years.

It would take time, and giving them time was one of the reasons she had agreed to postpone her marriage.

Bea met Kesgrave's gaze and knew his thoughts aligned with hers.

"As delightful as that would be, I'm afraid we must forgo the pleasure of viewing tonight's performance," she said, easily imbuing her words with the regret she genuinely felt.

"We have an appointment to dine with associates. Other investors, you see. But we will return tomorrow to resume our tour of the theater. Hopefully, Miss Andrews will be more composed then."

Miss Calcott lauded Bea's optimism but insisted it was sadly out of place. "It has begun, the long, dark descent into misery, and it won't end until she is prostrate with grief and wailing into the yawning chasm that is her future without the lying blackguard—dying in a stable! What could he have been thinking? Once again, I am grateful for the tawdriness of his end. Done in by a rake that he stepped on himself. If only she could appreciate the irony of his carelessly destroying himself," she said, ushering them down the hallway to the theater's exit on Adams Street. As they passed through the stairwell to the upper boxes, she lamented the undue suffering Hobson's death had caused her. During his life, he had been like a needle, pricking her arm, but now he was a thorn firmly planted in her side. "And yet his burlettas and farces!"

Chapter Thirteen

As soon as they were settled in the carriage, Kesgrave regarded Beatrice with a weary eye and asked if marriage to her would require him to produce many long-winded seminars on the history of random subjects at a moment's notice.

Amused by how genuinely aggrieved he sounded, she assured him he had risen to the challenge deftly. "Your ability to lecture on any given topic in stupefying detail is your particular skill," she added cajolingly. "No other man in London could have produced the theater of Epidaurus so easily or adroitly. I *gave* you the opportunity to shine. And you are very welcome. Now do stop angling for compliments and tell me what you think of our suspects."

"If I am angling for compliments, brat, it is only because your steady stream of insults has eroded whatever confidence I had," he said, his lips trembling in that familiar way. "And the name of the best preserved example of an ancient Greek theater is not a stupefying detail but a general fact known to any student with a classical education."

"You may deprecate all you want, Kesgrave, but I am

determined to find your vast wealth of knowledge very impressive," she said avidly. "There, you see, another compliment. Now may we discuss our suspects? I counted four."

"Fairbrother, Chatterley, Miss Drake and Miss Andrews," he said. "Obviously, Fairbrother's accident is too much of a coincidence not to be examined fully, and Chatterley does not seem like an entirely decent fellow. Too prankish. It's possible Hobson's death was a lark that somehow got out of hand. Miss Drake's plagiarism puts her on the list, as does her claim to have been in her office working on the play during the time in question. As she did not actually write the script, it seems unlikely that she was revising it. Furthermore, according to Smeeton, she was the only cast or crew member who did not appear when Fairbrother cried out in pain. Miss Andrews also had cause to wish Hobson ill, and her inability to produce either a pink or red ribbon makes her claim about shopping at Coddlington's doubtful. That said, she does not appear to be strong enough to overcome Hobson, but as I did not have an opportunity to examine the body, I cannot say how much strength was required. She could have stunned him with a hit over the head before running him through."

Bea was deeply gratified by this speech because it demonstrated not only how aligned their thinking was but also the rationality of her conclusions. Clearly, she had not made any outlandish leaps of logic.

"That is true," she said and admitted that her anxiety about being discovered in that dreadful situation by the stable yard's owner and Mrs. Norton's impatience to leave precluded a more thorough examination of the corpse. "He was lying on his back, and I did not turn him fully over to see what other wounds, if any, he'd suffered."

"I trust we will be paying a call on Mr. Fairbrother soon," he said.

Obviously, yes, the next step in their investigation was

to ascertain the precise nature of the actor's injury. The timing of that meeting was something that needed to be decided, and Bea appreciated having someone to discuss it with.

No, she thought immediately, not someone. Him. The duke.

During their visit to the theater, he'd been quiet. Aside from negotiating with Miss Drake over the particulars of their fictional financial investment, he had been almost silent. Indeed, he had withdrawn from conversation so thoroughly, she imagined some of the respondents had forgotten he was there.

But not Bea.

She had been aware of him the whole time and found herself a little in awe of his ability to fade into the background. It was not an impressive accomplishment on its own, for she herself had been sinking beneath other people's notice for more than six seasons. But it was disingenuous to pretend her ability to disappear was the same as his, for wallflowers were made to wilt and dukes to dominate. Decades of sycophancy had convinced Kesgrave of the supremacy of his thoughts and opinions, making it almost impossible for him to affect inferiority. His first attempt at playing a minion—a lowly law clerk during her investigation into Mr. Wilson's death—had yielded little success, for he could not abide being treated as a man of his purported station. When the Marquess of Taunton dismissed him as if swatting a fly, Kesgrave had stiffened his shoulders and snapped with commanding disrespect.

Bea had not expected him to show so much improvement in such a short interval and, hoping to encourage further growth, complimented him on how well he'd behaved.

"Behaved?" Kesgrave echoed, as if not entirely sure what the word meant, and he repeated it again as his lips curved into a smile. "Why do I suddenly feel like a faithful blood-hound being complimented on the hunt?"

"Because after several hours of containing your knowl-edge, a feat that is quite difficult for you, you are feeling churlish and require an opportunity to vent your discomfort," she explained with patronizing superiority before graciously offering herself as a target for his peevishness. "You may use me as your pincushion. Stick me with as many needles as you require to restore your good humor."

As unambiguous as the invitation was, Kesgrave, his ability to think perhaps compromised by the exertions of the afternoon, misunderstood it entirely, for in a moment he was sitting on her side of the carriage, arm curled around her waist and kissing her deeply. At once, Bea observed the clarity of her own thoughts begin to cloud as a longing to feel closer to the duke overtook her. It was not enough to simply revel in the sensation his embrace created.

Oh, no.

Her fingers itched quite desperately to slip under the fabric of his shirt and touch the smooth expanse of his back. Ah, but they could not get close with the blasted weight of his greatcoat. If she could just dispense with the offending obstacle....

Suddenly, her hands were encased in Kesgrave's firm grip as he groaned and shook his head. "As much as it pains me to deny you anything, especially when it means also denying myself, I cannot allow you to prosper in your efforts to take off my coat. It is difficult enough for me to remain in control when properly attired, and I fear the removal of any barrier, however slight, will make it all but futile."

Bea, whose understanding of her own actions had been clouded by passion, felt heat suffuse her face as she realized she'd been trying to undress him in a carriage with his groom only a few feet away.

Observing the rise in her color, Kesgrave shook his head decisively and returned to the other bench. "No, brat, no. You will remove that charming blush from your cheeks at once, for I will not allow you to endanger my virtue further with your utter delightfulness. Ordinarily, I am able to keep a tight grip on my appetites, but having never known love coupled with desire before, I did not comprehend what a challenge it would be to resist you. But I am resolved to remain pure until our wedding afternoon—you will note, I trust, that I have no intention of waiting until sundown—and to that end, I must insist that you present that wan complexion your aunt assures me is your customary appearance."

Obviously, it was impossible for her to comply with the request, for the indication of his impatience only caused her flush to deepen. Indeed, even as she ordered herself to think of something sufficiently mundane to say, her mind leaped forward three days as she tried to guess what the duke considered to be a proper interval. He meant hours, she thought, not minutes, for they could not say their vows in his grandmother's drawing room one moment, then hastily make their goodbyes the next. Such immoderate behavior would make their intentions apparent to everyone, which would be unbearable, would it not?

And yet the prospect of sitting down to a leisurely breakfast with the dowager whilst fully aware that all previously wicked and indecent activities were now deemed moral and upstanding by the church was in its own way intolerable. Her fingers began tingle again as she imagined running them along his heated skin with the full blessing of God and country.

"Beatrice!" Kesgrave growled, his voice shockingly feral, and she realized how easily he'd followed her thoughts.

Despite the ferocity of their recent embrace, she was mortified to discover not only the depths of her own lasciviousness but also her inability to hide it. Resolutely, she focused on the matter at hand, struggling to recall precisely the topic they'd been discussing when the duke had distracted her.

The interviews at the Particular with the theater company.

That's right, she thought. She had complimented him on how well he'd restrained himself during their visit, something she had not believed him capable of. Her tone had been ironical, but as she considered it again, she found herself genuinely grateful he had not felt compelled to take over the investigation. It was no small thing, she knew, thinking of all he commanded—the estates and vast wealth and the army of servants.

Keenly aware of that now, she thanked him for allowing her to conduct the interviews. "I recognize how difficult it is for you to hold back."

It was a sincere statement, earnestly felt, and she expected him to be gratified by her appreciation. Rather than respond in kind, however, he considered her with an amused expression in his bright blue eyes as his lips quivered. "At the risk of alienating your affections, for I know how much you cherish the image an endlessly pontificating duke, I must confess that I am not nearly as meticulous as you believe. I'm not beset by a constant need to represent the facts in a particular way."

Naturally, Bea found this statement to be among the most inaccurate in history—not quite on par with Ptolemy's insistence that the sun revolved around the earth but certainly in align with Louis XV's contention that after him would come the deluge—but she kept her expression bland as she responded with excessive sobriety. "Yes, of course, your grace. I am sure you are not in any way controlled by compulsion," she said before glancing down to stare at her hands, which were grasped lightly in her lap. Then she added softly, "HMS *Majestic,* HMS *Goliath,* HMS *Audacious.*"

'Twas a challenge, to be sure, a gauntlet thrown provokingly at his feet, and having issued it, she sat primly in her seat and began a mental count. As she'd expected, she had barely got halfway to the number ten before he said, "HMS *Goliath,* HMS *Audacious,* HMS *Majestic.*"

Determined not to be ruled by her own compulsions, Bea contained her laughter and merely allowed a small, knowing smile. Unrepentant, Kesgrave announced that it was maritime tradition. He said it firmly and with steadfast conviction, as if the practice of listing naval ships in the order they'd appeared in battle were an immutable force in the universe like gravity.

Aware of the direction of her thoughts, he calmly added, "Just because I refuse to flout tradition for the sake of willful dissent does not mean I'm pedantic. It simply means I have a healthy respect for the customs of the past."

Given that the Matlock family could trace its lineage back to the Peasant's Revolt of 1381, it was hardly surprising to discover he valued the institutions that ensured his wealth and status. If history had served her half as well, she would no doubt be as pompous as all the preening politicians she had encountered at Lord Pudsey's salon.

With exaggerated consideration, as if determined to correct a great disservice, Bea apologized for repeatedly calling him a pedant. "Clearly, you are a traditionalist, and that is a *wholly* different thing. I cannot say at this precise moment exactly *how* they differ, but as soon as I return home, I will consult my dictionary and acquaint myself with the disparities. I am sure there are dozens."

Although Beatrice had hoped to elicit an extensive list of the differences between the two, Kesgrave, who was accustomed to this sort of abuse from his beloved, blandly stated that he looked forward to learning the results of her research.

Then he said, "To return to my original point, which I will do now despite your attempt to lead me off on yet another absurd tangent, it required no great effort for me to hold myself back during our interviews at the Particular. As you had the matter well in hand, I saw no reason to interfere. Furthermore, I found it at once illuminating and entertaining to watch you neatly gather the information you required without alerting your suspects to your purpose. You have a true aptitude for it."

Bea, who had been formulating a mocking reply to his assertion that it was *she* who had a fondness for absurd tangents ("Yes, because *I* am frequently compelled to lecture on the tenets of maritime tradition" or perhaps more succinctly, "Damn all my pesky lectures on maritime tradition!"), felt her mind go suddenly blank at the lavishness of the compliment. It was stated plainly, simply, without adornment or embellishment, to be sure, but the sentiment it expressed—oh, yes, the sentiment. That was extravagant in its display of admiration, and Bea, who, sitting across from him at the dinner table at Lord Skeffington's, had never imagined rising even to his disdain, still felt slightly breathless at winning his esteem.

And yet how astonishingly easy it had been to earn, for he had taken her seriously from almost the very beginning. True, he had sought to dismiss her at first, seeing naught but a dull spinster with an indecorous curiosity. But his dismissiveness quickly gave way to thoughtful consideration and then grudging respect as they'd investigated Mr. Otley's murder. Despite five centuries of exaltation, he was remarkably free of the prejudices of his station, and it was that inexplicable open-mindedness that pulled at her with an irresistible force more than the corded muscles she had felt beneath his coat or the lush lips that could make her forget where she was or the gloriously blue eyes or—

"Bea," Kesgrave said impatiently, with a hint of warning, "I must insist you make some effort, for it is not—and if anything is a testament to the depths to which you have sunk me, it is this next word—*fair* that I have to bear the burden of abstemiousness alone. Now, if I am to have any hope of arriving at the altar with my virtue intact, you will cease staring at me as if you desire nothing more than to make quick work of my clothes."

Suffering none of the mortification of earlier, for the slight note of desperation in his tone made her feel powerful in a way she'd never experienced before, Bea tilted her eyes down in an approximation of modesty and vowed to look at him with the same benign indifference with which she contemplated blancmange.

Kesgrave drew his brows together, as if unable to determine if she was teasing him or not, but demonstrated his ability to resist a digression by returning the topic to Mr. Fairbrother. "Although I agree we should examine his wounds as soon as possible, the hour is growing late and your aunt is no doubt keeping an eye out for you. Even my grandmother will be wondering where I am, for she knows I cannot visit cousin Amelia this long without a strong desire to box her ears. Shall we arrange to call on him tomorrow morning?"

His reasoning was undeniable, and Bea, promptly agreeing with his suggestion, asked what subterfuge they would use the next day to evade the stifling concern of both their families. It was a damned irritating nuisance, having to invent pretext after pretext in order to sneak out of the house to ask relevant parties pertinent questions, and she decided the freedom that marriage offered was as appealing as the duke's lithe form.

Ah, but no, she thought, as annoyed as she was baffled by the ease with which her mind insisted on wandering again and again to the contemplation of the fine figure Kesgrave cut. Mere minutes ago, she'd promised to consider him a blandly sweet dessert she only mildly enjoyed and already she had broken her word. Had love really made her so facile?

Unaware of her failure to comply with his single request, Kesgrave insisted he had an infinite number of relatives they may profess to call on. "Tomorrow, we will bless my cousin Adelaide with our presence. She is an octogenarian with a notoriously bad memory. She has been known to forget my visit whilst I am still sitting in the chair opposite her. Neither the dowager nor your aunt will ever be the wiser."

Grateful for the duke's ability to keep a clear head, Beatrice agreed to this arrangement and proposed they leave at nine o'clock, which was a good half hour before her family typically presented themselves for breakfast. Not only would an early start allow her to avoid her aunt and Flora's awkward questions, but it would also provide them with enough time to call on Mr. Fairbrother before returning to the Particular to conduct more interviews and gather additional information.

With their schedule for the next day settled, Bea raised the issue that troubled her most: the fact that the state of Mr. Josiah's bedchamber clearly indicated a great search had taken place. "I cannot conceive what the murderer was looking for, and none of the motives we have ascribed to the suspects would account for it."

Kesgrave agreed it was puzzling and considered the matter for a long moment as the carriage rumbled down King Street. "Given that the scene, as you said, indicated a struggle, it is possible that the perpetrator lost something in the tussle that could reveal his or her identity—for example, a brooch Miss Drake always wore or a patch with her family's insignia. In that case, he or she would have been forced to retrieve it before leaving. But given that none of our suspects save Fairbrother show signs of an injury, it's also possible that the killer created the scene to give the appearance of a struggle and a search. He or she might have thought that leaving behind a chaotic mess would obscure their motive and therefore their identity. They are all theater people, after all, and know how to set a stage for dramatic effect."

Bea, who had not contemplated such a diabolical explanation, regarded the duke with the light of approval flashing in her eyes. "I had not considered it from that perspective, but it is logical and fiendish. Well done, your grace."

He laughed ruefully at her compliment and begged her not to sound so surprised by his ability to think critically and devise clever solutions. "I might not have the discovery of four murderers to my credit, Miss Hyde-Clare, but I have been overseeing an extensive estate for more than a decade, a situation that has provided me with an opportunity or two to hone my deductive skills."

Fluttering her lashes in a display of excessive admiration, she said, "Do tell me more about the size of your estate, my lord duke. Do you possess a large riding house, an observatory *and* a dozen-acre walled kitchen garden with recessed braziers to mature the pippins upon your command?"

"It's a pinery, brat," he said amiably, "and given your scorn for hastily ripened fruit, I will make sure you are not subjected to any pineapples."

Bea had only been teasing him with her invention of a generous enclosure with coals along the perimeter to keep the crops warm during the chilly winter, for such a contrivance had struck her as immoderately extravagant. She had not expected him to respond with a hothouse devoted to the cultivation of a fruit so exotic she had only read about it, and the fact that he did—the fact that he *could*—made her feel curiously small and inconsequential. The pinery, like the eighth footman, hinted at a magnificence so great she could scarcely comprehend its immensity. She knew there was more to him than this part she adored, this beloved ally who assumed costumes and identities to interrogate theater owners with her, and she worried that the piece she knew was merely a tiny sliver of the whole. Their life together could not exclusively be made up of intimate moments in a carriage. At some point, she would have to grasp the entirety.

"I take it back," Kesgrave said suddenly, sliding across the carriage to sit beside her again. "You may have all the pineapples you wish—every meal, every day. I will tell Stephens to arrange for daily delivery from Haverill Hall. Just please stop looking so desolate, my love. I cannot bear it."

Bea knew this to be true, and if she explained how demoralized and intimidated she was by the prospect of his pinery, he would leap to soothe her fears. He had done exactly that with the eighth footman, sneaking into her bedchamber while her family was abroad for the evening to speak frankly with her, and he would no doubt do it again and again and again—as many times as necessary until she was finally and truly at peace with the grandeur of his position.

But the deadening repetition of her insecurities was precisely the problem, and she could not imagine anything more tedious than being called upon to soothe the same anxieties over and over. A musical piece that endlessly replicated a single note was a monotonous bore, and she trembled at the thought of being an amateurish sonata composed by a middling talent.

To be sure, she would never embody the spritely imprudence of Beethoven's Piano Concerto No. 1, with its mischievous third movement, but she firmly believed she could eventually achieve a sort of deft and lyrical poise.

It would take time, of course, for her to overcome the debilitating timidity of her first six seasons and the crushing self-doubt. She could not undo in a day what her aunt and uncle had spent nearly a lifetime assembling. Inevitably, there would be setbacks, crises of confidence incited by pineries and footmen, and the thought of subjecting Kesgrave to every single one was horrifying.

Determinedly, she smiled brightly at the duke, which was not at all difficult, for she quite relished the prospect of the standoffish Mr. Stephens having to arrange for the regular transportation of pineapples to London, and announced she had always longed to try the pineapple tart described in botanist Richard Bradley's cookery book, *The Country House-wife and Lady's Director in the Management of a House, and the Delights and Profits of a Farm*.

Then, because they had once again strayed far from poor Mr. Hobson's untimely death, she lauded the shrewdness of his observation with renewed vigor. "It explains both the chaos and the fact that we have not encountered any missing items in our investigation. More baffling is the decision to use a bedchamber at a stable yard for the scene of the attack, but I suppose that explanation is far more mundane than the high theatricality of the suspects. It is probably merely the place where the murderer ran him to ground. Miss Andrews, for example, following him to the source of the lavender perfume and having her worst suspicions confirmed. That said, I wonder if Tavistock did not overplay his hand by making the scene so sordid. It was the very opposite of a young girl's fancy."

Kesgrave stiffened at the mention of the man who had sought to destroy her reputation, but when he spoke, his voice was mild. "I believe for his lordship's purpose, the tawdriness of the location was the point. He chose a stable yard because its vulgarity would have demeaned you further, making your ruination complete. He wanted you to be so thoroughly debased that I would have no choice but to cast you out. It would not have worked even if every detail of his plan had gone smoothly, but he could not have known that."

Although his tone remained calm and she could detect no visible sign of anger, she felt fury emanating from him like rays of sunshine. Firmly, she reminded him that Tavistock's scheme had already failed. "Recall, if you will, Mrs. Norton made a comment that revealed the nature of the ruse and I stopped in the middle of the corridor. If she hadn't screamed in terror at the sight of Mr. Hobson's bloodied corpse, I would have left the building without getting a single step closer to the scene of my destruction. Tavistock miscalculated. He severely underestimated us—you in your affection for me and me in my ability to detect a plot. He even underestimated poor Mr. Hobson by giving him no more consideration than he would a scullery maid. If he'd taken even minor pains to learn something about the man upon whom his entire plan hinged, rather than accepting a reference from his mistress and then requiring his steward to make the arrangements, he might have learned about his vulnerabilities. My impulse is to ascribe this oversight to the overweening confidence of an arrogant man, but you, my lord duke, are by far the most arrogant person I've ever met and you would never leave the ruination of a dowdy spinster to a subordinate. You would oversee every detail yourself to ensure maximum destruction of her reputation. And I do not say that merely because I am fond of you," she hastened to add.

Now Kesgrave's lips twitched with genuine humor. "You don't?"

"No," she affirmed, grateful that his rage had subsided. "I say it because it's the truth, and because it *is* the truth, I'm forced to conclude that Tavistock is stupid as well as sloppy. No doubt the people in his employ are too, as things like this tend to flow down from the top, which means while he was egregiously underestimating us, he was also foolishly *over*estimating his steward—witness, for example, how he tripled the offer at the first sign of resistance. His plan, therefore had exactly no chance of succeeding. So the next time you see his lordship, rather than planting him a facer, you should thank him for being an ineffectual dullard because it has given you and your betrothed something to laugh about."

Kesgrave examined her thoughtfully as he shook his head. "You would say that to him, wouldn't you—just those exact words to his face—and consider justice to have been served."

She nodded emphatically, fully aware of how much pain words could inflict because they had inflicted it on her. "He was always going to fail. I was never at risk," she said, then added with meaningful emphasis, "*We* were never at risk."

It was clear from the expression on Kesgrave's face that he remained skeptical of the retaliatory value of amused condescension, and Bea made no further attempt to convince him, for she cared little if Tavistock suffered a drubbing at the duke's hands. She believed wholly in his decency and knew his own internal sense of justice would not allow him to do grievous bodily harm to a man who had done none to her. Lord Taunton had tried to break her neck and throw her body over a balcony wall, and Kesgrave had contented himself with one beautifully landed blow and banishment.

At least, Bea believed he contended himself with a single punch. In actuality, she had not been there when the duke confronted the villain with his gambling debts and ordered him to leave the country or his family would suffer the indignities of poverty, so she could not say definitively that the marquess endured no additional blows. It seemed unlikely, however, that he'd—

But the thought...the thought...whatever it had been...was decisively lost as Kesgrave's lips crushed hers in a passionate kiss that instantly set her heart to racing and she had to grasp onto his shoulders to anchor herself, for she felt as though she were falling.

No, not falling, she realized dimly, as her back pressed

against the plush upholstery. Merely laying down and drowning in pleasure as the duke's hands roamed her body.

She arched, straining to bring herself closer to him, and thought, Oh, good, as his fingers skimmed the bodice of her dress.

No, not good, she thought.

Delightful...so delightful...and strong, she thought, feeling the muscles in his back contract at her touch.

But Kesgrave did not want this.

Well, yes, he very clearly did desire these very actions, but his plea for her help in maintaining his virtue had been sincere and just because his control appeared to have slipped now—

Slipped? she thought mockingly. Rather like fallen off a cliff.

Regardless of the description, Kesgrave had lost his footing and required her assistance in regaining his balance.

And she would help, she decided, as she felt his lips caress her neck, sending shudders throughout her entire body. She would...she would...soon.

But *soon* was a slippery notion and she worried that soon might be too late, so she ordered herself to pull back at once. It was difficult, almost painful, to break contact, and gathering her wits, she noted the wild confusion in his eyes. Her breathing labored, she tried to think of something to say that wasn't an expression of astonishment at what the human body could feel.

The case, the case, she thought, scrambling for coherence. Hobson. The fireplace tongs. The plagiarizing Miss Drake. Mr. Fairbrother's debts. Mr. Smeeton. The theater.

The theater!

That was right. They had introduced themselves as theater owners, and Kesgrave had made a surprisingly credible show of it.

LYNN MESSINA

Offer him a compliment.

"I must congratulate you, your grace, on your persuasive impersonation of an investor," she said, her voice still breathless from desire but firm enough for comprehension. "I knew perfectly well you were merely pretending, and yet I found myself fairly convinced you intended to sink capital into the theater. It was the specificity of your questions that made it particularly believable."

Kesgrave, his color still high but his searing blue gaze alert and coherent, accepted the praise. "I would point out again that I've been overseeing my family's extensive portfolio of investments for more than a decade, but I do not want to expose myself to further ridicule."

It was the ideal response, precisely the sort of drawing room banter she relished, and yet it felt wholly out of place in the charged atmosphere of the carriage. She had succeeded in distracting him, yes, but not in lightening the mood.

"It must be onerous indeed," she replied, "having to constantly hide your light under a bushel. Perhaps you should find another young lady who will have more respect for your consequence. You would have little trouble, as I understand that an extensive portfolio of investments *and* a pinery are a highly desirable combination."

Now a ghost of a smile appeared. "Such a course would mean foisting you on an unsuspecting *ton,* and that seems grossly unfair to my fellow men."

"Ah, a philanthropist," she said approvingly. "How very noble. I could recommend an association that advocates for the care and welfare of street urchins that would greatly appreciate your support. I say that with all sincerity, your grace, for Mrs. Palmer provided me with a name of such a group and I have sent pin money. It wasn't very much, as my funds are limited, but if I could persuade you to give, then my contribution would be considerable indeed."

As Kesgrave was in actual fact a philanthropist, he had many thoughts on the judicious allocation of wealth to groups working to alleviate poverty and suffering and he happily shared these with Beatrice as the carriage turned into Wardour Street. He had in his employ a solicitor who examined each organization to ensure its legitimacy and evaluate the quality of its program, and he urged her to refer Mrs. Palmer's association to Mr. Beazley.

"You do not have to content yourself with pin money," he added, "for as the Duchess of Kesgrave you will have access to unlimited funds. And do not forget you have your own investments, which were left to you by your father. Those could be quite valuable. I believe you mentioned something about a steam engine? We will put Mr. Stephens on the case, and he will find out. You are also not limited to only existing charity organizations. If you do not find one that fulfills your requirements, you may start your own."

The speech bore all the hallmarks of a Kesgrave lecture, and Bea realized the danger had passed. The duke was on solid footing, and whatever had pushed him over the edge—the threat of Tavistock's machinations or her contention that they had never posed a threat—no longer plagued him.

Instead, *she* was plagued by yet another indication of Kesgrave's grandeur, for it was impossible not to be unsettled by how carelessly he'd tossed off the suggestion that she start her own charity.

'Twas a monstrously egotistical way of looking at the world—assuming you were the solution to an enduring problem—and yet she did not doubt that for Kesgrave this perspective had borne itself out.

Bea, however, did not have five hundred years of accomplished ancestors to prop her up, and she found the prospect of adopting such an outlook inconceivable.

Nevertheless, Kesgrave continued to catalogue the benefits of founding her own organization, assuring her with unassailable confidence that it would not take seventeen years for her to earn a royal charter, as the wheels of government run much more smoothly now than they did seventy-seven years ago, when Thomas Carom sought to establish the London Foundling Hospital.

As Bea had no intention of doing anything for seventeen years, save humbling her husband, she found his reassurances unnecessary and, attempting to change the subject, interrupted his lecture to ask if he'd observed the smooth way she'd led him out of treacherous waters. "I neither pleaded for assistance in protecting your virtue nor suffered the humiliation of using the word *fair* to describe my burden. Rather, I fended for myself by providing a distraction. It is, I am convinced, an approach capable of replication, and in the interest of science, I am happy to submit now to your attentions in order to test the theory."

Whether the duke would have acted to advance the cause of science remained unknown, for at that moment the carriage arrived at number 19 Portman Square and Jenkins jumped down from his seat to open the door. Mindful of her aunt's interest in Kesgrave, she advised him not to come in or risk being embroiled in another conversation about the various varieties of beets.

"She has been reading *Mr. Fletcher's Guide to Edible Roots* in preparation," she warned, "which is a testament to her determination to impress you, for Aunt Vera is quite doggedly illiterate. You must tread carefully, lest my uncle grow jealous."

Kesgrave, who had had no intention of accompanying her inside, said he now felt compelled to greet her family briefly, for to do otherwise would appear cowardly.

As Bea had expected, her aunt met them at the door and quizzed the duke on the welfare of his cousin. Assured of Amelia's continued good health, she attributed the elderly woman's well-being to a nutritious diet, which naturally included beetroot. Thoughtfully, she listed the most nourishing types, noting with regret that she had been unable to find information on Kesgrave's favorite variety, the 'Audacious.'

Noting the depth of her disappointment, his grace, who had invented the 'Audacious' in an attempt to earn a distracted Bea's attention only the week before, announced that he might have possibly got the name wrong. He would consult with his chef on his preferred type of beetroot and report back to her posthaste.

It was, Bea thought, a tactical mistake, for now he would have to follow through, and if he thought complaining about having to bear more than his fair share of abstemiousness to his intended was humiliating, then he would find asking his chef what kind of beetroot he liked best utterly mortifying.

Kesgrave left a few minutes later, and Bea retired to her bedchamber to read a chapter or two of the Kepler biography before dinner. Although the family had planned to attend Mrs. Mortimer's rout when the invitation arrived the week before, they decided now to spend a quiet evening at home. They did this, Bea knew, because they wanted to protect her from the prying eyes of the *ton*, which remained fascinated by her confrontation with Wem.

Bea did not blame them—neither the members of the beau monde for wanting to know more nor her family for wishing to spare her. Having agreed with her aunt about few things in her life, Bea thought the other woman's strategy of maintaining a quiet existence while waiting for the scandal to die down was sensible. Alas, it was not only confirmed gossips like Mrs. Ralston who were talking about her but rather most members of society, and as Mrs. Norton's perniciousness had made plain, many did not consider the scene wherein her father's dearest friend confessed to his murder as definitive proof of her good character.

As such, Bea was content to remain at home and discuss Kepler with her uncle, which she did for fifty-five satisfying minutes. Then she evaded further questioning about Mrs. Norton from Flora by attempting to discover if Russell had thought about her suggestion that he take fencing lessons. Eschewing a simple answer of yes or no, he took the query as an opportunity to renew his complaint that his mother had cheated him, for agreeing to allow him to take lessons while refusing to supply the necessary funds to pay for them was a dirty trick.

"I cannot believe my own mother would play me foul," he muttered—at which point Flora began to list all the things she wanted that their parents would not bear the cost of and the evening devolved into a shouting match between the two siblings.

Listening to them bicker, Bea found it astounding that with all the breathtaking changes that had occurred in her life in the past two weeks, her cousins' antipathy toward each other remained impervious to alteration.

Chapter Fourteen

Although Beatrice had attended few plays in her life and was not, despite her recent claim to theater ownership, in any way associated with the acting profession, she knew a villain when she saw one. Frances Roland Fairbrother, with his gaunt face, pointy chin and jet-black hair, bore a marked resemblance to the image she carried in her head of Iago or Ludovico, the usurper of Milan. As he stood in the entryway of his Greenfield Road home, his heavy brows drawn impatiently as he glared down at her, he seemed to seethe a sort of irritable depravity from every pore, and she could easily imagine him ordering his brother's execution with all the moral vacuity of a Richard II.

Or, she allowed, noting the white knuckles with which he clutched the plain wooden cane in his left hand, he was a man suffering from a horrible wound and doing his best not to succumb to the pain as he greeted his possible future employers.

In any case, Miss Calcott's description of his appearance was accurate: He was striking in a compellingly interesting way.

"You must come in, yes, of course," he said, his words as stilted as his movements as he tried to lead them to a round table next to a small window overlooking a dark alley. Despite the compact dimensions of the room, the exertion of walking across it was too much and after a moment, he halted his progress and contented himself with a gesture. "Please, do sit down. I...um, yes...I was about to make myself a cup of tea. I hope you will join me."

It was, Bea thought, a brazen lie, for the man could hardly stand, let alone fill a pot with water and set it on the fire. No doubt, prior to their arrival, he had been lying in bed and moaning at regular intervals. And now, thanks to their sudden appearance, he was forced to play host.

'Twas quite rude of them to intrude on his convalescence.

Unless he incurred his injury whilst killing Mr. Hobson.

In that case, having to endure their ill-timed visit while his leg throbbed in pain was light punishment for his sins.

Either way, Bea did not desire a cup of tea, for it would just distract from their purpose.

"No, please, do sit down," she said with a vigorous shake of her head. "We can see you are already under a great strain and do not want you to injure yourself further, especially on our behalf."

Somehow, his thin face seemed to grow even more narrow as he considered her request, for it clearly presented him with a conundrum. As a member of the theater company, it was almost his duty to exert himself on their behalf, particularly when it came to their comfort over his own.

To settle the matter, she said that it pained her to see his suffering, and, sighing with relief, he took the seat across from her at the table.

He rested the cane against the side of his chair, then fiddled with the head as his eyes swept from Bea to Kesgrave and back again. "It is a pleasure to welcome you to my...uh... ah, humble abode," he said, then added awkwardly. "Your call is...um...much unexpected."

Yes, Bea thought, their visit was quite unusual, and she could only imagine how extraordinary it would be for true investors to venture to the heart of Whitechapel to meet an actor of only minor significance.

Bea decided to address the matter directly. "Mr. Harper and I believe in being scrupulously thorough with our investments and could not consider going forward with our interest in the Particular without discovering more about your accident."

Fairbrother flinched at the word *accident,* knocking the cane onto the floor, where it landed with a rattle. Flustered, he glanced apologetically at Bea as he leaned over to pick it up. His attention diverted, he did not consider the movement until his elbow rammed into his thigh. At once, his face lost every remnant of color, but he otherwise kept careful possession of himself, never once crying out in pain. Instead, he closed his eyes, as if absorbing the agony into his body, and when he opened them a few seconds later, he seemed almost unperturbed by the incident.

"Ah, yes, my accident," he said coolly as little beads of sweat formed around his temples, fully revealing the depth of his struggle. "I'm not sure what I can tell you about that. It was an unfortunate mishap."

It was a masterful performance, and Bea had to resist the urge to applaud. Instead, she said, "You have been an actor at the Particular for a long time, have you not, Mr. Fairbrother? Almost a decade?"

Whatever he'd been expecting, it was not a query about the length of his tenure in the company. "Well, yes...ah, that is true. I learned the trade from my mother. She performed at the Haymarket before marrying my father. She read Molière to me when I was in leading strings."

"Ah," Bea said with a nod of approval, although she was not entirely sure the playwright's impiety was appropriate subject matter for a small child, "so I don't have to tell you what a finely honed instrument a theater is. Everything must operate precisely according to plan, or the whole undertaking collapses. I trust you are familiar with the Globe?"

Once again, he seemed taken aback by the question. Nevertheless, he responded that, yes, he was familiar with it. "My father kept a small one in the parlor. He liked to point out the movements of French and British troops during the Peninsula War."

Bea did not know if this particularly obtuse response could be attributed to the deleterious effects of pain or guilt on one's mental faculties or if Mr. Fairbrother was simply not very clever.

"I meant the Globe theater," she explained.

"Yes, yes, of course you did," he said quickly, the color in his cheeks rising slightly in embarrassment as he stuttered an apology for misunderstanding. "Why would you care about the objects in my family's parlor," he mumbled before adding more clearly, "Yes, I know the Globe. Shakespeare's theater. My mother played Ophelia once."

"Then you know how it came to its disastrous end," she said.

Fairbrother nodded as if he did indeed know, but when he spoke, his tone was inflected with uncertainty. "A fire, wasn't it? It burned the theater down."

"And what caused the fire?" she asked.

"I'm not entirely sure I remember that detail," he admitted with a contrite smile. "Was it a candle? Did someone behind stage knock over a candle and the scenery ignited?"

It was, Bea thought, a reasonable guess and very likely the way several other profitable theaters had met their end. But not Shakespeare's. "It was a misfire of a cannon. All it took for the Globe to literally disappear was a single misfire of a cannon during a performance of *Henry VIII*."

The actor nodded as if confirming a detail he had all but forgotten. "Yes, of course. The misfire. Such an unfortunate accident."

"So you see now why Mr. Harper and I are here," she said firmly.

Exhaustion flitted across the actor's face as he contemplated this assertion, which, it was clear, eluded him entirely. Incapable of making a coherent reply, he shrugged his shoulders and dropped his hands into his lap in utter defeat. Then, as the agony seared through him, he cried out in pain.

Determinedly, he sought to hide the severity of his discomfort, and Bea watched him take several shallow breaths while smiling with aggressive insouciance. All in all, it seemed very uncomfortable for him, and she could only imagine how cross he was to have a visitor who insisted on quizzing him rather than stating her purpose forthrightly.

Taking sympathy on him, she said, "Theaters are vulnerable to human error. Four performances of *Henry VII* proceeded without issue. Four times at the end of act one, King Henry entered the stage for the scene in Cardinal Wolsey's home to the sound of stage cannons. Four times those cannons discharged harmlessly. But the fifth time during the fifth performance? A stray piece of flaming detritus landed on the theater's thatched roof, sparked a fire and destroyed the entire theater. We are here, Mr. Fairbrother, to ascertain if you are a stray piece of flaming detritus. I trust you will be so kind as to provide us with the details we need so that we may come to a conclusion on our own."

The request terrified him.

As with the pain, he sought to disguise his reaction with sheer self-control, loosening the smile that momentarily tightened, blinking eyelids that had gone suddenly wide. He reached out again for the cane, and realizing it was still on the floor, leaned to the side to pick it up. He kept his head down slightly longer than was necessary, no doubt to give himself a few extra seconds to gather his thoughts.

Bea, in no hurry, allowed him the fleeting respite, and, waiting until his back was straight, assured him that he may begin his explanation. "We are all ears."

Fairbrother flinched at the eagerness in her tone but gamely began his narration by setting the scene in exhaustive detail. "It is at the end of the third act, and Mysore has started to realize that all his plans would come to naught. His brother would marry the secret princess and ascend to the throne and he would be driven from the kingdom where he has lived his whole life. He is starting to feel desperate and alone, and the panic of those emotions turns to hatred because everything he has done has been out of love for his country and now his country is rejecting him. And the princess, who had professed to love him, has abandoned him because he isn't the rich merchant he pretended to be. It is devastating to him because he has fallen in love with her despite his determination to remain indifferent to her beauty. He only wanted access to the vast wealth she would command upon her marriage in order to lessen the suffering of the serfs who toiled in the fields. But all that has been undone by his brother's scheming. And that is where we pick up the scene, with Mysore by himself in the forest realizing he has a quiver full of arrows and his bow. He gives a wonderful soliloquy, full of fire and passion, and just as I am resolving to confront my brother once and for all, I take a step backward—because, as you know, I am facing the audience—and knock into a tree. The tree knocks another tree down and it feels as though the whole forest is falling on top of me, so I reach out to steady myself, grabbing hold of the rampart, which I pull toward me with great force, causing a rupture in the base, and then I hear a terrible cracking sound and the lower half of my body is suddenly trapped under a hundred pounds of wood and plaster and I can barely remain sensible for the ferocity of the pain."

Finishing his tale with that melodramatic flourish, Fairbrother slouched in his chair, visibly relieved. Alas, even that minor movement was too abrupt for his injury and he tried with little success to conceal the fresh wave of agony that overtook him. Bea, who had found his tale to be light on the details that mattered, waited patiently for the pain to subside before asking him to clarify exactly how he had reached for the rampart.

Kesgrave, however, required no further information to cry foul on Fairbrother's story. "The pain you are experiencing is too sharp and focused to have been caused by the injury you described. Rather than a bruise, you have a deep gash that runs several inches across your thigh."

Fairbrother raised his head at a defiant angle, as if to deny the charge, then crumbled under the weight of the duke's authoritative stare.

"It was Chatterley," he said, looking at his fists, which were clutched again around the cane. "It was Chatterley. He did it."

Briefly, Bea thought it was a confession—an admission that he had in some way been involved in the evil deed if not its principal architect—but that belief was immediately dispelled as Fairbrother continued.

"Damn his eyes, embroiling me in this madness! Chatterley knows I cannot resist a bet and that as soon as he made the proposition, I would be powerless to refuse," he said, the harsh lines of his face taking on a peevish childishness as he complained. "And, really, it was unsporting of him to keep offering me the opportunity to double my winnings if I could shave more and more seconds off my time."

Bewildered as to the exact nature of the wager, Bea glanced at Kesgrave to see if he had a better sense of what Chatterley had spurred the other man to do and, noting his blank expression, decided he was equally at sea.

"Shave time off what activity?" she asked.

Fairbrother's eyes darted around the room, clearly looking for an escape, and settled with thoughtful consideration on the window behind the settee, as if he were mobile enough to dash across the floor, leap over the sofa and climb through the casement.

Bea felt confident he would swoon from pain before he even got his first leg over the high back of the settee—a realization he must have arrived at himself, for he sighed as if in defeat and rounded his shoulders again, sinking further into his seat. The movement caused another anguish-filled pang that darted across his face before churlish defiance supplanted it and he looked fleetingly like a little boy being held to account by his nanny. A moment later, however, he seemed to recall Mr. and Mrs. Harper's position as possible investors at his place of employment and the rebelliousness fled.

"Slipping through the corner trap before it snapped shut," he said.

It sounded like madness, the challenge Chatterley had laid down, for although Bea did not know the details of how trap doors worked in general—or the corner trap in particular— she had gleaned enough information from La Clairon's memoir to realize that the area under the stage bore an oddly striking resemblance to a sailing ship, with its ropes, blocks and tackle. To raise a platform to the stage was no mean task, requiring an elaborate pulley system, a great drum, and a team of men to operate them. Even if the corner trap was a smaller, simpler version, it still seemed like an act of utter folly for a performer to play with the valuable and complicated apparatus for sport.

"Chatterley was operating it?" she asked.

"Yes, which is not an easy thing to do without help, but he handled the mechanism masterfully," he said, unable to smother the spark of admiration that entered his voice. "It was a golden opportunity because all the various people who would protest our...that is, who might *advise* us to reconsider our actions...were in assorted meetings: the stage mechanics, scene designers, the wardrobe executors. It would have been churlish to turn down the wager. All I had to do was pass through the trap within the allotted time, which would not have harmed the equipment because it was designed to open and close countless times during a performance. When I got through the door with twenty-two seconds to spare, Chatterley, as I said, suggested a revised allotment. I won that as well, and Chatterley, now out a shilling rather than a few pence, suggested we double the bet so that I would get either twice as much or nothing. I did this three times, each successfully. Then snap!"

He clapped his hands to emphasize the slamming of the door and winced either at the memory of the brutal blow or at a fresh stab of pain that coursed through him at the movement. "It sliced clean through my breeches and cut my thigh. Blimey, it hurt. Like a bug—er, like the devil, Mrs. Harper. It hurt like the devil. It was so painful, I thought I might faint right there on the stage. And the blood. There was so much of it, on the flap itself and dripping onto the floor under the stage. Chatterley, the miscreant, was no help. He was laughing. I could hear it over the dizzy throbbing in my head. I could barely see for the searing pain in my thigh and he was giggling like a lord up to his eyeballs in blue ruin. But then he saw the blood and sobered up. He knew what it would mean if Smeeton or Miss Drake found out we had been playing with the corner trap. We would be chucked out of the company so hard and fast, our feet wouldn't touch the ground until we hit Tunbridge Wells. That was when he came up with the plan to make it look like the scenery collapsed. 'Let's say the rampart fell on you, Fairbrother. It was the rampart!' I knew it wasn't quite sporting, but I went along with him because I didn't see any other way out."

He fell silent then, no doubt contemplating his imperiled future. All that fine scheming and he'd probably wind up as a minor player in some obscure theater company in the wilds of Yorkshire—damn interfering investors!

If Bea was astonished at all by this tale of wanton destruction, it was by how closely it matched her own speculation, for she had considered the possibility that Fairbrother had destroyed the rampart to disguise his involvement in Hobson's death. She wanted to attribute that fact to her talent for deductive reasoning but knew it had more to do with the inadequacy of the lie. The enfeebled scenery story had never made sense.

As for the veracity of the rest of his account, she had no idea and no amount of questioning would prove as conclusive as a single glance at his wound.

But how to contrive a look?

Given how eager he seemed to please his possible new employers, she decided to cower him with a mix of outrage and concern. "Goodness gracious, Mr. Fairbrother, I cannot believe anyone would behave with such feckless stupidity! Just think of the damage you could have done to the stage and to yourself! Several hundred pounds of destruction! And you—you're lucky to have suffered only a wound to your leg.

You might have severed a limb. Indeed, you might still. Come, let me take a look so that I may put my mind at ease."

Once again, his face lost all color as he stared at her in appalled dismay for several moments before stuttering, "Mrs. Harper...you cannot possibly mean...I cannot bring myself...it is not the thing to..." Unable to finish the horrifying thought, he trailed off.

Patently, Bea knew she could not make the observation herself, but she resisted his increasingly desperate pleas for discretion for a full minute simply to heighten his unease. Then she made a great show of succumbing to his appeals by reluctantly allowing Mr. Harper to make the inspection.

Although this offer was much better than the original, the actor continued to protest.

"There is nothing for it, Mr. Fairbrother, so you may cease your complaining," Bea said impatiently. "I am an altruistic and public-spirited woman, and as such I cannot leave you here without reassuring myself that you are not about to lose your leg to gangrene."

At the mention of gangrene, Fairbrother adopted an expression of abject terror and looked far younger than his six and twenty years. "Do...do you think that's possible?"

"Possible?" she asked, mercilessly pressing her advantage. "My good man, I think it's probable. I cannot imagine the physician you and Chatterley managed to find treated the wound properly. Now do remove your trousers so that Mr. Harper may take a look. He was a field doctor during the war. If you ask, he will rattle off the battles at which he performed surgery in chronological order."

Although Fairbrother was relieved to discover he was in the presence of a medical professional, the supposed medical professional himself was not as pleased about the news and glowered intimidatingly at its bearer. Bea stared blithely back, undaunted by his surliness, for she had no patience for his delicate sensibilities. Furthermore, she could not comprehend the source of his annoyance, as examining the wound had been the sole purpose of their visit. They would never discover the cause of the injury without looking at it. Would she have much rather made the inspection herself? Of course. There was nothing like knowledge personally attained to allow one to be confident in its accuracy. But her offer had been roundly rebuffed, making Kesgrave the only logical option.

Fairbrother, grateful now for her coercion, admitted he'd been deeply concerned about the thick yellowish substance that seeped through the sutures.

At this description, Kesgrave's scowl darkened but he noted calmly to his patient that sometimes pus was a sign of healing. "It varies depending on the particulars of the case," he explained as he offered his arm to the actor and helped him to his feet. Then he suggested he perform the examination in the privacy of the bedchamber, a proposal to which Fairbrother enthusiastically agreed before asking if he had attended to patients at Waterloo. The duke sent his beloved one final angry glare as he closed the door.

Bea had not sought the opportunity to search his rooms with abandon, but now that it had been presented to her, she lost no time in making a thorough review of his possessions. The space was small and contained mostly impersonal necessities like plates, baskets and candlesticks. In the cabinet, she found a yellowed tablecloth neatly folded next to a porcelain pitcher with a cracked handle. The items on the shelves near the stove were equally uninteresting, as were the articles in the small writing desk next to the settee.

A wooden box on the mantelpiece held a pair of small notebooks, the first of which detailed various household expenses, including how much Fairbrother had spent on apples and mutton in the past month. The second book recorded his gambling debts, which, at only eleven pounds and some shillings, struck her as minor, considering his reckless proclivities. Hobson held his largest debt at six pounds, with Chatterley close behind at four. Based solely on the numbers, killing the former was the better use of one's villainy, for eliminating him also meant eliminating the majority of his debt. But in actuality, Chatterley was the far bigger threat, for his impetuosity and the effortless way he provoked Fairbrother into impulsive and imprudent behavior presented a genuine danger to his well-being.

You are being too rational, Bea told herself as she returned the notebook to the box. Murder was rarely a highly considered affair. More often than not, it was a spontaneous act borne out of fleeting and overwhelming emotion. Such was the case with Lady Skeffington, who, in the moment before bashing Mr. Otley over the head with a candlestick, had had no thought at all of bashing Mr. Otley over the head with a candlestick.

In the rash version of events, Kesgrave's explanation for the chaotic state of the crime scene made sense, for what he proposed was little different from Chatterley's idea of destroying the rampart. A terrible thing happened that must be made to look like another terrible thing.

Diabolical indeed, she thought, examining a small stack of books on the pedestal table next to the settee. A varied assortment, the pile contained a guide to mastering piquet, a history of Persia, a collection of stories about the ancient art of pugilism and a slim volume on horse racing. The titles were as uninteresting as they were unenlightening, and she replaced them on the table. A moment later, the bedchamber door opened and Kesgrave stepped out.

"And you are *absolutely convinced* the wound is healing properly?" Fairbrother asked, the concern evident in his tone. "I would not keep asking but, you see, the expression on your face when you first looked at it indicated otherwise."

Firmly, the duke assured him his injury was mending very well. "As you know, it will take some time before you can put your full weight on it. I am sorry if my expression discomfited you. It has been some time since I have been on the battlefield, and the sight of your wound brought back many troubling memories."

Immediately contrite, Fairbrother apologized for exposing him to such unpleasantness and promised to be more thoughtful in the future. When Kesgrave reminded the actor that it had been his idea, the other man insisted he should have tried harder to discourage his interest. "As you are a busy theater owner with many important responsibilities and obligations, you cannot be expected to think of minor details such as the condition of my leg," he said with determined obsequiousness.

Having no desire to linger, Kesgrave accepted his apology and bid him good day. Fairbrother, delighted to be allowed his guilt, was nevertheless unsatisfied with the exchange, for he had no idea what determination Mrs. Harper had made.

"Determination?" Bea asked, slightly taken aback by the question. Surely, he did not know he was a suspect in her murder investigation.

"As to my status," he explained anxiously. "Am I a stray piece of flaming detritus?"

Oh, yes, of course, yes, Bea thought, his rambunctious dealings with the corner trap. "Mr. Fairbrother, Shakespeare's misfiring cannon was an innocuous mound of wrought iron compared to you and Chatterley. Nevertheless, I will hold my tongue and not mention what I have learned to Miss Drake, as your egregious injury is punishment enough for your exceedingly poor judgment. I can only hope your recklessness will be chastened by both my generosity and this painful interlude. Now, if you will excuse us, we have other matters to attend to. I wish you a speedy recovery."

"Yes, yes, of course," he said, his relief palatable as he surged forward to escort her to the door, briefly forgetting his condition and putting all his weight on his wounded leg. Incapable of swallowing the excruciating stab, he howled in agony as his face turned white.

"Do take a seat, Mr. Fairbrother," she said, "and we shall show ourselves out."

As soon as Bea and the duke started down the staircase, she sought to confirm her suspicion by asking him about the injury.

"It was grotesque," he said sharply. "The skin was apparently squeezed and sliced at the same time, creating bruising and a deep incision that was sutured with black string. I have no idea if it is healing properly and will send my personal physician at once to examine it."

Bea applauded this plan, as his description of the wound aligned exactly with the damage one would expect from a trap door. Then she hailed the success of their morning visit, for having eliminated two suspects, Chatterley alongside Fairbrother, they had to account now for only two. She recommended they hold a frank conversation with Miss Drake next and began to suggest the best manner with which to raise the issue of her plagiarism. Kesgrave, however, was not finished discussing Mr. Fairbrother's leg—or, rather, the brutal way he had been exposed to it without notice.

Naturally, Bea scoffed at the notion that he had not been warned, as the situation itself had made the expectation apparent to anyone with an awareness of logic. "If you choose to cultivate a healthy disregard for reason, then that is your decision and I cannot see how I am to be held responsible."

As the Duke of Kesgrave considered himself to be among the most rational men in the kingdom, if not *the* most, he took great exception to this charge, and while his carriage rambled along Fenchurch toward the Particular, he explicated in detail all the ways her assumption was incorrect. Delightedly, she refuted each one, sometimes descending into illogic just to provoke his pique, and by the time they arrived at the theater, Kesgrave was resigned to inspecting all gangrenous limbs as a condition of their marriage.

Chapter Fifteen

The pleasure that flashed in Miss Drake's eyes upon seeing the Harpers at her office door was quickly supplanted by a woeful frown, and she professed herself to be utterly despondent at the prospect of sharing unhappy news.

"It is my father," she explained, her head tilted down as if slightly embarrassed by her recalcitrant relative. "He could not be persuaded to accept your proposal. It was the amount you offered, you see. He did not think it was commensurate with the stake you require. I tried to convince him of its fairness, but he is fixed in his opinion."

As hopeless as the situation was, she invited her guests to linger by gesturing to the pair of chairs next to her work table —an indication, Bea thought, that the rejection was not so much an insurmountable obstruction on the road to an agreement as merely a slight bump to be navigated carefully. Miss Drake confirmed this suspicion a moment later when she sighed heavily and lamented her helplessness in the situation. "If only there was something *I* could do to change his mind."

Bea, who had perceived her meaning without the extra emphasis on the word *I,* was a little insulted the other woman thought they were too obtuse to understand. Nevertheless, she appreciated a tough-minded negotiating tactic and decided to return it in equal measure. Her original plan to introduce the issue of plagiarism had been to approach the topic gingerly by first gushing over the woman's skill and talent.

Now, settling comfortably into the chair, Bea smiled warmly and assured Miss Drake there was no cause for such dejection. "We had already decided not to invest in the Particular, and that is the reason for our visit. We did not want you to labor under a misapprehension for a moment longer than necessary, and a good thing, too, for it seems as though we may have created friction between you and your father."

Miss Drake, who had clearly mapped out a different version of the conversation in her head, stared in confusion at Bea, her eyelids fluttering as she sought to understand how her plan had gone awry so quickly. The Harpers were supposed to counter, not withdraw!

While the other woman gathered her thoughts, Bea explained that the Adelphi could not align itself with a theater that was tainted by plagiarism. "Obviously, you are welcome to operate the Particular in any manner you wish, and as the daughter of the owner, you are well within your right to ruthlessly appropriate the work of one of your subordinates and present it as your own. We would never presume to lecture you on morality, Miss Drake, however insufficient we find yours. But Mr. Harper and I have higher standards and cannot involve ourselves in something so sordid. We are, of course, grateful for your hospitality and think you run a very fine theater. I trust it goes without saying that we wish you the best of luck, and please do thank your father as well for entertaining our offer, as unsatisfactory as it was."

Bea wasn't entirely sure what reaction she'd hoped to

provoke with her speech, for she could not easily imagine a murderess feeling embarrassment or shame at being called a plagiarist. Perhaps astonishment that her infamous deed had been discovered or maybe anger at the temerity of a provincial theater owner daring to hold her to account. Certainly, she had acted with impunity for several years, and suffering little consequence for her dishonesty no doubt increased her own sense of self-worth. Bea would not have been surprised to discover that Miss Drake considered herself to be the actual author of the plays she stole.

A display of scorn, too, was not entirely out of the realm of possibility, for there were few better ways to dismiss an argument than to show it contempt. With all these viable options, Bea was not at all disconcerted when Miss Drake dissolved into a fit of giggles. She herself had used the ploy several times in her investigations and knew it to be an effective tactic.

Miss Drake, being of a theatrical bent, was somewhat more effusive in her simulation of amusement, and Bea waited patiently for the exhibition to end so that she could ask useful follow-up questions about her relationship with Mr. Hobson.

Finally, Miss Drake's laughter receded and she apologized for her unruly response. "I simply did not expect that matter to rear its head during this meeting. My focus was on persuading you to raise your offer so that I may return to my father, who is, I truly believe, intrigued by the prospect of investors despite his claims of utter indifference. But this"— she tittered again but held herself together—"came as a complete shock. It should not have, of course, for I have worked hard to make sure everyone in the theater knew my secret. Thank you for your strong disapproval, for I am much comforted by the rigidity of your morals. Plagiarism is a serious offense and should be treated as such. Now I am more eager than ever to work with you and will redouble my efforts to convince my father."

As she spoke, she lowered her chin and slipped the gold chain that hung around her neck over her head, revealing a key. Skillfully, she unlocked a compartment, barely discernable to the unknowing eye, in the side of the table and removed a neat stack of bound papers. She put the sheets down and slid them across for Beatrice to examine.

"As you are in the theater as well, Mrs. Harper, I am confident I will not have to explain all the ways this profession treats women differently from men," Miss Drake said pragmatically. "We will simply take it as an article of faith. That being the case I know you will understand the lengths I had to go to convince the actors in this theater to perform my work. I've written every word of my plays myself, sometimes to great difficulty and pain, for writing is not an easy occupation, but I was forced to hire Robert to appear as their author in order to induce the company to take them seriously," she explained as she nodded at the documentation before them. "Aware of the dubiousness of that claim, I have ensured that every aspect of the arrangement has been recorded and verified by a trusted legal source. Here is the agreement between Mr. Hobson and myself, with the name and address of my solicitor. Naturally, I do not expect you to take my word for it and encourage you to visit Mr. Potts for confirmation of all I've said. He is also in possession of all the originals of my plays, as well as every draft I have worked on. I have done this, not in expectation of convincing investors but with an eye toward posterity. I refuse to allow the annals of history to credit Robert Hobson with authorship of my plays. Marlowe made that mistake with Shakespeare and see where it got him?"

With a glance at Kesgrave, who seemed equally disconcerted by the development, Bea picked up the contract and read the first page. Clearly and concisely, it delineated everything Miss Drake had just said in slightly more legal terms. Page two detailed Mr. Hobson's responsibilities, among which was a requirement to let slip to the principal actor of the company—Daniel Latham—the truth about the works' authorship. Guidelines for how to make this revelation were provided alongside possible responses from his associates. The following page listed compensation—primarily a monthly stipend with quarterly opportunities to earn bonuses.

All in all, it was an astounding document.

It was also, she thought, persuasive.

Before Bea could respond to the agreement or even Christopher Marlowe's slide into partial obscurity, Miss Drake handed her a slip of paper with her solicitor's address. "I will send Mr. Potts a note alerting him to your intention to visit. He cares for his ailing mother and usually works in the morning, but of course he will make himself available at your convenience. I know he will be happy to answer any questions you might have. If you are satisfied with my morality, I would like to resume our discussion of your offer. As I said, there really isn't anything I can do to change my father's opinion. He is stubborn. If you are sincere in your intention and would genuinely like to invest in the Particular, I would recommend increasing your bid by a pony or two. It's a token amount but would go a long way in appeasing his vanity."

Bemused by the breakneck speed with which Miss Drake returned to the matter of their investment, Bea kept her eyes focused on the fourth page of the contract, which catalogued the number of plays Mr. Hobson was to produce each year and their particular genres. Before reentering into a counterfeit negotiation, she needed a moment to organize her thoughts, for she did not know what bearing Miss Drake's act of deliberate misdirection had on the situation. Did it make her less inclined to murder Hobson or more?

Thoughtfully, Bea handed the document to the duke to peruse and congratulated Miss Drake on her thoroughness. "Rarely have I seen such a meticulous contract. You appeared to have considered every possibility. Tell me, what is your contingency plan in the event of Hobson's passing?"

Now Miss Drake's face took on the first hint of embarrassment. "Ah, yes, that is the question, isn't it? It pains me to admit it, but the prospect of his dying before his usefulness was at an end did not occur to me. I made sure to tie him to the theater for ten years, at which point we would either go our separate ways or come to a new agreement, but as for the other...." Her voice trailed off as she lifted her shoulder in a sort of baffled shrug. "It simply did not, and now I am in quite a scrape. It's a terrible thing to say because a man has lost his life, and yet I cannot deny that his death is a great inconvenience to me. I have no concern for the immediate future because it will be easy enough to claim I found a cache of plays in a box beneath his bed or in the wardrobe. But how many can I realistically expect to find? Quite a limited number, I assure you. The only solution is to find another man who would be willing to go along with my scheme, which sounds simple but is actually complex. You will not be surprised to learn, Mrs. Harper, that most men are not eager to allow a woman to take credit for their work even when that work was hers to begin with."

Bea agreed that it sounded like a daunting task and asked if that was truly the only avenue open to her. "The Particular has been performing your plays for years to great acclaim. Have you not earned the company's respect? Would admitting the truth now really undo years of good work?"

Miss Drake laughed and shook her head at what she called Mrs. Harper's charming display of naiveté. "It is all about the setting of a thing. A worn swath of yellow silk that looks golden in candlelight appears faded in the full light of day. My work cannot bear the sunlight."

Once again, Bea found herself swayed by Miss Drake's argument, for it comported with her own experience. Indeed, just the week before she had looked on in disgust as male guests at Lord Pudsey's political salon listened with serious consideration to a weak-chinned man make the exact same argument against the elimination of the income tax that they had dismissed from her friend Mrs. Palmer.

It was a maddening set of competing standards.

Was it maddening enough, Bea thought, to drive the theater owner to murder? She had made her commitment to posterity clear—for the admiration of future generations she was willing to suffer the scorn of her contemporaries. What if Hobson had threatened to undermine her long-term plans by revealing the truth now? Her carefully constructed house of cards would tumble to the ground and she would never be able to rebuild it, for it was impossible to carry out the same deception twice.

In that situation, Miss Drake's alarmingly specific contract would be a strike against her because it demonstrated how deep her play went. Every single aspect of her game had been premeditated.

If Hobson had wanted to extract more money from her, all he had to do was threaten to publish their contract in the dailies. Nothing in Bea's research, however, indicated that he required immediate funds, and if he continued with the contract he would be compensated nicely without any risk of a negative outcome.

Ah, but need was rarely the basis for greed, she thought cynically.

Aware that she had allowed the silence to drag on a little too long, Bea admitted with feigned embarrassment that her observation had been uncharacteristically naïve. "Normally, I take a much dimmer view of human nature. Indeed, I would look at your arrangement with Hobson and wonder how long it would take him to realize he held the upper hand."

Bea, who firmly believed that even the most dyed-in-the-world villain would show some remorse when confronted with an unsettlingly accurate observation, such as an eye flicker or a muscle twitch, had no idea what to make of Miss Drake's glee.

Beaming with approval, the theater manager clapped her hands as if delighted by a performance and cheered happily. "Brava, Mrs. Harper! Do not tell me you aren't a gifted story-teller in your own right, for you have to have some experience in the craft to come up with a plot so insidious. Now, let me see, what did I do to poor Hobson to protect my secret? Run him through with the rake myself? Or perhaps the scene played out more impulsively? I sought to confront him about his threats, our conversation quickly became heated and I pushed him back and he tripped and fell on to the rake, impaling himself. Oh, cruel fate, making me a murderess when all I wanted to do was plead my case! Oh, but that is the way fate works, doesn't it, moving us around the board like chess pieces. We all think we are the queen, but we are merely pawns. I wonder why in your scenario I followed him to the stables," she said.

Miss Drake's demeanor turned thoughtful as she consid-ered the matter, and Bea could not decide if she was being mocked for an absurd suggestion or diverted from an insightful one.

"I suppose to make my participation appear more unlike-ly," Miss Drake continued in the same pensive vein. "Because the first question everyone would ask would be precisely that —why the stables—so doing it there makes the mystery itself more confusing. It muddies the waters, which should be any murderer's first goal. In that case it would be quite clever of me to do it at the stables because that makes no sense of all." She nodded with approval, as if genuinely impressed by her own deviousness. Then she sighed and looked at Beatrice with a sincerely woeful frown that bore no resemblance to the facsimile she had presented upon their arrival. "As much as I desire your good opinion, I cannot allow you think I am that ingenious when I'm in fact much more dull. Do let me prove it to you."

Miss Drake rose to her feet with a good-natured grin, opened the door and called to Smeeton to fetch the director. "I'm sure he will be along shortly. I saw him only a half hour ago pestering Mr. Vokes to make doubly sure the rampart is secure. Ah, there you are, Mr. Rowe. Have you met Mr. and Mrs. Harper, our visitors from Bath who are interested in investing in our theater? I was just telling them about Tuesday's morning rehearsal. It was during that rehearsal that you realized the jester's motivation was not clear and insisted I revise the scene right away."

Although her tone was neutral, holding no criticism or rebuke, Mr. Rowe responded as if he'd been censured and launched into a passionate defense of the eleventh-hour change, arguing that it was impossible to get a complete sense of a work's power until all the elements came together. "Scenery! Property! Costumes! The script is important, of course it is. Words are the walls that prop up the story. But they are just one aspect. The intensity of a performance comes from the combination of all these things, from the way they work in tandem to articulate meaning and encapsulate feeling. This is why I couldn't possibly know that the central conceit of the play did not work until I saw Jacopo, the soul of my story, standing among the trappings of royalty in his fool's cap and brandishing a bauble. There he was, the inane jester expounding on his desire to be a great tragedian, and with every jingle of his hat's bells, I could feel the folly of his dream. But I couldn't feel the pain because I didn't know where this deep and abiding longing came from. *That* was vital. Without accounting for the source of his pain, the story is only a mildly entertaining piece about a misguided fool. And that could not stand!"

As he spoke, Miss Drake, assuming the Harpers were equally familiar with the excessive fervor of ardently devoted directors, looked at them with pointed amusement.

When his spleen had been properly vented, she calmly reminded him that she had not objected to the changes. "In fact, I agreed that your critique was valid and returned to my office to rewrite the soliloquy during the break between rehearsals. I said the revisions would take about an hour. Did they take me an hour, Mr. Rowe?"

Now the director's expression turned slightly abashed and his shoulders slouched forward as he muttered no.

"Why not?" Miss Drake asked.

"Because I interrupted at regular intervals to gauge your progress," he admitted quietly. Then he added with renewed fervor, "Given how little time we had before the play's premiere to address my concerns, I did not think it prudent to allow you the opportunity to go off in the wrong direction. The situation called for strong oversight, and I will not apologize for providing it."

It was apparent from Miss Drake's patient expression that Mr. Rowe did not apologize for many things and with a firm nod, she thanked him. The gratitude was for providing the answers she sought, but Mr. Rowe assumed it was for his supervision with the script and immediately assured her it was all in a day's work.

"I cannot in all good conscience give you less than my absolute best, however that might inconvenience you," he added self-importantly.

"I know, Mr. Rowe," she said with a hint of resigned wryness. "I know. Now if you will excuse us? The Harpers and I still have much to discuss."

Although taken aback to find himself dismissed from the conversation, he left the office. Miss Drake closed the door behind him and sat down across from Bea.

"I trust that settles matters to your satisfaction," she said calmly. "I do not blame you, Mrs. Harper, for allowing your imagination to run amok. You came here today believing I was a plagiarist and, unable to accept the fact of my decency, invented a new crime to lay at my feet. I understand the impulse entirely and might have made the leap myself if I weren't so stubbornly practical."

Naturally, Bea could not bear the accusation of fancifulness without bristling, but she was too resolutely sensible to issue an objection. Instead, she smiled and apologized for making such an absurd and defamatory assumption.

"I sometimes speak without thinking," she explained while silently toying with the possibility that Miss Drake and Mr. Rowe were working in concert. If they both had a hand in Hobson's demise, then they would have established their stories in advance. An interview with either one of them would have yielded the same result.

How probable was it?

The answer depended on what the director had to gain from the murder. Could he have been another victim of Hobson's greed? Or had he acted out of a desire to protect Miss Drake?

Bea recalled the way the theater manager had treated Mr. Rowe and decided it was unlikely that they were romantically involved. There had been no hint of fondness in her exasperation, only impatience.

"You must not apologize," Miss Drake announced in blithe dismissal, "for your accusing me of murder is the best thing that could have happened for our future partnership. It has allowed me to demonstrate what a fair-minded and even-tempered associate I will be, and for that I'm grateful. I am confident that my easygoing nature has material value to you. Shall we say it's worth another fifty quid? Or am I being too modest? Perhaps one hundred pounds? Dare I go as high as one fifty?"

With each new amount, her voice altered a little, increasing in volume and excitement, like an auctioneer at Christie's trying to rouse the interest of buyers in the back of the room. Emboldened by her own game, Miss Drake raised her bid by another fifty pounds and, vowing to gain her father's compliance, lifted her right hand as if to ring an imaginary bell to proclaim the sale.

No, Bea thought, not a bell. Auction sales were marked by a hammer striking a blow against a rostrum. She'd never attended one, of course, for no Hyde-Clare would presume to gaze upon the treasured artifacts of a recently deceased aristocrat with interest, let alone with an eye toward possessing them herself, but she'd read enough descriptions to know how they worked.

Yet the idea of a bell persisted in Bea's mind, even after Miss Drake lowered her hand and pressed for a commitment. Kesgrave, incapable of treating the sham negotiation as the fiction it was, proposed the Harpers take a higher percentage of the profits in exchange for a larger investment that would increase annually at a fixed rate.

And still Bea heard bells—not, she realized, the deeply resonant clang of a church set, cast in thick alloy and pitched to draw worshippers to service. No, the sound was far more frothy, far more lighter and airier, tingly and tinny, like the giddy chime of a sleigh bell.

Yes, that was precisely it: a sleigh bell.

Ah, but not a sleigh bell, for only moments ago Mr. Rowe

had observed the effective juxtaposition of a jester solilo-quizing his longing to be a great tragedian while the bells of his fool's cap tinkled frivolously.

Clearly, it was a jingle bell that dinged in her head.

She had no sooner made the distinction, however, than she wondered if there was a difference. Were they not made in the same foundry and merely distributed varyingly for use?

Miss Drake suggested an annual increase of ten percent, to which Kesgrave scoffed dismissively as he countered with three, and Bea impatiently wondered why sleigh bells and jingle bells mattered at all.

Undeterred, Miss Drake tapped a ledger as if indicating that the book's contents justified her audacity, then proposed a modest seven percent, and Bea, who was firmly seated in her chair, felt curiously unstable as she recalled the sensation of slipping on a book in the bedchamber in Milford Lane.

The worn copy on the care of Thoroughbreds—it had rolled on a sleigh bell.

Not a sleigh bell!

As Bea's breath caught in her throat at the piece of evidence that attached Latham to the crime, she told herself it was not conceivable for him to be the culprit. He had been asleep in his dressing room during the time in question, Smeeton had said. Indeed, Smeeton had specifically stated that he had seen the actor resting on his sofa at two o'clock.

But *had* he?

Bea struggled to recall the stage manager's exact words, something about peering into the actor's darkened room.

Peering, which was usually done from the doorway.

Smeeton had definitely seen someone asleep on the sofa, but that did not mean he actually saw Latham. The actor could have recruited someone to hide under the blanket to give the appearance of his presence. From the doorway, in the dark, Smeeton would never have been able to tell the difference. It could have been one of the British Museum's stuffed giraffes for all he knew.

Well, no, that notion was absurd, for a giraffe's body bore no resemblance at all to a human male's. But another animal, like a zebra or a lion.

Yes, a lion, she thought, picturing the assortment of costumes that had hung from the wall in Latham's dressing room. A lion was among them.

Suddenly, Bea stiffened as she recalled seeing the other half of the lion regalia in the cellar.

A wildly implausible idea occurred to her.

Ah, but *was* it wildly implausible?

Yesterday, in the storage room, when she was unnerved by the hollow orange eyes of the demon, Miss Drake had praised the ingenuity of the wardrobe designer: *You see a demon head now, but this costume was originally a donkey's head* for A Midsummer Night's Dream. *Our wardrobe designer turned it into a lion's head for* The Flower or the Forgery, *and then, when our Dr. Faust needed to look like a demon in last year's production of* The Devil Awakens, *Mrs. Tapsell altered it again. And it will remain here until we have a new need for it.*

Oh, but it hadn't remained there, had it?

She recalled the thick layer of dust that coated the Pulcinella mask directly beside it on the shelf—a thick layer that had been absent from the demon head.

Absent because someone had retrieved it from the shelf, cleaned off its coating of dust and laid it on the sofa in Latham's dressing room.

The sequence of events made sense and yet it was madness, for what cause could Latham have to harm his fellow actor? By all accounts, Hobson was an enthusiastic and sycophantic presence, eager and determined to please. An accomplished toady, Miss Calcott described him, whose fawning was perfectly set to endear himself to Latham's vanity.

Short of calling Latham a mediocre actor who lacked the intelligence to comprehend the confines of his own limited range, she could not imagine how Hobson could manage to alienate his friend's affection. Furthermore, not a hint of a rupture had spread among the company, which was, Bea thought, meaningful, for Smeeton had observed that the theater was rife with gossip: *There are no secrets, so we are compelled to invent them.*

And the acoustics of the building were horrible, inexpertly designed to ensure that the wrong noises carried. How had Miss Calcott described them?

Sound barely travels from the stage to the upper boxes, and yet in the dressing rooms you can hear a script drop to the table.

Plainly, the two actors did not have a violent falling-out. If a rift existed, it was much milder in nature and spurred, most likely, by Latham's resentment, for dogged flatterers did not easily take offense. The only advantage Hobson had in the relationship was as the Particular's favorite playwright, for, as Steagle and Gofton had both attested, Latham was always angling for better roles.

Could that have been the source of the conflict? Latham demanded a better role—more lines, greater heroics, larger emotions—and Hobson, not actually being the author of the piece, was unable to oblige him? Peeved by the refusal and unaccustomed to being denied anything, especially by the servile Hobson, perhaps Latham had seethed bitterly over the insult, his anger growing by degrees until it was roiling with such fury he could do nothing but devise a scheme to demonstrate once and for all that he would not suffer a slight to his ego by an obsequious lackey who was lucky to bathe in the light of *his* glory.

It was a theory, to be sure, but Bea could not persuade

herself that anyone would respond so extremely to being denied a part in a play. Even a gleaming gem of a part would not justify—

Then, like the last puzzle piece snapping cleanly into place, Bea saw the complete picture.

Gleaming gem of a part indeed, she thought, as she realized Latham had overheard just enough of the conversation between Hobson and Lord Tavistock's steward to believe the Great Mughal diamond was real.

And he was not the only one. Fairbrother—he believed it too. That was why he had a book about Persia on the table next to the settee in his rooms. Inspecting the neatly stacked assortment, she'd thought he was varied in his tastes, but now she perceived how very out of step with his other reading material the history book was.

Urgently, instinctively, giving no thought to Miss Drake's good opinion, Bea grabbed the duke's forearm and squeezed tightly. Kesgrave, his voice mild despite the sudden and forceful pressure, thanked the theater owner for her willingness to be reasonable and suggested that he might be able to see his way to five.

"But that is my final offer, so I hope it can be made acceptable to your father," he said, rising smoothly from his chair after Bea leaped jarringly to her feet. "I trust you will not mind if we remain for a while longer to continue our observation? We did not have a chance yesterday to meet everyone."

Miss Drake, her expression bland despite her guest's oddly fitful behavior, stood as well. "Yes, please do. Inspect every aspect of the theater as closely and carefully as you like. We have no secrets here." But of course she had at least one secret, and remembering the elaborate ruse by which she garnered respect for her own plays by disavowing authorship, she urged them again to visit Mr. Potts. "He will confirm everything I told you."

Bea, struggling to appear unhurried in her rush to confirm her theory, calmly assured Miss Drake that they would call on her solicitor presently. She smiled graciously as the other woman escorted them to the door and waited patiently as the duke answered pointless polite queries about their fictional theater.

The effort it took—oh, the effort!—not to shout: Latham! Latham! Latham!

And then finally, *finally,* Miss Drake was content to return to her office, and she and Kesgrave were alone in the corridor. Refusing to waste another second, Bea grabbed him by the arm and led him down the hallway. "It is Latham," she said softly. "The fool thinks the Great Mughal is real and must have got into a violent altercation with Hobson when he wouldn't reveal its location. The diamond was what he was searching for."

Kesgrave refrained from comment as they arrived at Latham's dressing room door, and Bea knocked briskly once, then twice, then, just to be sure, a third time. When nobody answered, she opened the door and stridently marched across the room to the far wall, where Latham's costumes were haphazardly stored, some hanging from hooks, others heaped in bins and dumped on a chair.

It was here, she knew it, the fool's cap with its missing bell, for she had seen the jester's outfit just the day before, its motley coat trimmed in red and its breeches with the mismatched legs.

The duke, comprehending their purpose, asked what they were searching for and nodded knowingly when she answered.

"The sleigh bell," he murmured.

"Yes," she responded grimly, pushing aside a knight's tunic to find a king's robe underneath, "the sleigh bell."

There was, as far as Bea could tell, no discernable order to the jumble of items—a priest's frock piled on top of maharaja's dhoti covering a judge's gown beside a soldier's uniform. On and on she dug, deeper and deeper, her estimation of Miss Drake sinking lower and lower as she perceived the extent of the chaos that had been allowed to flourish under her lax supervision. She recalled the orderly shelves in the cellars and Miss Drake's pride at allowing nothing to go to waste.

Nothing? Bea thought snidely, as she pulled the wooden bin away from the wall to make sure the incriminating cap hadn't slipped behind it. Latham's dressing room was a wasteland of rumpled jackets and wrinkled coats.

Frustrated that the desired item was neither behind the bin nor under it, Bea swore hotly. "Goddamn it."

Then, as a softly amused chuckle sounded behind her, her heart skipped painfully in her chest and she turned to see Latham stepping deeper into the room, a gun held level in his hand and aimed straight at her heart.

"My thoughts exactly, Mrs. Harper."

Chapter Sixteen

The fear that surged through Bea at the sight of the gun—
the hot, spearing, paralyzing terror that threatened to
choke her—was for Kesgrave. Kesgrave, who was accustomed
to being in charge. Kesgrave, who considered himself the
master of every situation. Kesgrave, who sparred regularly
with Gentleman Jackson and would consider overcoming an
actor, with his battle scenes scripted down to the last step, a
feeble challenge. Kesgrave, who would feel compelled to do
something stupidly heroic to save her.

Kesgrave, who would get himself killed.

Bea was not worried for herself.

No, she'd been in scrapes before and managed to save
herself—not, she conceded, anything quite as dire as a flintlock pointed at her chest, but the Marquess of Taunton had
tried to break her neck and she'd successfully beat him back
with a torch, lighting his hair on fire and contriving to get
herself engaged to the duke in the same deft move.

She had handled that predicament with aplomb, as she
had the ramshackle shed in which she had been trapped by

Mr. Skeffington in the Lake District. Plank by plank, minute by minute, she had freed herself.

But this fix...

Oh, yes, *this* fix was different, she thought, noting the gleam of excitement on Latham's face—his darkly handsome gothic face, which now seemed sinister in its perfection. His fathoms-deep eyes glowed brightly, and her knees felt unsteady as she forced herself not to look at Kesgrave.

Kesgrave, who would see her terror and act impetuously to relieve it.

He was so near, only a foot or two to her left, and her fingers tingled with the unbearable urge to touch him. To resist, she curled her hands into fists.

Latham, his attractive features relaxed as he contemplated Beatrice over the double barrels of the pistol, laughed softly again and said, "I cannot claim to be surprised to find you rifling through my possessions. I have known you for a pair of imposters from the moment Steagle mentioned to me there was no Adelphi theater in Bath. A word of advice, my dears: The next time you impersonate theater owners, pick a theater that actually exists." He shook his head with feigned disappointment, as if genuinely saddened by their failure to present themselves properly. "Truly, I would have thought Tavistock could afford cleverer lackeys to do his bidding, what with his many acres and houses, but perhaps his pockets are to let just like mine. That would explain why he has gone to such lengths to recover the diamond."

It was strange and yet not at all strange to stand there with a flintlock pointed at her and hear Tavistock's name. The architect of her destruction, he'd sought her removal from the game, and if he had not anticipated it happening in such a brutal fashion, it was only because he hadn't cared enough to consider it.

She was a pawn and as such was to be disposed of easily and thoughtlessly.

But not Kesgrave.

Never Kesgrave.

The duke was a prized piece, a valuable piece, an important piece to be surrounded by knights and bishops, and that he would be swept off the board with the same broad stroke that removed her was an irony so exquisite Bea could hardly breathe.

Would Tavistock ever know what he had wrought, she wondered.

Forcibly, she drew air into her lungs and resolved that he would. She would tell him herself. Oh, yes, she would, for he deserved to know the damage he had done with his lies and schemes. How confident he had been that the actor's death had nothing to do with him!

And yet she knew, even with the line so plainly drawn linking Tavistock to this moment, the lord would be incapable of grasping the connection.

Latham, noting the change in her demeanor, cocked the gun and urged her to think very carefully before doing something stupid like trying to tackle him. "You might think this a stage prop, but I assure you it is the genuine article and will lodge a bullet into your heart. I secured it a week ago when I realized that Hobson could not be cajoled into telling me the location of the diamond. It was very vexing, I assure you, for he had never resisted me before. Even while we were in that dreary room in the stable, he continued to deny me. He even tried to fob me off with a bouncer about the diamond being a story to lure a woman to her ruin. To think I would believe such utter rot! The dunderhead! He was looking for the diamond too. I knew it and he knew it."

So many thoughts darted through Bea's head during this speech, one after the other, flashing and flittering—the flint-

LYNN MESSINA

lock was authentic because its weight was accurate (what an amazing invention: flint, steel, iron oxide), trying to reason with Latham would be a waste of time and effort, Hobson's death had been much more terrible than she'd imagined, she would not die over a fictional diamond—and landed on the unbearable incongruity of this man, this dull-witted villain who had killed over literally nothing, calling someone else, anyone else, a dunderhead.

In that moment in Miss Drake's office, when she'd comprehended Latham's motive for killing Hobson, Bea had believed she'd grasped the depths of his idiocy, but now she realized it was in fact bottomless. If a dying man clinging to his story could not convince him of its truth, then nothing would.

No, trying to reason with the handsome lackwit would serve no purpose at all.

What about bribing him?

The man had owned himself in Dun Territory, and the Duke of Kesgrave could hand over a small fortune without noticing the difference.

All Latham had to do was name his price.

As simple as the proposal sounded, she knew it wouldn't stop there. No, revealing their true identities would set off another chain of events, possibly more lethal than the sequence already in motion. Latham's candor was sparked by the belief that she and Kesgrave were nobodies, second-rate lackeys hired by Tavistock to locate the diamond, and there was no telling how he would react if he discovered he'd confessed his murderous crime to a peer of the realm.

Not well, she thought.

Latham, noting her concentration, tut-tutted with disapproval and ordered her not to be a clunk like Hobson. "Do you think I cannot tell from the way you are staring at my gun that you are trying to decide if you can knock me over

294

before I shoot, Mrs. Harper? Do you really not understand how blatant you are in your calculations?" He laughed, the sound hollow as his upper lip curled with contempt. "Truly, your incompetence forces me to wonder what dark little alley Tavistock found you," he said, taking one step toward her and then another and another. His left arm, darting out from his side with unnerving speed, seized her by the elbow, jerked her around and thrust the flintlock against her back between her shoulder blades. "There, I have provided you with the answer, and it is zero." Brutishly, furiously, as if she had in fact acted on an impulse to rush him, he dug the weapon in deeper, the pressure growing as his anger increased. "The odds of your knocking me over before I fire are zero. You see, I've learned from my encounter with Hobson. He knocked the gun out of my hand, causing an ill-advised struggle and requiring me to grab the fireplace tongs."

With his grip on her secure, he felt more in control of the situation, and when he spoke next, to announce a short stroll to the cellar, it was with the quiet assurance of a man who knew exactly what he was doing.

But it had been a mistake, Bea knew, spinning her around, because now she was looking at Kesgrave, now she was staring into his eyes, into that blue, all that deep, gorgeous cerulean, seething and steady, and the panic that had risen at the touch of the flintlock (oh, the amazing flintlock, so ingeniously devised with its tumbler and sear spring) immediately began to subside, soothing the jumble of thoughts, raucous and irrelevant, that had swiftly overtaken her.

The moment of eye contact was fleeting, for in an instant Latham had turned her again, jerking her toward the door and shoving her forward as he warned Kesgrave not to make a commotion in the corridor.

"If you make even the slightest peep, I will pull the trigger and lodge a bullet into your associate's heart," he said matter-of-factly. "It will, in all likelihood, kill her within a matter of minutes, if not seconds. That in itself should be discouragement enough for you, Harper, but if you still harbor hope of crying out heroically for help, I want to draw your attention to the gun's twin barrels, which will allow me to get off another shot quickly. You will both die horribly in a tragic accident when the false gun I took from the property closet turns out to be real. Imagine my horror when I discover the truth. The shock! The revulsion! To have to live with that stain on my soul. What heartbreak! What tragedy! Could I even bear to go on?" He sighed deeply, as if contemplating a very great misery. "Yes, yes, of course. It would be hard. I would suffer setbacks. Some days I would be too despondent to climb out of bed. And yet limb by limb I would slowly rise from my slumber because I would have no choice. My public would demand that I endure for their sake. And I would." He bowed his head as if accepting a burden so great he could barely stand under it. "I would."

Latham spoke so fondly of this fantastical future Bea began to worry that he would shoot them in the corridor simply to bring it about.

What an exceptionally stupid way to die.

To distract him from the role of a lifetime, she suggested they work together to find the diamond, as neither party had been successful on their own.

The proposal elicited a scornful laugh from Latham, who thanked her for confirming his suspicion—that Tavistock had no reason to expect loyalty from her or her associate. "He will have little trouble believing that a pair of scoundrels absconded with the diamond to the Continent. Upon learning of your betrayal, he will either cease looking for the diamond altogether or follow you to Italy and Greece or perhaps Portugal and France. I have not decided yet where I will send you. I briefly entertained passage to the New

World, but then I decided the destination should not be so far that he wouldn't be tempted to follow, for I rather like the idea of his lordship embarking on a wild-goose chase. Either way, he will clear the field, allowing me to search for the diamond unencumbered. And I am confident I will find it, as I have the letter sent by the old man to his granddaughter. Tavistock doesn't know that. No, he has no idea Hobson threw the letter away as if it were just another missive from an appreciative admirer. But I found it and know it is filled with clues. The old fool! Induced by a lightskirt who treads the boards at the ramshackle Athenaeum to trust a beef-witted slowtop like Hobson to find a priceless jewel."

Listening to him describe the letter Hobson had consigned to the trash due to insufficient luridness, Bea felt an overwhelming urge to laugh, for it struck her as almost fitting that she would lose her life over something so idiotic as a figment of Lord Tavistock's imagination. With a stroke of her pen, she had arranged the demise of Mr. Theodore Davies, a phantasm who had exceeded his usefulness, and it felt now as if he were enacting his revenge.

Without thinking, she turned her head to seek out the duke's gaze and share her amusement, for surely he felt it too —the absurdity of the moment. But Latham, resenting any movement he had not sanctioned, whipped his free hand across her cheek, throwing her head back, and Bea closed her eyes in terror because she knew how close the thing was: the pistol cocked, the sear spring engaged, the tumbler near release, Kesgrave's fury, Latham's agitation, a cough, a twitch, a jerk, a spasm.

Any or all could end it.

But the moment did not come.

That was all she thought when one second became two seconds became three seconds became four.

The moment did not come and she was alive.

Relief was like a ragged breath, difficult and painful, and she kept herself still as she tried to form a coherent thought. Latham, however, was eager to be gone and, as he opened the door, reminded them to stay silent.

"Remember, bang-bang, if you don't," he said, "and as I deplore violence, I will be doubly cross if you make me fire my weapon."

Outside the dressing room, the corridor was empty, but voices carried from the stage as Mr. Rowe and Mr. Vokes argued over the stability of the rampart. Less distinctly, Bea could hear Miss Drake denying that she had ordered a new package of nibs and Chatterley complaining about a tear in his costume.

It was difficult for her to walk down the hallway, feeling the flintlock pressed against her back while so much normal activity went on around her. Her body still shook from the recent terror, her knees watery and uncertain, and it was only the thought of the gun's hair trigger that propelled her forward, toward the cellar door and then down its dark, winding steps.

The light from the hallway at the top of the stairs was dim but just bright enough to reveal the sconce at the bottom of the staircase. Impatiently, Latham ordered the duke to light the candle, which he smoothly did using flint and tinder on top of the wall-mounted candle box. At once, a small circle of light illuminated the narrow corridor, which branched off in three directions. To the right, Bea recalled, was the costume closet Miss Drake had showed them during their visit the day before.

With his free hand, Latham removed the candle from its holder and instructed Kesgrave to walk down the hallway to his left. Bea followed, her steps cautious on the uneven ground, and her heart lurched painfully in her chest when

Latham shoved her roughly with the gun and commanded her to stop dawdling.

He was going to kill her by accident, after all, she thought in disgust, for he clearly had no idea how sensitive an instrument the flintlock was.

At the end of the hallway, Latham told Kesgrave to make a right, then a quick left, then a right again, and at every turn, Bea tried to figure out what part of the theater they were under. It didn't matter, of course, for no one above would hear them regardless of how loudly they screamed. The gravel floor and thick walls ensured no sound would escape the dingy cellar. The discharge of the gun would echo slightly, creating little more than a dull thump as it extinguished their lives.

Despite the felicitousness of the setting, Bea did not believe Latham intended to shoot them, for he had made his aversion to violence clear and there was a far easier way to dispose of them: lock them in a room and leave them to die.

As her sense of dread grew, she tried to tell herself that was not the case. Surely, Latham intended to lead them to some secret egress by which he could slip them out of the building unseen.

But that was a futile hope, and she knew it. With his talk of sending them to Portugal or France, he had made his intentions known and taking them to another location simply to end their lives there merely increased his risk of discovery.

Far better to find a distant closet in a forgotten corner and close the door.

Problem solved.

She had no sooner had the thought than they arrived at the end of the passage. There were no more lefts or rights to be made, and Latham, pushing Kesgrave to the side, opened the door himself.

"All the comforts of home," he said facetiously.

Compared with the storage room Miss Drake had shown them, with its shelves of grotesque masks and animal heads, Bea actually thought it was a good deal more comfortable. Its full dimensions were difficult to decipher in the limited light of the candle, but the space felt smaller, more compact, and contained fewer items. A large cabinet with bookshelves consumed most of the far wall, while dome-topped chests of various sizes lined the side walls. In the middle of the room, tilting drunkenly, was an old writing table that was missing its fourth leg.

All the items, even the storage chests, which had been designed to be stuffed and then forgotten, had a desolate feel about them, as if they had been forsaken decades ago. The impression contrasted sharply with the costume closet, filled with articles from the Particular's recent plays.

Bea was certain an examination of any surface would reveal a layer of dust two inches thick.

Latham stepped into the room and closed the door behind him, a cautionary measure that struck Beatrice as comical, for they were as deep in the bowels of the theater as the pharaoh Khufu was in the Great Pyramid of Giza.

This damp little room was their burial chamber.

Already, the air felt stale.

Opening a large chest to the right of the door, Latham retrieved ropes from its depths and Bea realized his plan to inter them in the cellar was not a spontaneous decision.

He had known from the moment he had awaken that morning that they would end up here.

For some reason, Bea found that notion more chilling that the hard press of the double-barreled flintlock on her back.

Hindered by the gun, Latham ordered Bea to constrain Kesgrave, first securing his hands at the wrists and then his feet at the ankles. It was a strange experience, at once sweet and sorrowful, to be so close she could feel the heat of his cheek and yet not be free to lay a kiss upon it. Their eyes met briefly in the dim light, and although she could scarcely read his expression, she felt comforted by the calm he exuded.

This damp little room would not be their burial chamber.

Although she was tempted to be clever with the knots, she knew Latham would check to make sure the bonds were tight and secure. Furthermore, the sophisticated art of nautical rope tying was another regrettable gap in her education.

If only she knew as much about the carrick as she did the flintlock.

Latham, satisfied with her effort, deposited Bea on the other side of the cabinet and, finally putting down the gun, tethered her hands and feet. He worked quickly and efficiently, causing Bea, who kept her eyes trained on the pistol as she waited—alas, futility—for an opportunity to seize it, to wonder if he had served time as a sailor. When he was done binding her limbs, he looped another cord through her arm and hitched her to the cabinet. He did the same to Kesgrave, making sure that neither one of them would be able to move around the room, however inelegantly.

Then he heaved a loud sigh, as if greatly relieved, and rose to his feet. "Now that everyone is in their final resting place, I can admit that this experience has been something of an ordeal. I thought it would be easier than disposing of Hobson, for I am not a vile monster to withstand the spillage of blood and feel nothing. It was quite horrible, what Hobson put me through, so I was resolved to do better. And I think I have," he said and then looked from Bea to the duke as if seeking confirmation. Finding none, he continued to expound on his own generosity, lauding his kindness in leaving them there to die peacefully. "And with a candle! For no man should expire in the smothering gloom of darkness. 'Light shines on the righteous and joy on the upright in heart.'"

The temerity of a murderer quoting Psalms while in the commission of a double homicide was so astounding, it literally took Bea's breath away. Sitting there, bound to the cabinet, her shoulders already sore from the awkward position of her arms, she gasped in shock and stared at him, the monstrosity of his soul hardening the angles of his face until he was as deformed as the demon head.

But Kesgrave—O, glorious, wonderful Kesgrave—found his audacity remarkably funny and laughed with unrestrained glee.

"My good fellow, how long do you think it will take us to die here?" he asked, amusement lacing every word. "Twenty minutes? Thirty?"

Latham had no ready answer, for his compassion did not require him to account for all the tedious details of his plan, and peeved at being called to account, he extinguished the candle as he swept out of the room. Then he slammed the door like a recalcitrant child refusing to eat jellied eels for dinner.

The moment he was gone, Bea, struggling against the confines of the ropes, tried in the pitch blackness to discover the condition of the leg she was bound to. If there was a jagged edge along any part of it, a spot that had begun to splinter, then perhaps she could wear away the cord.

Smooth...smooth...smoo—

Oh, wait, was that a rough patch?

Slowly, she slid the side of her pinky over the spot again and again. It was smooth all the way up and all the way down.

Bloody, buggering hell, the cabinet was in pristine condition! How had it not suffered a few dings and scrapes during its epic journey to this far-off spot?

Smothering a scream of frustration, she abandoned her efforts, leaned against the wall and sighed wearily. It had been a futile plan anyway. It would take many days to wear down the thick rope from friction, and while Latham's estimate of a candle's burning time was wildly off the mark, they would not last a full week. She had read enough biographies of explorers whose ships had been becalmed or wrecked by shoals to know how vital water was to survival. They could go only a few days without it.

Bea realized that in the absolute darkness, they would not be able to mark the time, to tell minutes from hours, to distinguish day and night.

Somehow that nothingness felt more wretched than the empty blackness she saw with her open eyes.

Feeling consumed by the void, she said softly, with sadness and sincerity befitting the hopelessness of the situation, "I'm sorry."

But Kesgrave, his rich baritone ringing so brightly in the darkness it was a small spark all on its own, asked with genuine surprise, "Whatever for?"

The calm in his voice, as if their detainment in the cellar were a minor inconvenience, such as cold tea in the drawing room, was a tonic. Bea had not thought it was possible to love him any more than she did, for her feelings for him already consumed the whole of her, but that had merely been a failure of imagination because she had never conceived of their being entombed together. Sitting there, consumed by oblivion, she felt herself sink even deeper.

Determined to match his nonchalant tone she said, "For getting us into this predicament. If I had paused for even a moment's thought rather than rushing headlong into Latham's dressing room to search his things, we wouldn't be trapped here."

"Ah, but think of all the things I've learned about you in the past half hour that a more temperate suitor would have most likely discovered before agreeing to marriage," he replied with unsentimental bluntness, "such as how well you tie a knot. I am sure that skill will be quite useful when you are securing a swing to a tree limb for our children. And then there's your ability to remain preternaturally calm while a deadly weapon is pressed directly against your heart. Surely, that cool head will pay great dividends in the future. If our son is anything like me, he will fall through the ice of the pond at Haverill Hall twice before he is seven."

Unbidden, the image appeared in her head of a small boy with unruly blond locks and cheerful blue eyes.

It was unbearably bittersweet, and she felt the first tears rise in her throat.

No. *No.*

She would not succumb to maudlin sentiment.

Exhaling deeply, she said, "I support the acquisition of knowledge however one attains it, but I feel compelled to point out that I have demonstrated grace under pressure before. There was the fire in Taunton's hair, for example, which I extinguished mere moments after he tried to break my neck. That incident occurred before you accepted my proposal so the information was available to you should you have wanted to factor it into your decision."

Kesgrave laughed, as she'd hoped he would, and said, "Who is being pedantic now?"

"Alas, you have thoroughly corrupted me," she said on a giggle, feeling momentarily lighthearted because it was still a wonder, this thing between them. How had they ended up here, so far from the dinner table at Lakeview House—and, no, she didn't mean in a cellar ten feet below a theater on Adams Street.

But even so, that was where they were, and he could be as gracious and irreverent as he wanted, but it was still her fault.

It was unfair—indeed, excruciatingly so!—that the imperious Duke of Kesgrave, proud Corinthian and undaunted leader of society, had somehow managed to overcome half a millennium of breeding and perfection to fall in love with an insignificant spinster with no fortune or conversation, only to find himself delivered to this new, horrible low. All those lords privy seal, all those clerks of the hanaper, all those exalted ancestors going back to the Peasants' Revolt, and he would die here anonymously, his grave unmarked, his fate unknown.

That was what her overweening confidence had wrought.

When the sobs came again, she was powerless to stop them and, slowly at first and then with increasing vigor, tears streamed down her cheeks. Breathing was difficult, and even though it made no difference in the utter blackness, she closed her eyes because it gave her a sense of control. Then she lowered her head to drip her tears onto the ropes because she hoped—futilely, maniacally—that the water would weaken or stretch the fibers.

In truth, she knew nothing about the care and composition of ordinary rope and again regretted the oversight. If only she had paid more attention to the rigging in Captain Cook's last journal!

"Fall silent?" Kesgrave asked.

Deep in her misery, Bea assumed she had missed the first half of his sentence and struggled to find meaning in this fragment. Lacking the larger context, however, it was impossible, and she took several calming breaths before responding. "Excuse me?"

She was relieved to discover her voice sounded almost normal despite her bout of uncontrolled weeping.

"During our discussion of your archnemesis, Miss Brougham, as she was known then," he explained, "you said that in the wake of her comments, you fell silent. I have been quite puzzled by that statement, as you have never been silent with me, and, at the risk of giving full leave to the pomposity you love to skewer, most people are. They are intimidated by my rank, stature and bearing and are deferential and quiet.

LYNN MESSINA

Indeed, I have deliberately cultivated a daunting demeanor to deflate mushrooms, toadies and fools."

When he first started speaking—when he brought up the dreadful Mrs. Norton and her own calamitous debut—Bea had felt a strange desolation, an unfathomable loneliness, at the realization that he would not allow them to talk about it: the minutes, the hours, the oblivion. They would discuss frivolities, as if awaiting the delivery of that fresh pot of tea, and meet their end with the stalwart indifference of proper English gentlemen.

Immediately, however, she apprehended the inaccuracy of her assumption, for he was indeed talking about it, sidling up to death sweetly by satisfying a curiosity before it was too late.

"I thought you were going to kill me," Bea said. "In the library."

Kesgrave chuckled lightly. "Yes, I recall your brandishing the candlestick."

Vehemently, she rebuffed his comment. "No, I thought you were going to *kill* me—not as an abstraction but as a fact. In those fleeting seconds, I believed myself truly to be dead, and I was disgusted by my timidity. I was *disgusted* by the fact that my voice had been so silenced I couldn't even raise it to save my life—and again, that was in the literal sense, not the figurative. That moment was transformative, you see, for I could not be as afraid of anything as I was of dying in silence. The drawing room in comparison was far less daunting," she explained, pausing briefly because that, too, was still a wonder. Then, her lips lifting in a grin that had seem inconceivable only a minute before, she added, "And then, of course, there was the fact that you annoyed me with your endless lectures and your boundless confidence and your impenetrable conviction that you know how to do everything better than everyone else and your—"

She gasped, the sudden intake of breath nearly choking her as she felt the air around her move and a soft brush on her arm.

"Such as freeing myself from ropes?" he said softly as his hand moved along her shoulder to cup the side of her face. "Is that what you mean by my impenetrable conviction? Perhaps in this instance the belief is justified?"

The sweep of his fingers against her cheek was so shocking she thought for a moment it was an illusion, a chimera willed into being by her fear and desire, but the boast was too resolutely Kesgrave to be anything but corporeal fact.

"How——"

But the question was never asked, for he had found her lips in the blackness and captured them eagerly, desperately, frantically. His hands clutched her shoulders tightly, as if to keep her in place, and Bea, giddy with relief, giggled at the ludicrousness, for she could not go anywhere with her legs bound at the ankles and her body tethered to the cabinet.

"Oh, well, you laugh," Kesgrave growled, as he pulled her roughly into an embrace. "You did not have to watch minute after minute as Latham's finger twitched on the trigger."

No, she did not.

"I'm sorry."

Kesgrave shook her lightly and told her to stop apologizing. "You cannot be held responsible for the behavior of a madman."

Complying meekly with his request, Bea asked how he'd managed to escape.

"I pocketed a quill knife," he said as he untied the ropes that held her. "If you recall, I was searching the bin next to the small table when Latham entered with the gun. There was a knife on the table, and thinking it could be useful, I slipped it into my pocket. It was easy enough, as he was distracted by you. Somewhat more challenging was maneuvering the knife with my hands bound in the dark. I nicked myself quite a few times in my efforts but ultimately prevailed."

It was on the tip of Bea's tongue to grumble about his withholding such pertinent information and allowing her to stew in her own fear for...well, she wasn't exactly sure how long but it had to have been at least twenty minutes. Or maybe only fifteen? Before she could complain, however, he released her hands and she was able to shift positions.

'Twas splendid to move around.

A minute later, her legs were also free and she expressed her gratitude by launching herself at him and setting off another fit of giggles as she landed awkwardly on his hip. Her amusement subsided as she found his face in the darkness and pressed her lips against his, whispering thank you over and over as the kiss grew deeper and deeper. Responding to her appreciation with equal fervor, he rolled her gently over and pressed his body enticingly against hers. She sighed in delight, aware yet uncaring that they were not entirely free yet, and tensed in anticipation when she perceived a noise and then a second later a light.

"The door," she whispered, pulling back slightly.

Uncomprehending, he laughed quietly as he continued to place soft kisses along her jaw. "No bother, I promise. Recall my upbringing in the Castle of Otranto. There is no lock I cannot open."

"No," Bea said firmly, "someone is at the door."

She had no sooner said the words than a lone candle illuminated the black room, revealing their position on the floor.

"Good God, Bea, what are you thinking," cried the voice in alarm, "to indulge in such an activity here? Is it even sanitary? Are you rolling around in rat droppings?"

Chapter Seventeen

B *ea's jaw dropped* as she observed the astonishing sight of her cousin Flora walking across the gravel floor. It was just...just...

But there were no words to describe the depth of her shock.

Unruffled, Kesgrave greeted her warmly and inquired after her mother. "I am correct in believing Mrs. Hyde-Clare has no idea you are here?"

Flora chortled with delight and assured him her mama thought she was lying in bed clutching her stomach in pain from spoiled oysters. "I left them out for an entire day to make sure they would be extra pungent."

"How clever," he said.

Bea stared at them in dismay as they exchanged niceties. "No," she said curtly, "we are not going to pretend this is a morning call."

"Of course not, dear," Flora said with a speaking glance at the duke, who did not bother to smother his smile. "You are in a cellar rolling around in rat droppings, something I am sure you would never do during a morning call."

Realizing her position put her at a disadvantage, Bea rose to her feet and dusted gravel off her skirt. "What are you doing here?"

"Saving you," Flora said, glancing again at Kesgrave with slight befuddlement at her cousin's inability to grasp the obvious.

"But why are you here? *How* are you here?" Bea asked snappishly, taking another step closer in the gloom and noting for the first time the outfit she wore. "Are those my clothes?"

Flora gestured lavishly to the ensemble and firmly said they were not. "They're Russell's."

"But you found them hanging in my wardrobe," Bea pointed out.

Flora conceded that was correct.

Bea growled.

"What my betrothed is trying to say with her guttural incoherence, Miss Hyde-Clare, is thank you for rescuing us," Kesgrave asserted smoothly.

"No, what I am *trying* to say," Bea clarified with an irate look at the duke, "is that it's much too dangerous for you to be traipsing through London on your own dressed like a man."

"And yet it's all right when you do it?" Flora asked scornfully.

"You are an attractive young lady who will make a brilliant match some day," Bea explained, "and I am a drab spinster of no consequence."

Having drawn in a deep breath to argue fiercely with her cousin, Flora let it out in a rush as she laughed with sincere amusement at this particularly fatuous statement. With a look at the duke, she said, "Will you break the bad news to her or shall I?"

But Bea did not need anyone to tell her that her days of

spinsterish obscurity were over. "Very well," she said with admirable calm, "please explain how you found us here."

Even in the dim light, she could see Flora's eyes gleaming with excitement to show off her ingenuity. "Well, it started with that faradiddle that you welcomed Mrs. Norton as a friend. It's insulting, Bea, that you would expect me to swallow such a plumper. Do you think I'm still in leading strings?"

As Bea did in fact consider her in many ways still to be a child, she did not respond to this query. Her cousin, however, noticed neither the pause neither its implied criticism in her eagerness to demonstrate how terribly clever she was.

"Knowing you could never count her among your friends and recognizing, more importantly, that *she* would never count *you,* I realized something very strange was afoot and set Harris upon you to follow, for I could not extricate myself from Mama without careful planning," she explained.

Bea was appalled. "You asked one of the footmen to follow me?"

"Well, technically not you. Kesgrave," she clarified helpfully, as if the distinction made a significant difference. "I explained that I wanted to send his cousin a gift and required the address. He was quite confused by your destinations, for neither the boarding house in Covent Garden nor the theater near the Strand befitted a residence belonging to an elderly relation of a duke. Nevertheless, he gave me the addresses and I reasoned the theater was your more likely direction today. And I was right, of course, which is why I was able to arrive in time to rescue you. If you are wondering how I disguised myself once I entered the building, the answer is I pretended to be a delivery boy from a stationary shop. I borrowed a packet of nibs, you see, from an office and then walked around the building as if trying to deliver them. That was when I spotted you in the hallway with that awful man.

He was directing you to the cellar stairs, which seemed odd to me, so I followed. At a safe distance," she hastened to add when she read the censorious expression on her cousin's face. "I am not a child and my rescue has been successful, has it not? Now do say thank you for saving us, Flora."

Bea smiled. "Thank you for saving us, Flora."

Her cousin dipped her head in thoughtful condescension, then ruined the effect by announcing she had spent all her pin money on the hack. "I did not realize it would cost quite so much to travel around London and will require either a loan or an escort back to Portman Square."

"There, your grace, see," Bea said self-righteously. "I hope now you will stop encouraging her."

Whether the duke would comply with her request, she was unable to ascertain, for at that very moment, Miss Calcott crossed the threshold and surveyed the room. Finding everything to her satisfaction, she nodded with approval and announced the heroic rescue she had planned would be much easier to achieve than she had anticipated.

"I assumed in order to locate you, I would have to check every room," she explained to Beatrice and the duke. "This is much better."

Flora, bristling at the intrusion, stepped into the other woman's line of sight and replied sharply that a heroic rescue had already been achieved. "By me. I am the heroine. Me. Miss Hyde-Clare. Not you."

It was an odd speech—part explanation, part tantrum— and Miss Calcott could be forgiven for finding it confusing, especially as the woman seeming to deny her claim of heroism was dressed as a man.

But the actress, demonstrating again how difficult it was to disconcert her, curtsied deeply and apologized for the presumption. "I did not realize you already had the matter well in hand. Thank you, Miss Hyde-Clare, for relieving me of the responsibility. Perhaps now that the rescue has been so wonderfully executed, we can return to the surface to apprehend our villain before he eats too many tea cakes and falls asleep, for it is rapidly approaching his naptime," she said, then looked at Beatrice for confirmation. "That is why you are here, isn't it? To seize him for killing Robert? I know you are not theater owners from Bath because there isn't an Adelphi in Bath. Steagle has pointed that fact out several times and wonders why you felt the need to obscure your origins. He suspects that you secretly own the Athenaeum and seek to eliminate your competition, but I know you cannot be theater people because you ask far too many questions. Actual theater people care only about reviews and receipts. What I cannot figure out is why you have concerned yourself with Robert's demise. Are you Runners or investigators hired by his family?"

"Concerned citizens," Flora volunteered as she lifted her chin to a noble angle. "We are merely concerned citizens who seek to right injustice wherever we find it."

"Yes, I see," said Miss Calcott in an unconvincing tone, for obviously she did not see at all. She darted a curious look to Bea, who, realizing she did not have a better explanation for their involvement, admitted that her cousin's answer was not entirely inaccurate.

"Tell me, Miss Calcott," Kesgrave said as he lit a third candle and the gloom receded to the corners, "how do you know Latham is our villain?"

"I know he is a *villain* because he is exceedingly vain," she said, "but I know he's a killer because he just told me. Not in so many words, you understand, for he did not announce plainly over tea cakes: I killed Hobson. But he has many habits, one of which is getting as chatty as a magpie when he is excited about something. Unable to find anyone else to talk to, he visited with me and Helen in my dressing room and he excitedly told us about his likely success with a new venture and that mean, awful Hobson would no longer be able to thwart him. As it was a strange thing to say because he and Hobson had always rubbed together well, I pressed him for his meaning and his answer indicated a hitherto unknown resentment. From there it was easier enough to decipher. Knowing your interest in the matter, I asked him if he had spoken to you today. He immediately looked guilty, because he is a terrible actor, and said you were 'storing'—ha ha!—up your strength. As he is a dimwitted clucklehead, his remark could mean only one thing, so I gave him additional tea cakes from my private supply and came down here to find you. Task accomplished."

"*My* task," Flora said.

Bea was impressed again when Miss Calcott, revealing no impatience at the absurd display of vanity, dutifully corrected herself and asked Flora if she would like to be the one who guided them out of the cellar. "Or shall I lead the way?"

Flora, perhaps abashed by the excessive courtesy, deferred to the actress and followed her silently out of the room. Bea trailed her cousin and noticed with unsettling surprise that the distance to the staircase was actually quite brief. With the flintlock at her back and the sobering sense of mortality, the walk had felt endless.

They reached the top of the staircase, and Bea, mindful of the powerful firearm, instructed her cousin to alert Miss Drake to the problem. "And summon Runners. I'm sure Miss Drake will know how."

"Miss Drake?" Flora asked confused.

"The theater owner from whom you stole the packet of nibs," Bea explained.

Her cousin looked prepared to argue, even opening her mouth as if to issue a protest, but then she nodded abruptly and repeated, "Miss Drake."

Kesgrave, no doubt also considering the destructive tendencies of the double-barreled pistol, suggested Bea show Flora where Miss Drake's office was—in case, he explained, she had forgotten in the excitement.

Flora, reminding the company that she had carried out a flawless rescue, professed herself deeply insulted at the implication she was a doddering child and marched down the corridor to the manager's office.

"She is a delight," Miss Calcott said without irony.

Bea withheld comment as she followed the actress to her dressing room. Although Kesgrave urged caution, Miss Calcott insisted they had no reason to be concerned.

"Latham is far too satisfied with how well he handled the matter to think for a moment he has failed," she explained, adding that she was confident they would find him in gentle repose on her settee. "Perhaps snoring lightly."

He was not, in fact, sleeping when they entered the room, but rather sitting at the table eating tea cakes and reading the newspaper. His lazy smile upon seeing the actress turned into a horrified gasp as he noticed the formerly entombed Harpers. He immediately began to choke and held up a finger as if to forestall comment while he struggled to regain control of his breathing—a process that was taking a suspiciously long time.

Indeed, the coughing fit, which presumably began in earnest, soon revealed itself as a ploy to allow Latham to retrieve his flintlock from an interior pocket in his coat. It was almost comical, the way he thought he was being subtle, rounding his shoulders and turning slightly to the side to hide his movements.

Straining for breath, he managed a weak apology.

Kesgrave, perhaps out of a malicious desire to allow the villain to believe he might actually succeed in his fumbling plan to escape, waited until Latham had one hand on the handle before striding fully into the room, raising his fist and knocking Latham out with one sturdy blow. The flintlock fell harmlessly to the floor, but the table suffered irreversible damage as the actor landed squarely in the middle, breaking it in half. Ever resourceful, Miss Calcott managed to save the tea cakes from the wreckage and held out the tray to Bea, who, having no appetite, declined the offer.

The booming crash of the table promptly drew curious onlookers, who expressed horror and confusion to find Latham lying unconscious. Smeeton wondered if he was napping, and Miss Calcott quickly and efficiently explained the nature of the actor's crime.

A collective gasp of surprise filled the room.

Miss Drake, pale and shaken, arrived to report that a Runner had been sent for and would be there soon. She then looked at Latham, sprawled on the broken table, with spilled tea in his hair, and sighed wearily.

"So handsome," she murmured, "so gifted, so brilliant at breathing life into heroic characters, so ruthless."

Miss Calcott, whose estimation of the actor's ability differed wildly, rolled her eyes but refrained from comment.

In due time, the Runner appeared, and Kesgrave quickly apprised him of the facts and succinctly answered his questions. Naturally, some confusion emerged as to his interest in the affair, especially when Miss Drake, determined to protect the dignity of her investor, insisted he was a theater owner from Bath and *had* no interest.

"His interest is in justice for the poor and helpless," Flora said indignantly.

A squabble ensued, and Bea grasped for the first time the pervasive awkwardness of a duke apprehending a killer while disguised as a theater owner. Clearly, they were obliged to reveal the truth, for the authorities were now involved, and regardless, it would not be kind to simply disappear from Miss Drake's life as if they had never existed.

No, an honest accounting had to be made.

Alas Bea, who, despite the satisfactory resolution of their entombment problem, still felt terrible that her rash behavior had subjected her beloved to ropes and darkness, was decidedly reluctant to do it, for divulging their identities would expose Kesgrave to further discomfort. It was above all things ridiculous—a duke masquerading as a provincial theater owner to pursue a murder investigation—and she had little hope of their exploits remaining secret. As soon as they left the Particular and returned to their carriage, word would spread, first slowly among actors and theater mechanics and then swiftly among the *ton*.

Naturally, the irony did not escape Beatrice, for the purpose of the one-week postponement of their nuptials had been to allow the gossip to die down and now she had managed to produce fresh fodder.

'Twould have been better for all parties involved if they had just allowed her and Kesgrave to marry last week as originally planned.

As always, Bea found strength in the sheer absurdity and, determined to brazen it out despite the unfortunate consequences, announced forthrightly that Mr. Harper was in fact the Duke of Kesgrave.

At once, the Runner's expression became deferential, while a look of anguish crossed Miss Drake's face as she realized the theater would not be getting an infusion of funds.

Perceiving yet another flaw in her plan, Bea rushed to apologize for disappointing the theater owner, but the other woman briskly dismissed her concerns, insisting that it made no difference in the end, for it was unlikely her father would have agreed to their offer of five percent.

Having disclosed everything they knew, Kesgrave gave his

card to the Runner and told him to contact his steward if he required any additional information. The Runner tucked the slip into his pocket as Miss Drake eyed it enviously. Bea, observing the look, promised to attend the premiere of *Jacopo the Courageous,* which, far from cheering up the manager, served only to remind her that she no longer had a lead actor.

Miss Calcott sought to comfort her by offering to find Latham's replacement herself. "To spare you the effort, for you are already so busy running the theater!"

Confident that the Runner and Miss Calcott could address any remaining difficulties, Bea made their goodbyes. Kesgrave was as eager as she to leave, but Flora wanted to linger, driving her cousin to tug forcefully on her arm to get her to the carriage—an act she instantly regretted because Flora wanted to talk about their investigation the entire way home. It was, Bea allowed, a reasonable impulse, for despite claiming ownership of the case, she knew very little about it. Her first question was: Hobson who?

Patiently, Bea answered her queries about the victim, Latham and Mrs. Norton, and, going back farther, about Wem and the true reason she had attended Lord Pudsey's salon. She even explained, when pressed, the events on the terrace during the Larkwell ball that had ended with her dress scorched by torch fire. It was only when Flora asked about Mr. Davies's untimely demise—had the carriage that had struck him really hit him by *accident*—that she grew evasive and asked by what method she planned to sneak back into the house.

Flora, unsettled by the question, for that aspect of the masquerade had not occurred to her, opened her eyes wide and requested her cousin's advice. Although Bea was reluctant to answer, for she did not want to contribute to her cousin's delinquency, she felt she had no choice, as it was she who had raised the issue in the first place.

"I am in awe of your cleverness, darling," Flora said, clapping with delight when she learned of Bea's trick of keeping a change of clothes in the closet along the hallway off the kitchens so that she could assume proper attire before returning upstairs. Her desire for more strategies was temporarily forestalled by their arrival at number nineteen, but she consoled herself with the prospect of learning more after dinner. "I am sure my stomach issues will have resolved themselves by then."

Bea, wondering if she could feign her own stomach ailment to avoid the conversation, slid forward to climb out of the carriage. Kesgrave, however, requested a private word, and she leaned back in the bench as Flora looked cautiously through the window next to the servants' entrance and then passed through the door. She hoped for her own sake the girl reached her bedchamber without Aunt Vera catching her, for there was no way she would not hold Bea responsible for the wildly inappropriate behavior.

She was imagining the vigorous reprimand she would get when Kesgrave sat next to her on the bench and banged the roof of the carriage. They pulled away from the curb at once.

"Where are we going?" she asked. "Never say we are actually going to visit with your cousin to give our story some verisimilitude. I must confess, I do not think I have the stamina necessary for an afternoon of polite conversation with a septuagenarian."

"That is extremely disappointing to hear," Kesgrave said, taking her hands in his, "for the activity I have planned for this afternoon requires quite a bit of stamina."

And yet, Bea thought, he did not appear disappointed. The gleam in his eyes, that flickering blaze of eagerness and anticipation, indicated the very opposite, and she felt her breath hitch.

"I fell silent," he said softly.

Uncomprehending, bewildered by his words, bemused by his gaze, she nodded.

"In the library, at Lakeview House, glaring at you across Otley's dead body, I fell silent," he explained, pressing his lips against her hands. "Not literally, you understand, but figuratively. Though I would not know it for months, that was it—the moment everything changed. For years, I heard naught but the sound of my own voice and then you started talking and all I could do was listen. From that moment, Bea, I have been struck dumb by you—by your wit and your fearlessness and your intelligence and your sense of humor, so mischievous and sharp, and your beauty."

Instinctively, she drew back, flinching at the lie—oh, yes, only a small lie, only a white lie, and yet large enough to infect all those gorgeous truths.

She did not need it, the appeasement of her vanity, because she had everything else. And she did, truly. She was no longer such a ninny as to believe one shortcoming negated all her strengths.

Resolutely, Kesgrave tugged her forward and tilted her head up until she was looking again into his eyes. "You have the right to your own opinion, my love, and I will not quarrel with your determination to consider yourself drab. I won't even ask you to accept compliments from the public at large—indeed, I am rather inclined to discourage them from Nuneaton—but if we are going to be married, then you will have to learn how to grow accustomed to my appreciation for your appearance, as I find your impish grin to be the single most beautiful thing in the whole of the world."

Obviously, Bea could not be expected to accept a compliment of such lavish excess without blushing prettily and averting her eyes—a provocation that the duke, in turn, could not be expected to resist.

When, several minutes later, Kesgrave released her lips,

he laid his head against her forehead and said softly, sweetly, with a note of reverence, "Struck dumb. And that damn fool with a pistol almost took it all away. When he cocked it, my heart stopped, simply ceased beating for nearly a minute. Just the slightest pressure and—" But he shook his head, unable to finish the thought. "I will wait no longer. I will take no more chances. We will settle this today. A promise not to pursue murderous scoundrels yielded no satisfaction, so I am raising the ante. Before God and my grandmother, you will *vow* to cease investigating."

Her heart tumbled.

Indeed, it somersaulted in her chest like a circus performer as she apprehended his meaning.

Giddy with happiness—no, *dizzy* with it—she stared at her bridegroom, at his gorgeous blond curls and searing blue eyes, and realized it was not just her wedding day but also her wedding night.

No, she thought, her blood pounding as she recalled his puzzling remark from earlier, her wedding *afternoon*.

"Bea!" he said on a strangled laugh, as keenly aware of her thoughts as ever. "Pay attention."

Flushing slightly, she said, "Your wits must be addled by lust as well, your grace, if you are commanding me to bring the full force of my intelligence to bear on your irrational request. You stand a much better chance of success if I am thinking of activities that require stamina."

Although his eyes flashed in awareness, he remained stubbornly focused on the matter at hand and countered that there was nothing irrational in desiring his wife not to be riddled with bullet holes. As she had never been at risk of such an immoderate fate, the flintlock having only two barrels and *riddled* implying "many holes," such as a sieve—a distinction she would think a pedant like him would not only respect but demand—she dismissed his request as an outrageous overreaction and suggested that it would be far more useful if they added a vow regarding the timely disclosure of secreted quill knives.

Kesgrave knew the comment for the purely distractive taunt it was and yet could not stop himself from rising to the bait, insisting he had not wanted to get her hopes up in case he was unable to a) reach the knife, b) maneuver the knife, c) slice the knife through the ropes.

"There is nothing wrong with a display of caution," he said, proposing they also add a vow requiring both parties to practice restraint before searching the private dressing rooms of suspects. Then, perceiving the disadvantages of specificity, amended it to searches in general. "Any room, carriage, stable or outbuilding."

"How willing you are to tinker!" she said with feigned surprise. "Does not the marriage ceremony deserve the same respect as maritime tradition? You won't play fast and loose with the order of warships in the Battle of the Nile but are perfectly content to rewrite the Book of Common Prayer?" She tsked in disapproval, her eyes sparkling with poorly suppressed humor. "Really, Damien, I am not sure I can reconcile myself to the change. I fell in love with a pedant, not an iconoclast."

Maddened by her illogic, Kesgrave glowered imperiously.

Delighted by his officiousness, Bea grinned impishly.

It was, by any account, an auspicious start to a very happy union.

A TREACHEROUS PERFORMANCE

My Gracious Thanks

Pen a letter to the editor!

Dearest Reader,

A writer's fortune has ever been wracked with peril ⁻ and wholly dependent on the benevolence of the reading public.

Reward an intrepid author's valiant toil!

Please let me know what you think of A Treacherous Performance on Amazon or Goodreads!

Keep reading for a sneak peek at Book 6 in the series *A Sinister Establishment!*

A Sinister Establishment

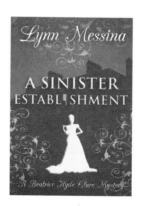

If Beatrice Hyde-Clare had realized that her refusal to consent to her betrothed's slight alteration in their marriage vows would allow his grandmother to assemble a roomful of people to witness the happy event, she would have agreed at once to his request. A promise made during one's nuptials was binding, to be sure, but she had little doubt she would have found a way to extricate herself from a pledge to cease investigating murders should the need arise—a development she deemed highly unlikely, though not impossible considering the recent spate of corpses in her life. Her confidence was owed to the fact that during her brief courtship of the Duke of Kesgrave she'd grown adept at making rhetorically persuasive arguments. If her logic did not quite meet his rigorous standards for accuracy, it was no matter, for it satisfied her own.

Alas, she had been too delighted by Kesgrave's audacity in rewriting the Book of Common Prayer—and why should he not take a liberal hand, for its lineage went back a mere three centuries while his own encompassed a full half millennium—to notice the dowager quietly scribbling messages at a table in the corner of the drawing room. It was only when the familiar trill of her aunt's strident disapproval wafted in from the entry hall that she recognized the tactical error.

"Well, no, Flora, I do not think Beatrice *chose* to have her wedding today with the *express* purpose of rousing you from your sickbed," Vera Hyde-Clare explained with just enough uncertainty in her voice to allow for the possibility, "as I believe she holds you in high esteem and would never *wish* for you to suffer a monstrous setback or have your health permanently damaged. And yet here you are, at Clarges Street, a shadow of your former self, barely able to hold your head up as you totter forward. Rather, I am merely calling attention to the misfortune of the timing, for it is so very unfortunate. It goes without saying that I would much rather you had *not* eaten a plate of spoiled oysters. But having made such an ill-advised decision—and an unusual one, too, as I would have sworn you detested the creatures—you should be allowed to bear the consequences in peace rather than summoned to attend a wedding that was not *supposed* to happen for another three days. I cannot condone the thoughtlessness. My poor dear, how terrifyingly pale you look. Do lean on me, so that you do not collapse onto the dowager's fine marble floor." She paused slightly in her speech, then added, "Oh, but it is very fine marble indeed, so elegantly veined. I wonder if it's from Italy. Livorno, perhaps. Or maybe Carrara."

As genuinely concerned as she was about her daughter's health, Vera's anxiety was no match for her instinctive admiration for quality, and Bea, noting the hushed tone with which she spoke, imagined the other woman running her fingers reverentially over the smooth marble. It was a visceral response to opulence, one Vera could no more control than the beating of her own heart, and, amused by her aunt's constancy, Bea envisioned her perched on the threshold of heaven too awed by the exquisite ornamentation of the pearly gates to enter.

'Twas an absurd picture, without question—Aunt Vera pestering poor St. Peter on the location of the seabed from which the jewels were harvested whilst he tried to find her name in the Book of Life—and Bea laughed despite her churlishness. She was further diverted when Flora, assuring her mother she felt quite sturdy, laid claim to a miraculous recovery. "Truly, I feel as though I was never sick at all, Mama. I cannot think of how to account for it save for your exceptional care. Thank you, darling, for attending to me so diligently."

As Flora's stomach ailment had been a ruse employed that morning to allow her to slip from her home at 19 Portman Square unnoticed, this assertion was decidedly false. Indeed, the whole scheme had been based on the assumption that her mother's sweeping discomfort with illness would keep her far away from the sickroom, a supposition that proved accurate when she prescribed several hours of uninterrupted rest for her daughter. Obligingly banished to her bedchamber, Flora had changed into her brother's clothes, crept out of the house through the kitchens and hailed a carriage to the Strand. There, she'd gained entry into the theater where Bea and the duke were investigating the murder of an actor and rescued them from a slow, agonizing death in the jet-black bowels of the building's cellars.

That Kesgrave had already freed them from their restraints and would have turned his attention to the door as soon as Bea had finished expressing her gratitude had no bearing on Flora's perception of herself as their heroic savior. As such, she took a sort of proprietary interest in them now as she strode into the drawing room, asserting that the only wretched thing would have been for the pair to wed without their guardian angel in attendance.

Vera, whose aversion to infirmity of any sort was so deeply ingrained even she realized there was something suspicious about her daughter's praise of her nursing skills, stared in confusion at this mention of a protective spirit and looked around the room as if expecting to see some secondary figure from the Bible standing by the fireplace, such as Noah or Job.

Fortunately, she spotted only her niece, whose customarily wan appearance reminded her why she was so cross in the first place, and she berated the girl with brusque impatience for breaking her promise to wait a full week before making her vows. "I cannot comprehend it. No, I cannot. If you were determined to ignore the wisdom of my counsel, then why do so *after* our visit to Madame Bélanger? Surely, courtesy demands that you openly rebel the day *before* a significant investment is made on your behalf? I find your behavior vexing, extremely vexing."

Since Bea resented the acquisition of the excessively lavish trousseau almost as much as her aunt, she thought this was a fair question and turned her unblinking gaze to Kesgrave for a reply, as the decision to diverge from the agreed-upon schedule had been his. Daunted by neither the presence of Vera Hyde-Clare nor the sting of her disapproval, he returned Bea's stare with unflinching calm, his own eyes, brilliantly blue and impossibly bright, glowing with a determination to see the thing done. How it might be contrived—with a modicum of dignity or amid an orgy of carping—was of no concern to him, and Bea, who knew his ability to think rationally had been corrupted by the sight of a murderous actor holding a pistol to her back earlier in the day, felt a strange sort of flutter in her belly at the implacability of his intent.

It was, in fact, much worse than a flutter, she realized, as color suffused her cheeks,

And how could she not blush, knowing all too well the thoughts that occupied his mind? She herself shared them, and well aware of how thoroughly unsuited they were for the dowager's drawing room, she felt her face grow uncomfortably warm.

What a wholly depraved creature she must be to entertain such ideas whilst in the presence of her family!

The case was hopeless indeed when even the shrill displeasure of her steadfastly censorious aunt wasn't enough to completely quell the anticipatory shiver of delight Bea felt at the inflexibility of the duke's resolve.

Naturally, she expected everyone in the room to notice the unusual blush, but Flora drew the occupants' attention by dismissing her mother's complaint with a brisk wave of her hand. "We could not possibly allow Beatrice to marry Kesgrave with only the rags on her back, for she is not some poor orphan in a fairy story who must sweep out the soot from our fireplace or sleep in a cupboard. She is a beloved member of our family, and I know you would never want her to take a turn around Berkeley Square in a dress marred by a stain of gooseberry jam. Why, one of the neighbors might notice! 'Tis not like this tear in my own gown, which is so small I'm sure not even the dowager duchess will note it."

As if of its own volition, Aunt Vera's index finger flew to Flora's lips as she tried to stop her daughter from speaking of such terrible things as stains and tears. Although the target of her apprehension was in the hallway conferring with her butler, she could not squelch the sensation of the peeress's eagle eye hovering somewhere over her shoulder observing her family's every minor imperfection. It was a familiar feeling, as she lived with the perpetual fear of falling short of the other lady's exacting standards—a dread her daughter routinely exploited in her pursuit of a wardrobe by Madame Bélanger.

Or, if not a full wardrobe, then several new gowns by the exquisite modiste.

Having witnessed Flora's efforts on multiple occasions, Bea knew exactly what she was up to and was disconcerted to discover she felt a pang of sympathy for Aunt Vera, whose panic prevented her from realizing her daughter's dress was without defects or blemishes. Bea was saved from succumbing to the odd compulsion to offer her relative comfort by Flora, who blithely continued her speech, insisting the couple had already demonstrated incredible forbearance by waiting so long.

"Instead of offering recriminations, let us be happy for them, Mama," she exclaimed with giddy assurance. "Life is a precious gift and we must be glad they are alive and well to enjoy this wonderful event, for no one's future is assured. Why, something dreadful might have happened to them this very day had some divine force not been watching over them. *Carpe diem quam minimum credula postero!*"

Vera, whose anxiety remained acute as she frantically inspected her daughter's dress for imperfections, inhaled sharply and called for their carriage to take them back to Portman Square posthaste. "We must return my dear girl to her sickbed, for she is babbling incoherently," she said, darting an angry look at Bea. "I knew it was too soon."

The unspoken charge hung in the air for only a moment

before her son strode into the room in the company of his father.

"There's no need to kick up a fuss, Mama," he said bracingly. "She's not incoherent, just speaking in Latin."

Although Russell had sought to reassure his mother with this comment, she was more unsettled than ever to discover Flora was proficient in a foreign language. For years she had despaired of her daughter's inability to learn French. If only the recalcitrant child would apply herself! The subjunctive was not *that* difficult to master.

Uncle Horace was just as astonished and stared at her as if trying to comprehend her unprecedented erudition. Finally, he said with bemused wonder, "He's right. It means 'seize the present; trust tomorrow e'en as little as you may.' It's from the *Odes*. I must confess, Flora, that I do not recall Miss Higglestone including Horace on your syllabus. And yet she must have, for your accent is uncommonly good."

Flora preened at the compliment while Vera extolled the virtues of their former governess, whose skills she had never doubted though she might have questioned them once or twice.

Unable to allow his sister to bask in the glow of filial approbation alone, Russell launched into a catalogue of the many Latin phrases he had learned during his brief yet distinguished career at Oxford: *Georgics, Eclogue, Aeneid.*

He had barely made it through the complete works of Virgil when the door opened and the Countess of Abercrombie swept into the room on a cloud of sweet-smelling perfume.

"Oh, my dear," she said with unrestrained emotion as she beheld Beatrice by the fireplace next to Kesgrave, "you are a most beautiful bride." She sighed deeply and dabbed delicately at her eyes, which may or may not have been filled with tears. Then she walked across the floor until she was mere inches from Bea, wrapped her in a gentle hug and murmured softly, "A most, *most* beautiful bride."

Familiar with her ladyship's penchant for drama, Bea submitted unprotestingly to this treatment. For her aunt, however, it was an irresistible provocation and she ceased trying to determine if her daughter had a fever to stare with wide-eyed amazement at the lovely widow.

"But...but...her cheeks are so sallow," Vera exclaimed in confusion, "and her dress is...is...so..." But she could not come up with the right word to describe the serviceable gown of an indeterminate blue and abandoned the effort, settling on a vaguely articulate grunt of despair. "You may see for yourself how inadequate it is. One does not have to wear one's presentation gown to one's wedding but surely something better than...than..." Again, her vocabulary failed her as she waved her hand at her niece. "We must send home for something more appropriate or—and I believe this is the more auspicious plan—wait for one of Madame Bélanger's lovely creations to be ready. I am sure you agree, my lady, that Bea cannot marry the Duke of Kesgrave dressed in that...that..." —here, finally, inspiration struck and she latched onto the word her daughter had used earlier—"*rag* of a gown."

Now it was her ladyship's turn to affect astonishment, for she could not perceive anything to complain about in Bea's appearance. Indeed, pushing the young woman back so that she may inspect her properly, she noted nothing but the radiance of excitement.

"Yes, yes," Lady Abercrombie said with blissful contemplation, "a most beautiful bride."

To say that Bea wanted the whole lot of them gone, that she wished they would simply vanish from the room at the waspish snap of her fingers, would be to grossly understate the case. She'd lived a mostly quiet life—quietly reading, quietly sewing, quietly listening to her aunt grapple with her children's unerring ability to increase her anxiety with their excessive demands for money and attention—and she could scarcely comprehend how it had altered so profoundly in such a brief span. A mere six months ago she had been sitting in the Skeffingtons' dining room in the Lake District quietly eating eels *à la tartare,* and now she was in the Dowager Duchess of Kesgrave's drawing room besieged by an almost painful cacophony.

All she wanted was to be alone with the duke.

And yet it was impossible to smother the gurgle of laughter that rose in her throat at the expression of utter bewilderment on Aunt Vera's face as her relative tried to make sense of Lady Abercrombie's stunning reversal. Only five days before, her ladyship had stood in the Hyde-Clare's breakfast room—entirely uninvited, of course, for nobody was ramshackle enough to entertain guests over eggs and kippers—and insisted that Bea and the duke wait until at least May to make their vows. First, she must throw a ball to introduce Bea to society with all the pride, pomp and circumstance befitting a future duchess, a development that her relatives had failed to anticipate when they hosted their own indifferent affair seven seasons before.

Naturally, Aunt Vera had found the prospect of her niece's reintroduction to society horrifying, for it would imply to all and sundry that she'd inadequately performed the task the first time around. Nevertheless, she was grateful for the countess's support in delaying the nuptials and felt her opinion had helped convince the pair to wait a week.

But now...now she was smiling fondly at Bea and wiping maudlin tears from her eyes as if nothing would make her happier than to witness her hasty marriage to Kesgrave.

Did her ladyship not understand what was happening? Was she incapable of comprehending how the passage of time worked? Perhaps she had fallen into a fugue state and believed she'd emerged a full week later?

Although the latter would provide a plausible explanation, it seemed highly improbable, for Lady Abercrombie appeared to glow with vibrancy and health. Her eyes sparkled with satisfaction as she murmured yet again, "A beautiful bride."

Vera's brows drew impossibly closer at each repetition of the sentiment, which was truly inconceivable, and Bea imagined her ascribing some very secretive, very cunning motive to her ladyship's behavior. Clearly, the countess was playing a deeper game than anyone could imagine.

Ah, but what could it be?

While Vera applied herself to detangling the many strands of Lady Abercrombie's wily scheme, Russell continued to demonstrate his extensive knowledge of Latin. Having exhausted the works of Virgil, he had moved on to Ovid —*Heroides, Ars Amatoria, Epistulae ex Ponto*—but his sister, whose education was more complete than anyone in her family had suspected, observed that titles of books did not count as actual phrases, let alone complete sentences. Resolutely, he dug deeper into his recollection of classical studies and emerged with Emperor Augustus's last words, which he promptly mangled.

"*Acta est fabula, plaudite,*" his father corrected impatiently.

As Flora laughed at her brother's humiliation, Lady Abercrombie tsked disapprovingly and insisted she would not applaud, for the play was just beginning. Uncle Horace rushed to explain that he was merely correcting his son's Latin, not declaring the actual end of something, certainly not Bea and Kesgrave's happiness, and Russell made another attempt at demonstrating his skill, this time misquoting Seneca's maxim about great fortunes.

Bea, taking advantage of the countess's momentary distraction, extricated herself from her ladyship's firm grip and looked at Kesgrave. "Do you see what you have wrought with your wrangling, your grace? If you had not attempted to rewrite the text of the marriage ceremony in service of your own selfish ends, we would have been wed by now and far from this madness. Indeed, we would have been back in your carriage and en route to Kesgrave House."

Although Bea expected him to protest this flippant characterization of his concern for her safety, he merely laughed and noted that she was overlooking one very obvious fact. "As much as I want to be all things to you, especially a pincushion when you need a target for your surliness—how did you put it to me yesterday in the carriage: you may stick me with as many needles as you require to restore your good humor—I cannot be both bridegroom and clergyman. In fact, even if I were not the bridegroom, I could still not administer the vows, for I have not taken holy orders."

Since Bea could not argue the validity of the point, she hastily asserted the difference between waiting patiently for the minister to appear in the calm of his grandmother's elegant drawing room and Bedlam.

As if to underscore the disparity, Lady Abercrombie addressed herself to the duke for the first time, noting that *his* attire seemed a trifle underwhelming for the occasion. "I say, Kesgrave, has love made you so addled you did not notice your tailcoat is a full decade out of style? That straight cutaway and broad lapels make you look like a bailiff collecting the village rents. Could this be your valet's way of expressing displeasure of the match? If so, you must give him his notice at once—although not before securing an ensemble appropriate for the occasion. Do dash back to Berkeley Square to change. Give no thought to us, for we are happy to wait."

Aunt Vera, whose keenly discerning eye extended only to the imperfections of her family, expressed surprise at this observation and then immediately lent her support to the plan. "We can wait for his grace to change, can we not? That is to say, there is no reason why we should rush the process. Perhaps he would like the opportunity to select the new tail-coat himself, which might take a while. We would not want him to feel rushed, certainly not on our behalf, and could return to Portman Square to indicate our patience. Further-more, we do not wish to take advantage of the dowager's hospitality. Yes, it is probably best if we leave this matter now and reconvene at a later date. I'm sure that's more convenient for everyone involved."

The hopeful note in Aunt Vera's voice, as if this propi-tious plan was the one that would make the couple fall in line, was more than Bea would withstand, and a peal of laughter escaped her. Truly, she could not fathom the cause of her rela-tive's irrational persistence. The marriage would take place either now or in three days from now, and as her cousin Flora had pointed out recently, a ceremony performed in indecent haste would do little to overshadow her more outrageous behavior of goading a murderer to confess in the middle of Lord Stirling's ballroom.

The new Duchess of Kesgrave would be notorious regard-less of her wedding date—and even more so when word of their newest escapade, at the Particular, began to spread, as surely it must. An august member of the peerage could not spend two days pretending to be a theater owner from Bath without causing a few dozen tongues to wag. If the actors themselves did not endlessly marvel over the dramatic revela-tion of a secret duke, then the Bow Street Runner who'd arrived to take custody of the villain, a confused young man who could not quite grasp the duke's interest in the matter, would discuss it at length with his associates.

It was because of their investigation that Kesgrave's tail-coat was several years behind the current mode, and while he ordinarily endeavored to turn himself out as a proper Corinthian, he did not believe his garments necessitated a postponement. Nevertheless, he thanked Mrs. Hyde-Clare for her consideration.

Naturally, the insistence that his wedding of all things did not require the first stare of fashion confounded Bea's aunt, but her uncle appreciated the practicality and assured him his coat was nothing to frown at. Lady Abercrombie, taking exception to this statement, began to specify in earnest the many details that were not au courant. Flora, who knew why the duke was dressed in an old tailcoat but was determined not to reveal the secret, hinted wildly at his being preoccupied with concerns of much greater importance than conforming to the latest rage, and Russell, in a bid to redeem himself, announced with fastidious articulation, "*Non omnia possumus omnes.*"

Bedlam, Bea thought with regret tempered by amusement, was no doubt a placid sea in comparison.

"Ah, there he is," Kesgrave murmured softly as he tilted his head, and Bea, assuming he meant the man who was to marry them, looked up gratefully. But it was not a minister who'd entered the room. No, it was Viscount Nuneaton, and she felt a frisson of alarm as she watched his lithe form stroll unhurriedly across the floor. His sudden appearance now too closely resembled his sudden appearance several days ago, and she trembled in panic at what struck her as an inauspicious omen.

It was absurd, of course, to compare the two situations, for they bore no relation to each other. On what was originally meant to be her wedding day, she'd allowed herself to be swayed from a hasty marriage by nascent familial affection and Kesgrave's evenhanded response to delay. Today, neither of those conditions prevailed. To be certain, she was fond of her family—particularly Flora, whose florid estimation of her own heroics possessed an unexpectedly endearing quality—but the affection she felt for them was but a tepid cup of tea compared with her consuming regard for Kesgrave. The duke's tractability, as well, had undergone a dramatic alteration that could be attributed only to the well-aimed double-barreled flintlock that had bedeviled their morning.

Even if Prinny himself arrived at Clarges Street to halt the proceedings, Kesgrave would briskly sweep him to the side like a flea-ridden mongrel.

Truly, she had no reason to be concerned, and as her heart resumed its normal pace, she smiled at the dandy, who was as exquisite as ever in his satin breeches and elegant cravat.

"I could not be any more delighted for you, Miss Hyde-Clare," he said warmly as he bowed over her hand. "I have never envied another man's situation, for I have always found my own to be quite complete, but I would be bending the truth if I denied feeling a tinge of jealousy at Kesgrave's good fortune. You are an original, my dear."

Naturally, Bea could not accept such a lavish compliment without demurral, and she immediately called his lordship's sincerity into question by hinting at an ulterior motive. "Still currying my favor in hopes of discovering what happened at Lakeview Hall, I see," she said with gleeful cynicism.

His interest in the matter was hardly surprising, for he had also been a guest of Lord and Lady Skeffington when Mr. Otley was murdered, and he could not figure out how a plain spinster with no consequence or conversation had managed to identify the killer. Intrigued, he had made several attempts in the months since to learn the whole story, but Bea had resisted revealing all—first because she did not trust him with information potentially damaging to her reputation and then later because she enjoyed the game. In her six and twenty years, she'd had few games with anyone, let alone handsome dandies, and she was reluctant to see this one end, even now, on the verge of her wedding to Kesgrave.

Striving for an archly satirical note, she complimented Nuneaton on his relentless determination, assuring him that all young ladies simply adored being pestered. "We consider it a very appealing trait in a gentleman."

Although the viscount was famous for his languorous affect, barely bestirring himself to wince at the *ton*'s many ill-considered sartorial choices, he laughed with full-throated appreciation and promised Bea that she would soon find him irresistible. "For I do not mean to relent until I know everything about your many investigations."

Bea opened her mouth to insist that five investigations did not exactly rise to the level of *many*—a remark that would have been unintentionally revealing, for even if the viscount suspected there was more to the Taunton affair than a simple accident with a torch, he could know nothing of her involvement in Fazeley's brutal stabbing—but Kesgrave interrupted their conversation with a pointed cough. "As much as I enjoy watching my betrothed flirt with another man, you have a more vital reason for being here, Nuneaton. I trust you secured the item?"

His grace spoke calmly, even languidly, and yet Bea could not help but detect a hint of annoyance in his tone, which baffled her. He'd objected previously to the viscount's interest in her, yes, but she'd assumed he had only been teasing, a supposition bolstered by the almost comical way he commanded their attention now. Surely, a man who possessed every advantage of wealth, privilege and breeding was immune to the coarser emotions like jealousy.

'Twas beneath him in every way.

If Nuneaton noticed anything amiss in his friend's conduct, he gave no indication as he reached into his pocket and withdrew a small silk purse. "I did, yes. It was not without its challenges, for the jeweler had yet to finish repairing the clasp and had to be induced to work more quickly. If left to himself, I suspect it would have taken several more days."

Curiously, Bea wondered what could be so important to Kesgrave that he required its delivery to his grandmother's drawing room only minutes—at least she hoped it was only minutes—before his nuptials, and then she saw the glint of gold followed by a flash of blue.

Astonished, she stared at the beloved sapphire bracelet her mother had worn every day of her marriage until a murderer tore it from her wrist after snuffing out her life with a pillow. The last time she had seen the heirloom was barely more than a week ago, in Lord Wem's study, its delicate links tethering his lordship's watch to his waistcoat. She had paid it little heed as it shimmered in the sunlight, for she had naturally assumed it was a lovely adornment, a pretty chain with a practical purpose. But later, when she spoke to him amid the jubilant hubbub of Lord Stirling's ball, she recalled it again, the flicker of sapphire, and perceived at once its significance.

In the days since the ghastly encounter with Wem, she hadn't thought of the bracelet a single time. So many things had provided distraction: first her wedding, then the postponement of her wedding, then Mrs. Norton's missing diamond, then the murdered corpse of an unfortunate actor who had been hired to ensure her ruin.

All these events, one after another, had kept her mind too busy to return to the bracelet, and although Bea knew it was merely an object—only gold and gems—she could not squash the devastating sensation that what she had really forgotten was her mother. Having finally discovered the truth about her parents, their lives as much as their deaths, she'd turned her attention to other matters, allowing them to fade in the distance like a ship sinking below the horizon.

It was terrible, the remorse she felt at her callous disregard, and yet she could not regret anything that demonstrated so plainly Kesgrave's grace and goodness.

Incapable of speech, Bea raised her head and stared into his eyes, dazzling and blue. How could she possibly express the strange and unsettling mix of shame and pride she felt?

It was all so much more than anything she'd ever imagined.

She'd had fantasies, of course. Like any schoolroom miss on the precipice of her first season, she'd pictured her ideal suitor and conceived of something vague and benign: a kindly gentleman with even features, modest manners, and an interest in biographies and travelogues. The details of their life together were equally nebulous and consisted mostly of pleasant afternoons passed in companionable silence, each of them engrossed in their book whilst sitting shoulder to shoulder on the settee. Deeply contented, she would pause every so often in her reading to sigh happily over his quiet decency.

But this breathtaking surge of admiration, this rush of emotion, wild and overwhelming, was dizzying in its intensity, and to feel it now, again, anew, on this day of all days, when he had already awed her with his insouciant unraveling of the ropes that had bound them in that pitch-dark cellar under the Particular, was truly unbearable.

It was only luck, she knew, that placed her in the drawing room in Clarges Street with the Duke of Kesgrave, a fickle act of an indifferent god, and she felt in her bones the fragility of fate. One slight alteration in the fabric of time—if she had chosen to read the *Vicar of Wakefield* rather than seek out a biography in the Skeffingtons' library on the night Otley was killed—and she would have lived her entire life without him.

Gratitude for the capricious hand of fortune almost

crushed her, and determinedly pushing it aside, she struggled to come up with the words to express her appreciation for his thoughtfulness in remembering her mother's bracelet.

Alas, when she opened her mouth to thank him, her composure deserted her completely and all she could manage was a low, distraught plea. "You must stop doing this!" she said desperately.

It was not the response Kesgrave anticipated.

Oh, no. Having been impressed by Bea's pluck and daring from the very first, even while her refusal to abide by his authority drove him mad with frustration, he'd never imagined that the presentation of a simple band could have such a disastrous effect on her self-possession.

Kesgrave's confusion, so readily apparent in the way he drew his eyebrows together and pursed his lips, helped relieve some of Bea's distress. After two decades of falling short of her aunt's unreasonable expectations, it was still revelatory to exceed his.

Taken aback by her discomfort, Kesgrave immediately complied with her request, promising never to repeat the event. "I could not even if I desired to," he assured her, "for the bracelet is the only item of your mother's in need of reclaiming."

It was perfect, Bea thought, the characteristic pedantry of his reply, and under ordinary circumstances, it would have elicited from her a fond mocking rejoinder. But everything about the moment felt remarkable, even the sunlight filtering through the window, bathing them in a golden glow, and she answered instead with terrifying honesty. "You must stop making me love you more, Damien. The feeling is already so overwhelming, I can scarcely breathe."

His features remained steady but his eyes—oh, yes, his eyes—blazed with emotion and he raised his hand as if to touch her. Mindful of their situation, however, he let it drop before he made contact, and his lips curved slightly as he shook his head to deny her request. "I fear I cannot, Bea, no. Your brief spells of breathlessness are the only advantage I have in this relationship, and I am not prepared to relinquish it."

The duke spoke softly, emphatically, and Bea waited for amusement to enter his eyes, for she knew he was teasing, but his expression remained fervent. Warmed by his gaze, she longed to move closer, to draw his lips to hers, and it was only the presence of her family that kept her firmly rooted to the spot. Vaguely, she realized Nuneaton had stepped discreetly away and was now correcting Russell's pronunciation of *vixere* ("It's a *W*, my dear chap, not a *V*"). She heard Aunt Vera thank the viscount for his attention to her son, who grumbled that he knew how to speak Latin, thank you very much. Flora laughed at her brother's embarrassment and asked Lady Abercrombie about the contents of Bea's trousseau.

Unaware that he could strike Bea dumb with a single, searing look—another advantage he had in their relationship, she thought wryly—Kesgrave held up the strand and said, "May I?"

"Yes, please," she said, offering her arm and immediately admiring the delicate band as it encircled her wrist. It was, without question, a beautiful piece of jewelry, with its heart-shaped links and marquise-cut stones, but what made it truly extraordinary was the way it traversed time and space to deliver her mother there, on her wedding day.

Oh, how you would have loved him, Mama, she thought, her throat constricting painfully as her grace entered the room with the minister in tow.

Briskly, as if she were hosting a second ceremony later in the afternoon and needed to move the first couple along, the dowager arranged the occupants of her drawing room in a half circle beside the fireplace and directed Beatrice and

Kesgrave to stand in the center. She positioned the clergyman in front of them, just slightly to the left of the lavish bouquet that adorned the mantelpiece.

Bea had no idea why the dowager suddenly felt compelled to rush them to the altar—less than a week before hers had been one of the many voices urging restraint and caution—but the older woman's matter-of-fact attitude was like a balm to her heightened emotions, soothing the intensity of her feelings and allowing her to think coherently. Calmly, her gaze fixed on Kesgrave's vibrant features, she waited as the minister opened the prayer book and began the Solemnization of Matrimony. He spoke slowly, carefully, his tone earnest and somber as he explained the ordination of marriage, and Bea, who thought his solemnity was a trifle overdone, felt her heart turn over in giddy delight when the duke rolled his eyes in impatience.

Even England's most zealous pedant had his limits.

She smothered the giggle that rose in her throat and marveled again at the wonder of marrying a man whose thoughts aligned so perfectly with her own. Yielding partially to sentiment and partially to the strain of mischievousness she didn't know she possessed before confronting the Duke of Kesgrave in the Skeffingtons' darkened library, she decided to comply with his request to make a change to the ceremony. Clearly, he had not thought the matter through, for if he had paused for even a moment to consider the impact on their guests, he would never have made the suggestion.

Patiently, Bea listened to Mr. Bertram's seemingly endless litany of vows—obey, serve, love, honor, keep, forsake—and agreed to abide by them all. Then she announced she had one minor alteration to make.

The minister looked up from his prayer book and raised a quizzical brow. "An alteration?"

Bea nodded soberly. "I would like to add a vow."

Much taken aback by this presumption, the clergyman tilted his head to the side and sought to confirm that he had heard her correctly. "*You* would like to *add* a vow?"

"I would, yes," she said, her tone mildly conversational as if discussing something utterly benign like the weather. "If you would be so kind, please say, 'Wilt thou vow to cease investigating the horrible deaths that keep crossing thy path?' Then I will answer, 'I will.'"

The effect this entreaty had on the company was immediate—of course it was. To tinker with the Book of Common Prayer was already an intolerable impertinence but to suggest such a shocking addition was the height of impudence! The temerity of inserting the wretchedness of death into a joyful event! The audacity of undermining the sanctity of marriage with irreverent humor!

Mr. Bertram glowered fiercely at the bride before directing his passionate disapproval at the dowager for allowing such disrespect to prosper in her drawing room. Her grace opened her mouth to protest the unspoken accusation but failed to say anything coherent. Flora giggled knowingly, Lady Abercrombie clucked censoriously, and Russell called out, "I say, Bea, that's not quite the thing." Nuneaton murmured, "Brava," while Uncle Horace looked around as if not entirely sure what had just happened.

But it was Aunt Vera's response—a gasp of horror so deeply felt it seemed to rise from the tips of her toes—that caused Bea to look up at her husband and grin impishly.

About the Author

Lynn Messina is the author of almost two dozen novels, including the Beatrice Hyde-Clare mysteries, a cozy series set in Regency-era England. Her first novel, *Fashionistas,* has been translated into sixteen languages and was briefly slated to be a movie starring Lindsay Lohan. Her essays have appeared in *Self, American Baby* and the *New York Times* Modern Love column, and she has been a regular contributor to the *Times* parenting blog. She lives in New York City with her sons.

Also by Lynn Messina

The Fellingham Minx

The Bolingbroke Chit

The Impertinent Miss Templeton

Stand Alones

Prejudice and Pride

The Girls' Guide to Dating Zombies

Savvy Girl

Winner Takes All

Little Vampire Women

Never on a Sundae

Troublemaker

Fashionista (Spanish Edition)

Violet Venom's Rules for Life

Henry and the Incredibly Incorrigible, Inconveniently Smart Human

Welcome to the Bea Hive

FUN STUFF FOR BEATRICE HYDE-CLARE FANS

The Bea Tee

Beatrice's favorite three warships not only in the wrong order but also from the wrong time period. (Take that, maritime tradition *and* historical accuracy!)

The Kesgrave Shirt

A tee bearing the Duke of Kesgrave's favorite warships in the order in which they appeared in the Battle of the Nile

Available in mugs too!

See all the options in Lynn's Store.

Made in the USA
Middletown, DE
15 September 2024

60999526R00213